The Islamorada Murders

by

Owen Parr

Copyright © 2022 by:
Owen Parr Published
in the United States

ISBN: 9798354858583

This is a work of fiction. Names, characters, businesses, places, events, and incidents are the products of the author's imagination or used in a fictitious manner. Any resemblance to actual persons, living or dead, or actual events is purely coincidental.

DEDICATION

I want to dedicate this book to each one of you, my beloved grandchildren, who fill my heart with hope and optimism for the future of the next generation. As I write these words, I am overwhelmed with gratitude for the joy and inspiration you bring into my life.

In a world that constantly undergoes change and presents its share of challenges, you stand as beacons of hope. Your presence reassures me that the future holds promise and that remarkable individuals like yourselves will shape it for the better. Your compassion, empathy, and inclusivity serve as a testament to the values that will guide you in creating a brighter tomorrow.

"All men make mistakes, but a good man yields when he knows his course is wrong and repairs the evil. The only crime is pride."

—Sophocles, Antigone

THE ISLAMORADA MURDERS

Part 1
1
Monday, 6:40 p.m.

After our previous case, my wife Marcy and I felt the need to escape the fast-paced life of New York City. So, we hopped on a flight to Miami International Airport, rented a car, and drove south to the Topsider Resort in Islamorada, Florida.

Just two days in the Florida Keys had already transformed our mindset as if we had taken Jimmy Buffett's advice to heart. The Topsider Resort was the perfect setting for our getaway, with its laid-back atmosphere and a friendly community of long-term residents who knew each other well.

Marcy had recently retired from the FBI's White-Collar Crime Division in New York and had joined Mancuso and O'Brian Investigative Services, our small but thriving enterprise located in Manhattan's Financial District. In addition to our investigative work, we also owned a pub and cigar bar.

As the sun began to set, we found ourselves on the resort's private beach, enjoying a couple of local craft brews alongside fellow Northerners seeking respite from their daily routines. However, the tranquility was momentarily disrupted by a minor incident involving two individuals poaching lobsters just off our beach, drawing the attention of the Florida Wildlife Patrol.

Out of the blue, a man approached us, sporting large, dark sunglasses, which he must have purchased at an Elton John garage sale, a Miami Dolphins cap, a black T-shirt, jeans, and a medical mask.

"Are you Joey Mancuso, the private detective?" the mysterious man inquired, scanning the group of sunset admirers and the impending arrest of the lobster poachers.

I glanced at Marcy and then turned my attention back to our unexpected visitor. He didn't seem threatening or aggressive; instead, he appeared timid and visibly afraid.

"Yes, that's me. Who's asking?" I responded.

"Could we talk privately, Mr. Mancuso?" he requested, ignoring my question.

"Are you from Boston?" I asked, noticing his accent.

"Salem," he replied.

His response immediately triggered a reaction in Marcy, evident from the expression on her face as she subtly shook her head.

"How about we take a walk?" I suggested, reluctant to bring the mysterious man into our unit. He nodded in agreement.

I turned to Marcy and informed her that I would be back shortly. She acknowledged me with a nod, taking a sip of her beer.

We strolled along a gravel path that led to the front of the resort, running parallel to US 1. I decided to break the silence. "What's your name?" I inquired.

He hesitated for a moment before responding, "You can call me Ted." Sensing his hesitation, I pressed further, "Ted, what? You already know my name."

"Ah...Williams, Ted Williams," he finally revealed.

"Alright, I think I'll call you Mickey. Now, how did you know I was staying here? And why are you still wearing the mask?" I probed.

Ted glanced around, then removed his mask but opted to keep the Elton John glasses on. "You had dinner at the

Square Grouper last night, and someone you met is a close friend of mine. That's all I can disclose," he explained.

The only person we interacted with was our server, Dianne, who hailed from Brooklyn, just like Marcy and me. We engaged in casual conversation, and I probably mentioned my profession, although I couldn't recall the specifics. It was after enjoying two Tito's martinis at their upstairs raw bar.

As we reached the halfway point toward the front of the resort, I halted my steps. "What's the issue? Why me?" I questioned.

"I understand you handle murder cases," Ted stated.

"That used to be my line of work with the NYPD, and now I continue in private practice. But why?" I inquired.

"I need you to solve a murder," he whispered, glancing around cautiously.

"Whose murder?" I asked, my curiosity piqued.

Ted approached me, his voice barely audible. "Mine."

I instinctively took a few steps back. "Could you take off the sunglasses? Eyes can reveal a lot, and I need to see yours," I insisted.

After performing a quick scan of his surroundings, Ted complied and removed his shades. His bloodshot eyes showed signs of exhaustion, with heavy redness and dark circles beneath them.

"What do you mean? Are you saying you're going to be murdered?" I questioned, startled by the revelation.

"I need to speak in confidence. Can we establish something akin to attorney-client privilege?" he requested, his voice filled with urgency.

I remained silent, observing Ted closely. "Listen, Mickey, my wife and I are here to take a break. You sought me out, so if you want to share your story, go ahead. Otherwise, I'm missing out on a beautiful sunset, and my beer is getting warm. So, what's it going to be?" I emphasized my patience was wearing thin.

Ted took a deep breath before speaking. "I own a charter fishing boat out of Bass Pro Shops World Wide Sports Marina. Four guys chartered my services for a full day of fishing," he began, then paused.

"And?" I prompted, growing increasingly impatient.

"Right. When we reached a GPS destination given by my guests, another boat approached. I positioned my boat side by side with theirs, and I noticed they had weapons, although they weren't brandishing them," Ted explained, pausing again. He began breathing erratically, lowering his head and resting his hands on his knees. "Give me a minute."

I couldn't comprehend what was happening to this man. "What happened next?" I inquired.

Ted straightened up and continued, "One man from the other boat said, 'Let me see the money.'"

"And?" I pressed for more details.

"One of my guys replied, 'Let us see the drugs.'"

"One of the individuals on my boat retrieved a duffel bag from under my center console, where there's a restroom and a small storage compartment. He opened it and showed them the contents," Ted explained.

"Did you see what was inside?" I asked.

He nodded, saying, "Lots of money."

"Then what?" I probed further.

"The two men who hired me boarded the other boat, demanding to see the drugs. Then they started arguing in Spanish. A scuffle broke out. Meanwhile, one of the two men left on my boat jumped over to the other boat and shot one of them while the altercation continued," Ted recounted, pausing briefly.

"What were you doing during all this?" I questioned.

"I was just watching, unsure what was happening or what I should do. Then...then the man left on my boat said something like 'gringo pa Cuba' as he looked at me. Shit, I understood that to mean 'take me to Cuba.' I freaked out," Ted admitted, his voice filled with anxiety.

"So you panicked. What happened next?" I inquired.

"The remaining man on my boat boarded the other vessel and retrieved a package from the fish well. He threw it onto my boat. I could see through the packaging that it contained cocaine or fentanyl. It was a white substance," Ted revealed.

"So now you have both the money and the drugs on your boat, correct?" I summarized, trying to grasp the situation.

"Correct. Mind you; we were in the middle of the ocean with no one else around. I was concerned, expecting a Coast Guard boat, DEA, or someone to show up," Ted explained. "Then they threw the man who had been shot into the water, and one of them started approaching my boat."

"And they just let you go?" I questioned, skeptical of Ted's account. Was he trying to deceive me?

"Mr. Mancuso, I panicked. As the guy was boarding my boat, I hit the throttle at full speed and made my escape. Their guy fell into the water," Ted clarified.

"So you managed to get away? I don't know, Ted, it sounds like you're spinning me a tale," I expressed my doubts.

"No, no, sir. They chased after me, but I was able to seek refuge at Bud and Mary's Marina, and they eventually gave up," Ted assured me.

"And now they're searching for you?" I questioned further.

"Yes, them and the police," Ted admitted.

I tilted my head, seeking more clarity. "Why would the police be involved?"

"Well, the police and the DEA," Ted replied, glancing around cautiously. Lowering his voice, he continued, "It turns out my fishing guests were under surveillance, and the DEA was anticipating their return. Then, another charter boat discovered the body of the man they had shot. So now, the suspicion is that I killed them and kept the money and drugs."

"Why do you think these individuals brought drugs on board if they were going fishing? Are you certain you weren't part of a drop-off?" I probed, trying to piece the puzzle together.

"No, sir," Ted responded promptly. "As I mentioned earlier, they provided me with coordinates where a friend said he had recently caught tunas. They wanted me to take them there at noon."

"So it was a drop-off," I concluded, connecting the dots.

I walked back, the sunset now over, and Ted seemed somewhat more at ease as dusk settled in. "Now, tell me; how do you know that all these people are searching for you?"

"I left my boat at Bud and Mary's, and a friend gave me a ride to the place where I've been hiding for the past three nights. I've been told that strangers, the DEA, and the local police are asking about me at World Wide Marina," Ted disclosed.

"Where exactly are you hiding?" I inquired.

Ted hesitated before replying, "I...I'd rather not say."

I nodded in understanding. "Understood. So, what exactly do you want from me?" I asked, curious about his expectations.

"I want you to find the people who are trying to kill me," Ted pleaded, his voice filled with desperation.

"I understand that you're in a difficult situation, Ted, but what you're describing sounds like an ongoing criminal investigation. It's important for you to contact the local police department and share all the information you've shared with me," I insisted, trying to steer him in the right direction. "They are better equipped to handle this kind of situation."

Ted's expression became pleading, and he countered, "Your website says you're the last advocate of the victims. And I am a victim." He then revealed a burner phone and handed me a matchbook with his number inside. "Please, call me here," he pleaded. "Mr. Mancuso, if you don't help me, I'm afraid I'll be fish food in a day or two."

I felt a pang of sympathy for Ted, but I knew the limitations of my expertise. "I appreciate your trust in me, Ted, but I am not equipped to handle an active investigation like this. It's crucial that you involve the proper authorities."

I decided to shift the conversation slightly. "Regarding the phrase 'gringo pa Cuba' you mentioned, what do you think it means?" I inquired, hoping to gather more information.

Ted hesitated, displaying signs of discomfort. He blinked rapidly and bit his lower lip before finally replying, "I'm not sure. I thought it meant me, the gringo, to Cuba."

I could sense that Ted's response wasn't entirely truthful, raising further questions in my mind. What was the truth behind his story? What was his true motive? I couldn't ignore my instincts, but at the same time, I questioned how I could assist him or whether I should help him at all.

2
Monday, 7:40 p.m.

As I made my way back to Marcy, I noticed Ted strolling out of the resort on the gravel path. The sun had dipped below the horizon, casting a magnificent display of colors, but Marcy seemed more intrigued by the events I had just witnessed.

"You missed another breathtaking sunset and the apprehension of the poachers. What was that all about?" Marcy inquired, her curiosity piqued.

"He approached me with an unusual request," I began, taking a seat next to her on the beach lounge chair. I reached into the cooler, pulled out a beer, and offered one to Marcy. "He wants me to solve a murder."

Marcy's eyes widened, her disbelief evident. "Whose murder?" she asked, leaning forward.

"His own," I replied, causing Marcy to look at me as if I had lost my mind. Sensing her confusion, I took a sip of my beer and began recounting the encounter with Ted Williams while the sky lanterns illuminated the dock in the distance.

Uncertainty clouded Marcy's face as she pondered the situation. "What do you plan to do?" she inquired, her curiosity urging me to reveal my next move.

I crushed an empty beer can and tossed it into the cooler. "Honestly, I'm not sure yet. But I think it's worth stopping by the Square Grouper to speak with Dianne. If she's the one who mentioned me to Ted, we might uncover more about this mysterious individual."

Marcy reminded me of our dinner reservation at Kayo-Grill for sushi. "We can still enjoy our meal, but let's make a quick stop at the Square Grouper for a drink and to chat with Dianne," she suggested, finding a balance between curiosity and practicality.

"Sounds like a plan," I agreed, and we headed back to

our place to freshen up for the evening.

After forty-five minutes, we found ourselves seated at the upstairs bar of the Square Grouper. Amidst the lively atmosphere, we spotted Dianne attending to her tables. Marcy waved her over as our martinis arrived.

With warm greetings exchanged, I wasted no time getting to the heart of the matter. "Dianne, do you have a couple of minutes? There's something we need to discuss with you."

Dianne managed a smile but conveyed her busyness. "I'm really slammed at the moment. What's this about?"

Taking a moment to assess the situation, I pressed on. "It's about a potential friend of yours who might be in trouble. We suspect you may have mentioned me to him. Can you recall anything of the sort?"

Recognition flickered across Dianne's face. Sensing the urgency of our request, she swiftly glanced around and asked another server to cover for her temporarily. "Follow me," she said, motioning toward a quieter corner of the bar with a tilt of her head.

We complied, the three of us huddled together in the corner, the ambiance providing a semblance of privacy as we leaned in to hear each other better. The anticipation grew as we waited for Dianne's response, hoping for any clue that could shed light on the enigma of Ted Williams and his connection to us. Dianna's face betrayed a mix of fear and concern, her raised eyebrows and darting glances revealing the gravity of the situation.

With a sense of urgency, I asked, "Can you confirm if you told your friend about me? He's in serious trouble, and I need to help him."

Dianne hesitated, apprehension evident in her eyes. "I don't think he wants me to reveal his name," she confessed, shaking her head.

Understanding the severity of the situation, I emphasized, "Dianne, if what he said is true, he needs all the help he can get. I can't assist him if I don't know who he is."

Her eyes widened, realizing the gravity of the matter. "Are you really going to help him? Because what he said...it's true," she admitted.

Gently pressing for more information, I persisted, "Please, tell us his name."

Glancing around cautiously, Dianne moved closer and whispered, "Paul Reinhard."

Curious, I inquired further, "Is he from Boston?"

Dianne clarified, "Salem. I have to go."

Eager for more details, Marcy asked, "Where is he hiding?"

Dianne shook her head rapidly. "No, no, I can't say."

Reassuring Dianne, I assured her, "We won't bother him. But I need to know."

Taking a deep breath, Dianne mustered the courage to disclose, "He's in a boat in dry dock outside, in the front yard. Second row up from the bottom. That's all I can tell you. I gotta go."

With that, Dianne swiftly departed to attend to her duties. "I'll settle the bill, and then let's go have dinner," I suggested, taking charge of the situation.

We descended the stairs, and as we made our way out, Marcy shared additional information that Dianne had revealed during the payment.

As we walked through the parking lot, divided into north and south sections, I noticed the long steel racks holding numerous boats stacked two stories high in dry dockage. Marcy paused, and with a hint of concern, she said, "By the way, Dianne also mentioned that she's pregnant with Paul's child."

Pausing to absorb this new information, I started the rental car and merged onto US 1. "He might find temporary refuge here," I pondered aloud.

Marcy glanced at me, her eyes filled with worry. "Maybe, but what about Dianne? How long before they discover her relationship with Reinhard? Do you think they won't extract that information from her? I'm more concerned about her safety than his."

We both contemplated the precariousness of the situation as we drove away, leaving behind the Square Grouper and the secrets that lay within its walls.

"Damn, you're right," I exclaimed. "Do me a favor, text Agnes. Give her this guy's name and where he's from. Let her do her thing and call us back."

Agnes, our brilliant researcher and hacker who worked for our investigative services, was the perfect person to dig deeper into this mysterious case. Two hours later, as we relaxed on the balcony of our octagon villa overlooking the bay, Agnes sent us an email with her findings.

"Do you want me to read it?" Marcy asked, holding up her illuminated iPad.

"Yes, please," I replied eagerly.

The bright light from the iPad filled our cozy surroundings as Marcy began to read. She skimmed through the initial paragraphs before exclaiming, "This is so interesting."

"I thought you were going to read it out loud," I reminded her.

"Hold on, bobo, I am," she chuckled. "I just glanced through the first few paragraphs. Here we go. Paul Reinhard, twenty-nine years old, born in Salem, Massachusetts. Graduated from MIT with a doctorate in computer science. During his final year at school, he created three successful apps, which he sold to a company for millions. Then, Dr. Reinhard started a company focused on sorting and aggregating algorithms, which he sold to a private equity firm for ten million dollars three years ago, even before fully developing it. Are you listening?"

Taking a puff of my cigar, I turned my gaze from the starry sky to Marcy. "That can't be my Ted Williams, no way. This guy is a multimillionaire running a fishing charter boat in the Keys?"

"Here's a picture of our PhD," Marcy said, shining the bright light of the iPad toward me.

"Son of a bitch, that's him. I can't believe it," I muttered in disbelief.

"I'll keep reading. Get us a couple more beers," Marcy requested.

Reaching into the cooler I had brought up from downstairs, freshly filled with ice and local brews, I retrieved the beers. There was something about the taste of beer when it was nestled in ice, as opposed to being in the fridge. "You want a Channel Marker or the Sandbar Sunday?" I asked Marcy.

"Sandbar," she replied without looking up from her iPad.

After a few moments, she continued reading. "Anyway, our boy is a millionaire and receives monthly royalties from his algorithm program, estimated to be around one million dollars per year."

"I still can't believe it," I murmured. "Although, if I had millions in the bank and a yearly income of one million for doing nothing, I might be tempted to do the same."

Marcy chuckled. "No, no. I can't picture you being a captain on a fishing charter. You don't even know how to put a hook on a shrimp, and you get violently sick if we take the Brooklyn ferry."

I was about to retort, but my cell phone rang. The caller ID displayed Agnes Persopoulus. "This is incredible stuff you found out about this guy," I greeted her on the phone.

"I know, but listen, I just received a forwarded call from the office. A Ted called. He asked you to call him back on the burner phone. He said it's an emergency. Do you know who that is?" Agnes explained urgently.

"Yeah, thanks. Bye," I replied abruptly. My heart raced as I rushed inside our villa, frantically searching for the matchbook. Panic set in as I couldn't locate it. I dashed back out to the balcony, calling to Marcy, "Do you know where the matchbook is that I had in my trunks?"

"Why is it that men can never find anything?" Marcy quipped, not looking up from her reading.

"It's an emergency," I pleaded, scanning the surroundings.

"What's the emergency?" she asked, finally glancing up. "And the matchbook is in the top left drawer of the bedroom dresser, where you keep your humidor."

Ignoring her question, I hurried inside, following Marcy's instructions. I located the matchbook and quickly dialed the number of the burner phone.

3
Monday, 11:45 p.m.

After just one ring, Reinhard answered the phone, sounding frantic. "Mr. Mancuso," he gasped. "I have...an enormous problem."

"I know," I replied, bracing myself for what he was about to say.

"No, you don't know," Reinhard insisted. "My girlfriend has been abducted." He paused, the weight of the situation evident in his voice.

Sitting on the bed, I motioned for Marcy to join me. She entered the room, concern etched on her face. "What's going on?" she whispered.

I covered the phone and whispered back, "Dianne was abducted." Marcy's hand flew to her mouth, and her eyes closed in disbelief as she sat down beside me. I pressed the speaker button on the phone. "Are you still there?" I asked Reinhard.

"What am I going to do? She's pregnant with our child," he exclaimed, his voice filled with desperation.

I didn't want to disclose that we had spoken with Dianne, fearing that Reinhard might suspect us of tipping off the abductors, even though we had no involvement in their actions. "What do they want?" I inquired, seeking Marcy's support.

Reinhard paused for a moment before responding, "A trade. Me for her," he said, his voice trembling.

"I think it's time you tell me your real name."

He took a brief pause, gathering his thoughts, before answering me. "Paul Reinhard," he declared, and then added, "and my girlfriend is Dianne, the one you met at the restaurant."

"Thank you, Paul. Did they give you a specific time?" I asked, glancing at Marcy.

"I have to turn myself in tomorrow before six in the evening, or they'll kill her," Reinhard revealed, his words laced with urgency. "Are you going to help us?"

"Hold on for a moment," I replied, placing the call on mute. Turning to Marcy, I sought her input. "What are we going to do?" I whispered.

"We have to help. I can't bear the thought of this pregnant girl losing her life," Marcy responded firmly.

I unmuted the call. "Paul, do you recall the name of the people who chartered your boat?" I inquired while Marcy began scouring the internet for any relevant information.

"They paid with a Platinum American Express. It had a corporate name. R...A...something Trading...wait, wait, RAJO Trading," Reinhard recalled, his voice fraught with anxiety.

"Do you have any idea where they might be from?" I probed, hoping for any clue we could use to aid our investigation.

"I don't know, Mr. Mancuso. I can't think straight," Reinhard admitted, his distress evident.

"You're doing fine. Do you remember any details they mentioned about places or travel destinations?" I probed further, hoping to extract more information.

"They talked about getting away during Mardi Gras. That's all I remember," Reinhard responded, his voice filled with uncertainty.

"Great," I whispered, conveying the newfound lead to Marcy. She nodded and continued her search.

"Are you in a safe location?" I asked Reinhard, concern evident in my voice.

"I'm moving around. I'm sure they forced Dianne to reveal my hiding place," Reinhard confessed, his fear palpable.

"Stay cautious and keep your phone with you at all times," I advised, emphasizing the importance of his safety.

"So, you're really going to help us?" Reinhard asked, a sense of relief creeping into his tone.

"Buddy, I'm going to have to involve the local police department. I can't handle this alone. Do you understand? You're entrusting us with your lives, Paul. We'll do everything we can," I assured him, fully aware of the gravity of the situation.

We ended the call, and Marcy and I regrouped in the living room. "Did you find anything?" I inquired.

"There's a company called RAJO Trading in New Orleans. They specialize in seafood imports. However, it's unlikely that drug dealers would use their real names to rent a fishing boat for a drug deal," Marcy shared her findings.

"We both know that it's often the small mistakes that criminals make that expose them. Perhaps these guys genuinely intended to go fishing and do the drug deal," I speculated.

Marcy chimed in, "But it seems like they got greedy and double-crossed the other party involved. Another body might surface soon unless the sharks got to him first."

"Well, that was another mistake on their part. And if Reinhard hadn't escaped, he would have likely been the next target," I analyzed the situation.

Marcy's tone grew serious as she asked, "You know what's going to happen if he trades himself for her, right?"

"There's no real trade happening here. I'm afraid this doesn't have a happy ending for either of them," I responded, a tinge of sadness in my voice.

"Make that three lives," Marcy remarked, acknowledging the unborn child.

I glanced at Marcy and simply closed my eyes, taking a moment to gather my thoughts. "I know," I whispered.

Marcy handed me the iPad, directing me to the Monroe County Sheriff's website. "They have a Special Investigation and High Drug Traffic Division in Key West. There's also a satellite office in Islamorada. You should call them now," she suggested, passing me the device.

I glanced at my watch, realizing it was almost midnight. "The hell with it," I muttered to myself. With determination, I dialed the local number. After four rings, a slightly groggy woman's voice answered, "Monroe County Sheriff's Department."

"Hi, this is Joey Mancuso. I'm a former detective with the homicide division in New York City. May I ask who I'm speaking with?" I inquired politely.

"Sure, I'm Colleen Baranova, former beauty queen and Wimbledon champion. What can I do for you?" came the sarcastic reply.

I couldn't help but chuckle, appreciating her quick wit. It was likely that they received prank calls frequently. "Well, Mrs. Baranova," I responded, "I have information regarding a murder and a drug deal that occurred a few days ago."

"It's 'Miss.' Did you say your name was Manuso?" she asked, clearly not taking me entirely seriously.

"Man...cuso," I clarified.

"Alright, Man...cuso. Who was murdered, and what's this about a drug deal?"

I decided to get straight to the point. "Your department is searching for Paul Reinhard, and I have information about him."

"Hold on a moment," Colleen replied, and I could hear a muffled conversation in the background. "Can we call you back on this number?"

"Yes, it's my cell number," I confirmed.

"And where are you located?"

"I'm staying at the Topsider, mile marker seventy-five, Unit one."

"Stay where you are. I'll arrange for someone to call you back," Colleen said before abruptly ending the call.

Turning to Marcy, I relayed the information. "They said someone will call."

Marcy looked concerned. "Do you think they'll come here?"

"She mentioned a call back, not a visit," I reassured her.

"But you know what they'll want, right?"

"Yes, I do," I replied. "Let me call Reinhard."

Realizing that the sheriff wouldn't be of much help unless Reinhard turned himself in, I made the call.

On the second ring, Reinhard picked up. "Mr. Mancuso, any news?"

"Paul, I've contacted the sheriff's department. They'll call me back. But here's the deal, buddy. They'll want you to turn yourself in before they take any action. It's standard procedure," I informed him.

"Oh no, I can't do that," Reinhard protested. "I need to surrender to these people, not the sheriff. If they arrest me, Dianne and the baby are as good as dead. You know that," he pleaded.

"I'll see what I can do. If they call again, make sure they let you talk to Dianne," I instructed, avoiding the explicit mention of a "proof of life" verification.

"Okay," Paul responded before ending the call.

"Joey, I'm going to bed. Let me know if something happens. Is that alright with you?" Marcy asked, seeking my permission.

"Not a problem. There's no need for both of us to stay up," I assured her.

Uncertain about how to pass the time, I debated whether to have a cup of coffee, grab a beer, eat something, or simply zone out in front of the TV. Opting for some fresh air, I settled on the balcony and waited for the anticipated call. The ambient noise was almost nonexistent, save for the gentle swishing of the waves caressing the shore. The bay waters appeared serene, resembling a glassy surface with a shimmering path leading to the horizon, accompanied by the moon shining above. Three sizable sailboats were anchored approximately three hundred yards away, their masts adorned with small flickering lights. In the far northeast, a faint glow illuminated the sky above the city of Miami.

Around two in the morning, I heard the sound of gravel crunching as a car approached our unit. I walked down to the rear of our unit, where the gravel road spanned the length of the resort.

A sheriff's car pulled up near me, and I patiently waited. Two officers emerged from the vehicle, their flashlights switched on. Thankfully, the car's blue and red lights remained unlit. I didn't want to cause a disturbance in such a peaceful setting.

The driver approached me. "Are you Mancuso?"

"Yes, officer, Joey Mancuso," I confirmed.

"Can I see some identification?" he asked, without introducing himself or his partner.

Anticipating the request, I had both my New York private detective and NYPD consultant IDs handy. Retrieving them from my shirt pocket, I handed both IDs to the officer. He shone his flashlight on them before passing them to his partner for inspection.

"You're retired from the NYPD?" the second officer inquired.

"Yes, I served twenty years with the force," I replied.

"So, where can we find Paul Reinhard?" officer one asked.

"Can we walk toward the dock? I don't want to disturb anyone here," I requested.

Both officers directed their flashlights toward the dock and its surroundings.

"You lead the way, and we'll follow," officer one instructed.

They were dealing with a murder investigation in the Atlantic Ocean and a drug deal, so they took extra precautions to verify my identity and ensure they weren't walking into a potential disaster.

Once we reached the dock, I took a seat on a bench while the two deputies stood in front of me.

"Guys, may I have your names?" I asked, wanting a formal introduction despite having glimpsed their name tags.

"I'm Deputy Kris, McCullum and this is Deputy Greg Leavitt. Now, what's going on here, and where is Reinhard? There's a warrant for his arrest," Deputy Kris responded.

"Yes, I'm aware. Please have a seat. It's a long story," I replied, gesturing for them to sit. However, they both remained standing as I began recounting the events from the moment Marcy and I first met Dianne.

For a good twenty-five minutes, I detailed the events, with both deputies listening attentively. Once I finished, Kris spoke up. "Two things need to happen here. First, we'll bring in our SID team from the Keys office. But before that, we need to take Mr. Reinhard into custody."

"I understand. However, Reinhard is prepared to surrender himself in exchange for his girlfriend, who, as I mentioned, is pregnant with their child. The deadline for this exchange is 6 p.m. tonight," I explained.

"Where is he now?" Kris inquired.

"I don't know. He was hiding in a boat, but he's been moving around," I replied.

"You sure he's not upstairs in your unit?" Greg asked.

"No, the only person upstairs is my wife, who is sleeping," I assured them.

"Do you mind if we take a look?" Greg requested.

"Follow me," I replied, standing up and leading them to our unit.

As we approached the unit, I noticed that Marcy was already awake and preparing coffee. I knocked lightly, cracked the door open, and asked, "Are you decent?" knowing well that she probably wasn't. Her preferred sleeping attire was simply one of my T-shirts.

"Just give me a minute," she replied, rushing into the bedroom.

A couple of minutes later, she opened the door, offering a warm smile to everyone. "Good morning. I just made coffee. Would anyone like a cup?"

The three of us walked into the unit.

I introduced Marcy, saying, "This is my wife, Marcy." To provide further credibility to the deputies, I added, "She retired just four days ago as a special agent with the bureau in New York. Marcy, this is Deputy Kris and Deputy Greg."

Everyone exchanged nods. Kris then asked, "May we have a look around?"

"Feel free to have a look. It won't take long," I responded with a chuckle. The unit consisted of two bedrooms, two bathrooms, and the living, dining, and kitchen area where we were gathered. It wasn't spacious, but it was functional and practical.

Both deputies swiftly inspected the bedrooms and returned within ten seconds.

"Coffee, anyone?" Marcy offered again.

"Sure, thank you," Kris accepted.

We sat around the dining table, each with a cup of coffee in hand. Greg took the opportunity to strike up a conversation. "How long were you with the bureau?" he asked Marcy.

"Almost twenty-one years with the White-Collar Crime Division," Marcy replied.

"Have you had enough?" Greg probed further.

"We just had a daughter, but I'll be working with our own investigative team now, which offers more flexibility with hours," Marcy explained, giving my arm a reassuring squeeze.

Turning the conversation back to the matter at hand, I asked, "What happens next?"

Before Kris or Greg could respond, Marcy voiced her concern, "I'm worried about Dianne and her baby. We can't allow them to harm both of them."

4

Tuesday, 6:15 a.m.

While Marcy had gone back to bed, I found it difficult to get a proper rest. In the past couple of hours, I had taken several short naps in the easy chair in the living room. However, restlessness consumed me as I tried to formulate a plan. Each time I heard the sound of gravel crunching, I would rush to the balcony, anticipating the arrival of a sheriff's car. Yet, at this early hour, many residents were using the boat ramp below us to put their boats in the water. We had less than twelve hours to locate Dianne, assuming she was still alive.

We had provided the deputies with our research on RAJO Trading, but it was likely they had already delved deep into the company and its owners. However, we had an advantage in the form of our skilled hacker, Agnes, back in New York. Marcy had sent her a text with the company's name, hoping she could uncover the owners. We knew that they had used an American Express card to charter the fishing boat, so it was possible they had also used the same card to book accommodations in the area. But where? And how could we find out? Reinhard didn't have access to his records, which would contain the Amex number. Although Agnes was talented, this task seemed nearly impossible for her to accomplish. We needed names, and we needed them quickly.

Deputy Kris had assured me that someone from their Special Investigation division would drive up from Key West to meet with us this morning. However, it was hard to anticipate their arrival before ten o'clock at the earliest.

In an attempt to keep myself occupied, I made fresh coffee, toasted two bagels, and prepared scrambled eggs with diced ham. I wasn't particularly hungry, but the activity prevented my mind from overheating.

Marcy entered the kitchen. "I could smell the food. Are you hungry?"

"Not really, but we might as well eat something. It's going to be a long day," I replied.

"Have we heard from Agnes?" she inquired.

"Not yet. I'm expecting a text and email from her any moment now, I hope," I responded.

"She'll come through. I told her about Dianne and the baby. She's just as worried as I am."

"Please have a seat. I'll serve you breakfast."

We sat down to eat, but it was clear that neither of us had any appetite. We mechanically went through the motions, pushing the food around on our plates.

"So, once we get the names from Agnes, what's our next step?" Marcy asked, her voice filled with concern. "Are we supposed to assume that the key players of RAJO are the ones currently fishing here? It could be any employee from their company. And where do we even begin searching? There must be countless motels to call, not to mention listings on Airbnb and other platforms."

"I've thought about that," I replied, taking a sip of coffee. "They used a corporate Platinum Amex card. I highly doubt that regular employees have access to such a card. As for accommodations, do you remember my case when I was with the NYPD, where I located the Colombian drug lord at The Plaza?"

"No, but I'm sure you're about to enlighten me," Marcy responded, a hint of amusement in her voice as she took a sip of her coffee.

"We had evidence linking him to the murder of another drug dealer in New York City. As we were brainstorming where to find him, I blurted out, 'The Plaza.' And believe it or not, when we called the hotel, he was there. The SWAT team apprehended him just an hour later."

"You guessed it, right?" Marcy asked, clearly intrigued.

"No, it wasn't a guess. I had previously interviewed him when he was a suspect. He was immensely wealthy and a foreigner. The Plaza has a longstanding reputation, especially among wealthy foreigners. So my observation of the man led me to believe that he would choose The Plaza as his destination."

"Okay, Sherlock. So where do you think our suspects from New Orleans would be staying here?" Marcy inquired, a playful grin on her face.

I stood up to refill our coffee cups. "When you were doing your research before coming down here, which were the most luxurious places we couldn't afford?"

"Correction, we could afford them if it weren't for your frugality," Marcy retorted. "But the top ones were The Moorings Village and Cheeca Lodge and Spa."

"Just as my brother always says, it's wise to be thrifty. I have a hunch that our suspects are staying at one of those two places. I'd bet anything on it."

"I hope you're right, not just for our sake, but for Dianne's well-being," Marcy said, her tone filled with concern. "I'm going to call Agnes now."

Just as she said that, a notification sounded on my phone. "Hold on. Agnes says we should check our email."

"Let me grab my iPad," Marcy said, dashing into the bedroom to retrieve it.

Opening the email, she read, "Rafael 'Rafa' Galiano serves as the president of RAJO, while Jorge Castellanos is the COO. Both are from Honduras and immigrated to the US on B-1 visas in 2010. They established RAJO in the same year, specializing in importing seafood products from various South American countries, including Mexico, and so on."

I couldn't help but smile. "We've got them."

"I wish I shared your optimism," Marcy replied.

Glancing at my watch, I saw that it was already seven forty-five. "Where on earth is our contact from SID?"

"Call Deputy Kris while I contact these two places to check if they have a room there," Marcy suggested.

I dialed the sheriff's office in Islamorada, but my friend Coleen and the deputies had finished their shifts. Unfortunately, I couldn't obtain their cell numbers, as the desk deputy informed me. Restlessly, I drummed my fingers on the dining table as Marcy made her calls.

"No rooms at the Cheeca Lodge under any of their names or the corporate name. Let me try The Moorings."

As I heard the sound of gravel crunching, I rushed outside. Our SID operatives had arrived, parking under our unit. Two individuals stepped out of the car. "Up here!" I called out.

Both of them looked up and nodded in acknowledgment.

I waited for them and noticed our awake neighbors giving me concerned looks. One of them asked, "Is everything okay?"

I flashed a reassuring thumbs-up in response.

The two deputies reached the landing, and I introduced myself. "This is my wife, Marcy," I said, turning to Marcy and adding, "And these are Sergeant Leone and Deputy Susan Joyce."

Marcy smiled and subtly gestured toward her iPad. She had found something.

"Please have a seat. I still have some hot coffee. Would you like some?" I offered, but both of them declined.

Leone turned to Marcy and inquired, "You're the FBI agent?"

"I was a special agent, yes. Until four days ago," Marcy confirmed.

Leone nodded, then turned to me. "And you are the former homicide detective from New York?"

I maintained my smile and gave a nod of agreement. Leone appeared slender, weighing maybe a hundred and fifty pounds at most and standing no taller than five-five. He sported a small pencil mustache above his barely noticeable upper lip, and he was bald. I estimated his age to be around fifty-two. Joyce, on the other hand, was younger, possibly in her forties, and taller than her partner. She had short blond hair, complemented by striking blue eyes. Her appearance went beyond mere attractiveness, with high pink cheeks and a disarming smile. We had two paths to tread. They could perceive us as arrogant law enforcement agents from the big city and treat us with disdain, or they could show us respect and acknowledge our expertise. Naturally, I hoped for the latter. I was weary of the common perception of "smart-ass, big-city cops."

Leone commented, "This is good," and asked, "Does everyone know the procedures and protocols moving forward? Are either of you carrying a weapon?"

Marcy responded, "No, Sergeant. We are unarmed."

I inquired, "How much do you know?"

"We believe we have most of the information," Leone replied. "Deputy Kris provided a detailed report via email last night or early this morning."

I nodded and added, "Good. Let's get up to speed. Our researcher in New York obtained the names of..." I proceeded to inform them about Galiano and Castellanos.

"That all seems plausible. Now, we need to locate these two individuals in the Keys," Joyce remarked.

"Well, we believe we've made some progress on that front as well," I said.

Leone and Joyce exchanged glances, and Leone's grin made me wonder if they thought we were fabricating everything.

"What kind of progress have you made?" Leone asked. I glanced at Marcy and nodded.

"RAJO Trading has rented a three-bedroom cottage at The Moorings Village on 123 Beach Road, around mile marker eighty-two," Marcy stated.

Leone questioned, "How can you be sure this Reinhard fellow isn't making all this up? He could have easily killed the other guy and attempted to keep the drugs and money for himself."

"Seriously, Sergeant? One man against six?" I retorted.

Leone raised another concern, "How do you know the two men they encountered weren't working with Reinhard? He could have easily radioed them to meet up and concocted this entire story. Except it played out differently."

I glanced at Marcy. Was it possible? Were we being deceived?

Marcy asked sternly, "And what about Dianne's abduction?"

Leone responded, "Have you spoken to her since the abduction?"

Damn, he had a point. Everything they said made sense.

"Could you at least check The Moorings?" Marcy pleaded.

"I can't go charging in there based on a hunch," Leone replied. "Right now, our only suspect is the potential fictional author, Paul Reinhard. We need to locate him first before taking any further action."

I glanced at my watch. It was already ten o'clock. "Sergeant, if Reinhard is a true-crime author and not a fictional one, his girlfriend and unborn baby have only eight hours left."

"We'll see about that," Leone retorted. Shaking his head, he added, "You know, for two seasoned law enforcement professionals, I'm surprised you didn't consider the option I presented."

They both stood up, heading toward the door. Joyce chimed in, "We'll keep you informed."

I could sense Marcy's anger. She clenched her lower lip, holding back her frustration. Finally, as they reached the landing, she couldn't contain herself any longer. "If anything happens to Dianne and the baby, you'll bear the responsibility," she exclaimed.

5
Tuesday, 11 a.m.

Marcy watched with frustration as Leone and Joyce casually descended the steps. "These two clowns have completely twisted everything around on Reinhard," Marcy vented, seething at their lack of urgency.

"It's their job to be skeptical. However, their unwillingness to investigate the story is concerning. But we have a car, and we can handle this," I reassured her.

"Do what?" Marcy questioned.

I reached for the car keys. "We're going to The Moorings."

"That could be risky. We're unarmed, and we know there are at least four of them," Marcy pointed out.

"We'll adapt as we go," I replied as we made our way down the steps and headed for the car.

As I started the car, Marcy said, "I was afraid you'd say that."

We drove north on US 1 for about five miles, then turned right onto Beach Road and continued until we reached the entrance of The Moorings.

Pulling up to the guard gate, I rolled down my window, smiled at the young woman in uniform, and said, "Hi, we have some friends staying here, and we wanted to surprise them, but I don't have their cottage number."

"I'm sorry, sir. I can't provide you with that information or allow you in without their approval," she replied. "I can call them. What's their name?"

Glancing at her name tag, I said, "Stacey, that would ruin the surprise, wouldn't it? They're registered under their corporate name, RAJO Trading, or perhaps Mr. Galiano."

Stacey punched a few keys on her computer. "Yes, I see RAJO Trading. I'd be happy to give them a call."

I turned to Marcy and asked, "Do you still have any of your FBI business cards?"

"Maybe a couple. Do you want one?" Marcy replied.

I nodded to Marcy and then turned back to Stacey. "Hold on a moment, Stacey." Marcy handed me a business card.

As Marcy and I entered the premises, we couldn't help but feel a mix of excitement and nervousness. The elaborate ruse we had concocted with Stacey had worked, but the weight of our deception lingered in the back of our minds.

We followed Stacey's directions and made our way toward cottage six, walking hand in hand as we blended in with the other vacationing couples. The atmosphere around us was serene, with the sound of waves crashing against the shore and the gentle rustling of palm trees in the warm breeze.

As we approached cottage six, we noticed its distinct three-bedroom layout, nestled amidst the lush surroundings. It was an idyllic spot for our covert surveillance operation, offering ample opportunities to remain inconspicuous while gathering crucial information.

With Marcy's card safely back in my possession, we exchanged a smile, momentarily easing the tension that had built up during our interaction with Stacey. Despite the risk of impersonating FBI agents, we knew the importance of the mission, and the potential consequences were not lost on us.

"Let's focus on the task at hand," I said, my voice laced with determination. "We've come this far, and we need to make the most of this opportunity. Dianne could be inside, and we must gather any evidence we can."

Marcy nodded, her expression serious. "Agreed. We need to act swiftly and discreetly. Let's keep our cover as a couple planning our honeymoon and explore the area while keeping an eye out for any suspicious activity. We must remain unobtrusive, just like the seagulls."

With renewed resolve, we embarked on our mission, walking leisurely around the pristine grounds, taking in the natural beauty that surrounded us. The meticulously manicured lawns, the coconut trees swaying in the breeze, and the colorful wildlife all created a picturesque facade that belied the secrets hidden within.

Time seemed to both speed up and slow down as we maintained a watchful eye, searching for any signs that would lead us closer to Dianne and the truth we sought. Every passing minute brought a heightened sense of anticipation, knowing that each step could bring us closer to a breakthrough.

As we discreetly observed the other cottages and their occupants, we hoped to catch a glimpse of someone who might be connected to our investigation. Every detail mattered; every interaction and conversation potentially held a clue.

The sun warm glow over the landscape, and we continued our surveillance, our dedication unwavering. We remained vigilant, ready to adapt our strategy at a moment's notice, prepared to face any obstacles that might arise.

In this paradise of beauty and tranquility, we sought to expose the truth that lay beneath the surface. As shadows grew longer, we pressed forward, determined to find the secrets, and perhaps Dianne herself, that the cottage held captive.

"There it is, unit six," Marcy whispered, her eyes fixed on the white wooden cottage adorned with a charming front veranda, embraced by the vibrant greenery of meticulously landscaped plants and flowers.

"Quite a beautiful cottage," I remarked, my gaze captivated by its quaint allure. "Do you have any idea how much these units rent for?"

Marcy nodded, a glint of mischief in her eyes. "This time of year, it's over four thousand dollars a night. I happened to check when I was researching this place."

I chuckled softly. "And you still think I'm being cheap for not wanting to book a week here?"

She shrugged off my comment, her focus shifting to the absence of any signs of activity. "I don't see anyone. Do you think they've checked out?"

A sense of ambiguity hung in the air as we stood before the silent cottage. Without any visible indicators, it was impossible to determine if it was vacant or hiding secrets within its walls. I contemplated the situation before suggesting, "Should we knock on their door?"

Marcy's eyes gleamed with a hint of mischief as she proposed a better idea. "Wait here," she instructed, turning back toward the maid we had encountered earlier.

I positioned myself in front of the unit, taking a few steps toward the shoreline, facing away from the cottage. Moments later, Marcy rejoined me, and I turned to face her, my curiosity piqued. "Well?"

"They haven't checked out, but they're not currently here. The maid hasn't been granted access to the cottage; she only leaves towels on the porch," Marcy informed me, her voice tinged with uncertainty.

My mind raced, contemplating the implications of this new information. "Has she seen Dianne?"

"She mentioned spotting a group of men and a woman leaving before our arrival, but we can't be certain if it was

Dianne or someone else. Do you think they left to rendezvous with Reinhard for a trade?" Marcy speculated.

Glancing at my watch, I noted that it was already twelve-thirty. "But why would they do that? Reinhard has until six tonight," I countered, turning halfway to steal a glance at the enigmatic cottage.

Marcy pondered for a moment before suggesting, "Perhaps Reinhard grew anxious and contacted them to expedite the trade. He might think that we are incapable of intervening before the deadline."

Shaking my head, I acknowledged the urgency of the situation. "Regardless of their intentions, we need to gain access to the cottage and thoroughly search it for any evidence. Do you think we can persuade the maid to provide us with a key?"

Marcy hesitated, her face contorted with concern. "Impersonating a federal agent again isn't a wise course of action."

I smirked at her playful remark. "I was referring to the idea of searching the unit, not impersonating an agent.

"Let's abandon both ideas, Mancuso. Instead, let's contact Reinhard. I have a growing desire to meet him and exchange crucial information."

Curiosity etched across my face, I questioned her, "Why, though? What's driving this sudden urge to meet Reinhard?"

With a determined glint in her eyes, Marcy responded, "I believe that meeting Reinhard will provide us with valuable insights and help us unravel the enigma surrounding our investigation. There are still many unknowns, and we can't afford to leave any stone unturned."

Agreeing with her assessment, we began to retreat, preparing to regroup and strategize for our upcoming meeting with Reinhard. The mysterious cottage stood as a formidable enigma, and the secrets it held would only be uncovered through careful planning.

Give him a call, just to ensure he's not already on his way to the trade. Plus, I'm eager to meet him in person," Marcy said, emphasizing the importance of our upcoming rendezvous with Reinhard.

Dialing his burner phone, I anxiously awaited his response. "Mr. Mancuso, any good news? Have you found Dianne?" Reinhard's voice came through the line.

"Not yet, Paul. We need to meet. Can you tell me where you are?" I urged, my voice filled with determination.

Confusion-tinged Reinhard's voice. "Meet? Why? I'm in the vicinity."

"Has anyone contacted you?" I pressed, hoping to gather any additional information.

"No, I reached out to them. I spoke with Dianne. She assured me that she's fine. The trade is still scheduled for six. I don't know what to do," Reinhard confessed, his voice laden with worry.

"Where can we meet?" I inquired, eager to discuss the situation face to face.

"Alright. Are you familiar with the History of Diving Museum? It's located next to Ziggie and Mad Dog's steak place," Reinhard suggested.

"Yes, I know the restaurant," I replied.

"Meet me behind the restaurant. They're closed at this time," he instructed.

"I'll be there in five," I assured him before ending the call. As we left the Moorings, I waved at Stacey, acknowledging her unwitting involvement in our undercover operation.

Driving a few miles north on US 1, we arrived at Ziggie & Mad Dog's on the left side of the road, across from the museum. I bypassed the front parking area and parked the car on the side of the road behind the restaurant. Both Marcy and I scanned our surroundings, searching for any sign of Reinhard.

"Do you think he's playing games with us?" Marcy questioned, her tone laced with skepticism.

"He's likely just being cautious, ensuring we aren't being followed," I reasoned, my eyes scanning the area for any movement.

A minute later, Reinhard, disguised with a hood, emerged from behind the bushes at the back of the restaurant. He swiftly approached our car, opened the back door, and slid inside, hunching down to maintain a low profile.

"Drive out of here. Head north toward Publix," he directed, his voice laced with urgency.

Marcy turned around to catch a glimpse of Reinhard as I pulled out of the parking area and drove north. She then glanced at me, a faint smile playing on her lips, likely amused by Reinhard's choice of Elton John sunglasses as a disguise.

We traveled another mile or two until we reached the Publix parking lot. I parked the car and switched off the engine, signaling that it was safe for Reinhard to sit up and remove his disguise.

"Reinhard, you can sit up now. They won't come here," I assured him. "And please, take off the glasses."

Reinhard complied, sitting up and swiftly scanning his surroundings before removing the sunglasses. "This is my wife, Marcy. We have some questions for you," I introduced Marcy as she turned to face him, ready to delve deeper into the intricacies of our ongoing investigation.

Marcy posed the question, her curiosity piqued. "Are you the same Paul Reinhard who graduated from MIT and sold his company for millions?"

Reinhard nodded in confirmation, his intrigue evident. "How did you know?"

"We do our due diligence," Marcy replied, her tone confident. "Tell me about what happened that day, starting from the beginning."

Reinhard began recounting the events. "It was like any other day when I have a charter. I woke up at 5 a.m. and headed to the marina to prepare the boat. My guests were supposed to arrive at six."

Marcy inquired further, "Did they arrive on time?"

"They got there a little after six thirty," Reinhard admitted.

Curiosity burning in me, I questioned Reinhard, "Why did they choose you? How did they know to contact you?"

"They met Dianne at the Square Grouper, just like you did," Reinhard explained. "They asked her if she knew a fishing captain, and she gave them my card. That's all."

Marcy and I exchanged glances, silently acknowledging the significance of this information. "Please continue," I urged Reinhard.

"This isn't the first time she has done this," Reinhard admitted. "She often refers clients to me."

Marcy pressed on, her questions probing deeper. "How long have you been involved with Dianne?"

"About six months or so," Reinhard replied.

Curiosity still burning, Marcy questioned, "How far along is Dianne in her pregnancy?"

Reinhard replied, "She said she's about a month along. Why all these questions about her?"

Marcy maintained her focus, her tone steady. "Was the pregnancy planned? Did both of you intend to have a child?"

Reinhard's gaze darted around the parking lot, his nervousness palpable. "It wasn't something we actively sought, but neither of us wants to terminate."

"Understood," Marcy acknowledged. "Did Dianne have any prior acquaintance with these individuals?"

Reinhard's eyes widened in surprise. "What are you suggesting? I don't know. But do you think..." Reinhard's words trailed off, leaving the implication hanging in the air.

Marcy interrupted him, her voice firm. "Now, Reinhard, focus. Tell me about what happened when you went out fishing."

Reinhard obliged, recounting the details of his fishing excursion. "First, I headed a few miles out, baiting and casting to attract fish. Then we began searching for dolphins and any signs of tuna. After a while, they requested that I meet up with these other guys, and..." Reinhard reiterated the same story he had previously shared with me.

With the conversation drawing to a close, Marcy had one final inquiry. "One last question, Reinhard. Does Dianne know about your wealth?"

"My wealth? Well, yes," Reinhard admitted. "Initially, I didn't disclose it to her, but when she told me about the pregnancy and expressed her concerns, I wanted to alleviate her worries."

Marcy pressed further. "So you told her that you're a millionaire?"

"I didn't want her to be anxious about our situation, so yes," Reinhard confirmed.

As Marcy glanced at me, I understood her intent. Addressing Reinhard, she continued her line of inquiry. "Now, tell me about the sea conditions on the day you went fishing."

Reinhard appeared surprised by the question, momentarily unsure. Did he not understand, or was he attempting to gather his thoughts?

"The sea conditions," Marcy clarified. "What were they like?"

Reinhard began to respond, offering details. "The past few days had been very calm. The waves were one to two feet high, which isn't ideal for dolphin fishing. That day, it was a beautiful but calm day. Do you think I'm making all of this up?" Reinhard's tone carried a mix of frustration and disbelief.

I couldn't help but voice my own doubts. "Are you?"

"Why the hell would I seek your help if I made it all up?" Reinhard retorted, his gaze scanning the parking lot anxiously.

Marcy interjected, exploring another possibility. "Perhaps you double-crossed these individuals, not anticipating that they would come after you or abduct Dianne."

Reinhard's expression shifted to one of shock. "Oh my God, are you both serious? It's almost two o'clock, and I only have four hours left. What are we going to do? Did you meet with the sheriffs?"

"Yes, Paul, we did," I replied, pulling out of the Publix parking lot and heading south. "But they suspect that you orchestrated this entire situation to retain the money and drugs and evade prosecution for two murders."

Reinhard's disbelief was palpable. "That's insane! And you think I would involve Dianne in the middle of all this?"

"Call us the moment you receive the call to arrange the trade," I instructed, determination lacing my words. With that, we left the Publix parking lot, our sights set on what lay ahead.

6
Tuesday, 2:20 p.m.

We dropped Reinhard off behind Ziggie's and made our way back to our place. Along the route, we decided to stop at a convenience store to purchase two burner phones. I had a nagging feeling that using my regular phone wouldn't be safe in this situation.

"What are your thoughts on Reinhard?" I asked Marcy, curious to hear her assessment.

"To be honest, I believe he's being truthful. I found the way he presented his story to be well-balanced," Marcy replied thoughtfully.

"Balanced? What do you mean?" I inquired, eager to understand her perspective.

Marcy explained, "When someone fabricates a story, they often embellish insignificant details while downplaying the important aspects. It creates an illusion of providing answers without actually revealing the truth. Unless you're a psychopath, lying becomes difficult. Liars tend to focus on nonessential information and neglect to add important details. It's a form of deception."

"Like politicians," I interjected, briefly turning my gaze away from the road to meet Marcy's eyes.

She chuckled and nodded. "Exactly. If Reinhard were lying, he would have gone into great detail about his breakfast, how Dianne kissed him goodbye at 5 a.m., the specifics of the bait he used, and so on. However, he didn't exaggerate or omit any key details related to the actual crime."

"He provided the same information to you as he did to me, word for word," I added, emphasizing the consistency of Reinhard's account.

"That's precisely what leads me to believe he's telling the truth. If he had fabricated the story, it would have likely changed in some way. You know how we question suspects separately when working with Father Dom? It reveals a lot. So, based on that experience, I think Reinhard is being genuine," Marcy explained.

I nodded, appreciating Marcy's insights. "So, you trust him?"

"Yes, I do. However, I can't help but wonder about Dianne's involvement. It's possible she's part of a scheme to extract a substantial sum of money from Reinhard. Despite his brilliance, he appears somewhat gullible," Marcy voiced her curiosity.

"An easy mark, a patsy," I mused, considering the potential motives at play.

"Exactly," Marcy confirmed, her gaze fixed on the passing scenery outside.

"In that case, if your theory holds true, either Reinhard won't receive a call to make him sweat it out, or they'll contact him to demand a ransom," I speculated, steering into the parking lot of the Topsider.

"But if I'm wrong..." Marcy trailed off, her voice filled with concern, leaving the outcome hanging in the air.

"Don't go there. They still need Dianne alive to bring him to them," I cautioned Marcy, emphasizing the importance of keeping Dianne safe.

"Should we call Leone and Joyce again?" Marcy suggested, considering reaching out to the local law enforcement once more.

"And what? They'll want Reinhard in custody before taking any further action," I replied, recognizing the limitations of involving the authorities at this stage.

Just as we contemplated our next move, my phone rang. Hastily retrieving it from my pocket, I saw that it was the Monroe County Sheriff's Office calling. Putting the call on speaker, I answered, "This is Mancuso."

"Leone here. We need to pick up Reinhard. A second body floated in at the sandbar. We think it's the second person he killed," Leone informed us without wasting time.

Curiosity sparked, I questioned, "How do you know it's a victim related to this crime?" Marcy and I ascended the stairs to our unit, keeping the conversation going.

"Executed with a close-range shot to the forehead, forty caliber, just like the first victim. Oh, and he's missing a leg. Likely became shark food," Leone revealed grimly.

Seeking more information, I asked, "Do you have any identities?"

"They didn't have IDs, but we matched prints for one of them—a Cuban citizen deported two years ago for drug trafficking. We assume the other is Cuban as well. Your guy killed these two, kept the drugs and the money," Leone concluded, presenting a theory that aligned with their investigation.

Resolute in our belief in Reinhard's story, I interjected, "That's one theory, but not the only one. We believe his account. Moreover, his pregnant girlfriend was abducted by the killers you're after, and—"

Interrupting me, Leone retorted, "Oh, excuse me! The retired New York FBI special agent and retired NYPD detective have solved our case. I can go back to Key West and go fishing myself. Look, Mancuso, if you don't tell me where I can pick up this guy, I'm arresting both you and your wife for obstruction. Got it, buddy?"

Leone's typical reaction was expected. Small-town local law enforcement often harbored animosity toward big-city cops, especially those associated with the FBI. Admittedly, their theory held merit, but we had the advantage of conversing directly with Reinhard—an opportunity they had not yet had.

"We've spoken to him, and he's constantly on the move, so we don't know his current location. Listen to me. I understand your perspective. We haven't solved the case either, but if Reinhard is telling the truth, he has less than four hours to trade himself for his pregnant girlfriend. If you arrest him now, we'll lose any chance of finding these people," I explained, trying to make him see the bigger picture. Inside, I wanted to add, "You understand, asshole?"

Leone's tone softened slightly as he responded, "Okay, Mancuso, assuming these people exist, what's your plan?"

"We know where the four guys are keeping Dianne," I revealed.

Joyce was eager to know the details. "And you found out how? And when?" she inquired.

"We made a few calls this morning and located them at The Moorings. They're holed up in a three-bedroom cottage," I explained, providing the specifics.

"I see. So you've already been there yourself, conducting your own investigation. Is that how things work in New York?" Leone questioned, his tone laced with suspicion. "Why didn't you inform us before taking matters into your own hands?"

Suppressing my frustration, I diplomatically replied, "I apologize for not informing you beforehand. It was an oversight on our part. However, you can still go there and check it out for yourselves."

Leone retorted, his hostility palpable, "Yes, sir. Any other orders?"

To diffuse the tension, I injected a touch of humor, saying, "Don't call me sir; call me chief."

Leone chuckled, and I thought I heard Joyce joining in. "Okay, Mancuso, if they're indeed there, we'll bring them all in. Then, I expect Reinhard will willingly turn himself in. Agreed?"

"We'll personally deliver him to you. Thank you," I acknowledged, stepping out onto the balcony.

Our unit boasted a magnificent 180-degree view of the bay, stretching from west to north to east. It was a truly glorious day. Below, other guests of this idyllic paradise were enjoying various activities—paddling, kayaking, snorkeling, or simply basking in the sun on our private beach. The desire to join them gnawed at me. We had come here seeking rest and relaxation, yet we found ourselves entangled in a web of murder, abduction, and drug investigation.

Marcy joined me on the balcony, holding a beer and a cigar. A smile formed on my face as I reached for the offerings. "Thank you. Do you think your parents can look after Michelle Marie for a few more days?"

Curious, Marcy asked, "Why? Do you want to stay here a little longer?"

"Look at these people," I gestured toward the vibrant scene below. "We should indulge ourselves in the same leisure. Instead, we're caught up in work."

"I'll call them and see if we can extend our stay here," Marcy offered, understanding my longing for a brief reprieve from our responsibilities.

I savored the taste of the beer and the rich aroma of the cigar as I took a leisurely puff. "Do that. We could really use some genuine time off," I expressed to Marcy.

An hour later, my phone rang, and it was Leone on the line. From the tone of his voice, it was clear that he was not pleased. "Mancuso, were you and your wife posing as FBI agents?" he demanded.

Oh no, what had transpired now? "Why would you say that?" I responded, trying to gather my thoughts.

Leone retorted, his frustration evident, "The guard at the front gate of The Moorings reported that two agents had already been there, inquiring about these individuals pretending to be their friends. The four men and a woman returned, and she informed them that friends had stopped by. Long story short, they became suspicious and left. Now tell me it wasn't you and your wife."

"I believe there must have been a misunderstanding. Do you have any information on their whereabouts?" I inquired, hoping to salvage the situation.

Leone scoffed, clearly doubting my explanation. "Sure, Mancuso. You messed up big time. If..."

As Leone continued speaking, I noticed another incoming call coming through, transferred to me by my office in New York. Ignoring it for the moment, I wrapped up my conversation with Leone.

Using the burner phone, I dialed Reinhard's number. He answered on the third ring. "Paul, take note of this number. It's a burner phone. Did the kidnappers contact you?" I asked, my tone urgent.

"I have twenty-four hours to come up with four million dollars, or they'll kill Dianne," Paul revealed, his voice filled with desperation.

7
Tuesday, 4 p.m.

"Did you get a chance to speak with Dianne?" I inquired, eager for any updates.

"Yes, I did. She seems worried, but overall she's alright," Reinhard replied. "It seems like she might have mentioned our wealth to them.

Can you gather that amount of cash within twenty-four hours?"

"I explained to them that it's not feasible. I need to sell securities and wire the money to a bank—they'll provide further instructions. However, it takes at least two days for trades to settle before the funds become available," he explained.

"What was their response?" I asked anxiously.

"They simply hung up," Paul responded with a sense of dread. "They're threatening to kill her, Mr. Mancuso."

"I don't think they'll follow through with that, Paul. She's their leverage for the money. Stay strong and keep us updated," I reassured him before ending the call.

At this point, I was grappling with conflicting thoughts. Was Dianne somehow involved in this situation? If so, their initial plan might not have been to harm Reinhard during the drug deal. Instead, they would have likely targeted him afterward. Alternatively, could Dianne herself be a victim caught up in this twisted ransom scheme?

"Is there an FBI office located in the Keys?" I asked Marcy, sharing the details of my conversation with Reinhard.

"I believe there's one in Homestead, about fifty miles from here. Why? Are you thinking of involving them?" Marcy inquired.

"We're dealing with two murders and now a kidnapping for ransom. Shouldn't they be informed and involved?" I questioned, recognizing the limitations of our own resources.

"It's quite a change of heart, considering you're usually the one who prefers handling things on our own. Now you want to bring in the Feds?" Marcy remarked, slightly surprised.

"I know. But without our team and with limited resources, it's the logical choice. And if Dianne is indeed a victim in all of this, I don't want to risk her life," I explained, my concern for Dianne's safety growing.

"Leone should be the one to contact the bureau. You should call and update him on the latest developments," Marcy suggested, emphasizing the importance of involving local law enforcement.

I followed Marcy's suggestion and acted accordingly. Leone wasn't particularly pleased with my proposal to involve the FBI. He mentioned that he would consider it but had already deployed all his personnel to search for Reinhard in Islamorada, Marathon, Tavernier, and Key Largo. Leone believed that if Reinhard was ready to proceed with the original exchange, he wouldn't have ventured too far north or south of these four keys. He was correct in his assumption, but now Reinhard faced a larger predicament—there was no way to deliver the money within twenty-four hours.

After recounting my conversation with Leone, I remarked to Marcy, "He might decide against involving the bureau. I don't think he wants to relinquish control of the case."

"That sounds like someone I know," Marcy quipped.

I understood who Marcy was referring to. "I think we all become possessive when it comes to our cases. However, he doesn't have enough personnel to handle everything."

"If they arrest Reinhard, he won't be able to deliver the money to the abductors, especially if they don't believe his story."

"It's disheartening to think he might lose all that money," I replied.

"Wouldn't you be devastated if I were abducted?" Marcy asked.

"You were once, and I saved you,"

Marcy reminded me. "Except my abductor didn't want money; he wanted to keep me with him forever and start a family.

"I would have done anything to rescue you, even if it meant robbing a bank," I confessed, gazing into her eyes.

"You're sweet, Mancuso, and that's why I love you," she responded.

"I know."

"You're also full of it," she teased. "Anyway, why don't you reach out to your friend Jack Ryder in Miami for assistance?"

"Sure, that's all we need—to further aggravate Leone by involving an author of murder mysteries in the case."

"He's actually a consultant for the Miami Beach major crimes division, and quite a good one," Marcy revealed.

I met Marcy's gaze. "I fail to see how Jack can help in this situation. He doesn't possess any more resources than we do."

"Regardless, we should have called him when we arrived here. He's always hanging around Islamorada, with his boat docked somewhere in the bay. He'll be disappointed we didn't reach out to him," Marcy reasoned.

After contemplating it for a moment, I dialed Jack's number on the disposable phone. After exchanging a few pleasantries, he exclaimed, "You son of a bitch! You're in the Keys and didn't bother to inform me?"

"We had intended to call you once we arrived here," I replied while Marcy made a disapproving face. "Are you currently in Miami Beach?"

"No, I've got the Easy Ryder moored in the usual spot, right off Robbie's on the bayside. I'm just a few miles away from the Topsider," Jack informed me. "I'm flying solo this time, working on a tight deadline for a new novella. Just putting the finishing touches on it before sending it off to the editors."

Suddenly, it clicked in my mind. "You still have a Zodiac on your boat?"

"Of course I do. I can swing by and meet you and Marcy in fifteen minutes. Would you like me to do that?"

"You know where we're staying?" I questioned.

"I know precisely where the Topsider is. Head to the dock in fifteen minutes. Make sure you have some cold beers ready," Jack confirmed.

I grabbed a few beers and placed them in a cooler. Marcy and I walked down to the dock, placing the cooler on a nearby table as we waited for Jack. True to his word, fifteen minutes later, he skillfully maneuvered his boat into a dock space, and we warmly greeted him.

Jack Ryder and I had crossed paths during a case I worked on for the NYPD several years ago. Back then, he had been a highly successful investment banker. We instantly clicked and developed a strong friendship during the course of the investigation. Despite coming from different worlds, our personalities were remarkably similar, and we quickly formed a bond as if we had known each other for ages. We were around the same age, but Jack was taller than me, with blond hair—a quintessential all-American athletic type.

One morning, his wife announced that she needed space, space that didn't involve him. After a contentious divorce, they divided their assets and settled custody arrangements for Max, their beagle.

The following day, Jack walked into his office in New York's Financial District and handed in his resignation. He had grown tired of investment banking, bosses, suits, ties, and all the other nonsense that came with it. Together with Max, he headed to Miami Beach, where he purchased an old fifty-four-foot yacht and pursued a successful career as a bestselling crime author.

"Marcy, how have you been? And how's your beautiful daughter doing?" Jack inquired, stepping onto the dock.

Marcy embraced him warmly. "We're both doing great. Thanks for asking.

"And how's your older son behaving?" Jack asked, affectionately ruffling my hair.

"He's doing fine for now," Marcy replied, laughing.

Jack playfully hugged my shoulders and added, "If you ever kick his ass out, you know where I live."

"Okay, stop hitting on my wife, or I won't give you a beer," I teased, chuckling.

We settled down at a picnic table outside, cracking open three beers. The conversation meandered through our past cases as we updated each other on our lives. Jack had gone through several romantic partners since our last encounter, and Marcy was relieved to hear that he was no longer strictly adhering to his "expiration date" rule for dating.

"So, how long will you be staying?" Jack inquired.

"Probably until Wednesday of next week, depending on whether we can extend our stay beyond Saturday," Marcy answered.

"I'm more than happy to have you stay on board as long as you want," Jack offered.

"Which brings me to the case we're working on," I interjected, launching into an account of Reinhard and his escapades.

As I finished my story and we emptied our second beers, Jack asked, "Let me make sure I've got this straight. You want me to harbor a fugitive wanted for two murders who allegedly stole cash and fentanyl? By the way, how much fentanyl are we talking about?"

"About fifteen pounds, worth around one million four in street value," I informed him.

"You do realize that if I get caught doing this, we could all end up in prison, right?" Jack pointed out.

I smiled and replied, "Look at it this way—you might just find the plot for your next bestselling novel. Besides, how much in royalties have I contributed to your bank account by asking for your help in the past?"

"I'll babysit this guy as long as he doesn't talk too much. I've got work to do," Jack agreed.

Marcy ordered pizzas for the three of us, and we remained outdoors to partake in the daily tradition of watching the sunset along with the other guests. I brought Jack up to speed and informed him that Marcy had retired from the bureau and was joining our team.

"So, where is this Reinhard hiding now?" Jack inquired.

"He's laying low, but this island is small, and he's likely to be spotted and arrested. That's why stashing him in the Easy Ryder is the perfect solution," I explained.

"Does he know about your plan?" Jack asked.

"Not yet. I thought we should move him tonight when there's less chance of him being spotted," I replied.

"You're going to ask him to come here?" Jack questioned.

"I have a feeling this place is being watched. The deputies are aware that we've been in contact with him," I explained.

"In that case, tell him I'll pick him up at the small beach in Robbie's marina," Jack suggested.

I dialed Reinhard's burner phone, and he answered on the fourth ring. "Hello?" he greeted.

"Paul, it's Mancuso. Are you still in Islamorada?" I asked.

"Yes, why?" he responded.

"I have a plan for you to stay hidden. Have you already sold your securities?" I inquired.

"I've sold them, but I won't have the funds ready to wire until tomorrow. The earliest would be Friday morning. I'm afraid that won't work for them," Reinhard explained.

"If they want the money, they'll have to wait. Now let me explain what I have in mind," I said, outlining the details of Jack and the Easy Ryder.

Initially, Reinhard wasn't enthusiastic about the plan. However, realizing that hiding aboard a yacht was likely his best option at the moment, he reluctantly agreed.

After ending the call with Reinhard, we continued to marvel at the stunning sunset. A golden river seemed to form between us and the descending sun while the clouds above appeared ablaze. Shades of blue emerged, adding the final touches to the magnificent canvas. The sun began to set behind the three sailboats moored near the Topsider. I framed the breathtaking scene with my phone and snapped a photo, which could easily qualify for National Geographic.

"Alright, Jack, Reinhard will be ready for pickup at nine," I informed him once the tranquility settled in.

"What's your plan?" he inquired.

"I need to get a step ahead of these guys. Since we can't rely on any help from the sheriff, I'm going to have Agnes dig deeper into RAJO Trading. I want to find out who these individuals, Galiano and Castellanos, really are," I explained my strategy.

8
Wednesday, 7 a.m.

Marcy joined me in the dining room and asked, "What time did you get up?"

"I was up at six, emailing Agnes. I've made coffee, bacon, and hash browns," I replied.

"I know. The smell of the bacon woke me up. I'll make the eggs and toast. I assume everything went according to plan last night," Marcy said as she took charge of preparing the rest of the breakfast.

"It did. Jack texted me on the burner. Max and Reinhard are getting along just fine. No one saw the pickup," I confirmed.

Curious, Marcy asked, "So, what's the plan now?" as she refilled my coffee and poured herself a cup.

"Well, my plan is to make a plan. I'm not sure where to go next. Hopefully, Agnes can provide some insights into who these guys are. I'll see where that leads us. I was also thinking about calling Jote and Tico."

Marcy burst into laughter. "Oh, my God. The local deputies will lose their minds if you bring in 'The Pirates of the Caribbean.'"

Jote and Tico were undercover vice cops from the Miami Criminal Investigation Division who had worked with us on multiple occasions in the past, both officially and unofficially. They were great guys but certainly stood out with their vibrant personalities and unique style.

Jote, a slender fellow, adorned both ears with gold earrings and sported a Pancho Villa-style mustache that concealed his upper lip and drooped an inch on each side. His arms were covered in sleeve tattoos, and if you looked closely, you'd spot a nearly indistinguishable neck tattoo, usually hidden by his thick, solid-link gold chain. His gold Presidential Rolex was renowned in the drug world as a symbol of having completed one's first job or being "crowned." Additionally, he wore a gold wristband on his other arm. He always donned tight jeans and colorful T-shirts featuring the Grateful Dead.

Tico, his partner, was younger, a bit heavier, and taller than Jote. He had a closely cropped haircut that concealed his premature baldness, a gold tooth, a scar under his right eye, and a Fu Manchu mustache. Like Jote, he also sported a gold Rolex and gold chains as part of his ensemble. Every time I saw these guys, I half-expected Johnny Depp to be just around the corner, ready to join them. Their vice-mobile was a souped-up Volkswagen van equipped with all the surveillance gadgets and tools they needed for their undercover work. These guys were skilled and, like me, operated in the gray areas of the rules.

"If Leone is unwilling to involve the bureau, then calling our two boys for help seems like the only choice," I said, contemplating our options.

"There's only one way to find out," Marcy replied, pushing my cell phone closer to me.

I dialed Leone's number, and he answered, "You're bringing Reinhard in?"

"I don't know where he is. Did you call the Feds?" I asked, seeking more information.

"No, Mancuso, I didn't call the FBI. All I know is that I have two dead bodies in the morgue, shot and killed. The only suspect I have is Paul Reinhard, who is on the run for a reason. As long as he's out there, I can't confirm the truth of the story you're telling me. Got that?" Leone responded firmly.

"So, you're sticking with one theory and not considering any alternatives?" I questioned.

"I'll gladly consider other theories once Reinhard is in custody. But for now, I won't waste any effort on anything else, and I won't embarrass myself by involving the FBI. You can help by bringing in Reinhard," Leone stated.

"Alright, I'll see what I can do," I reluctantly agreed, frustrated with Leone's narrow perspective.

Fed up with their lack of support, I decided it was time to bring in fresh reinforcements. I dialed Jote's number from my cell phone contacts.

"*Hermano Jote*, how are you, buddy?" I greeted him as he answered on the third ring.

"*Coño* Mancuso, always a pleasure to hear from you. What's up, bro?" Jote responded cheerfully.

"Marcy says *hola*. And by the way, she's out of the bureau and now part of my team," I informed him.

"*Carajo mano*, now you've got a professional investigative team. Say hi and give her my best wishes," Jote exclaimed, excited about Marcy joining our ranks.

Jote's excitement was palpable as he chimed in, "*Hijo de puta*, why didn't you call me before? Tico and I love fishing down there. How long are you going to be in Islamorada?"

Marcy replied, "We're not sure yet, maybe a week. We came down here for some rest, but we got caught up in a murder, an abduction, and a drug case."

Jote burst into laughter, saying, "Shit, man, you've got a fucking magnet for these things. I hope you're investigating and not involved in any of those three things."

With a chuckle, I responded, "Definitely investigating. But let me tell you what happened and run a couple of names by you." I proceeded to explain the story from the day Reinhard visited us.

As I mentioned the company name, RAJO Trading, Jote interrupted me, exclaiming, "Get the fuck out. RAJO stands for

Rafa Galiano and Jorge Castellanos, right? Forget about alleged perps, brother. These are bad *hombres*. We heard the DEA was after them."

Surprised, I asked, "So you know them?" Marcy served us fresh cups of coffee as we continued the conversation.

"Mancuso, we were all over their asses here in Miami. In our case, the company name was NONOS Trading, another play on their names. They were running the same shady business from the Miami River. Unfortunately, someone tipped them off before we could gather enough evidence. They closed down shop and disappeared three years ago. And you're telling me these guys have the balls to come back to Florida with a new company name?"

"Well, actually, they're operating out of New Orleans now. They claim to be on vacation here in the Keys," I explained, starting to connect the dots.

Jote scoffed, "Vacation, my ass. That encounter at sea was a test and a way to showcase the merchandise. Something went wrong because the plan would have been a second meeting with the actual load. Fifteen pounds of fentanyl is just an appetizer to these guys. I'm sorry, but your guy is not telling you the whole story."

The revelation added another layer of complexity to the case. It was clear that there was more at stake than we initially thought, and Galiano and Castellanos were not to be taken lightly.

As Jote expressed his doubts about the ransom situation, I couldn't help but feel a pang of concern. He had a different perspective on Galiano and Castellanos, labeling them as ruthless individuals who wouldn't resort to abduction for ransom. I admitted that I had believed most of Reinhard's account so far, prompting Jote to playfully tease me about my romantic nature.

After a brief exchange of banter, Jote inquired about the investigation and the involvement of the FBI. I informed him that the local sheriff was skeptical of Reinhard's story and had no interest in pursuing it, as he was solely focused on the two deceased individuals.

Understanding the sheriff's perspective, Jote took a moment to discuss the matter with his captain. There was a brief pause on the line, and then Jote returned with news. He revealed that they were going to seek permission from their captain to investigate the case quietly, aiming to avoid tipping off Galiano and Castellanos once again. He emphasized the potential magnitude of the operation, indicating that the initial sample of fifteen pounds of fentanyl could be just the tip of the iceberg.

Curious about the timeframe, I asked how long it would take for them to receive confirmation. Jote assured me it would be less than an hour. However, he sternly advised us to stay away from dangerous individuals, emphasizing the high stakes involved.

Taking a moment to process the conversation, I sipped my coffee and turned to Marcy, sharing my concerns about Jack hiding Reinhard aboard the Easy Ryder. We both agreed that it might be best for Reinhard to find an alternative place to stay, away from the boat.

I reached for the burner phone and attempted to contact Jack, but there was no answer. Worried, I immediately dialed Reinhard's number, only to be met with silence once again. The lack of response intensified our apprehension about their safety.

9
Wednesday, 10 a.m.

Marcy's concern mirrored my own. The possibility of Galiano and Castellanos discovering Reinhard's location at Robbie's and witnessing Jack's retrieval of him in the Zodiac weighed heavily on my mind. The path between Robbie's and the Easy Ryder was exposed, leaving them vulnerable.

"But it was nighttime when he was picked up, right?" Marcy asked, searching for reassurance.

"The Zodiac has navigation lights," I responded, my voice filled with worry.

"Oh God, what should we do? Let's try calling them again."

I dialed both Jack's and Reinhard's numbers, but there was no answer on either line. It felt surreal, like a nightmare unfolding before my eyes. This wasn't the first time I had put Jack in danger, and guilt gnawed at me for jeopardizing the safety of one of my closest friends.

"We need to get to the Easy Ryder," I blurted out, my mind racing for a solution.

"There are three boats docked nearby. Why don't we ask one of the owners for a ride?" Marcy suggested, trying to offer a practical option.

Without wasting a moment, I rushed downstairs and headed to the dock, desperately seeking assistance. I approached the various boat owners, anxiously inquiring about their vessels. Thankfully, a man who had been snorkeling with his kids responded, "The deck boat is mine; well, I rented it. Why do you ask?"

"It's an emergency. I need to reach a yacht that's moored just five minutes from here. Can you take me?" I pleaded, hoping he would understand the urgency.

"No problem, I'll take you. Come on, kids, let's go for a ride," the man said, including his children in the plan.

My heart sank. I couldn't endanger innocent children. I turned to the man, grateful for his willingness to help, and explained, "I truly appreciate your offer, but I'd rather not have your children on board. It's a dire situation, as I mentioned before."

Glancing back at his kids, my benefactor decided. "You heard the man. Stay with your mom. We'll go out later."

"Hi, my name is Chris," he introduced himself, stepping onto the deck boat. I followed suit, feeling a mix of relief and gratitude. "I'm Joey, and I apologize for the inconvenience with the kids."

"Don't worry about it. I could use a break from them anyway if you catch my drift," Chris replied with a laugh.

"Thank you so much for this. I really appreciate it."

"Where are we heading?" Chris inquired, starting the boat's engine, ready to embark on our urgent mission.

"Do you know the channel that connects this side of the bay with Robbie's marina?" I asked Chris, hoping he was familiar with the route because I had no clue. "Of course. It's right over there," he replied, pointing in the direction.

As Chris started to pull out, I heard someone calling my name from the entrance to the docks. It was Jote and Tico, my buddies from Miami. "Hold on a second, Chris. I want these guys to join us," I said, knowing that Jote and Tico's appearances might unsettle him.

Chris, who had been smiling moments ago, now looked at my friends with furrowed brows and tense body language. "Wait, wait. Who are these people?" he asked, visibly concerned and turning to his wife, who was in the water near the boat.

"Chris, what's happening?" she inquired, her gaze shifting between her husband and my companions.

"These two are undercover police officers from the Miami Police Department. I know them," I explained, hoping to alleviate Chris and his wife's worries.

"Chris, ask for their IDs. I don't think you should go anywhere," his wife suggested, displaying her concern.

Jote, unaware of the tension, jumped into the boat and exclaimed, "We're coming with you. Marcy informed us."

"Do you guys have your credentials with you?" I asked Jote and Tico.

"Yeah, brother. Why? What's going on?" Jote replied.

"This is Chris, and that's his wife," I introduced them, pointing to each person. "Would you mind showing them your credentials?"

Jote and Tico reached for their credentials and flashed them to Chris and his wife. "We're undercover with the Miami Police Department," they affirmed. Then, in a more serious tone, Jote added, "As long as you two don't have any vices, there's nothing to worry about."

Chris didn't grasp the humor in Jote's remark. Sensing the tension, I intervened, saying, "He's joking. We need your help to get to the yacht."

Turning to Chris's wife, who was holding onto the boat, I assured her, "I'll have him back in fifteen minutes."

"Chris," she called out.

"I'll be right back. Everything is fine," Chris reassured her, gently pulling out of the dock space. His concerned wife moved back and held onto the kids.

Jote looked at me and made a facial expression that conveyed, "Oh shit."

The boat's maximum speed was twenty-five knots, which wasn't bad considering the seventy-five-horsepower engine and the four of us onboard. During the journey, no one spoke, the tension palpable in the air.

As we navigated through the channel, I spotted the Easy Ryder positioned about three hundred yards north of us. Pointing in its direction, I said to Chris, "That's where we're headed."

Chris nodded, skillfully maneuvering the boat around some buoys that marked the channel, steering us toward our target.

As we approached the Easy Ryder, I noticed the Zodiac tied to the side of the boat. Relief washed over me. Perhaps Jack and Reinhard had gone off for food or a short trip. "Chris," I said, "pull up next to it, and we'll disembark. You can head back to your wife. Thanks, buddy. I owe you a couple of beers."

Once we climbed aboard the Easy Ryder, my calls for Jack and Paul went unanswered, except for Max's barking from inside the salon. I couldn't help but worry again, but I kept my concerns to myself. I opened the salon door, greeted Max with a pat on the head, and he calmed down, wagging his tail. Stepping inside, I was relieved to find no bodies. However, there were three staterooms below that needed to be checked.

"Guys, let's check the three staterooms downstairs," I instructed. We descended the short stairs leading to the staterooms, and once again, anxiety gripped me. Would I discover Jack lifeless? My legs felt weak, and my heart raced.

Each of us entered a different stateroom, and in the manner of a typical police procedure, I heard "Clear and clear" from my companions. Thankfully, I could add a third confirmation after examining Jack's personal stateroom. That was the good news, but it meant that both Jack and Reinhard had been taken.

Silently, we made our way back up to the salon, and I sank onto the sofa with Jote seated across from me. "I'll walk around the exterior, looking for any signs of foul play," Tico stated.

What he really meant was signs of blood.

"Are you carrying any firearms, Joey?" Jote asked, breaking the silence.

I didn't respond, my head bowed as I gazed at Max, who sat in front of me, seemingly asking, 'What happened to Jack?'

Jote asked again, his tone insistent, "Brother, do you have a firearm?"

Raising my gaze toward Jote, everything appeared blurry and out of focus. Shaking my head, I replied, "No, I don't carry."

Jote produced a small .38-caliber Smith & Wesson that was holstered on his ankle and tossed it to me. "Now you do."

I stared at the gun, unsure if I wanted to possess one. "What are we going to do?" I asked, still feeling dazed and disoriented.

"Tico and I are officially taking over this case. We've been after Galiano and Castellanos for quite some time. Call the deputies and let me speak to them. They need to set up checkpoints on the way out of Islamorada in case these guys try to make a getaway," Jote instructed.

I retrieved my phone and found Sergeant Leone's number in my recent calls. I pressed the redial button and handed the phone to Jote while Tico returned, shaking his head.

Before Jote made the call, I voiced my concerns, saying, "There are four guys, plus Dianne, Reinhard, and Jack. They don't need Jack or Dianne. They have Reinhard. You know what that means, right?"

"Jack can handle himself," Jote reassured me. "He's a capable guy."

I glanced at Tico, then back at Jote. "He's a freaking author. He has no idea how to deal with four armed thugs."

Jote remained silent, fully engaged in his conversation with Leone, asserting his authority and introducing themselves. Meanwhile, Tico retrieved three bottles of water from the galley and handed one to me. After Jote disconnected, I asked eagerly, "What did he say?"

Jote opened his water bottle, took a sip, and replied, "He initially gave me some grief about jurisdiction, but I informed him that we're part of a DEA and FBI task force actively pursuing these individuals. So paper beats rock."

I chuckled, briefly wondering what would have happened if Leone had chosen scissors. "Are you really part of such a task force?"

"Not at the moment, but we have been in the past. I don't give a damn. We'll sort out the details later," Jote answered confidently.

Curious, Tico inquired, "Is he arranging roadblocks?"

"That didn't sit well with him either. He's worried about creating massive traffic congestion for miles. But that's the advantage of these islands – there's only one way in and one way out," Jote responded.

I asked for my phone back, called Agnes, and requested that she text pictures of Galiano and Castellanos to Leone just in case they hadn't thought of it themselves.

"Does Leone know about Jack?" I inquired.

"Yeah, I told him, and he's pretty pissed at all of you for concealing this guy, Reinhard," Jote replied.

I couldn't care less about Leone's reaction. My sole concern was Jack Ryder. What had I gotten him into?

This was supposed to be a leisurely week in Islamorada. Just relaxing, enjoying some beers, indulging in delicious seafood and fresh fish, and basking in the sun. On Saturday, Marcy and I had plans to go fishing with an acclaimed expert, Captain James from Catchalottafish Charters, based at the Wide World of Sportsman Marina on mile marker 81.5. It was the same marina where Paul Reinhard docked his boat. But now, instead of experiencing a carefree time, a close friend was possibly kidnapped, the life of a young pregnant woman hung in the balance, and a brilliant computer whiz faced the threat of being killed. Instead of savoring craft beers and avoiding stress, I found myself on the trail of ruthless drug dealers. Jote had once remarked that trouble had a way of finding me, and unfortunately, he was right.

10
Wednesday, 1 p.m.

Jote asked, "Where to next?"

As I was formulating a plan, he interjected, "Listen, I don't know that I want to carry a firearm. My New York concealed-carry license is not valid in Florida."

"You're with us, and my captain was arranging to make you a temporary consultant with our team. I told him about your background with the NYPD. Just hold onto it; you may need it," Jote insisted.

I hesitated. Marcy and I had made a pact when I left the NYPD after both of us had close brushes with death. No more firearms. But he had a point. Our adversaries, as Jote referred to them, were playing for keeps. "Let's take the Zodiac back to the Topsider. From there, we can regroup and plan our next move," I suggested.

Tico took the lead, boarding the Zodiac, followed by Jote and myself. Then it dawned on me that we were leaving Max behind. "Hold on a second, come here, Max," I called to the little dog. "You're coming for a ride with us, buddy."

Tico skillfully navigated the Zodiac through the marked buoys and the narrow channel, steering us back to the Topsider. We scanned the bay waters and the overgrown mangroves lining the channel for any sign of bodies. There was nothing to be seen. After docking and securing the raft, I carried Max back to our unit with Jote and Tico. Waiting for us were Marcy, Sergeant Leone, and Joyce, who were seated in the living room.

Leone stood up and, with a hint of sarcasm, said, "Well, Mancuso, what a fine mess you've gotten us into." He then scrutinized Jote and Tico, his smile fading away.

"Deputy," Jote began, reaching for his credentials, "I'm Jote, and this is Tico. We're with the vice squad of the MPD and part of a joint task force with the DEA and FBI."

"You could have fooled me," Leone retorted.

Tico replied with a smirk, "That's the idea."

Joyce chimed in, "We've set up roadblocks both north and south, from Tavernier up to Marathon. These guys aren't going anywhere."

"I hope you're right, Mancuso. The traffic jam we've created is worse than any hurricane evacuation order," Leone remarked. "Now tell me the complete story."

We gathered around the dinner table in the dining area while Marcy stayed in the living room with Max. I recounted the story once again, starting from Reinhard's visit to us on Tuesday to our boarding of the Easy Ryder.

Jote then shared the details of their surveillance and the failed attempt to apprehend Galiano and Castellanos in Miami. They suspected that someone within their own department, the DEA, or the FBI had tipped off the criminals, giving them enough time to shut down operations and escape, only to resurface in New Orleans and establish a new base.

"There's one thing we're overlooking," Jote interjected. "These guys didn't come here to kidnap Reinhard for ransom. They're involved in a much bigger operation. That means they won't leave until it's completed."

"So Reinhard is insignificant to them, except for his ability to identify them," Leone observed, adding, "assuming he actually saw them shoot the two Cubans."

"I'm going to take Max for a walk. I'll be right back," Marcy announced, then expressed her concern, "I hope they don't ask about Max. Pets aren't allowed here."

"Just tell the manager that Max is a retired drug-sniffing member of the NYPD," I suggested. "He's here on official duty."

"He's one of us?" Jote inquired.

"He was," I replied, holding back a thought that had crossed my mind.

Leone and Joyce stood up, signaling their departure. Leone stated, "We're heading back to the local station. Let us know if anything develops on your end."

Jote, Tico, and I remained behind. I waited until Leone and Joyce had left.

"You know what?" I began, sharing my suspicion. "I think Reinhard is playing me. He's somehow involved, maybe unintentionally. Here's what I believe: After these guys shot one Cuban and took the other, Reinhard fled. But the fifteen pounds of fentanyl was still in his boat. Perhaps he didn't intend to take it, but he ended up with it. Now, these guys want to kill him, but they also want their drugs back."

"You think he has the one the money Galiano brought, to pay for the fentanyl?" Jote questioned.

"Indeed, it's possible. If that's the case, it's no surprise they intend to extort more money from him. After all, their motive is greed, not drugs," I replied, contemplating the situation. "Let's head downstairs and wait for Marcy and Max to return. I have an idea."

We descended and stood by my car, preparing ourselves for whatever would unfold next.

Suddenly, I spotted Marcy rushing toward us, her voice filled with urgency. "Joey, shots were fired at the front of the resort!" she exclaimed.

Jote and Tico swiftly took off, running while drawing their weapons. I instructed Marcy, "Stay here," and followed closely behind, making my way toward the front. I reached for the firearm Jote had given me but decided against brandishing it.

As we approached the front of the resort, we came upon a body lying face down on the grass, roughly fifty yards from US 1, right in front of the tennis court. Drawing nearer, I noticed the victim's blond hair. Damn, was it Jack?

Jote knelt beside the body while Tico maintained a vigilant watch over the surrounding area.

"Is this Jack?" Jote inquired, slightly turning the victim's head.

I closed my eyes for a brief moment before responding, "Yes, it's him. Is he dead?"

Jote urgently shouted to Tico, "Get the van! He's alive, but he's losing a significant amount of blood."

Marcy joined us, informing us, "There's a hospital at mile marker ninety-one point five, just sixteen miles north of here."

Jote positioned Jack face up and applied pressure to the front and back of his left shoulder, where it appeared he had been shot.

"There's also a fire station much closer. We should consider stopping there for first aid, and they can assist in transporting him to the hospital," I suggested. Kneeling next to Jack, I called out, "Jack, Jack, can you hear me?"

He mumbled something inaudible in response, then lost consciousness. A small crowd from the resort had gathered around us, with mothers holding their children back. Most people wore expressions of disbelief, their hands covering their mouths, unable to comprehend that such a violent incident could occur in this serene and picturesque setting.

Marcy remained with Max while Jote swiftly departed the resort in the hippie-era Volkswagen van. Tico affixed blue-red lights to the roof and activated the siren. Undoubtedly, the scene must have carried a somewhat comical tone for onlookers—an oxymoronic sight of a police hippie-style Volkswagen van tearing down US 1.

Marcy called asking for an update on Jack's condition and informed me that a guest had witnessed the shooting. According to the witness, Jack had jumped out of a car while it was moving south on US 1. The only description available was that the car was a dark-blue, four-door sedan.

I immediately dialed Leone and briefed him on the situation, urging him to have his team on the lookout for the car. We waited anxiously in the small emergency waiting room.

After about twenty minutes, a doctor in scrubs emerged from the emergency room. He addressed us, asking, "Are you family?"

Before I could respond, Jote intervened, saying, "No, doctor, we are police. How is he?"

The doctor provided us with some reassurance, saying, "We managed to stop the bleeding. Fortunately, the bullet passed through underneath the glenohumeral joint, only causing damage to the tendons in the teres minor area."

Seeking clarification, I inquired, "What does that mean, doctor?"

With a smile, the doctor replied, "He's going to be fine. However, he'll have limited use of his left shoulder for some time and will require physical therapy. Luckily, no bones were affected."

Curious about Jack's status at the hospital, I asked, "Will he be staying here?"

"Just overnight. He can be discharged tomorrow around midday," the doctor informed us. Anticipating our next question, he added, "Give him an hour. He's currently sedated and sleeping. A nurse will inform you when you can speak with him."

We expressed our gratitude to the doctor and resumed our seats. Leone arrived shortly after, alone. He inquired, "How's your friend?"

I gave a reassuring response to Leone, "He's going to be fine. Any luck in locating the car?"

"Not yet, but there are numerous places they could be hiding. I'm arranging for a helicopter to assist with the search," Leone replied.

Jote then brought up the idea I had mentioned earlier, asking, "Joey, you were about to share an idea before Jack was shot. What was it?"

Glancing at Leone and then back at Jote, I feigned forgetfulness and shrugged, responding, "I completely forgot amidst all the commotion." In truth, I hadn't forgotten, but I wasn't ready to share it with Leone just yet.

11
Wednesday, 4:30 p.m.

Leone had left, and Jack was now awake, albeit still groggy. He requested water, and the nurse provided him with some crushed ice to ease his thirst. "I'll leave you two to talk. Call me if he needs anything," she said before leaving.

Standing by Jack's bed, I reassured him, "You're going to be fine. You might need physical therapy and may have to postpone your next book for a while."

"I have a deadline," Jack mumbled.

Smiling, I replied, "Don't worry, we'll write a note to your publisher."

We shared a moment of lightheartedness amidst the seriousness of the situation. Then, I introduced Jote and Tico to Jack.

Curious about the progress in apprehending the assailants, Jack asked, "Did they catch those guys?"

"Not yet, but there's a 'be on the lookout' order issued for them and their car. How did you manage to escape from the car?" I inquired.

Jack took a deep breath and replied, "It's a long story. I'll tell you later. By the way, where's Max?"

"He's with Marcy at our place. He was concerned about you," I answered.

Jack closed his eyes and expressed his gratitude before drifting back to sleep.

Before leaving the room, I had one more question. "Just one thing, what's the command to have Max search for drugs?"

Cracking his eyes open, Jack looked a bit confused but managed to respond, "Search, Max." He then fell back asleep.

As Jote, Tico, and I made our way back to the van in the emergency parking area, Tico inquired, "Why did you ask about Max searching for drugs?"

"Hold on a moment," I said, dialing Marcy's number. She picked up on the first ring. "He's going to be fine. Only some tendon damage," I assured her. "Listen, can you meet us at the Square Grouper with Max?"

We parked and waited for Marcy to arrive. Once she joined us, I explained the idea I had to Jote and Tico. "Reinhard hid here in one of these boats," I pointed to the row of boats on the dry dock. "If he took the drugs, I'm willing to bet they're stashed somewhere up there."

Both Tico and Jote gazed up and surveyed the area. Jote asked, "So Max is trained for this?"

"He worked in customs at the Newark Airport before Jack got him," I replied.

Jote voiced his concern, "Dude, there are over fifty boats here. How long will it take to search them all?"

"Let me have your badge," I responded firmly.

I located the marina manager and inquired about the boats owned by out-of-towners who visited only once or twice a year. The manager pointed out four such boats, all located in the upper row.

"Excellent," I said. "I'm going to need you to bring them down, one by one. We need to conduct a search."

The manager seemed irritated. "Don't you need some kind of warrant for that?"

Jote stepped in, taking charge. "I can haul your ass to the station and get a warrant if needed. But if we find drugs on any of these boats, you'll be arrested for being part of a drug distribution cartel. Do you understand?"

"Cartel?" he exclaimed. "I have nothing to do with that."

"Then do as we asked and bring those boats down," Jote instructed.

As the forklift started to lower the first boat, Marcy and Max arrived on the scene.

One by one, the boats were brought down. The first one was a Sea Ray Sundowner, about twenty-four feet long. I took Max onto the boat, opened the cabin door, and dropped him inside. "Search, Max," I commanded.

Max diligently explored every inch of the boat, sniffing for any trace of drugs. However, he came back empty-handed, wagging his tail.

Next, we moved on to a twenty-seven-foot Chaparral. Max repeated his search routine, but once again, no drugs were found.

Our third boat was a thirty-five-foot Invincible Catamaran equipped with four three-hundred-horsepower engines. It was partially covered with a tarp, so I waited for the attendant to remove it. I placed Max inside and gave the command, "Search, Max."

After three minutes, Max started barking, indicating a positive find. He still had his skills intact. I climbed into the boat and discovered Max barking, sitting, and wagging his tail near the door to the head and storage area under the center console.

Opening the compartment, I revealed two duffel bags—one blue and one black. "We've found something," I announced.

My intuition had proven correct, although I must admit that Reinhard had initially managed to deceive me.

Jote entered the boat and began taking pictures with his phone, while Tico captured images of the parking lot, the stacks of boats, and the surrounding area.

"Joey, open them. Let's confirm our suspicions," Jote urged.

I carefully opened the blue bag, revealing stacks of neatly packed hundred and twenty-dollar bills. Then, I moved on to the black bag, which exposed the dangerous fentanyl powder.

"Don't touch the drugs. They could be deadly. Let me take pictures," Jote cautioned.

The marina manager, who had been standing nearby, exclaimed, "I had no idea this was happening. Believe me."

I glanced at the manager and reassured him, "Don't worry about it. We know you weren't involved."

Passing Max over to Marcy, I watched as Jote closed the duffel bags and returned them to their original position. He then addressed the manager, saying, "Cover the boat as it was and put it back in its place."

Jote and I climbed down from the boat, allowing the attendant to replace the cover. Jote requested that I call Leone. "We're going to need his team."

I made the call and provided Leone with our location. "Are you thinking what I'm thinking?" I asked Jote.

"These guys will want to retrieve their money and drugs. I'm certain they'll try to get it out of Reinhard. So, let's set a trap," Jote replied.

Twenty minutes later, Leone arrived with Joyce and four other officers from the sheriff's department, including Kris and Greg. Jote showed Leone the pictures of the drugs and money, explaining his plan for twenty-four-hour surveillance of the marina.

Leone turned to me, and I knew what was coming. "So, Mancuso, your boy Reinhard isn't as innocent as you thought, right?"

I still wasn't sure whether Reinhard had intentionally been involved or if he had stumbled upon the hidden stash. However, the incriminating evidence of the drugs and money couldn't be ignored. Perhaps Reinhard believed he could use them as leverage to save his own life. Regardless, now wasn't the time to argue.

"I guess not. My mistake, deputy," I admitted.

Leone smirked, clearly satisfied. He had scored a point against the big-city detective, at least in his own mind.

Joyce interjected, "Where are the drugs and money?"

"They're still on the boat. We want to catch these guys red-handed," Jote replied. "Here's our plan."

Jote proceeded to explain his strategy for apprehending the perpetrators if they showed up, considering the drugs and money as bait.

12
Wednesday, 8 p.m.

The Square Grouper, a marina and restaurant situated on the bay side of US 1, featured a prominent dry dock area at the front where boats were stored. The main building stood near the water's edge, and the marina extended to the south, offering dockage options and a forklift for launching boats into the water.

Leone had organized a team of eight undercover officers from the sheriff's department, each disguised in unique ways. One officer positioned himself on the grass near the restaurant entrances, posing as a panhandler to keep an eye out for any suspicious individuals. The remaining officers strategically positioned themselves, some in the front and others in the back, ready to spring into action when needed.

Two unmarked police vehicles were stationed approximately one hundred yards from the restaurant entrance, ready to block any escape routes if our targets were spotted.

Jote, Tico, and I occupied the front porch of the restaurant, appearing as though we were waiting for a table inside. Leone and Joyce maintained a vigilant watch from upstairs in the raw bar, ensuring they had a clear view of the entrance and parking lot.

Our primary concern revolved around the continuous influx of guests frequenting the restaurant. We were mindful of the potential risk to innocent patrons if the apprehension of our targets turned violent.

The operation had commenced in full swing at seven o'clock, with the belief that our culprits wouldn't attempt to retrieve the drugs and money until after sunset. As the clock struck eight, we remained on high alert, fully prepared for any developments.

At nine-fifteen, our lookout communicated through the coms, "White van entering the parking lot with at least two suspicious individuals."

We all observed the van's arrival, maintaining patience as we waited for the situation to unfold.

The van parked next to the row of stacked boats, positioned conveniently beneath the Invincible, where we had discovered their hidden stash. The driver stepped out, raising the hood as if inspecting the engine, feigning car trouble. After conducting a quick scan, he nodded to the passenger, who then exited the vehicle and disappeared from sight.

Leone's voice came through the coms, "The passenger has moved behind the stack of boats and is making his way up to the top row. Be prepared."

We were unable to witness the individual climbing in from our vantage point, relying instead on Leone and Joyce's surveillance updates.

"He's removed the tarp and entered the boat," Leone relayed, providing us with a real-time account of the unfolding events.

Our plan was proceeding smoothly. The driver remained occupied, pretending to tend to the engine while keeping a watchful eye on his surroundings. Guests continued to arrive at the restaurant, parking their vehicles and making their way to the porch where we sat, putting their names on the waiting list.

The lingering question was whether anyone else was in the van. I doubted Galiano and Castellanos would risk being present alongside Dianne and Reinhard, but uncertainty lingered. Perhaps they were ready to make a hasty escape, intending to dispose of their two captives. But where would they go? I was certain they had noticed the roadblocks.

"The guy on top just tossed down the two duffel bags and is climbing down. This is it. Be ready," Leone alerted us.

I noticed the driver closing the hood and scanning the area before opening the side door of the van closest to the boats.

Leone announced, "I'm coming down. Block the entrance."

The individual swiftly loaded the duffel bags into the van, slid the doors shut, and the driver returned to the driver's seat. However, he was at a disadvantage, needing to maneuver through the parking lot to exit. I witnessed the unmarked police cars blocking the exit, but the van's driver had yet to spot them.

Standing alongside Jote and Tico, who quickly concealed their faces with black ski masks, I yelled loudly to the guests on the porch, "Get inside quickly!" A frenzy ensued as people rushed toward the interior. We approached the van from behind as it passed in front of us. Deputies Kris and Greg drew their firearms, keeping them lowered, positioned in front of the driveway just before the exit, facing the van.

In a commanding voice, Joyce ordered, "Stop the van, turn off the engine, and step out with your hands raised."

The driver came to a halt, surveying the scene as he observed deputies closing in from all directions, with Kris reiterating the demand.

Tico advised, "Move to the sides. Don't stand behind the van."

The driver appeared noncompliant, straightening himself in his seat and exchanging a few words with the passenger.

The van inched forward a few yards.

Two sheriff's cars positioned themselves behind the van, positioned sideways in the hopes of shielding the guests at the restaurant entrance from any potential gunfire.

Kris issued a stern warning, "Stop the van, or we'll shoot," she and Greg raised their Glocks and assumed a solid shooting stance with their feet shoulder-width apart and perpendicular to their target.

The passenger extended a pistol out the window, and the van accelerated, bullets flying haphazardly as the passenger fired at Kris and Greg. In response, both deputies returned fire, emptying their clips into the van.

Blood splattered across the inside of the windshield as the driver slumped forward onto the wheel, crashing into a parked car at the side. Deputies swiftly surrounded the van, their weapons trained on it.

Greg commanded, "Throw your weapons out and step out of the vehicle with your hands raised."

After what felt like an eternity, a pistol was tossed out of the passenger side, and a wounded man emerged, his hands raised before he collapsed onto the pavement.

The man was immediately swarmed by deputies, who conducted a search before placing him on his back. I approached the injured shooter, noticing the blood streaming from his left shoulder and forehead.

Leone's voice came over the comms, "Establish a perimeter and ensure that everyone remains inside the restaurant."

"Damn it, we need this bastard alive. He can provide us with information on the whereabouts of the others," I remarked.

Leone didn't respond, simply nodding in agreement.

Susan Joyce approached me, inquiring, "How did you know the drugs were here?"

"I had a hunch," I replied.

"A hunch? Based on what?" she pressed. "I believe you've been withholding crucial information that could have led to a smoother arrest and prevented all this gunfire, including the injuries sustained by your friend, who could have easily been killed."

"Deputy Joyce," Jote interjected, his hood removed, "ease up on Mr. Mancuso. We're all under immense stress right now. We were here for dinner and acted upon a tip from a restaurant guest who thought she had spotted Reinhard hiding on a boat a few days ago."

Joyce locked eyes with Jote but remained silent, eventually turning away and joining Leone a few yards away.

Jote patted me on the back. "She's one tough woman. Let's get out of here. Is there a place nearby where we can grab a pizza or something? Maybe we can take it back to your place. Do you still have some brews?"

"Sure, let's go," I replied.

The operation had achieved a partial success. We needed the surviving suspect to divulge the whereabouts of the rest of the gang and clarify whether Reinhard and Dianne were involved. Jote was determined to dismantle Galiano, Castellanos, and their entire operation. They had already evaded capture once and were resolute in their pursuits. The flow of fentanyl into our country continued unchecked, resulting in the deaths of over one hundred thousand people in the past year due to overdoses or lethal combinations of fentanyl with cocaine, marijuana, heroin, and methamphetamine. The urgency to stop them grew with each passing day.

13
Wednesday, 10:30 p.m.

We picked up two large pizzas from Tower of Pizza, along with some craft beers to replenish my cooler, and made our way back to the Topsider. As I set the table and got plates ready, I asked Jote, "What's your plan?"

Jote took a seat and replied, "I've already contacted the agent in charge of the task force. Special Agent Michael Donnelly from the Miami office. He'll be joining us first thing tomorrow morning."

Marcy chimed in, "I don't know Agent Donnelly. Will he be of any help?"

Jote shrugged and said, "Can't say for sure. He's a nice guy but a bit rigid. We'll see. By the way, Marcy, do you mind if we stay here tonight? You have an extra room with two beds."

Marcy smiled and responded, "That'll be great. You're welcome to stay."

Jote added, "We can figure out accommodations tomorrow."

With the pizzas laid out before us, we dug in, devouring the food as if we hadn't eaten all day, which was partly true. The room fell into a contented silence as we enjoyed our meal and drinks.

After wiping his mouth and hands, Jote spoke up, "Tico and I are meeting Agent Donnelly at the hospital tomorrow morning at eight. We want to question the surviving suspect, assuming he makes it through the night."

I turned to Marcy and said, "We'll come with you. We want to visit Jack. And I hope Donnelly allows me to remain involved in the investigation."

Jote shrugged again and replied, "I doubt it, brother. Donnelly can be a bit by-the-book. But knowing you, I have a feeling you'll find a way to stay in the loop."

I smirked and nodded. "You know me too well. Right now, my theory is that Galiano and Castellanos will try to extort the four million from Reinhard before disposing of him and Dianne. I don't think they'll risk sticking around with one of their own in custody."

Marcy closed her eyes and shook her head, clearly burdened by the situation. I shared her sympathy for Dianne and perhaps an unborn baby. The truth seemed elusive, with Reinhard having deceived me. Did Dianne also feed me a pack of lies?

Jote broke the silence, "If you have a couple more cigars, bring the cooler, and let's sit out on the balcony. It's a beautiful night."

I stood up and replied, "Take the cooler. I'll grab the cigars."

We headed out to the balcony, enjoying the cool breeze and stunning night sky. Opening four more beers and clipping three cigars, we resumed our discussion.

Tico leaned back and asked, "Is this place a rental resort, by the way?"

"No, it's a time-share. The guy I rented from has five weeks during the year. He bought them thirty years ago, but he couldn't make it down here this week," I explained.

Marcy turned to Jote and asked, "So, what do you think these guys are going to do?"

Jote leaned back, crossing his legs, and replied, "I agree with Joey regarding Reinhard and Dianne, but if the other two are here, there's a much bigger deal at play. And trust me, they'll follow through with it."

Marcy observed, "All the roads are being patrolled, and there are still roadblocks in some locations."

Jote added, "This deal isn't happening on land. I'm sure it's an exchange out in the ocean. That's why I'm going to alert the Coast Guard tomorrow to be on the lookout for any suspicious boats."

"Hopefully, Jack remembers more about these guys. Maybe he overheard something that can lead us to a clue. I doubt the guy we have in custody will willingly give up Galiano and his partner," Jote continued.

Tico chimed in, "Plus, there's more to it than just these four individuals. They had a significant operation in Miami, and I'm certain it's the same in New Orleans."

Curious, I asked, "So, what do you think that failed deal the other day was? Was it a separate, smaller transaction? Or were the two guys who got killed selling the fentanyl as a sample, hoping to secure the big deal?"

Jote took a deliberate draw from his cigar before responding, "Mancuso, this is where I differ from your theory. Reinhard told you that his guests, Galiano and Castellanos, were the ones buying the drugs, right?"

"Exactly. And he claimed that his guests killed the Cubans to keep the drugs and the money," I affirmed.

Jote exhaled a puff of smoke and continued, "Well, here's a fact: those two Cubans were associated with a Mexican cartel. The sheriff uncovered that information. The Mexican cartels have an abundant supply of fentanyl. They primarily get it from China in powder form, process it into pills, and smuggle it across the border."

Marcy leaned forward and suggested, "Perhaps Reinhard made a mistake in identifying the ownership of the drugs. Maybe his guests had the money and were purchasing the fentanyl as a sample."

"Okay, let's assume he made a mistake," I pondered. "Why would Galiano have the two Cubans killed and risk jeopardizing the bigger deal?"

Jote raised an eyebrow and replied, "Exactly, it doesn't make much sense, does it?"

I took another swig of beer, contemplating Jote's words. "So, what you're suggesting is that Reinhard, at some point, had both the drugs and the money on his boat. He then shot the Cubans and made off with everything?" I asked, trying to piece it all together.

Tico smirked, revealing his white teeth and a single gold tooth. "I think your boy Reinhard is more deeply involved than he let on. If he took the money and drugs and killed the Cubans, he royally screwed up the big deal for Galiano and his crew. That's why they're hunting him down and making extortion demands. They're furious."

Marcy interjected, seeking clarity. "But how does Dianne fit into this? Is she an innocent victim, or is she somehow involved with Reinhard?"

I pondered for a moment before responding, "Either she's an innocent victim caught up in all of this, or she's somehow connected to Reinhard. It's hard to say for sure."

Just as the conversation was heating up, Jote's cell phone rang, interrupting our discussion. I glanced at my watch and saw that it was already twelve-thirty.

Jote answered the call and said, "Hello." He listened intently before asking, "Where?" There was a brief pause, and then he replied, "We're on our way."

Curiosity piqued, I inquired, "What just happened?"

Jote glanced at Marcy, gauging her reaction before answering, "They found a woman's body in the parking lot of the Turtle Hospital at mile marker forty-eight point five."

Marcy's eyes widened, and she gasped, "Oh my God, is it Dianne?"

14
Thursday, 1:30 a.m.

We raced toward the location in what I jokingly referred to as the "vice-mobile," the vibrant, multicolored Volkswagen van adorned with police lights flashing blue and red on top. It must have been a peculiar sight for anyone witnessing our high-speed drive down US 1. However, there was nothing amusing about the urgency of our mission.

After an hour of driving, we arrived at The Turtle Hospital, where the woman's body had been discovered. The hospital was set back from the front parking lot, which faced US 1. The sheriff's department had cordoned off the area, and we parked on the median just beyond it.

From our vantage point, we could see a covered body in the parking lot. Deputies were diligently working around it, some taking photographs and collecting any potential evidence. One of them, Deputy Johnnie, as indicated by his nametag, caught sight of us and walked over.

I called out to him, and he approached, greeting everyone. Then he turned to me and asked, "You've met this woman, Dianne, right?"

"Yes, both Marcy and I know her from the restaurant, The Square Grouper," I confirmed.

"Okay. Our deceased person has no identification on her. Could you take a look and let us know if it's Dianne?" Johnnie requested.

I glanced at Marcy, seeking her confirmation. With a nod from her, we all proceeded under the crime scene tape and made our way to the body.

Carefully, Deputy Johnnie uncovered the face, revealing it to us. Marcy gasped and instinctively shut her eyes. "Oh my God, that's her," she whispered.

I looked down at Johnnie and nodded, confirming Marcy's identification. "I'm afraid it is her. How was she killed?"

Deputy Johnnie gently replaced the covering, and we noticed blood on her blouse, centered in the middle of her chest. Upon closer examination, it became evident that she had been shot twice.

Shaking my head in disbelief, I scanned the parking lot. "There's no blood here. It seems someone shot her elsewhere and then dumped her here in a drive-by fashion."

"That's our initial assessment as well. We have a witness who was walking his dog around midnight and saw a dark sedan pull into the parking lot, depositing the body," Johnnie informed us.

"Is he the one who called?" I inquired.

"Yes, but unfortunately, he didn't manage to get the license plate number. All he knows is that the perpetrators drove north on US 1," Kris explained.

"Is he still around?" I asked.

"No, we released him. He's a local, and we have his information. He lives up that street," Kris pointed in a direction about one block away.

Marcy interjected, "Please inform the Medical Examiner that she may have been pregnant. This could potentially be a double homicide."

Kris nodded in agreement and then inquired, "Do you have a last name for her?"

"No, but the Square Grouper, where she worked, can provide you with more details, including possibly her next of kin," I responded.

Kris jotted down some notes on a small pad. "She's the one you believed was being held for ransom, right?"

I nodded. "Possibly for ransom, yes. Initially, they wanted to exchange her for Reinhard. That was their original intention. But when they captured Reinhard, she became expendable."

Marcy asked, "Where is the ME's office?"

"Right here in Marathon, about ten miles north of us. We'll transport her there shortly," Kris answered.

I inquired about Deputies Leone and Joyce, "Where are they?"

"They went back to the Keys office," Kris replied. "They had an urgent matter to attend to. They'll be back in the morning."

Curious, I asked, "Did they find any forensic evidence in the van at the Square Grouper?"

"They're working on that. But things move at a slower pace around here. However, they did discover long blond hair, which we believe could be from our victim," Kris informed us.

"You mean Dianne? Victims have names, not just a body," I wanted to emphasize.

"Yes, and now we can match it," Kris confirmed.

We made our way back to the van. There was nothing more we could do at the scene. I turned to Jote and asked, "Can you try to obtain Dianne's home address from the Square Grouper?"

Was I at fault for this mess? Should I have turned Reinhard in from the get-go? These questions weighed heavily on my mind. I couldn't help but wonder if things would have turned out differently if I had reported Reinhard to the authorities immediately. Perhaps if he had been in custody, none of this would have happened. He would have surrendered the drugs and money, and there would have been no reason to kidnap Dianne. Her life could have been saved, and Reinhard's fate might not have been so grim.

Jote's voice interrupted my guilt-ridden thoughts. "Nothing else to do here. Let's drive back," he suggested.

Silence filled the van for half of the journey. There wasn't much to say, I suppose. Yet, I still had lingering questions for which I had no answers.

In the back seat, Marcy reached for my hand. "I meant to tell you there are no vacancies after Saturday. We'll need to check out by ten."

I turned my gaze from the window to face Marcy. "I don't think we'll need to stay beyond that point. If we have to help Jack, we can always stay on his boat."

Jote chimed in, "This drug deal is happening today or tomorrow. They can't afford to postpone it any longer."

"Do you really think they'll go through with it after everything that's happened?" Marcy asked.

Jote glanced at Marcy through the rearview mirror. "There's a boatload of fentanyl and who knows what else waiting to be unloaded. Galiano and his crew probably have their own boat, likely a discreet-looking vessel. They'll load it up and head north through the Gulf, along the west coast of Florida toward Louisiana."

Tico added, "What doesn't make sense is for them to draw more attention by killing that poor woman."

"Actually, buddy," I interjected, "it makes sense for them to create a distraction by dumping her body where it can easily be found. They have no idea that you guys and the task force are after them. They probably think the local authorities are focused on solving the murders."

Marcy raised an important question, "Aren't they worried that their guy at the hospital might talk and expose their plan?"

"Wait a second," I said. "Do you have Kris's number?" Jote handed Tico his phone, and he quickly located the number from Jote's recent calls, passing it to me.

I dialed Kris's number and put her on speaker. "This is Mancuso. Who is guarding your prisoner at the hospital?"

"Deputy Rattner," Kris replied.

"You mean that older woman who answers your phones?" I asked, my tone filled with concern.

Kris responded, "It's the night shift, Mancuso. We don't have thousands of personnel like New York City. She's capable. We have the prisoner in the room next to your friend, the author. Why? What's the urgency behind your call?"

I wanted to suppress my jealousy about the NYPD and focus on the matter at hand. "Get someone else over there immediately," I demanded, emphasizing my words. "I'm afraid our guys might send someone to silence the prisoner and prevent him from talking."

Jote attached the red light to the roof of the van, and Tico followed suit with the blue light. The "vice-mobile" accelerated, racing toward the hospital.

15
Thursday, 3:30 a.m.

"Did anyone enter before us and inquire about the patients' whereabouts?" I inquired.

"Approximately forty minutes prior to your arrival, a man claimed to be the prisoner's private doctor from Miami and insisted on seeing him," Tom, the attendant, responded.

"Did you request identification?" I probed further.

Tom hesitated momentarily before replying, "No, sir. The man asserted that he had been driving for two hours and needed to examine his patient immediately."

"Did you inform the nurses' desk upstairs about the impending arrival of the doctor?" I asked.

His eyes widened in realization. "Yes, yes. I promptly notified the night nurse upstairs."

At least he took that precaution. "Has the doctor left?" Marcy inquired.

"No, not yet. I believe he is still upstairs," Tom answered.

"Is there another exit besides the front door?" Marcy pressed.

"Yes, there's an exit at the rear," Tom confirmed. "Should I contact the police?"

I hope you're not aspiring to be a brain surgeon. No, I didn't say that. Instead, I responded, "We are the police."

"Mancuso, come here," Jote called out from the elevator. Marcy and I hastened over.

"What's the situation?"

"Jack is in the operating room with the nurse attending to Deputy Rattner, who sustained a grazing bullet wound," Jote informed me.

"Damn. Is Jack alright?" I inquired.

"Yeah, yeah," Jote reassured me.

When Jack caught sight of us, he smiled and embraced Marcy, followed by me. "Are you two trying to get me killed?" he jokingly asked.

"No, brother. Just spicing up the plot for your next best-selling novel," I quipped.

"I'd rather make that shit up and not have to experience it firsthand," Jack remarked, placing the deputy's weapon on a nearby counter.

"What happened?" Marcy probed.

"I had just finished a solid ten hours of sleep and was wide awake. It must have been around two forty-five in the morning. I was conversing with Deputy Rattner and the nurse outside my door when the phone at the nurses' station rang. The nurse was informed that a doctor was en route," Jack recounted.

"That alerted you that something was amiss?" I leaned on the counter, seeking further details.

"You're kidding? That was an alarm. No legitimate doctor would visit a patient at three in the morning for a shoulder wound. I alerted Rattner, but the man was already sprinting down the corridor, brandishing a firearm," Jack recounted.

Curiosity filled my voice as I inquired, "What did you do?" My gaze shifted between the nurse and Rattner.

"The only option I had was to pull the nurse and Rattner back into my room and shut the door. Unfortunately, there were no locks," Jack explained.

Marcy leaned in, seeking clarification. "That's when Deputy Rattner got shot?"

"No, no. We were uncertain of his intentions. I suspected he wanted to eliminate his accomplice. But about fifteen minutes later, he tried to enter my room. That's when he and Rattner exchanged gunfire. She was grazed on her left arm, as you can see," Jack said, acknowledging her injury. "I believe she managed to hit him once. After that, everything went silent, so we cautiously emerged around ten minutes later and made our way here. I've been guarding the room while the nurse tended to Rattner's bleeding."

Realization dawned upon me as I voiced my analysis. "This man didn't come here to rescue his accomplice. He intended to kill him, which he succeeded in doing. And you could have been his next target."

Jack nodded solemnly. "You arrived just minutes after he made his escape."

"We entered through the front door, so it's likely he fled through the back," Marcy added.

Concern etched Jack's face as he mentioned Reinhard. "What about Reinhard?"

"They still have him, but they murdered Dianne. We discovered her body a few hours ago," I informed him.

"Damn, that's a tragedy. Reinhard's up next," Jack lamented.

"They need him to execute the wire transfer, and the funds won't be available until Friday because he had to sell stocks. That's the earliest possible timeframe," I explained.

Marcy turned to Jack, seeking any recollections. "Jack, what do you remember about them?"

"There were two guys who kidnapped Reinhard and me. They kept mentioning their boss, so I never met this guy, Galiano, or his partner. One of the guys was actually my neighbor here," Jack recounted.

"So you're unsure of where they might be holding Reinhard," I concluded.

Jack responded, "I think we were heading in that direction when I managed to escape. We were getting close to the Topsider. I wasn't restrained, and the guy sitting next to me in the backseat held a weapon, although it wasn't pointed at me. They handcuffed Reinhard to the front door of the car. I shoved the guy on my left and bolted out of the vehicle. That's when he shot me, and that's when you came to the rescue."

Jote interjected with a pertinent question. "Did you happen to overhear any conversations about a specific location or a boat?"

"No, no," Jack replied, glancing at Jote. "The driver did mention that Friday was a significant payday."

Marcy chimed in with a suggestion, "That could be Reinhard's money."

"The money Reinhard is involved with is an additional benefit for them. Their primary motive is the drug deal," I interjected, exchanging a knowing look with Jote.

Jote nodded in agreement. "I agree."

"If we're fortunate, we might be able to apprehend them with both the drugs and the money," Marcy proposed optimistically.

"Getting our hands on the drugs will depend on locating the boat. However, the money is likely to be digital, involving cryptocurrencies like Bitcoin, Ethereum, or others," I explained.

Jote made a practical suggestion. "Let's leave this place and take a brief break at your location for an hour. I need to inform the Coast Guard and alert them to the situation."

Jack expressed his concern. "I can't leave Rattner and the nurse alone here."

"We'll wait for the deputies to arrive, and once they're here, we can make our move," I assured him.

Although I regretted losing the suspect who could have provided valuable insights into Galiano and Castellanos, I was relieved that Jack was unharmed. While I was unsure of how to safeguard Reinhard's life and apprehend the culprits, I had faith in Jote and Tico. I knew they would devise a plan. These criminals wouldn't elude the "Pirates of the Caribbean" a second time.

16

Thursday, 6:30 a.m.

Marcy and I crashed in the comfort of the master bedroom while Tico and Jote settled in the second bedroom. Meanwhile, Jack stayed up in the recliner in the living room, engrossed in a backcountry fishing TV show with Max curled up on his lap.

As the sun rose, Jote was the first to stir, taking the initiative to brew a fresh pot of coffee for everyone. Following suit, Tico hurriedly prepared a scrumptious breakfast using the leftover eggs and toasting a loaf of bread.

The commotion from the kitchen roused Marcy and me from our slumber, prompting us to join the others at seven o'clock.

"Good morning, sleepyheads. Breakfast is ready," Tico cheerfully announced.

I inhaled deeply, savoring the enticing aroma of the strong coffee. With a satisfied exhale, I declared, "Damn, I'm hungry."

Jote shared an update, saying, "I've already notified the Coast Guard. They'll be on the lookout for any suspicious boats."

"They'll have their hands full with all the fishing boats out there," I remarked.

"They know what to look for, and they have the entire day. After all, Jack mentioned that Friday is the big payday," Jote assured us.

Marcy turned to me, voicing her thoughts, "Are we planning to return to New York? We have to vacate this place by Saturday."

"I want to see this case through. What about you?" I asked Marcy.

She pondered for a moment before replying, "There aren't any fresh cases waiting for us back in New York. But finding affordable accommodation is a challenge."

With a knowing glance at Jack, I pointed toward him. Before we could ask, Jack preemptively offered a solution, saying, "All of you can stay on the Easy Ryder with Max and me. However, Jote and Tico will have to share a queen-size bed. But there are rules."

Tico swiftly declined, saying, "Oh no, thank you. We can find a rental somewhere. We're still on the clock with the FBI-DEA task force."

"That works for me," I agreed.

Amused by the mention of rules, Jote questioned Jack, asking, "You have rules for guests?"

"Rule one: Nothing goes down the head unless you ate it. Rule two: Guests on board are mates. They cook and bartend. Got it?" Jack declared, prompting a chuckle from Jote.

Curious about the bar situation, I asked, "You have liquor on board?"

"Oh, that's rule three. Guests must stock the bar," Jack replied, remaining comfortably seated in the recliner.

Shifting the topic, I inquired about Jote's meeting with Special Agent Donnelly, the task force's leader. Settling down with my coffee and a plate of scrambled eggs, I listened attentively to his response.

"We're meeting at eight at the sheriff's office here," Jote informed me from across the table.

I voiced my concern, asking, "You don't think he'll allow me to continue working on this case?"

"He's a nice guy, but he prefers to keep things within his circle. He's bringing six other agents, both FBI and DEA. We're only involved because we reached out to them—sorry, brother," Jote explained.

My expression soured as I replied, "I uncovered this mess. I'm sure he's interested in the drug case, but Dianne's murder might not concern him as much."

Marcy, sipping her coffee, chimed in, "And you're the last advocate for the victims. You can't just let this go."

I nodded in agreement with Marcy's words, adding, "I feel responsible for her death. She mentioned me to Reinhard, and we became involved. And then she was killed. No, I can't hand this off."

Jote apologized, saying, "I wish Tico and I could help, Joey. But I know he won't agree."

I turned to Jack, who was still engrossed in a fishing show in the living room. "Jack, is the Easy Ryder seaworthy?"

Without looking back, Jack confidently replied, "Of course she is."

As Jote went to refill his coffee, he urged me, "Joey, don't interfere. I've got the task force and the Coast Guard working on this. You don't want to get caught in the middle of any potential chase. If we find them, they won't outrun us."

"'If you find them' are the key words. We won't get in the way. We're just doing research," I reassured him. "Take the firearm you gave me before you leave," I added.

"Just be careful, my friend," Jote said, settling back into his seat next to Marcy. "Marcelita, don't let this guy do anything foolish."

Marcy smiled in response, giving her assurance.

Tico and Jote finished their breakfast and packed up their belongings, placing their plates in the dishwasher. As they prepared to leave, I joined them on the balcony and returned Jote's firearm.

"Just keep me updated on your whereabouts and let us know if you discover anything, okay?" Jote requested before heading downstairs.

"You got it," I replied as they descended. Suddenly, I remembered something else I needed from Jote. Approaching their van, I called out, "Hey, Jote, do you have any files on Galiano and Castellanos that you can share with me?"

Jote pondered for a moment before responding, "I'm not sure if I can."

"But your captain approved of me working with you before, right?" I inquired as Jote started the engine.

"Yeah, but Donnelly is likely to revoke that now that he's here," Jote explained.

"He hasn't done so yet," I pointed out.

Jote grinned. "I'll have Tico send them to you. They're all digital."

"Thanks, brother," I said with a smile.

"Likewise," Jote replied, pulling out and driving onto US 1 via the gravel road.

Returning to the unit, I found Jack sitting at the table while Marcy was in the bedroom. Curious about our available resources, I asked Jack, "Do you have any firepower on your boat?"

Jack smiled and replied, "Some legal, some not so much."

"Let's keep that between us. I don't want to worry Marcy," I whispered.

"By the way, it's a vessel or a yacht, not a boat," Jack corrected me.

"Yes, sir, Captain Jack," I responded playfully.

Just then, Marcy emerged from the room and asked, "What do you want to do? I'd like to make the most of our time here before we leave tomorrow."

Jack inquired, "What is there to do?"

"I've heard that snorkeling under the dock is fantastic. There are plenty of fish, including barracudas, manta rays, a small sand shark, and sometimes even manatees," Marcy suggested.

"Go for it. I'm waiting for Agnes to get into the office and do some research for us. I'll join you in a little while," I replied.

"You snorkel?" Jack asked, a smirk on his face.

I chuckled and asked, "How hard can it be?"

Excited about snorkeling, I changed into my swimsuit and sat at the dining room table to call Agnes.

Jack playfully commented, "For an olive-skinned Italian American, your legs look like vanilla ice cream. Get some sun, dude."

Ignoring his remark, I proceeded to call Agnes. "Good morning, boss. How are the Keys?" She greeted her.

"We've been busy. Lots going on. I need you to do some research," I responded.

"Are you flying back tomorrow?" she inquired.

"No, we haven't scheduled a return yet," I informed her.

"Okay, I'm ready," she replied.

"In Marathon, Florida, I want you to find motels with marinas that can accommodate a large vessel," I instructed, glancing at Jack. "Perhaps a forty-footer or larger. Also, check if there are any bookings under the names Galiano, Castellanos, RAJO Trading, or NONOS Trading. Got it?"

"Anything else?" Agnes asked.

"And if you can, check on Paul Reinhard, the person you already researched. See if he makes any wire transfers of funds from his brokerage account, possibly involving digital coins," I added.

"That's going to be a bit challenging. I'm not sure if I can," Agnes hesitated.

"If anyone can do it, I know you can," I reassured her.

"I take it you're working on the case?" Agnes asked.

"Playing from the sidelines. But yes," I confirmed. "How's Father Dominic?"

Father Dominic O'Brian was my half-brother, a pastor at Saint Helens in Brooklyn, and also my partner at Captain O'Brian's Irish Pub and our investigative service.

"He can't believe you went down there to relax and got involved in all this. But he said it's par for the course for you guys," Agnes shared.

"I guess so. Can you have the results by the end of the day?" I inquired.

"I think so. I'll text you as soon as I have something," Agnes assured me before ending the call.

"Are you heading to the beach? I'll join you if that's the plan," Jack offered.

"For a while. But I also want to visit Dianne's and Reinhard's places," I replied.

"They're probably sealed by the sheriff," Jack warned.

"I have a knife," I responded with a wink, implying my resourcefulness in gaining access if needed.

17
Thursday, 10:30 a.m.

The Keys greeted us with yet another stunning day. The temperature soared in the high seventies, accompanied by a gentle easterly breeze. The water shimmered like a polished mirror, beckoning with its refreshing allure. However, my snorkeling attempts were futile. The mask kept flooding, and the incessant taste of saltwater dampened the experience.

I reclined in a beach lounge chair alongside Jack while Marcy continued her aquatic expedition beneath the dock, channeling her inner Jacques Cousteau. If left undisturbed, I could have easily dozed off for a couple of hours. Other guests reveled in kayaking and swimming, but there was a couple who seemed to believe they were professional disc jockeys, subjecting the rest of us to their blaring music.

"What's our next move?" Jack inquired, breaking the tranquility.

"Where's your Zodiac?"

"I hope it's still at the small beach near Robbie's marina," Jack replied.

"Let's go check out Reinhard's and Dianne's homes. They reside in a duplex in Tavernier, around ten or fifteen miles north of here. Then tonight, we can move in with you on the Easy Ryder," I suggested.

I strolled along the dock's length to where Marcy was leisurely navigating the water, informing her of our plans. She was thoroughly enjoying her underwater adventure and intended to join a group heading to a drop-off location further along the coast.

Clad only in our swimsuits, polo shirts, and sandals, Jack and I hopped into the car and drove to the address I had for Dianne and Reinhard. True to my expectations, yellow crime scene tape sealed off the entrance to the front unit—Dianne's residence—with Reinhard's abode situated toward the back.

"Didn't you mention that Reinhard is a millionaire?" Jack asked, his voice tinged with incredulity upon witnessing the modest dwelling.

"Like many brilliant minds, this guy has eccentricities. He craves a simple, laid-back lifestyle, and the Keys offer the perfect haven for that. Everything here operates on a 'later' or 'tomorrow' basis," I explained.

Jack chuckled. "I may have simplified my life, but 'later' or 'tomorrow' isn't my style. What do you think he's going to do with all those millions in the bank?"

"Right now, if we don't help him, he's losing a few millions," I said.

Cutting a piece of tape on Dianne's door, we maneuvered under it after I managed to open the door. As expected, the place was in disarray. It was evident that our gang had searched for the money and the duffel bag containing drugs.

"It still doesn't make sense to me that Reinhard would steal the money and drugs," I commented, surveying the unit. "He has more money than he'll ever need. Why would he risk his life for a few million?"

"Maybe he was bored and seeking some excitement. As the genius that he is, perhaps he thought he could outsmart these people. Who knows why people do the things they do?" Jack speculated.

"Nah, I don't buy it. I still think he fled to save his life and didn't realize he had the stash on his boat. Or should I say vessel?" I mused.

"Technically, it's a vessel. But his is a boat. What about Dianne? Was she an innocent victim or a co-conspirator?" Jack inquired.

Just as Jack asked that question, Jote called me. "Yes, Jote?"

"Marcy is not going to like this. The young woman, Dianne, was two months pregnant. We just received the report from the ME. I'm sorry, man," Jote relayed.

"All right," was all I managed to respond before ending the call. I turned to Jack. "Dianne was an innocent victim—she was pregnant. Shit, Marcy is going to be devastated."

"I know. There's nothing here. Let's check Reinhard's unit." We found no trace of anything significant in Reinhard's unit. The gang had turned the one-bedroom living-dining area upside down. All we discovered was an abundance of fishing gear and related paraphernalia.

"Let's take another look. This guy must have a computer or laptop somewhere," I suggested. "Keep an eye out for any cables."

"They might have taken everything. I don't see anything. Did he have a car?" Jack queried.

"I'm certain he did, but it's not here," I replied. "Keep searching."

After an extensive second search, we came up empty-handed. If Reinhard had a computer, it was either in the possession of the sheriff or the bandits, as Jote referred to them.

"Jack, let's go check if your Zodiac is still there. If it is, take it back to the Topsider, and I'll meet you there."

Fortunately, the Zodiac remained untouched and undamaged. I set off, and Jack would follow suit. I dialed Agnes's number and waited for her to answer.

"Any progress, young woman?" I inquired impatiently.

"Working on it. There are a few places in Marathon that meet your requirements. I'll email them to you. As for the brokerage account, I'm unable to access it," Agnes replied.

"Okay, keep trying. I'm sending you a file on our suspects that my friend Jote sent me. See if you can dig up anything else on Galiano and Castellanos. I need any clue about their plans, operations, or whatever you can find," I instructed.

"Are these official files?" Agnes asked.

"Yeah, but I'm cleared to review them," I assured her.

"I didn't mean it that way. I meant that if they're official, it's likely they've already been thoroughly analyzed by law enforcement," she clarified.

"I'm looking for the smallest details we can find. Maybe there's something we can uncover. Do they have any social media presence we can explore?" I asked.

"No, none at all," Agnes confirmed.

"They seem to be running a large operation. I can't imagine it's just the two of them. Two of their associates are dead, and dead people can't talk. If they have a significant amount of fentanyl, there must be more individuals involved," I reasoned.

"How's your friend Jack Ryder?" Agnes inquired.

"He's doing well. We're moving to his boat, or vessel, tomorrow. We'll be operating from there," I replied.

"Father Dom wants to speak with you," Agnes mentioned.

Dom came on the line, and we exchanged pleasantries.

Then he asked, "What's your plan?"

"We're working on the case to some extent. Jote is part of a task force with the FBI and DEA," I explained.

"What can you possibly do that they aren't already doing? This seems like a major drug deal. People are dead, and even Jack was almost killed. I'm worried about Marcy and you," Dom expressed his concerns.

This was typical of Dom—always concerned about our safety and cautious in his approach. And, as usual, he was right. We had limited resources and lacked knowledge about the suspects' habits or past actions.

"Dom, I understand your concerns, and I appreciate them. But I put this young pregnant woman in harm's way, and now she's dead. The task force is focused on drug dealers. I'm searching for the damn murderers," I emphasized.

"Yeah, well, I was afraid you would say that. Just be careful," Dom warned.

"I will, Dom. We'll be cautious," I assured him, and before ending the call, I added, "Tomorrow is a crucial day, based on the information we have. See if you can assist Agnes with her research. I've given her quite a lot to work on," I said.

"How about we bring Jimmy Johnson, JJ, the young kid I mentioned before, on board? We were planning to hire him to drive and assist Agnes once you returned. But now, he can start immediately and lend a hand," Dom suggested.

"Do it. We definitely need all the help we can get," I agreed.

With JJ joining our team, we hoped to boost our resources and increase our efficiency in gathering information and working on the case. The following day would be critical, and having an extra pair of hands would be invaluable.

18
Thursday, 2 p.m.

The day felt never-ending, and exhaustion weighed heavily on me. However, there was no time to waste if we wanted to save Reinhard's life. Once he transferred the funds, he would be in grave danger.

Marcy had finished her snorkeling adventure and was now refreshed after a shower. I quickly took a shower myself to rejuvenate. Jack joined us after safely docking his Zodiac downstairs.

We gathered in the dining area, enjoying the sandwiches Marcy had prepared. Between bites, I shared the latest update with Jack.

"Agnes is doing her best to gather more information on these guys," I said. "Right now, I have a plan."

"Go ahead and tell me," Jack replied, his mouth still partially filled with ham and cheese.

I swallowed a piece of sandwich and took a sip of water before continuing. "Agnes sent me a list of marinas and motels with marinas in Marathon. I think we should head there and show the photos of Galiano and Castellanos I have. Maybe someone will recognize them."

Marcy interjected, raising a valid point. "But aren't you assuming they're in Marathon? They could be in any key, north or south of us."

"I'm aware of that," I acknowledged. "However, while looking at nautical charts on my phone, I noticed a significant opening between Marathon and the next key south, Big Pine Key. It's called Florida Bay. With that route, they could sail north-northwest, hugging the Florida coastline, and potentially reach ports like New Orleans or others along the way."

I noticed Jack glancing at me, his expression a mix of surprise and disbelief. "You were looking at nautical charts?" he asked, his voice tinged with amusement.

Marcy couldn't help but laugh. "I'm surprised you're not feeling dizzy," she teased.

I defended my choice, saying, "What's so strange about it? A nautical map is no different from a road map."

Jack, intrigued, gestured for me to show him. I borrowed Marcy's iPad and opened the same app I had used on my phone. Handing it to Jack, I said, "Alright, Captain, take a look at this."

After a few minutes of exploring the nautical charts, Jack nodded in agreement. "Yeah, it makes sense. They could be in Marathon, right before the Seven Mile Bridge."

"Now, let's switch to Google Maps and look up Marathon, Florida," I suggested.

Jack followed my instructions, opening the satellite view that revealed a network of canals, waterways, and labels for motels and marinas. "Marcy, take a look at this," he called out, zooming in on the map. "See all those boats moored in Boot Harbour? It's a potential hiding spot for them, along with countless other vessels docked at various locations," Jack said, his tone filled with concern.

"We won't be able to check every boat. We'll have to rely on basic police work and knock on doors, asking questions," I replied.

Curious, Jack asked, "Which doors should we start with?"

"First, Agnes is trying to find out if they registered under their corporate or personal names," I explained.

Interrupting our conversation, Marcy pointed out, "If they did that, they would be the most foolish drug dealers ever. They've made that mistake before."

"I'm aware," I acknowledged, grabbing a beer and placing my empty plate in the sink. "That's why I thought we could begin by visiting food markets and showing their pictures. They'll need supplies. Then, we can move on to small motels where they might check in and pay in cash, avoiding names and IDs."

Jack voiced his concern about the time, asking, "Are we going to do this now? No time for sleep?"

"No time for sleep. We can rest later. Tomorrow is the crucial day," I replied. "However, if you're not up for it, you can stay here. Marcy and I can start the initial inquiries."

"No, no. I'll come with you," Jack decided.

We embarked on the hour-long drive south to Marathon. One additional reason I believed the suspects might be there was because Dianne's body had been disposed of in Marathon. If they had acquired a boat by now, they could have used it to dump the body into the ocean. However, they wanted the body to be found, as it would divert the attention of the sheriff's office toward searching for killers rather than drug dealers. Dumping the body in the ocean would have hinted that they had a boat, or it would have taken days, if not longer, to locate it.

Now that we knew Dianne was pregnant, I couldn't fathom her involvement in the drug deal or the ransom scheme against Paul Reinhard. My belief was that she had been unwittingly caught up in the initial faux fishing trip while Reinhard was a useful yet innocent bystander. The small fentanyl exchange during the trip served as an opportunity for Galiano and Castellanos to establish rapport with the dealers and test the product before the larger exchange took place.

As we arrived in Marathon, we began our search by stopping at every gas station with a food market and any place that sold ice or food. Each of us took turns at every stop, but after visiting six places, we had no luck in finding anyone who recognized Galiano or Castellanos. Of course, it was possible that they had other associates purchasing supplies on their behalf.

"Joey," Marcy said upon returning to the car after an unsuccessful stop at a small food market, "it's almost five, and you guys haven't slept for nearly twenty-four hours except for a quick nap. I suggest we head back, grab something to eat, and get some rest. We can start fresh early tomorrow morning."

On our way back, I noticed a Cuban restaurant in Islamorada, a couple of miles from the Topsider. "Habanos, what do you say we eat there?" I suggested, reading the sign.

"I'm fine with that," Jack replied.

"Sure," added Marcy.

It was a little after five, and the restaurant seemed to have an early-bird special as it was bustling with locals, many of whom appeared to be fishing guides.

We settled into a booth with a view overlooking the Caloosa Cove Marina. As I perused the menu and observed the plates of food being served, it became apparent why this restaurant was so popular.

"There's a motel over there," Jack pointed out, gesturing behind me.

"Hah, not the most obvious one, is it?" I chuckled.

A server approached our table to take our drink orders. To our pleasant surprise, we learned that the restaurant had a full bar.

"I'll have a Tito's martini, dry and up," Marcy requested. The server noted it down and looked at me.

"Make it two," I said.

"Make it three," Jack chimed in.

The server smiled and promptly turned around to fulfill our requests.

After the server returned with our martinis and took our food orders, I took the opportunity to show her the pictures of Galiano and Castellanos. Flashing the images, I asked, "I'm trying to meet up with some friends. Have you seen these two guys?"

Initially, she responded with a "no." However, upon taking a closer look, she leaned down and reconsidered. "Maybe that one, but I'm not sure," she said.

As the server walked away, Marcy chimed in, "Could've been Castellanos. They might have stopped here for food, just like we did."

"Exactly," I agreed. "Before we leave, we'll make sure to check out that motel."

We continued sipping our martinis, eagerly awaiting our meal while keeping our eyes peeled for any signs of Galiano and Castellanos. The tantalizing possibility of a breakthrough in our search filled us with a renewed sense of determination.

19
Thursday, 6:30 p.m.

Having indulged in a lavish meal accompanied by multiple rounds of martinis and a satisfying *cafecito*, fatigue started to creep over me. Despite my weariness, I couldn't afford to rest just yet. I had to follow up on my intuition and investigate the Caloosa Cove Marina and Resort. Its location and amenities seemed ideal for the likes of Galiano and Castellanos.

As we stepped out of the restaurant, I turned to Jack and advised, "You better wait in the car. These guys might recognize you."

Jack chuckled and replied, "The only two guys that saw me are dead."

I couldn't help but raise a skeptical eyebrow. "What about the shooter at the hospital? He could have caught a glimpse of your face," I pointed out.

"He never saw my face, and I never saw his. We're good," Jack assured me.

Before reaching the resort, my attention was drawn to a man diligently cleaning a boat nearby. I approached him and politely asked, "Excuse me."

He glanced up, curious. "Can I help you?" he inquired.

I scanned the marina and queried, "Is there a dockmaster here?"

He scanned the area as well and nodded. "Yeah, Captain Sandy, but he's gone for the day. He'll be back at seven in the morning. Chubby guy, red-faced, always wearing a captain's hat."

Expressing my gratitude, we continued walking toward the resort, anticipation building with each step.

Upon entering the resort, I made a beeline for the reception desk. A young woman greeted us with a friendly smile. "Good evening. Do you have a reservation?" she inquired.

"Not quite," I replied. "I'm supposed to meet up with some friends for a fishing trip tomorrow, but I'm uncertain which resort and marina we're supposed to gather at."

She contemplated the situation for a moment before suggesting, "Could you try calling them?"

I sighed, explaining, "I'm afraid these guys prefer to disconnect from reality when they come down here. No phones or internet. But could you please check your bookings to see if they happen to be here?"

The attendant hesitated. "I'm sorry, sir. I can't disclose the names of our guests. I hope you understand."

Nodding, I reached into my wallet and retrieved a crisp hundred-dollar bill. Placing it on the counter, I gently set my phone on top, revealing Galiano's picture. Sliding the phone toward her, I politely inquired, "Perhaps you could tell me if you've seen my friend?"

The young woman's gaze shifted between the money and the photograph, contemplating her decision.

She glanced around once more, then slowly reached for my phone, dragging it closer on the counter. With her index finger, she delicately slid the bill out from under the phone, curling her hand around it. "Mr. G, yes. Maybe the other guy, as well," she finally revealed.

Eager to confirm their presence, I pressed further, "Are they still checked in? Because if they are, I want to catch them by surprise."

Her eyes darted around nervously as she replied, "I really can't disclose that information, sir."

I retrieved another fifty-dollar bill and slid it discreetly across the counter, silently emphasizing my intent. Without uttering a word, she covered it with her palm, crumpling it slightly, and then glanced at her computer screen. Typing a few words while still holding the balled-up bill, she nodded affirmatively when our eyes met.

"Room number?" I inquired.

Just as another person approached the reception desk, my young accomplice chuckled and commented, "My birthday, hah, it's two twelve. Is there anything else I can assist you with?"

"No, thank you," I responded, flashing a grateful smile before swiftly rejoining Marcy and Jack by the large plate-glass windows overlooking the Atlantic Ocean. The setting sun painted the sky in mesmerizing hues of orange, red, and blue, creating a breathtaking view despite facing eastward.

"They're still here," I announced, satisfaction evident in my tone.

Marcy interjected, "Are you going to call Jote?"

"Let's head back to the car," I suggested, leading the way.

As we made our way to the vehicle, Jack voiced his concern, "You are calling for reinforcements, right?"

"Absolutely," I reassured him. "I just needed to step away and gather my thoughts."

Handing my phone to Marcy, I requested, "Can you dial Jote and put him on speaker?"

She complied, dialing Jote's number while activating the speakerphone function. After a few rings, Jote's voice filled the car, "Mancuso, what's up?"

"You're on speaker with Marcy and Jack. We found Galiano and Castellanos," I relayed the exciting news.

"No shit. Where are they?" Jote inquired eagerly.

"Mile marker seventy-three point eight at the Caloosa Cove Resort and Marina. Ocean side, room two twelve," I divulged, my excitement growing with every word.

Jote wasted no time with pleasantries, getting straight to the point. "Did you see them?"

"No, not yet. But I have confirmation that they're registered there," I responded, navigating onto our gravel road and heading toward our unit.

Jote's voice remained on the line, filled with anticipation. "You still there?"

"No, back at our place," I confirmed.

"Good. Stay there. I'll let Special Agent Donnelly know. I'll call you later. And thanks, man," Jote acknowledged gratefully.

With that, I hung up the phone, feeling a mix of relief and anticipation. The situation was now in the hands of the professionals, and there was a glimmer of hope that this ordeal might finally come to an end. Our vacation had turned into a whirlwind of chaos and danger, with only a couple of peaceful days at the start. Paul Reinhard's unexpected request to solve his own murder shattered our plans of a relaxing getaway in the sun and surf of the laid-back Keys, replaced by a frantic search, multiple murders, and a high-stakes investigation.

Perhaps we could extend our stay for another week, but the thought of being confined to a boat with cramped quarters didn't appeal to me. Despite the Easy Ryder being a spacious and comfortable yacht, I yearned for my personal space.

As the evening wore on, we dozed off on the sofa, exhaustion finally catching up to us. It was around nine-thirty when Max, our faithful canine companion, started barking, alerting us to the ringing of my phone. Rubbing the sleep from my eyes, I answered with a dry mouth, "Yes?"

"Mancuso, we have a team ready to raid the location at five in the morning," Special Agent Donnelly informed me.

"We're piecing everything together as we speak. You're welcome to be present, but you're to remain as a spectator. ¿*Entiendes*?"

"Yes, I understand," I replied, my voice still groggy. "See you there."

With the call concluded, I roused Marcy and Jack, informing them of the upcoming raid and our role as mere observers. It was a relief to know that professionals were taking charge, but the tension and uncertainty lingered. We had come a long way from our initial plans of a carefree vacation, and now we were entangled in a dangerous web of crime and deception. Only time would tell how this gripping saga would ultimately unfold.

20
Friday, 4:45 a.m.

The time marked the pivotal moment when law enforcement was poised to move in. As we made our way to the Caloosa Cove Resort, we witnessed a formidable sight—a convoy of sheriff's department cars and personnel, accompanied by unmarked black SUVs indicating the presence of the FBI-DEA task force. It was a coordinated effort ready to strike.

Parking our car in the nearby restaurant lot, we positioned ourselves for observation. From our vantage point, we could see deputies assembling from different directions, armed with long guns at the ready. I surmised that a significant number of them had been deployed to secure the beach area, forming a tight perimeter. I hoped they were aware that there might be an innocent party among the group—if Paul Reinhard was still alive.

Out of nowhere, a deputy appeared, rapping on the window and causing us all to startle. Rolling down the window, I confirmed my identity as he inquired, "Are you Mancuso?"

"Yes, Deputy," I acknowledged.

"Stay put until we wrap things up. We'll let you know when you can join us," he instructed.

"Thank you," I replied, stealing a glance at Jack and Marcy, who were seated behind me.

While we couldn't see the resort's entrance, I imagined the tactical operation unfolding inside. Agents storming the building, swiftly ascending the stairs to the second floor, announcing their authority as the FBI, and forcefully breaching the target's door. Shock and awe was the standard protocol.

With bated breath, we awaited the expected sight of the perpetrators being escorted out in handcuffs. However, moments passed, and the only movement we witnessed was deputies gradually exiting the resort. Disquiet settled upon us as we noticed some of the deputies outside lowering their long guns, a troubling sign.

A procession of law enforcement officials approached, and among them were Jote and Tico, making their way toward our car. The three of us stepped out, eager for an update.

"The suite is empty. No sign of them. But they were here," Jote relayed the disheartening news.

"Damn it. What do we do now?" I exclaimed, frustration lacing my words.

"We're conducting a thorough search of all the boats in the marina. The Coast Guard is stationed at the exit, ensuring no one slips away," Jote informed us.

"Do you think they're hiding on one of the boats?" Marcy asked, her concern evident.

"No, my gut tells me they've already made their escape," Jote replied, his tone tinged with resignation.

The realization sank in—we had missed them. The trail had gone cold, and our adversaries had eluded capture once again. The pursuit for justice continued, but now we faced an even more daunting challenge of tracking down Galiano and Castellanos in the vast expanse of the open sea.

"But they are registered," I interjected, hopeful that the registration details might provide some leads.

"They paid cash through Monday. The suite is registered under a bogus name, Oscar Smith," Jote informed us, emphasizing the frustrating obstacle we faced.

"We need to contact Captain Sandy. He's the dockmaster here. He comes in at seven," I suggested, glancing at my watch to note the time.

"Okay. I'm sure some of the charter captains have his number. We'll wake his ass up and get him here," Jote agreed, acknowledging the importance of gathering more information.

"Can we go to the marina?" I inquired, eager to explore any possible clues.

"Follow me," Jote responded, taking the lead.

As we strolled around the restaurant, we reached the U-shaped marina. Mates were busily preparing boats for the day's fishing trips. We positioned ourselves near a white storage box in front of an unoccupied dock space. Ahead of us, a food market bustled with activity as lights were switched on in preparation for the day. Some deputies headed in that direction, while others diligently searched one boat after another.

A sense of tranquility permeated the surroundings. There was no sense of urgency or rushed movements among the law enforcement officers. The realization that we had collectively missed our targets began to sink in.

At six thirty, Captain Sandy arrived. Sporting a sunburned red face, he donned his worn-out white captain's hat, black Bermuda shorts, and a vibrant Caribbean shirt adorned with flamingos and other exotic birds. A smile crept onto my face as I observed his appearance—a unique blend of Mr. Pat and the little Professor Persopoulus, Agnes' husband, whom I affectionately dubbed a mini-Jimmy Buffett.

Spotting Jote amidst the search party on the docks, I called out to him and gestured toward Captain Sandy. Jote approached the captain, engaging him in a conversation filled with inquiries.

While we waited, Marcy raised some pressing questions. "So, they took off. What happened to the big drug deal happening today, and is Reinhard dead?"

Taking my attention away from the ongoing search, I turned to Marcy. "Two valid questions. Maybe the drug deal did take place, and perhaps we'll find Reinhard's lifeless body floating in the Atlantic Ocean. I wanted to avenge Dianne's murder and save Reinhard. It seems like I've fallen short."

"The day has just begun. If Reinhard is wiring money, it can't be done until the banks open. And as for the drug deal, it could still be in progress," Jack chimed in, offering a glimmer of optimism.

"Honestly, Jack, while I despise the inflow of drugs into our country, that's not our primary concern here. The double homicide of Dianne and her unborn child was my main focus. I put her in harm's way," I admitted, grappling with my own sense of responsibility and regret.

"Hold on a second here," Marcy interjected, her voice filled with conviction. "The events that unfolded before Reinhard contacted us were already set in motion. He took the money and drugs, whether intentionally or not, and sought refuge at the Square Grouper. You, Mancuso, had nothing to do with that. Reinhard is the one who put Dianne in harm's way, not you."

Her words lingered in the air, causing me to pause and reflect. "I suppose you're right. But I still can't shake the feeling that we failed to intervene at the right time."

Marcy shook her head gently. "We need to focus on the present. Maybe there's still a chance for us to help bring these criminals to justice," she asserted.

I shrugged, acknowledging her point yet uncertain of our potential impact. Deep down, I held onto the hope that the combined efforts of the FBI and Coast Guard would be instrumental in resolving the situation.

Jote concluded his conversation with Captain Sandy and exchanged a few words with Special Agent Donnelly before making his way toward us. I noticed Donnelly issuing rapid commands into his walkie-talkie, prompting a surge in activity among the law enforcement personnel.

"What's happening?" I inquired as Jote approached.

"Captain Sandy provided us with valuable leads, and everything is being mobilized swiftly," Jote informed us.

"Care to share?" I pressed, eager for any glimpse of the unfolding plan.

"It's on a need-to-know basis," Jote replied, his voice laced with a hint of amusement.

"Are you kidding me? We discovered Reinhard's hiding place, located these individuals here, and connected with Captain Sandy. Your special task force hasn't achieved much, and now you're shutting us out?" frustration seeped into my words.

Jote raised his hands in a calming gesture. "Hold on. I'm just giving you a hard time. Take a breath."

"I don't need games. I need information and results," I retorted, my impatience evident.

Jote placed his right hand on my shoulder, a gesture of reassurance. "You're right; I apologize. Here's what's going on," he said, shifting his gaze to include Marcy and Jack, preparing to reveal the crucial details.

21
Friday, 7:30 a.m.

Jote shared the valuable information he had gathered from Captain Sandy. "Captain Sandy recognized both of these guys. They chartered a sixty-five-foot Hatteras yacht called The Queen of the Seas, with a captain but no mate. Supposedly, they planned to enjoy a fishing weekend in the Lower Keys and Key West, returning on Sunday," Jote revealed.

"That's helpful intel," I acknowledged, but the absence of a mate on the fishing trip raised my suspicions.

Jote continued, "There's more. Captain Sandy spotted Galiano being dropped off here at the marina in a forty-eight-foot, bright-red MTI go-fast boat. We suspect that's the boat they intend to use for smuggling drugs into the US."

"So, the go-fast boat, favored by drug runners, is the perfect vessel for drug smuggling," I commented.

Jack chimed in with a suggestion, "You should check the clubs of offshore racing boat owners who gather on weekends, riding between various locations for enjoyment, not for a race. Many of them ride between Miami and Key West, stopping overnight at places like this. It could be an ideal cover for disguising a drug run."

Marcy sought clarification, "Is it similar to bikers but with boats?"

"Exactly," Jack affirmed. "It's just a lot of fun for a weekend."

Jote chuckled and looked at me, saying, "Sounds good. I'll have the task force, who haven't accomplished much so far, focus on that. Meanwhile, we have Coast Guard helicopters dispatched between here and Key West, scanning for the Hatteras yacht. If it's out there, we'll catch them."

"What about the go-fast boat? My guess is it's heading north along the Florida coastline," I added.

"We're on it," Jote assured me. "I believe every Coast Guard helicopter between here and New Orleans will be in the air at some point."

Feeling a sense of urgency, I asked, "What can we do to help?"

Jote smiled and responded, "Hey, man, enjoy your place today. Relax, and have a nice dinner. We're on top of this, and I'll keep you posted. There's nothing for you to do now. Frankly, you guys have done most of the work so far."

"You know we have," I replied, teasingly calling him an "*hijo de puta*" as Jote and Tico walked away. We shared a moment of laughter before settling into a state of anticipation, awaiting further updates.

"We should do that," Marcy suggested. "Enjoy our last day, then pack. But the question is, should we go back to New York or stay on the Easy Ryder?"

"I say we stay to see this through. But hopefully, without offending you, Jack, I think Marcy and I should stay here at this resort. There's a little more room for everyone," I proposed.

Jack agreed, "I would love to have you stay over, but I think you would enjoy this place more. I'll come to visit."

With everything having settled down, most of the deputies and task force personnel had left. We made our way back to the resort. Marcy and I approached the reception desk, where the same young woman greeted us.

"You again," she remarked. "You're with law enforcement, right? And you were gathering information yesterday?"

Suppressing the urge to respond sarcastically, I confirmed, "Yes, I was. You made a few extra dollars, and all's even."

She smiled at Marcy and asked, "Can I help you with something else today?"

"Yes, how about a reservation for tomorrow?" I inquired.

"We were booked, but suite two twelve just opened up. Would you like that one? It's our biggest suite; it sleeps five or six," she offered.

"We'll take it," I replied. "And what time does Habanos open?"

"They open at eleven for lunch. No breakfast. But if you want great pancakes and incredible grits, try Midway Café or The Green Turtle," she suggested.

"Thanks. Here's a credit card to hold the room," I said, taking care of the reservation. With that settled, we headed south.

"How about pancakes and grits, Jack? Are you in for breakfast?" Marcy asked.

"Carb it up. I guess we're going to The Green Turtle?" Jack confirmed.

"Then we can relax by the water. I think I'll give snorkeling another try if I can manage to stop swallowing saltwater," I shared.

"Hmm, I'm surprised you don't want to go to Key West after these guys," Marcy commented.

I shifted my gaze from the road to Marcy, who sat next to me. "That's because I doubt these guys went to Key West. I need some rest and time to let my little gray cells work, as Hercule Poirot would say."

"So, snorkeling or sleeping?" Marcy asked, considering our options.

After breakfast, we returned to the Topsider. I decided to make a call to Agnes and see if she could research something for me. Marcy planned to take a power nap before our snorkeling adventure.

"In that case," Jack said, "I'm going back to the Easy Ryder to settle back in. Maybe I'll start working on my novel. I do have a deadline. If you come up with something to do, let me know."

Jack left, and Marcy and I finally had some time alone in our unit. I asked Marcy how she was feeling.

"I'm tired and saddened about Dianne and her baby. I can't stop seeing her body in the parking lot. I don't know if I'll ever forget that scene," Marcy shared, her voice filled with sadness.

Closing my eyes, I could vividly picture the gruesome sight as well. "I wonder if we had done anything differently, could we have saved her?" I questioned, opening my eyes to meet Marcy's gaze. "Maybe..."

"Don't go there. It happened," Marcy interrupted. "And no matter how much guilt we feel or how much we second-guess ourselves, it will not bring her back."

"I know," I sighed. "I just hope that justice is brought upon these guys."

With that, I walked into our bedroom and, within minutes, fell into a deep sleep. Two hours later, I woke up feeling refreshed. Marcy had already prepared our snorkeling equipment.

"Agnes called. She has some information for you," Marcy informed me.

I stepped out onto the balcony, waved at some of our neighbors, and dialed Agnes's number. After three rings, she answered.

"Hey, young woman, how are you?" I greeted her.

"Hi, Joey, let me go to the cigar club to talk to you," she replied. Then I heard her say to someone, "JJ, I'll be back in a few minutes."

I waited patiently, enjoying the view from the balcony.

"I'm back," Agnes said two minutes later. "I wanted some privacy."

"JJ is working already? That was quick," I remarked.

"Father Dom brought him in yesterday after you guys talked. This kid is what, nineteen or eighteen? Let me tell you, he's an expert coder and a wiz with the internet."

"I can't believe he's any better than you," I chuckled.

"He should work for one of our government intelligence departments. He's ten times ahead of me in terms of his skills."

"Wow, I never expected that," I responded to Agnes's revelation about JJ's skills.

Agnes continued, "Anyway, he could crack into our genius, Paul Reinhard's, account. And guess what? No money movement of any kind, no wires pending or requested. Over fourteen million dollars sitting there, sixty percent invested in stocks and bonds."

Glancing at the time, I saw that it was already fifteen past noon. "I don't know why I had a feeling about that. But it's still early. Maybe a request to transfer is still coming."

Agnes assured me, "If it happens, JJ set up an alarm to notify him of any wire transfers. I don't know how he did it, but he did."

"That's great. Let me know if it triggers anything. We're going to hang here for a few more days. An FBI task force is on top of this. Not much for Marcy and me to do but relax. Thanks."

As I ended the call, thoughts swirled in my mind. Was there more to this than just a big drug deal? I wasn't sure, but I had a feeling that there might be. But what could it be? The pieces of the puzzle were still scattered, and I needed to put them together to uncover the complete picture.

22
Friday, 5 p.m.

After enjoying some snorkeling and being visited by a friendly manatee, Marcy and I relaxed on beach chairs under our unit, sipping cold beers. I decided to reach out to Jote and left him a message regarding our current status.

Twenty minutes later, Jote returned my call. "Mancuso, how are they hanging?" he asked.

I chuckled and replied, "They're hanging wet but loose. Any news?"

Jote filled me in, "We haven't located The Queen of the Seas anywhere between here and Key West. The Coast Guard tried calling the yacht, but there has been no response."

Curious, I asked, "Do we know what time they took off?"

"According to witnesses at the Cove Marina, they departed at four-thirty this morning, before the raid. The trip should have taken them about three and a half hours, so they should have arrived by now," Jote explained.

I glanced at Marcy as I continued the conversation. "Any bodies recovered from the ocean or elsewhere? Specifically, what about Reinhard?"

Jote responded, "No, nothing reported on land or at sea regarding Reinhard."

I inquired further, "And what about the go-fast boat? Any updates on that?"

Jote replied, "Nothing so far. We're expanding the search north along the west coast of Florida. What about the wire transfer? Have you found out if it took place? Don't tell me you have no way of knowing."

I chuckled again, replying, "Very funny. No, there has been no money transfer."

Jote pondered, "So, do you think your boy is floating out there somewhere?"

I took a moment to consider the possibilities. "It's hard to say. There are still a lot of unknowns in this situation. We'll have to wait and see how things unfold."

Jote concluded, "Alright, keep me posted if you hear or discover anything else. We're doing our best to track them down."

With that, we ended the call, leaving me with a mix of anticipation and uncertainty about what was yet to come.

As I opened another local craft beer, Marcy asked me about the thoughts I hadn't shared yet. I took a moment to ponder before responding, "I don't know. But what if they didn't go to Key West? What if Galiano, Castellanos, and their new goons went east to the Bahamas or south to Cuba?"

Marcy seemed skeptical, questioning the idea of going fishing in the middle of a drug deal. I clarified, "I've ruled out fishing. Taking that many people on a large yacht without a mate doesn't make sense. Usually, in a drug deal on the high seas, there's a yacht acting as a controller for the transfer, often disguised as a fishing vessel. They supervise from a distance, even do some fishing to maintain the facade upon their return."

"But these guys aren't planning to return to Islamorada, especially with the murder of Dianne hanging over their heads. So, where are they going and why?" I pondered.

Marcy suggested we have dinner at Kayo Grill, enjoying sushi. We agreed to shower and get dressed, but not before watching and enjoying the sunset. However, Marcy misinterpreted my words and thought I had a different idea in mind.

"I meant watch and enjoy the sunset before the shower," I clarified, grinning.

With that settled, Marcy sprinted up the stairs, challenging me to a race. I followed suit, enjoying the playful moment between us.

Later, at the restaurant, despite arriving late, we managed to secure the last orders of tripletail and wahoo grilled fish. We indulged ourselves with sake, a California roll, a lobster roll, the fish dishes, and a delectable homemade bread pudding dessert served with vanilla ice cream. It was a feast fit for our appetites after an eventful day.

Back at the Topsider, I sat in the living room, feeling a sense of contentment after a restful sleep, intimate moments, and a satisfying meal. With my mind preoccupied with a persistent thought, I composed a text message to Agnes, requesting her and JJ to delve further into Paul Reinhard's activities following the sale of his company. Aware that he had come down here to escape and operate a fishing charter, I wanted them to uncover any additional information. The message read, "Agnes, between you and JJ, see if you can dig deeper into what Paul Reinhard was doing after the sale of his company. We know he came down here to get away and run a fishing charter but see if there's more. Thanks."

I pressed the send button, hoping that Agnes and JJ would be able to uncover any hidden details or connections that could shed light on Paul Reinhard's post-sale endeavors. It was an important lead that could potentially reveal crucial information for our investigation.

23
Saturday, 11 a.m.

Having bid farewell to the friendly individuals we had spent the week with at the Topsider, we treated ourselves to breakfast at The Green Turtle before managing to secure an early check-in at the Cove Resort through some persuasive charm. The day in the Keys was once again filled with beauty, although locals predicted scattered showers and high winds in the afternoon.

Anticipating Agnes's call regarding my text, I decided to take a walk to the Cove Marina, located next to the resort. After making a few inquiries, I was directed to Chris "Lite" Hackley, the usual mate on The Queen of the Oceans. Lite, a rather petite figure weighing only one hundred fifty pounds, had an unlit, unfiltered cigarette perpetually attached to his lips. His green eyes bulged, encircled by dark circles, while his pale face displayed deep, vertical lines resembling trenches. His long, thinning brown hair, reaching his back, was tied in a ponytail. The aroma of his breath indicated a fondness for his favorite drink, the source of his nickname. It was difficult to discern whether his weathered appearance was due to years in the sun, smoking, drinking, substance use, or a combination of factors.

Lite quickly expressed his dissatisfaction at not being part of the fishing-charter trip. He believed the captain should have insisted on his presence. Little did he know that the captain's decision may have saved his life. Upon showing Lite the photos, he confirmed that Galiano, Castellanos, Reinhard, and two others had been aboard The Queen of the Oceans. Lite mentioned that the group had only packed enough water and snacks for a maximum of two days with no bait. However, he speculated that they might have restocked their supplies somewhere in the Lower Keys if that was their intended destination.

So, what did all this imply? Limited water and supplies for a week-long trip? Was Reinhard destined for a burial at sea? Or was there more to this mystery than initially met the eye?

Returning to our room, I found Marcy preparing to relax by the pool. "If we want to enjoy the day, we should make the most of it now, as rain is expected later," she advised.

"I know, but the rain usually passes quickly in this area. I'm just waiting for Agnes's call. I spoke with the mate of The Queen of the Oceans," I replied to Marcy, sharing the details of my conversation.

"I'm not sure what it means," Marcy pondered.

"Perhaps it was a brief trip to transfer to another boat or disembark somewhere and disappear if they were involved in drug trafficking. These guys seem to be done for. There's an airport in Key West. Maybe that's their destination," I speculated. "Speaking of which, I hope the task force is investigating that. Let me call Jote."

Jote answered on the third ring. "Mancuso, are you still here?" he asked.

"We're at the Cove Resort for a few days. What's up?" I inquired.

"Nothing, brother. No sign of The Queen of the Oceans. It's like a ghost ship," Jote responded.

"Did you guys check Key West International Airport?" I asked.

"Mancuso, you should know better than that. We had Sergeant Leone and Deputy Joyce check that first thing. They stationed deputies at the airport, screening everyone who's flying out. These guys won't be able to escape by plane from there."

"What about the go-fast boat?"

"Again, nothing. Everyone here thinks this whole drug deal is bullshit. I don't know how long we can keep the Coast Guard and helicopters flying around. The plan is to wrap this up on Sunday if nothing develops."

"Damn it, Jote, what about the murders? Dianne and her unborn child?" I inquired urgently.

"Like Freddie Prinze said, 'Not my job.' Hey, I don't mean that personally. But the task force was organized for drug seizures, not murder investigations. We'll leave that to the local authorities."

"Shit. I assume the coverage was extended north as well, right?" I asked.

"Both the ocean side and the Intracoastal. All the way to Miami. Like I said, it's a ghost ship. But hey, man, this is your kind of case, murder investigations," Jote reassured me.

"Yeah, thanks. I'm here with no resources, just a mask and a snorkel. I'm sure that will be very helpful," I remarked sarcastically.

"Sorry, buddy. If Tico and I had available time off, we would stick around and help. But we don't. Maybe something breaks today, and we can move forward. I'll keep you posted," Jote offered.

Jote meant well, but his hands were tied. The responsibility was back in my court, but I wasn't even sure which game we were playing anymore.

As Marcy enjoyed the pool, I joined her after 9putting on a swimsuit. My pale legs were in dire need of some tanning, just like the rest of me.

"I spoke to Mom. Michelle Marie is doing well. Mom and Alberto are enjoying having her there. They said we can take as much time as we need," Marcy informed me, updating me on the conversation.

"That's good to hear, but I miss her and our diaper duties," I replied with a hint of longing.

"Hah, I never thought you would say that. Any good news from Jote?" she asked.

"They've got nothing. And they might wrap it up tomorrow," I shared with a hint of frustration.

"So what do we do?" She pondered aloud.

"If we can't find these guys, we can't solve Dianne's murder or maybe even Reinhard's. I hate being stuck like this."

Just as I voiced my concerns, my phone vibrated, indicating an incoming call. I answered promptly, "This is Mancuso."

"Mr. Mancuso, this is JJ from the office in New York," came the voice on the other end.

"Hey, JJ, good to hear from you. You can call me Joey. Any recent developments regarding the wire transfer?" I inquired.

"Mr. Joey, no money has been withdrawn from Paul Reinhard's account. There have been no sales of securities or loans against the account. However, I did some further research on Mr. Reinhard," JJ reported.

"Excellent. What did you find out?" I asked eagerly.

JJ continued, "I came across some highly secured servers that I haven't been able to crack yet. However, it seems that Mr. Reinhard, who is quite skilled in aggregating algorithms, had received an offer to work on a project for the Department of Defense. He was working on the project alone but eventually quit after realizing that it had adverse consequences, ones that could potentially be used by governments to spy on people."

"How do you know he quit because of that?" I inquired curiously.

"Let's just say that in my research, as Agnes taught me to say, I stumbled upon an email in which he confides in a friend about it. He expresses his desire to have nothing more to do with coding or programming and ends the email by stating, 'Going fishing,'" JJ explained.

"The Department of Defense, huh? Fantastic work, JJ. I look forward to meeting you in person soon. Please continue to monitor the accounts and let me know if anything changes. Where's Agnes?" I asked.

"Thank you, Mr. Joey. Agnes went out with her husband to pick up lunch. Would you like her to call you?" JJ offered.

"No need for now, JJ. Just have her get in touch when she's back. Thanks again," I replied, appreciating JJ's efforts.

As the conversation ended, I couldn't help but feel a glimmer of hope. The Department of Defense project and Reinhard's sudden departure from coding seemed like significant leads. Perhaps they could provide us with the missing pieces of the puzzle.

After my conversation with JJ, I decided to share the interesting details with Marcy, who was relaxing by the pool. Sensing that I needed some privacy to make a call, I excused myself and headed toward the marina in search of Mr. Lite.

I found Lite engrossed in a conversation with another captain, probably trying to secure a job as a mate. He had a Yeti in hand, although I was certain it wasn't filled with cold water.

"Can I talk with you for a minute?" I asked him, and he nodded, excusing himself from the conversation and joining me.

"Congrats on getting a job," I remarked. "Listen, do you know if there's a way to locate The Queen of the Oceans?"

"You mean like a GPS?" Lite inquired.

"Exactly," I confirmed, taking a seat on a storage box by the dock.

"No, there's no GPS on the boat," he replied.

"What about Captain Tony? Is there a way to locate him?" I asked, hoping to find a lead.

"Locate him? I don't know how," Lite responded, taking another sip from his Yeti.

"Is Captain Tony married?" I probed further.

"Is he ever? His wife is like that government agency that tracks your every move. The NAACP, or something," Lite replied with a belch.

I chuckled. "You mean the NSA, the National Security Agency."

"Yeah, that's the one," he confirmed.

"Has the captain given her a reason to be so cautious?" I asked, curious about Captain Tony's situation.

"The captain is quite the ladies' man. Sometimes his fishing charters don't require any bait, if you catch my drift. He's got a couple of friends who bring paid ladies on board for a two-day fishing trip. So when I say 'fishing,' you know what I mean," Lite explained, leaving no room for ambiguity.

"I understand perfectly," I said, getting the picture. "How can I get in touch with his wife?"

"They live a few miles south in Marathon. The address should be in the office," he revealed, pointing toward a nearby convenience store.

I made my way to the office/store and managed to obtain Mrs. Tony's address without much difficulty. If she was as jealous and cautious as Lite described, I was confident that she had a way to track her husband's phone. It seemed like a promising lead to pursue in our quest to uncover the truth.

24
Saturday, 3 p.m.

As I arrived at Captain and Mrs. Tony's home in Marathon, the weather took a turn. Dark clouds rolled in from the northeast, and the wind grew stronger, creating whitecaps on the water. Having left Marcy to enjoy the resort, I approached Tony's residence.

The house was a small, worn-down white stucco rancher with a dilapidated red tile roof. The lawn was neglected, littered with trash, and the stucco showed signs of cracks, likely due to foundation issues. It wasn't a well-maintained property.

I knocked on the door and took a few steps back. After a short wait, a plump woman opened the door, holding a beer can in one hand and a cigarette in the other. Mrs. Tony's sundress was two sizes too small, revealing more than I cared to see. Her blondish hair was messily wrapped in a bun, partially undone. Stained teeth, with a missing one on the left side, dominated her large mouth.

"If you're here to collect for the electricity, I have no money until next week," she grumbled, assuming the worst. "So turn it off if you must."

"No, ma'am, my name is—" I began introducing myself, displaying my private investigator credentials, which she didn't bother examining.

"Who are you working for? The loan company?" Mrs. Tony interrupted, suggesting they were struggling financially and likely behind on their payments.

"It's nothing like that. May I come in?" I asked politely.

"You're fine where you are. What is this about?" she responded with a sigh, clearly uninterested.

"I'm trying to locate an individual who chartered your husband's boat for a week-long fishing trip," I explained. "I was wondering if you have a way to locate your husband using the Find My iPhone app or any other means. It's an emergency."

Mrs. Tony's curiosity seemed piqued as she considered my request.

I understood Mrs. Tony's frustration with her husband's infidelity and the difficult choices she felt she faced. Sensing her willingness to help, I explained the situation further.

"No, there's no crime involved," I assured her. "It's just that this individual's wife had a heart attack, and we need to find him urgently."

Mrs. Tony expressed her sympathy, realizing the seriousness of the situation. She agreed to retrieve her phone, asking if I wanted a beer, which I politely declined, making a mental note of the potential profitability of beer distribution in the area.

After a few minutes, she returned with a fresh beer and an unlit cigarette. She tapped on her phone, and I observed a red dot with a pulsing circle appear on the screen, indicating the location. It read, "Havana Harbor."

Curious, Mrs. Tony asked, "Where is my scoundrel of a husband?"

"He's in Cuba," I replied, returning her phone. "Yes, you can go fishing there."

Expressing my gratitude and bidding her farewell, I rushed back to my car and drove back to the Cove Resort. Along the way, I called Jote once again, eager to share the news.

"Jote," I greeted as he answered. "I found The Queen of the Oceans."

Jote couldn't help but make a sarcastic remark. "Using your mask and snorkel, Sherlock?"

"No, just deductive detective creativity," I chuckled. "They're in Havana Harbor, Cuba."

"What the fuck? Shit, man, we're screwed. Why there, you think?" Jote exclaimed, expressing his frustration.

I proceeded to explain JJ's findings about Reinhard and his potential involvement with the Department of Defense.

"You can do things we can't with your research skills, Mancuso," Jote acknowledged.

The revelation of the boat's location in Cuba raised more questions and deepened the mystery surrounding the case.

As I continued driving, I emphasized the need to connect the dots and consider the possibility of government involvement, even if it went beyond what they publicly admitted.

Jote questioned the connection between the Department of Defense (DOD) and the abductors, Galiano and Castellanos, who were known drug dealers. I explained that Paul Reinhard, the genius coder, had been working on a project that he abandoned due to the potential negative consequences if misused by a government. The DOD then approached him to continue working on it, which led him to quit the entire endeavor.

Jote wondered if the DOD was somehow behind the events. I urged him to connect the dots, pointing out that Galiano and Castellanos were dealing in fentanyl, and while the Mexicans processed it, the Chinese were the world's biggest suppliers. Given the Chinese government's extensive social control measures, such as surveillance cameras and facial recognition programs, it was plausible that they would be interested in Reinhard's work.

Jote grasped the implications and realized the equation had changed, bringing other agencies into the mix. I arrived at the resort, and I parked the car.

Jote questioned if the original fishing charter with Reinhard was merely a cover to abduct him. I agreed, suggesting that the fentanyl exchange might have been a down payment for the abduction, but Reinhard's escape had disrupted their plan.

Jote inquired about the two Cubans who were killed while delivering the drugs. I speculated that they had likely become greedy and wanted to keep both the drugs and the money, leading Galiano to dispose of them.

As we contemplated the situation, it became apparent that Dianne had unknowingly become a means to lure Reinhard in and had tragically become collateral damage in the process, along with her unborn child.

The pieces were starting to come together, shedding light on the complex web of events surrounding the case.

Jote expressed concern that pursuing Reinhard and the larger implications of the case could put us in danger. He suggested passing the information on to other agencies but remaining anonymous in our involvement.

I paused for a moment, considering Jote's warning. However, a determination to see justice served and prevent further harm compelled me to stay involved. I reassured Jote, "Maybe I do want a part in this. Just make sure to let them know."

With our decision made, I ended the call and headed toward the resort, ready to take the necessary steps to locate Reinhard and ensure his safety before he fell into the wrong hands. It was a dangerous path we were embarking on, but the pursuit of truth and justice often came with risks.

25
Sunday, 10 a.m.

It was Sunday morning, and Marcy and I found ourselves at the Midway Café, a bustling little breakfast spot. Our time in Florida was coming to an end, and we were scheduled to fly back to New York on Tuesday. It felt like our mission was accomplished—we had successfully located the key players in the mystery. However, circumstances and our current location had seemingly removed us from the active playing field.

As I drove us back to the Calusa Cove Marina and Resort, ready to soak up some more sun, my phone rang, interrupting our thoughts. I glanced at the caller ID and whispered to Marcy, "DOD calling."

A mix of curiosity and apprehension crossed Marcy's face as she frowned, closed her eyes, and shook her head. She stared out of her window, lost in contemplation. Sensing her unease, I assured her.

"Mr. Mancuso, my name is Joseph John. I'm with the Department of Defense. I was wondering if we could meet today?"

"I'm in Islamorada, Mr. John," as I answered the call.

Joseph John, introducing himself as a representative of the Department of Defense, explained that he knew our exact location and inquired if Marcy was with me. I found his question peculiar but confirmed that she was indeed present.

"Good. We would like to speak with both of you. How about meeting at the Cove Resort at two in the afternoon?" John proposed.

Considering the invitation, I replied, "Sure, we'll be waiting by the pool."

Silence filled the car for a few moments as Marcy and I processed the conversation. Eventually, Marcy broke the silence, her voice reflecting her skepticism. "What was that about?"

"I believe they're seeking additional information," I pondered aloud. "Although, you're right. They already have everything we've discovered. And yes, they specifically mentioned wanting to talk to you as well."

Marcy expressed her displeasure with the situation, emphasizing her reluctance to get further entangled with the agencies who saw us as expendable pawns. Her concern was understandable, but I couldn't shake off my own sense of responsibility and curiosity. Looking out my window as we passed the Topsider, I shared my thoughts. "Perhaps we should at least hear what they have to say?"

Resigned, Marcy returned her gaze to the passing scenery. "I suppose we don't have much choice," she conceded. "Just so you know, I've already booked our return flights for Tuesday at three in the afternoon."

"Perfect," I replied, grateful for Marcy's practicality and readiness to handle the logistics.

As we approached the resort, our minds filled with a mixture of uncertainty and anticipation for the meeting with the Department of Defense later that afternoon. Little did we know what revelations and challenges awaited us in the hours to come.

We quickly changed into more presentable attire and settled by the pool, sipping on our beers. With just three minutes to two, three individuals dressed in dark suits and black ties approached us. Thankfully, this wasn't a scene out of a science fiction movie, or I would have half-expected them to whip out ray guns and erase our memories of the entire case.

"Mr. and Mrs. Mancuso, I'm Joseph John. This is Albert Richard and Alex Tuck. Can we have a conversation in your room?" Mr. John introduced his companions standing beside him.

Observing the trio, it struck me that they all appeared remarkably similar. Mr. John seemed to be the oldest, possibly in his early fifties. They were neatly groomed, impeccably dressed, and exuded an air of professionalism. The only notable distinction was Tuck's slight weight around the waist.

It didn't immediately click, but as we entered our room, it dawned on me. Prince John, King Richard, and Friar Tuck—characters from the legend of Robin Hood. With a playful nod, I quipped, "Should we wait for Mr. Hood?"

Mr. John couldn't help but smile. "You catch on fast. No, Mr. Hood is back in Sherwood Forest. He won't be joining us."

Motioning for them to take a seat, I asked Mr. John, "Why the cloak-and-dagger routine?"

"We're dealing with an incredibly sensitive matter. Our agency is extremely cautious," he explained.

"So, you're not really from the Department of Defense," I remarked.

"We can certainly show you our credentials. They are official DOD credentials. But ultimately, the initials don't matter, do they?" Mr. John responded.

"No need for that. How can we assist you?" I inquired.

Mr. John nodded to Alex Tuck, signaling for him to speak. "We don't know how you obtained the information, but you've uncovered something highly classified."

"We handed everything over to the task force," Marcy interjected.

"Yes, we're aware," Tuck acknowledged. "That's precisely why we're here."

Marcy raised an eyebrow. "So, what do you want? Are you going to ask us to sign a non-disclosure agreement?"

Tuck chuckled, exchanged glances with his partners, and replied, "No, there's no need for a non-disclosure agreement. We understand that you are professionals and fully grasp the classified nature of this situation. We simply require your verbal commitment to keep everything confidential."

"That goes without saying from our end," I assured them, emphasizing our dedication to discretion.

"Perfect, enough said on that. I'll let Mr. Richard explain the rest," Tuck stated and gestured toward Richard.

"The work Mr. Reinhard was doing for the DOD—" Richard began.

"Hold on a second. If I recall correctly, Mr. Reinhard chose not to collaborate with the DOD, right?" I interjected.

Richard lowered his head and reluctantly responded, "Well, yes, he hadn't signed a contract with us yet, but—"

"But that's beside the point. Reinhard stopped working on his project because he was concerned about potential misuse by any government, foreign or otherwise. Isn't that true?" I pressed.

Richard sighed and glanced at his colleagues before answering, "Yes, it's true. There is a risk that the program could be misused by a foreign government. You are correct."

"Not our government, of course. But please continue," I urged.

Richard frowned, clearly irritated by my interruptions. "Look, Mancuso, we've reviewed your file, and it strikes me as a bit peculiar that you, of all people, would pass judgment on what is correct. Based on our findings, you seem to be someone who views others as a means to an end. So—"

Mr. John swiftly intervened, cutting off Richard's retort. "Let's put all that aside for now. Instead, let's focus on getting to the bottom of this with Mr. and Mrs. Mancuso. There's a cargo ship in Havana Harbor scheduled to sail for Shanghai on

Tuesday at one in the afternoon. We believe that Mr. Reinhard will be taken to China on that ship. Our government cannot allow his work to fall into the hands of their government."

"What makes you think he's not already on the ship?" Marcy inquired.

Mr. John responded, "We have very limited resources in Havana, Cuba. The information we have suggests that he is currently residing in a home in the Miramar neighborhood."

"And what do you want from us? We don't have any resources there ourselves," I stated.

"Due to your training and law enforcement background and Mrs. Mancuso's fluency in Spanish, we need assistance from both of you to extract Mr. Reinhard from Havana," Mr. John explained.

26
Sunday, afternoon

I leaned back, observing Marcy's reaction as her eyes widened, and she instinctively covered her mouth with her hand. She glanced at me and subtly shook her head, silently conveying her doubts. I understood her unspoken message.

Turning my attention back to the three agents, who were eagerly awaiting our response, I could sense that they had picked up on Marcy's hesitations.

"So, you're suggesting that the two of us should infiltrate Havana and extract Paul Reinhard?" I clarified, seeking confirmation.

Before they could respond, Marcy spoke up, "Can I have a moment alone with my husband?"

Mr. John nodded and said, "Sure, we'll step out for a moment."

However, I interjected, "No, you can stay here. Marcy and I will step outside." With that, we left the unit and made our way to the pool area.

"You're not seriously considering this, are you? Why on earth would they choose us? They have agents who are fluent in Spanish and far better trained for this kind of operation," Marcy voiced her concerns.

"I understand your reservations," I replied, glancing back at our unit. "Let's hear their plan first and evaluate it. Only then can we decide. We owe it to Reinhard."

"No, we don't owe him anything. Remember, he initially came to us and lied about almost everything. I thought our focus was seeking justice for Dianne? This situation has nothing to do with that," Marcy argued.

"Let's at least give them a chance to explain. We can always decline," I suggested.

Marcy visibly displayed her anxiety about the whole ordeal. She sat down and continued, "You do realize that if we get caught by Cuban authorities, we'll be treated as spies. We could face a firing squad or end up in some remote prison for twenty years or more. Do you understand the gravity of that?"

Taking a seat next to her, I reached out and held her hand firmly. "We don't have to commit to anything right now. All we need to do is listen to their proposal. After that, we can decide whether or not to get involved."

"If you insist on helping these people, I want your brother's input. Can we agree on that?" Marcy requested.

"Of course," I replied without hesitation.

I knew exactly what Dom would say. He was the voice of reason, always cautious and grounded in reality, whereas I tended to act on instinct, weighing risk and reward and always ready to take the next step in bringing offenders to justice.

Returning to our unit, we found the three agents standing anxiously, waiting for our response.

"Tell us your plan," I said, addressing Mr. John.

Marcy added, "But let's be clear, we haven't committed to anything."

Mr. John nodded, scanned the unit, and suggested, "Shall we sit at the dining table?"

We all gathered around the table as Mr. John pulled out a map from his coat pocket and unfolded it. He asked, "Are you familiar with Havana or Miramar?"

I shook my head, indicating my lack of knowledge.

Marcy replied, "My parents lived in Miramar, but that's the extent of my familiarity."

Mr. John turned the map around so that we could see the street names and details. Both Marcy and I leaned forward, eager to understand the plan.

Pointing to a particular area on the map, Mr. John said, "This little strip is a rocky beach called La Puntilla at the entrance to the Rio Almendares. Mr. Reinhard is being held with minimal security in a home on Fourth Street." He moved his finger to pinpoint the location.

Marcy's eyes widened as she looked up from the map and exclaimed, "Oh my God, my parents lived on Fourth Street, maybe just three doors away from that home."

Curious about the plan, I asked, "So, what's the strategy?"

Mr. John proceeded to explain, "At two in the morning, we can drop both of you and an agent at La Puntilla. A waiting car will drive you four blocks to Reinhard's location. Once there, two agents will enter the home and neutralize the two guards. Then, all of you will leave, return to La Puntilla, board the waiting boat, and head back to the Keys. That's the basic outline."

Curious about the term "neutralize," I inquired, "When you say 'neutralize,' what exactly do you mean?"

"We have no intention of causing harm or taking lives. 'Neutralize' simply means making them unable to resist," Mr. Tuck clarified.

Marcy voiced her skepticism, saying, "You're making it sound like we're picking up a pizza at Domino's. If it's that straightforward, why do you need our help?"

Mr. John responded, "Reinhard knows and trusts you. He doesn't know who our agents are and is likely terrified of being taken to China. We want to minimize the risk of him overreacting or resisting."

It was a lot to take in, and I glanced at Marcy, awaiting her reaction and knowing that Dom's input would also be crucial in making our decision.

Marcy posed a thought-provoking question, "How do you know Reinhard is not there because he wants to do this? Maybe he does."

Mr. John shifted his gaze to Marcy, acknowledging the validity of her question. "Good question, Mrs. Mancuso. But if he truly wanted to pursue this, he could have boarded a flight to China months ago. He made a deliberate choice to quit the project," he replied.

I chimed in, connecting the dots, "It was only after the DOD tried to recruit him that the Chinese likely became aware. Your interest in him inadvertently exposed him."

Mr. Tuck interjected, clarifying the nature of Reinhard's project, "His project wasn't a classified secret. However, its potential implications attracted both domestic and foreign attention."

Leaning forward, I refocused the conversation on the operation itself. "Returning to the operation, I assume the two individuals guarding Reinhard are armed," I asserted.

Mr. John assuredly replied, "We have strategies to handle that."

I pressed further, seeking more information. "Understood, but how can we be certain there aren't additional guards or unforeseen complications?" I inquired.

Mr. Tuck responded with confidence, "Our surveillance has been diligent. Two guards are stationed at a time, rotating their shifts at eleven in the morning. They work twelve-hour shifts."

Concerned about the potential risks, Marcy voiced her apprehension, asking, "What if we get caught?"

"In such a scenario, both of you will remain in the car while our agents enter the house. Once the guards are neutralized, you'll join them to retrieve Mr. Reinhard. If any complications arise during the entry, the car will swiftly transport you out of the area," Mr. John explained, outlining their contingency plan.

Considering the circumstances, I contemplated the necessity of both of us being directly involved. "Speaking Spanish doesn't seem crucial for this mission. Knowing Reinhard is," I observed, looking at Marcy.

Mr. John acknowledged our point, stating, "Ideally, we prefer both of you, but you're right—one of you would suffice."

Curiosity piqued, I turned my attention to the agent assigned to accompany me. "Is the agent who will be with me American?" I asked.

"He is a Cuban-American. He possesses extensive knowledge of the area," Mr. John confirmed.

Curious about the backgrounds of the support team, I further inquired, "And what about the driver and others? Are they also Cubans?"

Mr. John assured us, "Yes, they are Cubans who work for us, and we trust them implicitly."

Observing the need for discretion, I remarked, "Clearly, you aim to avoid leaving an American footprint on this operation."

"Indeed," Mr. Tuck concurred.

Feeling the weight of the situation, I leaned in closer to the map on the table. Engrossed in the details, I asked, "Can you arrange for Italian passports for both Reinhard and me?"

Mr. Tuck, intrigued by my request, sought clarification, "That can be arranged, but may I ask why?"

Recognizing the potential benefits, I responded, "It's a precautionary measure, providing an additional layer of protection and plausible deniability if necessary. While we'll strive to minimize risks, having the option to assume different identities could prove valuable."

I directed their attention to the location of the Italian Embassy on Fourth Street and Fifth Avenue, emphasizing its proximity. "If things go south, your car can drop me off right there," I asserted, fixing my gaze on the three agents.

Exchanging glances among themselves, they silently communicated their agreement. Mr. John then posed the crucial question, "So, are you in?"

27
Sunday, 3 p.m.

I glanced at Marcy and noticed a look of consternation on her face. "I'll let you know later," I replied.

Mr. Tuck interjected, "How much later, Mr. Mancuso? We're ready to proceed tonight. If you're not on board, we'll have to make alternative arrangements."

Mr. John chimed in, adding, "The sooner we extract Reinhard, the safer it will be. They're completely unaware that we know his whereabouts."

Assertively, I responded, "I said later. You're asking me to embark on some impromptu off-the-books operation you cooked up in just two minutes. I need time to think and discuss this with my wife. So, later means later. Understand?"

The three of them exchanged glances. Mr. John shrugged and said, "Fine. I'll text you my number. We need to know before five today."

Glancing at my watch, I confirmed, "Five it is. Now, if you'll excuse us."

Marcy and I remained in our quarters, a heavy silence hanging between us. I knew she was worried, and truth be told, I was worried myself. But something inside me urged me to proceed.

Finally, after twenty minutes of silence, as we sat in the living area, she broke the silence, asking, "Why would you even consider this? Extracting someone from foreign soil is not our responsibility. They have specialized operatives for that. But no, Joey Mancuso has to handle it all. Why?"

Sincerely, I admitted, "Honestly, I don't know why. I just feel compelled to do it. It seems like something we can accomplish swiftly—in and out."

"Of course, Joey Mancuso, the eternal champion for the victims," she retorted. "I know I won't be able to change your mind, and neither will your sensible and mature brother. I just want you to think about our daughter and me if something happens to you. We've both had our share of close calls, and we've managed to survive. I can't bear the thought of losing you."

I closed my eyes, deeply affected by Marcy's words, "Your daughter and me." It struck me with a powerful realization that I had been selfish, failing to consider the potential harm to my family if things went awry. As a police officer, and similarly, in the military, you can't approach dangerous situations with the expectation of death; it would paralyze you and hinder your ability to carry out the mission. Ignoring fear is not the answer either, as it can lead to overconfidence and a loss of vigilance. Instead, you plan meticulously, trust your comrades to do the same, and execute the operation.

Standing up, I moved to sit beside Marcy and held her tightly. "I love you both. Nothing is going to happen to me. I'll be back tomorrow morning in time for chocolate chip pancakes at the Green Turtle."

Marcy began to sob, and I held her even closer, planting a gentle kiss on her cheek. "Listen to me. This will be over before you know it. By this time tomorrow, we'll be sipping margaritas at Morada Bay."

"No salt," she managed to say amid her tears.

I smiled and replied, "No salt."

She turned to face me, our eyes meeting, and she kissed me passionately on the lips. Her emerald-green eyes were watery, and the sun's rays streaming through the window highlighted the shimmer of her platinum hair, casting a warm glow in our living room.

"Promise me you won't do anything reckless, and you better be back in time for breakfast," she whispered.

We remained seated, my arms wrapped tightly around her until her sobs gradually subsided.

"Are you going to call Father Dom?" Marcy inquired.

"I'm debating whether to do so. I know he'll interrogate me relentlessly if I tell him what we're involved in with Reinhard. He may not understand the level of our commitment," I pondered aloud.

"Do what you think is best. But just like a preemptive strike, his preemptive prayers might provide some assistance," she suggested.

"I know. He seems to have a direct line to Him," I replied with a hint of a smile.

"We all do, in a way. Maybe he just has VIP seating," Marcy mused.

Dom had played an immense role in my life. We shared the same mother, Briana. Despite being fifteen years my senior, he had become a second father to me, a mentor, and a moral compass after my own father's murder. He guided me away from following in my father's footsteps in organized crime. We were more than just half-brothers.

Being the coward that I was, I decided not to call Dom. Exhausted from comforting Marcy, I couldn't bear going through the entire explanation again. I had a strong suspicion that Marcy, who was extremely close to Dom, would dial his number the moment I stepped out the door.

I made the call stepping out of our unit and dialing Mr. John's number. "I'm in. What's the plan?"

"Good. Be at the Cove Marina docks at ten tonight. Bring nothing. We have everything you need," he replied.

"How about a firearm?"

"You don't need one. We got this," Mr. John assured me.

His confidence was palpable, suggesting he had experience in these types of operations. But could it really be as simple as ordering a pickup from Domino's? I had my doubts, but they made it sound straightforward. Land on the rocky beach, proceed four blocks in a car, neutralize the target, drive Reinhard back to the beach, then hop onto the getaway boat, and voilà. I half-expected a drumroll to accompany their explanation, but none came.

For the remainder of the afternoon and early evening, Marcy and I tried to distract ourselves by spending time at the pool. We engaged in idle conversation, had a virtual video call with our baby girl, Michelle Marie, and chatted with Marcy's parents. Neither of us wanted to broach the topic of the operation, so we carefully avoided it.

As six-thirty rolled in, we strolled back to our unit. Marcy discarded her swimsuit, pulling me close by the waist and leading me into the bedroom.

At nine forty-five, I made my way to the marina, where I spotted the three amigos along with two unfamiliar faces. My fate rested in the hands of Diego and Arturo for the next ten hours.

Part 2
28
Sunday, 9:55 p.m.

Diego Bermudez, our captain, skillfully maneuvered the forty-three-foot Midnight Express out of Cove Marina. The sheer sight of the vessel left me in awe, and the roar of its red Quad Mercury engines, all five of them, each boasting 450 horsepower, was nothing short of impressive.

Diego, in his thirties and affiliated with the Navy, although not clad in uniform for obvious reasons, possessed jet-black hair, captivating amber eyes, and a formidable mustache. His bulging muscles threatened to burst the seams of his T-shirt, emphasizing his strength.

Curiosity getting the better of me, I inquired, "How fast can this thing go?"

He flashed a smile and responded, "Up to ninety miles per hour if necessary. However, we won't be pushing it to that limit on the way in. I want to conserve fuel in case we need to make a swift getaway."

"A getaway?" I asked, a hint of unease creeping into my voice.

Diego exchanged a glance with Arturo before answering, "Cuba has gunboats patrolling the coast—only a few, but if we happen to come across one, we'll need to kick it into high gear."

"And how fast can they go?" I inquired further.

"They can't match our speed, but they do carry firepower," he replied, his tone carrying a note of caution.

As I surveyed our vessel, I noticed no guns mounted anywhere, which prompted my next question, filled with concern, "Do we have any weapons?"

"Not for defending against gunboats, no," Arturo chimed in. "But Diego can navigate us out of any trouble smoothly. There's nothing to worry about," he reassured me.

Arturo Hernandez stood at an imposing six foot five, his brown hair and beard adding to his commanding presence. His dark eyes and bushy eyebrows, coupled with his apparent age of thirty-something, exuded a sense of confidence.

Damn. I was already anxious about potential seasickness, and now I had to contemplate dodging .50-caliber bullets. Bring on the barf bags.

"Don't the Cubans have radar to detect unauthorized boats entering their waters?" I voiced my concerns.

"They do," Diego confirmed. "But they don't pursue every vessel. We have our own radar system to track their positions. We're well-prepared."

"But guys, I don't see any radar equipment installed on our boat," I pointed out, a tinge of worry lingering in my words.

"Up in the sky, Mancuso," Arturo interjected. "We have a Navy AWACS all to ourselves. This guy you're picking up must be a high-value VIP."

I gazed upward at the vast expanse of the star-filled sky, not expecting to spot the AWACS but finding solace in its presence. Still, I couldn't shake the feeling that we should have some means of defense if things took a turn for the worse.

Curiosity getting the better of me, I directed my question to Arturo. "Who are you affiliated with?"

"The less you know, the better, in case we get caught. But rest assured, this is not our first extraction mission," Arturo replied, his gaze steady. "Neither is it Diego's."

That assurance brought me some measure of comfort. However, I couldn't help but inquire, "Have you carried out operations like this in Cuba before?"

Arturo exchanged a knowing look with Diego before responding, "Not in Cuba for me, but Diego has been in and out of the country multiple times."

I surmised that both of these skilled individuals were likely Navy SEALs. Nevertheless, revealing their true identities to the enemy, if captured, would be a grave mistake.

"So, I assume you've had some practice runs for this operation?" I inquired further.

Arturo shook his head. "Not for this one. It was put together hastily. But don't worry, they've briefed us thoroughly on the plan. Did they go over the details with you?"

I scanned the calm seas around us, estimating the wave height to be around one to two feet, a smooth ride contrary to my initial expectations. "Yes, they did," I confirmed.

"Good. Let me walk you through it," Arturo began. "Diego will drop us off at La Puntilla, a few blocks away from the extraction site. He'll then move a few miles out to sea and await my signal. We'll have a car and driver waiting for us. The driver will take us to the target's location. Once there, I'll proceed inside while you stay in the car. Understand?"

I pondered his words for a moment. "So, you're going in alone?" I clarified.

Arturo nodded. "Yes."

I couldn't help but express my confusion. "Alone, to neutralize two armed guards?"

He maintained his composure. "Yes. If you say so. After I neutralize the guards, I'll notify you, and you'll join me to secure our target. You know the man, right?" Arturo asked.

"Yes, I do. But perhaps I could assist you as you enter. I have experience with firearms," I suggested, eager to contribute my skills to the operation.

"Using firearms will be a last resort for me. Your role is to stay in the car," Arturo emphasized.

"Right, I'll stay in the car," I confirmed.

"In the event that something goes awry, the car will take you to the Italian Embassy. Did you bring your new passport?" Arturo asked.

"Yes, I have it with me. However, I don't have the target's passport," I replied.

"I have that covered. If all goes well, we'll return to the car and make our way back to the boat, where Diego will be waiting for us," Arturo explained.

I couldn't help but voice my concerns. "And then we make a run for it?"

Diego chimed in, his voice steady. "We'll make our exit discreetly. We don't want to draw any unnecessary attention unless we're being pursued."

At the thought of bullets flying toward us, I couldn't help but inquire about the driver. "Do you trust this driver?"

"I trust only my teammates. This driver works for us, but I don't know his true identity," Arturo responded.

"Will I be armed?" I questioned, eager to know if I would have a means of defense.

"I have a Glock 19 for you. However, if you find yourself in a situation where capture seems imminent, discard it. Understood?" Arturo instructed.

The plan they outlined didn't sit well with me. Placing our trust in an unknown Cuban national to be our driver, Arturo venturing into a secured home while I remained in the car, waiting for a call to retrieve Reinhard—it felt far from foolproof. Arturo's words about the operation being put together hastily only added to my unease.

I noticed the boat slowing down slightly, prompting me to inquire, "What's happening?"

Diego's voice came over the intercom reassuringly. "I'm about three hundred yards away from the drop zone. Everything looks clear, according to our eyes in the sky."

Glancing at my watch, I noted that it was ten minutes to one in the morning.

"Proceed," Arturo stated, steeling myself for the mission ahead.

29
Monday, 2:20 a.m.

La Puntilla, far from a beach, was a treacherous stretch of rocky terrain leading to the inlet of Rio Almendares on the left. To the right, there were houses and a dimly lit street, but the absence of streetlights made it feel desolate and abandoned. Navigating through the darkness with jagged rocks protruding from the ground was a challenging task. With every step, I had to be cautious not to stumble and risk impaling myself on the sharp peaks. This was no walk in the park; it felt like traversing an alien landscape that was neither welcoming nor forgiving.

"Be careful," Arturo whispered, his voice barely audible amidst the sound of crashing waves and my own labored breath as I struggled to maintain my balance on the treacherous path.

"How much farther do we have to go?" I whispered back, my voice filled with a mix of fatigue and apprehension.

In a hushed tone, Arturo replied, "Just a few more yards, maybe twenty."

As we continued our cautious progress, Arturo suddenly raised his arm and clenched his fist, signaling me to halt. I froze in place, squatting down to maintain stability on the uneven surface. "What now?" I whispered, my voice tinged with impatience.

Ignoring my question, Arturo directed a tiny beam of light in the direction of the street. The initial attempts yielded no response. He tried again, and this time, a faint flash of light emanated from the same direction. "Is that our guy?" I inquired, barely audible.

"Yes, now stay quiet and stay low for the remainder of our approach," Arturo instructed, his voice a mere whisper.

Remaining low came naturally to me as I crawled forward, feeling as though I were moving on all fours. The lack of stable ground beneath me made it impossible to find a firm footing on the unforgiving rocks. This was a stark departure from my usual experiences navigating the streets of New York and solving murders. Extracting a person from a foreign country, in the company of a seasoned Navy SEAL, was uncharted territory for me. Even the weight of the firearm holstered at my side, a sensation I hadn't experienced in years, carried both a sense of reassurance and a reminder that danger could be imminent, with bullets possibly headed my way if I needed to draw my weapon. How did I end up in this situation? Marcy's words echoed in my mind, "They have specialized operators for this. But no, Joey Mancuso has to do it all. Why?"

As we continued our stealthy approach, I couldn't help but question the choices that led me here, mindful of the risks involved and the potential consequences awaiting us.

In that moment, there was no time for contemplation or second-guessing. I had to rely on my instincts and carry out the task at hand. Reinhard was an innocent individual who had unwittingly attracted the attention of governments always hungry for any advantage. His advanced program had caught their interest, but he had the foresight to halt its development before completion. What would our own government's intentions be? Would they force him to finish the program or dismiss it as inconsequential? I couldn't say for certain, but those concerns would have to wait until tomorrow. For now, he was being held captive, mere hours away from being shipped off to China.

The weight of failure loomed over me. If we didn't succeed, would the United States resort to a daring SEAL rescue operation, intercepting the cargo ship on the high seas? My friend Jack Ryder could easily write a book about that scenario.

"Shit," I muttered aloud, abruptly jolted back to reality as I stumbled once again, rousing from my brief daydream.

"Keep your voice down, brother. Are you alright?" Arturo whispered, his concern evident.

The pain shooting through my body was unbearable, easily registering at a fourteen on a scale of one to ten. It was akin to a swift kick to the groin. Unable to immediately respond, I grumbled, "I'll be fine. Just give me a moment."

"We've arrived. Our next stop is the car. Come on, move quickly," Arturo urged, leading the way.

I followed Arturo's lead as he climbed into the backseat of a 1962 Chevy Nova while directing me to take the passenger seat. The driver greeted us. "I'm Miguel. I'll be your driver. Stay low if you can. We only have a few blocks to cover."

Arturo inquired, "And your last name?"

"Salazar," came the driver's response. It seemed to be a prearranged code, providing reassurance that Miguel was indeed our designated driver.

Miguel, as he shifted the car into gear, continued, "We're on C Street. I'll be driving through B, then zero, two, and four. That's our destination."

Arturo spoke from the back, asking, "Do you know what to do once we arrive?"

"Of course," Miguel replied confidently.

I surveyed the car's interior, which was shrouded in darkness. Despite the limited visibility, it appeared to be in impeccable condition. Miguel, in his late twenties, had a jovial demeanor, his tone resembling that of a tourist guide rather than an operative engaged in a clandestine operation.

"We've arrived," Miguel announced, pulling to a stop after five minutes of driving and making a left turn. Arturo stood up from the back seat, giving me a reassuring pat on the shoulder. "You know what to do. Stay put until I give the green light. Got it?" he reminded me.

"Got it," I replied, adjusting myself on the seat. Miguel glanced at me and smiled. "*¿Americano?*" he asked.

"*Nessun, Italiano,*" I responded, indicating that I was Italian.

"*¿Habla Italiano?*" he inquired.

Quite a talkative fellow. Why all the questions? "*Sì, ma dobbiamo stare ziti,*" I replied, telling him that we needed to stay quiet. "*¿Comprende? No hablar.*"

He nodded, shifting his gaze to the house outside the window. I followed his line of sight, but from my peripheral vision, I noticed Miguel placing his right hand on a firearm holstered at his waist. Was he feeling uneasy, or did he have a different agenda in mind?

We waited in suspense, although only four minutes had passed since Arturo left the car. Suddenly, two flashes, likely gunfire, illuminated the window. Shit. I thought Arturo said no gunfire. Did something go wrong?

Unexpectedly, jovial Miguel swiftly drew his .38-caliber Smith & Wesson revolver, pointing it directly at me. "Your gun, *señor,*" he demanded.

"Really? You're going to do this?" I responded, locking my eyes with his.

"In this equation, you're meaningless. I can kill you right here and leave your body on some street. You'd simply be another dead Italian tourist, another victim of crime in Havana," he menacingly declared in flawless English.

"Okay, okay. I'm taking my firearm out slowly. Only two fingers," I assured him, showing him my index and thumb.

"Good," he acknowledged. "I don't want blood on my seats."

That was a relief. He had no intention of killing me in his car. I could discern from his demeanor that the last thing he wanted was bloodstains on his seats.

As I cautiously slid out my Glock, I remarked, "I was hoping to enjoy a *cafecito* and purchase some fine Cuban cigars."

Miguel responded, his tone dripping with sarcasm, "Well, it seems your visit to Cuba is coming to an abrupt end. No time for sightseeing now."

"Not on this—" he started to say, but I swiftly struck his gun hand against the wheel, causing his weapon to tumble to the floor. His gaze shifted downward in desperation as I forcefully pounded the butt of my Glock against the right side of his head, near his ear.

Miguel slumped unconscious, blood streaming from his right ear. Well, there goes the no-blood-in-the-car rule, Miguelito.

I retrieved Miguel's revolver and exited the vehicle. Arturo's anticipated green light for me to proceed had not materialized. Ten minutes had already passed, and it was high time for me to act. But what should I do now?

30
Monday, 3:10 a.m.

I proceeded cautiously toward the house, taking measured steps in the darkness. Thankfully, the streetlights were either out or non-functional. I couldn't help but wonder why Arturo had taken so long to give me the green light and what had caused those two flashes that resembled gunfire.

As I approached the house, using the walkway that led to the front door, I noticed it was partially open. Swiftly, I darted to the side and concealed myself behind an overgrown hedge. Two men emerged from the house, but they were not Arturo and Reinhard.

Damn it. Could Arturo and Reinhard be dead?

I waited until the two men had passed by my location, heading toward their car. Silently, I entered the house, gripping my Glock tightly, preparing for the worst. Time was of the essence, as these individuals would surely discover Miguel's presence within minutes.

The sparsely furnished living room appeared empty, save for a lamp casting its light on a side table. However, there was a motionless body lying face down on the terrazzo floor. My heart skipped a beat. Squatting down, I kept my Glock pointed toward the hallway, but upon closer inspection, I realized the body was too large to be Reinhard. This provided some relief. I gently pushed on the left shoulder, revealing the face of an unfamiliar person. Checking for a pulse, I discovered that the man was still alive. Then, something completely unexpected happened—he grabbed my hand and uttered, "*¿Que paso?*" (What happened?)

I couldn't afford to have this man raise an alarm, so I retorted, "*Esto paso*" (This happened), swiftly striking his temple with the butt of my Glock. I figured Arturo must have employed similar tactics before, given his expertise, and this man was about to experience a likely double concussion.

A hallway stretched ahead, with what appeared to be a kitchen on the left and a dining room on the right. I decided to explore the kitchen first, but it was vacant. The same held true for the dining room, which showed signs of recent food consumption—plates with leftovers and four water bottles.

Four bottles. Two men outside, the incapacitated stranger in the living room—that made three. Considering someone was likely guarding Reinhard, that would account for four. Or were there more of them lurking within the confines of the house?

Continuing down the hallway, I entered a bedroom where a small lamp illuminated the night table situated between two beds. To my dismay, Reinhard and Arturo were bound, their hands tied behind their backs, and they lay gagged on the beds. The only other piece of furniture in the room was an empty chair.

Arturo locked eyes with me, widening his gaze, and then subtly gestured toward the closed bathroom door. Just as I processed his signal, the sound of a flushing toilet reached my ears. Taking a position to the left of the bathroom entrance, I prepared myself.

A man emerged from the bathroom, occupied with zipping up his pants. Seizing the opportunity, I swiftly pivoted and delivered a powerful right-handed uppercut to his chin, reminiscent of the blows I had once received during my days as a boxer. The man staggered backward, his head colliding with the porcelain sink. Score one knockout for "Canvasback."

I disarmed the man and discovered a knife secured to his belt. With the blade, I cut Arturo free first, then proceeded to release Reinhard, who sported a relieved smile.

After removing his gag, Arturo spoke urgently, "There are two more of them."

"I'm aware, and they'll return any moment. What happened here?" I inquired.

"We'll discuss it later," Arturo replied, swiftly adding, "Reinhard, get into the bathroom and close the door. Mancuso, get into his bed. When they walk in, shoot first and ask questions later."

"Just shoot them?" I questioned.

"Put the gag in your mouth, hands at your sides. Yes, it's a matter of us or them. Understood?" Arturo instructed, switching off the light from the small lamp.

Thirty seconds later, a voice called out, "Claudio?"

Arturo responded, "Here, Pepe. Everything's fine."

Both men entered the darkened room, one veering right and the other left, passing right in front of the beds.

"Now," Arturo whispered.

He fired the first shot, and I swiftly followed suit. Each of us delivered two rounds to the chests of the approaching men, the impact propelling them back against the wall before they crumpled to the floor.

"We need to get the hell out of here quickly. Is the car still outside?" Arturo asked.

"It should be," I replied.

"Reinhard, let's go," Arturo commanded, opening the bathroom door. He retrieved his Glock and phone from a dresser drawer in the bedroom.

Arturo took the lead as we hurried past the living room, where one man still lay unconscious. We swung open the front door and stepped out into the open.

Suddenly, we found ourselves face to face with two men who were rushing back toward the house. A tense standoff ensued as we all froze in our tracks, assessing the situation. However, Arturo's reflexes were quicker than anyone else's, and I instinctively mirrored his actions, swiftly raising my weapon and firing shots that struck both men in the abdomen.

Making a dash for the car, we were relieved to find it still parked there. "Is he dead?" Arturo inquired.

"No, he should be unconscious but alive," I clarified.

Arturo dragged Miguel out of the car, dropping him onto the street. "Reinhard, get in the back seat and keep your head down. Mancuso, take the shotgun, and I mean it."

The engine of the Chevy Nova roared to life immediately, and Arturo accelerated, heading up Fourth Street toward Fifth Avenue while he made a phone call.

"Diego, we're on our way, and things are intense," Arturo spoke into the phone, waiting for a response. "Damn it, what now? Plan B?"

Without uttering a word, Arturo pressed harder on the accelerator and made a sharp right turn onto Fifth Avenue.

"If I'm not mistaken, our original extraction point should be on the left down the street," I commented.

"Mancuso, they knew we were coming. Our extraction point has been compromised. Diego will pick us up west from here," Arturo explained.

"Do you both know where?" I asked.

Arturo looked at me with a grin. "Unless you'd prefer to stay at the Italian Embassy."

"I'm good. Where are we heading?" I replied.

"There's another beach area about twenty minutes away. We'll take a zigzag route to get there, avoiding the main roads. By now, they know we've escaped the house, so they'll be searching for us," Arturo outlined our plan.

Reinhard spoke up for the first time. "Thank you, guys. I definitely didn't want to end up in China."

"We're not in the clear yet," I warned. "Do you know where Galiano and Castellanos ended up?"

"I overheard them saying they planned to stay here fishing for a while, then return to Sarasota via Mexico," Reinhard shared.

"And what about Captain Tony?" I inquired.

"I'm afraid he didn't make it all the way to Cuba. They kept me locked in the boat's salon, but I heard a struggle, and I think he was thrown overboard," Reinhard replied solemnly.

"Damn it, was he still alive?" I muttered.

"I believe he was," Reinhard confirmed, his voice filled with concern. "And what...what about Dianne?"

I turned to face him, and without uttering a word, the expression on my face conveyed the devastating news. "I'm sorry, Paul. She didn't make it," I whispered softly.

Reinhard's face sank, and tears welled up in his eyes. His voice trembled as he choked out his next question. "Was she...pregnant?"

Maintaining eye contact with him, I nodded somberly. "Yes, she was. I'm so sorry."

Reinhard succumbed to grief, his tears flowing freely as we continued our journey toward the new extraction point. Arturo skillfully maneuvered between Fifth and Third Avenues, his driving focused and determined.

After a few moments of silence, I asked Reinhard another question, seeking any information that could shed light on the situation. "Do you know if there was supposed to be a drug deal taking place?"

"It was set to happen in the Straits of Florida. These men were overseeing the entire operation. It involved a Mexican cargo ship and another yacht," Reinhard disclosed.

"Not a go-fast boat?" I inquired, seeking clarification.

"No, it was another fishing yacht, similar to the one we were on," Reinhard clarified. "As for the destination, I didn't catch that part."

Remaining vigilant for any signs of pursuit, I scanned the surroundings for any suspicious vehicles. So far, we seemed to be free of any unwanted attention. The Italian Embassy was no longer a viable option. Our choices were narrowed down to escaping this place with Diego's help, finding a place to hide, or risking capture by the Cuban government, with Reinhard potentially being sent to China and one Navy SEAL held captive by the Cubans.

31

Monday, 4 a.m.

Arturo maintained a cautious speed of around thirty miles per hour, not wanting to draw unnecessary attention, although the streets were mostly deserted at this early hour. Along Fifth Avenue, there were charming older homes, some dilapidated and boarded up, while others appeared to have undergone restoration. The avenue itself was wide, with a spacious grassy median running through its center.

As we passed the entrance to the Havana Yacht Club, I noticed a roundabout ahead, adorned with a statue of a military figure in its center. Though I couldn't read the sign, I couldn't help but wonder if it was Fidel Castro's statue gracing the site.

Arturo picked up on my curiosity and provided an explanation. "That's General Calixto Garcia, a Cuban hero from the Spanish-American War for Cuba's independence in 1895."

Our moment of reflection was abruptly interrupted when Arturo's voice rang out, filled with urgency. "Reinhard, keep your head down."

On the other side of the median, a military jeep drove by and slowed down, its occupants casting curious glances in our direction. I kept a vigilant eye on the rearview mirror as the jeep executed a U-turn and began trailing us.

"The jeep is following us," I alerted Arturo.

"I noticed," he replied, his tone steady.

The soldiers in the jeep maintained a distance of approximately thirty yards, not yet accelerating to close in on us. However, my heart raced as the situation intensified. Suddenly, the soldiers activated their emergency lights, flashing from high to low beams three times, and increased their speed.

"What's the plan?" I asked, hoping Arturo wouldn't suggest a violent resolution.

"We'll play it by ear, but be prepared to engage if necessary," Arturo responded, his voice calm yet resolute.

Arturo continued driving for another block, with the persistent jeep relentlessly flashing its lights. Eventually, he slowed down and pulled over to the side of the road, yielding to the pursuing military vehicle.

I quickly assessed the situation and considered the potential consequences of engaging in a firefight with the soldiers. Killing them would undoubtedly trigger a relentless pursuit, and law enforcement would spare no effort to apprehend us. I questioned whether Arturo could talk his way out of this encounter and whether our escape had already been exposed to the authorities.

Arturo brought the car to a complete stop, and I noticed him discreetly tucking his Glock under his left armpit, ready to act if necessary. The jeep pulled up right behind us, and its occupants exited. I turned my gaze to see that only two individuals had emerged. The passenger remained positioned at the rear of our car, his long rifle aimed in our direction. I realized I didn't have a clear shot at him, so I discreetly placed my Glock beneath my legs. The driver approached Arturo.

In a hushed tone, Arturo whispered to us, "Act as if you two are drunk."

The driver inquired, "*¿A dónde van?*" (Where are you going?)

Understanding the question, Arturo responded, "*Estos dos estaban de fiesta, los llevo a una casa que tienen alquilada.*" (These two were partying, and I'm driving them to a house they rented.)

Suddenly, the soldier positioned behind us with the rifle interjected, "*Sargento, nos llaman por la radio.*" (Sergeant, we're being called on the radio.)

"One moment," the driver, presumably the sergeant, replied. He then asked, "*¿Son turistas?*" (Are they tourists?)

"*Si, Italianos,*" Arturo replied.

I noticed the soldier behind us return to the jeep. "*Pasaportes,*" the sergeant requested, demanding to see our passports.

Loudly, the soldier in the jeep exclaimed, "*Tenemos una emergencia en Miramar.*" (We have an emergency in Miramar.)

The sergeant exchanged glances with his partner, then turned his attention back to Arturo and said, "*Dale,*" before swiftly running back to the jeep.

Arturo started the engine and slowly pulled away from what could have escalated into a deadly confrontation.

"Shit, that was close. They're going to figure out it was us as soon as they arrive, right?" I expressed my concern.

"Hopefully, we'll be riding into the sunrise before that happens," Arturo replied.

We continued driving for another five minutes, and I noticed a body of water ahead that appeared to be a lake. "Is this where Diego is?" I inquired.

"Just ahead. We'll have to swim out to him. This area is too shallow. I trust both of you can swim," Arturo confirmed.

I glanced at Reinhard, and he reassured us, saying, "No problem here."

"Let's make haste," I urged. "What should we do with the firearms?"

"Bring them along for now, but we'll dispose of them in the ocean," Arturo replied.

As the clock struck five in the morning, a faint ray of sunlight pierced the eastern horizon. Time was of the essence;

we needed to escape before the sun fully revealed our presence, vulnerable like a deer in an open field.

Leaving the Chevy Nova hidden among some bushes, we ventured into the inviting warmth of the water.

"Follow my lead," instructed Arturo, as he embarked on the swim toward the open sea.

Reinhard and I followed suit, but it was evident that Arturo, with his SEAL training, was more adept and faster. The weight of my waterlogged jeans tempted me to shed them, an unexpected hurdle in this rescue mission that caught me off guard despite having a SEAL as my partner.

Arturo paused, allowing us to catch up. "How much farther?" I inquired.

"Perhaps a hundred yards. Diego has my location on his GPS. You can do this. Let go of the weapons; they're weighing you down," Arturo advised.

Taking his suggestion, I discarded my firearms, but it was my jeans and shoes that posed the greatest challenge. After another twenty yards, I stripped down to my boxer shorts, not caring about the peculiar sight I presented. The priority was to swim unencumbered.

As we covered another fifty yards, the sound of an engine reached my ears each time I lifted my head from the water. "I hear an engine," I announced.

"That should be Diego. Stay put for a moment," Arturo directed. Retrieving a flashlight, he began signaling into the darkness. The crescendo of engines grew louder, and I fervently prayed that it was Diego and not a Cuban gunboat.

Emerging seemingly out of nowhere, the Midnight Express, propelled by its four engines and with Diego at the helm, appeared just ten yards ahead. It felt as if the entire Navy had arrived to pluck us from the ocean's clutches. With one final effort, we swam the remaining distance. Reinhard ascended the ladder first, followed by me and then Arturo.

Diego glanced at me and burst into laughter. "What happened to your pants?"

"They were too heavy," I replied. "I left them behind."

Arturo interjected, "You mean they're floating out there?"

"I'm not sure if they float or sink. Why? Is that a problem?" I inquired.

Arturo exchanged a disapproving glance with Diego. "Let's not dwell on it," he said firmly. "We need to leave."

Diego swiftly equipped himself with communications headgear, entered a series of commands into the console panel, and declared, "Strap in; we're taking off."

As the sun ascended in the east, its rays began to paint the sky with a breathtaking display of colors. Shades of orange, red, green, yellow, and a gentle blue haze transformed the fading night into a magnificent canvas.

Would this journey be an exhilarating adventure? Did we have enough fuel to outrun any pursuing gunboats if the need arose? The questions lingered in my mind as we prepared to embark on our escape.

32
Monday, 6:30 a.m.

"Do we have eyes in the sky?" Arturo inquired, referring to the presence of the Navy AWACS that had guided us thus far.

"They're with us. All clear for now, headed to Key West," Diego replied, momentarily removing one ear from his headset.

Arturo, sensing my concern about my floating jeans, turned to me. "Listen, the coastline is vast. But tell me, where is your Italian passport?"

A sense of worry crept over me. "I left it in one of the pockets," I admitted.

"Well, if they find it, all they'll know is that it belongs to a tourist. Maybe they'll assume the tourist was having a wild night on the beach and lost his pants," Arturo remarked, offering a reassuring smile.

I couldn't help but confess, "I actually told Miguel that I was Italian."

Arturo shrugged. "Too late to worry about that now. If they discover it, it'll only reveal our point of departure. I'm sure they already know we're headed to the US."

Curiosity compelled me to ask, "How many miles until we reach US territorial waters?"

Diego responded, "If we maintain a direct course, we have approximately 105 miles to cover. The US claims a twelve-mile radius around its borders."

Eagerly, I followed up, "And what about Cuba? Do they have a twelve-mile limit too?" I hoped their restrictions mirrored those of the US. With our boat's impressive five engines, covering twelve miles would be a breeze.

"Cuban authorities don't adhere to the same rules. They could make our journey hell all the way to US waters," Diego revealed, dampening my optimism.

Feeling a wave of unease, I pressed further, "Can we outpace their gunboats, at least?"

"As I mentioned earlier, Mancuso," Diego began, "we can outrun them if we have enough fuel. However, evading their .50-calibers is a different story. Furthermore, if they bring in their air force..." Diego paused, leaving the potential consequences unspoken.

Gazing up at the sky, I uttered a brief prayer and closed my eyes. Father Dom would be immensely proud of me if he knew how fervently I had prayed on this journey, surpassing the cumulative prayers of many years.

Reinhard spoke up, his voice filled with determination, "Fellows, if it comes to that, I'd rather surrender myself than risk all of your lives. Too many have already died because of me. I'll be fine."

Arturo's response was firm, "I apologize, Mr. Reinhard, but our orders do not involve turning ourselves in. We will ensure your safety and get you home."

It was clear that China had likely issued orders to Cuba to capture Reinhard. If the Chinese couldn't have him, their instructions were probably to eliminate him. They didn't want the US to gain access to his valuable computer program. It seemed that either they would obtain it or no one would.

As our fast boat sliced through the small waves of the Atlantic, the Cuban coastline grew increasingly distant, and a sense of relief washed over me. I retrieved my phone from a storage cabinet near the console where I had left it. Seeing multiple missed calls and text messages from Marcy, I dialed her number.

She answered on the fourth ring, her voice tinged with sleepiness. "Hello?"

"Hey, sleepyhead, good morning," I greeted her.

"Are you back?"

"We're on our way. How are you?" I asked, eager to hear her voice.

"I'm fine. Is Reinhard with you?" Marcy inquired, her concern evident.

"He's unharmed," I assured her, stealing a quick glance at Reinhard. "I saw that you called and texted."

"I figured your phone was on the boat. Plus, I guessed you were a little preoccupied," Marcy replied with understanding.

"Are you okay?" I asked, my voice filled with genuine concern.

"I'm good, really. Anyone injured?" Marcy queried, her worry extending to the entire team.

"No injuries on our side," I replied reassuringly. "We're headed to Key West."

"So you're not coming directly to Islamorada?" Marcy asked, a hint of disappointment in her voice.

"No, unfortunately. Our breakfast plans at the Green Turtle will have to be postponed. Maybe we can do lunch instead," I suggested, hoping to lighten the mood.

As I continued speaking with Marcy, I overheard Diego talking into his communication device. Then, he announced to the rest of us, "We have a problem," while pointing to the south.

I turned to look and noticed a rapidly approaching boat. Sensing Marcy's concern, I quickly reassured her, "It's nothing major. I'll call you later."

Before ending the call, Marcy expressed her love, saying, "Mancuso, I love you."

I replied sincerely, "I love you too," before disconnecting.

As Diego pushed the throttle to full speed, Arturo reached into the storage compartment under the console, gripping it tightly to maintain his balance. Both Reinhard and I glanced back, watching as we distanced ourselves from the approaching Cuban gunboat.

Arturo pulled out a box and a thick briefcase, catching my attention. I raised my voice to be heard over the roaring engine, "What do you have there?"

"M20 grenade launcher. Bring the box," Arturo instructed, moving toward the stern of the boat.

I clung to the box, struggling to keep my footing amidst the bumpy ride. "What's the effective range?" I asked, curious.

"About three hundred fifty meters, or just over a thousand feet," Arturo replied.

"That's good to know," I said, hoping it would provide us with an advantage.

Arturo gave me a knowing look. "It's not easy to hit a target with this thing on solid ground, let alone on a wavy boat going ninety miles per hour."

"Do you have any other weapons?" I inquired.

"No, just three M16s," he responded. "But let's hope we don't need them."

"Why's that?" I questioned.

"Because if we do, it means we're dangerously close to the enemy," Arturo explained. "Go back and grab the helmets. We might need them."

I sighed inwardly. So now I would be wearing a helmet and underwear. "Do you have any spare pants?" I asked, hoping for a miracle.

Arturo chuckled and shook his head. "I don't think so, buddy. Your legs look fine. Maybe a shave would help."

I glanced at my hairy legs, grateful they were no longer as pale as my exposed rear end. "Thanks," I muttered.

Making my way back, I gathered the helmets, clutching onto anything I could to maintain my balance. I handed one to Diego, one to Reinhard, and secured one on my own head.

Here we were, roughly eighty miles from Key West, and if death found me, I would be adorned in a black T-shirt, white underwear, and a helmet, barefooted.

"Are we out of Cuban waters?" I asked, hopeful for some respite.

"Yes, but like I said, they couldn't care less," Diego replied grimly. He shouted back to Arturo, "We've got two gunboats pursuing us!"

Glancing behind, I saw what was once a single vessel on the horizon now multiplied into two. Suddenly, a trail of white smoke erupted from one of the gunboats.

"Incoming!" Arturo warned, his voice filled with urgency.

Reacting swiftly, Diego executed an abrupt right turn, causing me to lose my footing and tumble to the deck.

As I regained my composure and sat next to Reinhard, I glanced back and witnessed a harrowing moment. A missile whizzed by our boat, followed by the deafening impact of a fifty-caliber round hitting the exact spot we had occupied moments before Diego's maneuver.

"Damn, that was too close," Diego muttered, his voice filled with frustration. He immediately initiated a series of wide zigzag movements to throw off our pursuers.

My heart pounding in my chest. I looked back, observing Arturo bracing himself on the stern and launching a grenade. Within seconds, it fell short of the lead boat. Just as the grenade landed, another puff of smoke erupted from the same boat. Anticipating the danger, I exclaimed, "Incoming!"

Diego maintained our current course, and the fifty-caliber round missed our location by a significant margin, landing far short and to the left. Although Arturo's grenade had fallen short, it had managed to divert the boats from their original path, causing the misfire.

Now, the gunboats had positioned themselves roughly one hundred yards apart and were closing in on us from opposing angles of about thirty degrees. Our intended route from the extraction point had been north with a slight westerly tilt. However, based on Diego's recent maneuvers, it seemed we were now heading more toward the north-northeast, veering away and eastward from our original Key West destination.

Suddenly, Diego shouted, "Brace yourself!" The Midnight Express roared as he executed a sharp turn back in a northerly direction. Once the boat settled on the new course, we surged forward at high speed. I held on to anything I could find, trying to maintain my balance, and directed my question to Diego amidst the cacophony, "How's our fuel situation?"

He shook his head, a look of concern on his face. "At this speed, not good."

I turned my gaze back to the gunboats trailing behind us. They remained at a considerable distance of around three hundred yards. While our engines churned out a turbulent wake, it was too far away to have any effect on our pursuers. The bow of the boat sliced through the slight chop of the water like a hot knife through butter.

"How far are we from US waters?" I shouted over the noise to Diego.

He consulted his controls and replied, "About twenty miles."

Quickly calculating the remaining distance, I estimated that at our current speed of ninety miles per hour, with twenty miles left to cover, it would take us slightly over thirteen minutes. "Can we at least make it to US waters?" I shouted, hoping for a glimmer of reassurance.

Diego looked at me, his expression uncertain. "If I stay on course, probably. But there's no guarantee these guys will give up the chase."

As I settled back next to Reinhard, the gravity of our situation sank in. We were like sitting ducks in the vast expanse of the ocean, with two relentless gunboats hot on our trail, determined to eliminate us. Reinhard gripped his helmet tightly, his knuckles turning white.

"Are we going to make it?" Reinhard asked, his voice filled with concern.

I pondered his question for a moment, then replied, "Do you believe in the power of prayer?"

Reinhard shook his head. "Not particularly," he confessed.

"Well, maybe you should reconsider," I urged him, realizing that desperate times called for desperate measures. I silently offered my own prayer, hoping for a divine intervention to guide us safely through this perilous ordeal.

Suddenly, Arturo's voice cut through the tense atmosphere, shouting, "Two incoming!" The urgency in his tone spurred a surge of adrenaline within me as I braced myself for whatever lay ahead.

33
Monday, 7:30 a.m.

Simultaneously, a round landed just ten yards to our left, while another perilously close, about five yards ahead and to the right. The impact of the first round caused the boat to violently veer about forty-five degrees off course.

Diego, standing in front of Reinhard and me, nearly lost his balance but managed to grip the wheel tightly, swiftly correcting our course. Meanwhile, Arturo had fallen during the commotion, and his launcher was now pointing straight up.

Gathering himself quickly, Arturo regained his footing and unleashed two grenades, aiming one at each of the gunboats. Although his shots missed the mark, they served their purpose in keeping the enemy vessels at bay.

"Mancuso, come back here for a moment!" Arturo's voice shouted over the chaos.

I hurried back to the stern, asking, "What do you need?"

"I'm going on the offensive. Hand me the grenades as I fire. We still have seventeen left. I'll launch ten in rapid succession. Ready?" Arturo explained determinedly.

As Arturo began firing one grenade after another, I swiftly passed them to him, maintaining a steady supply. Though none of the grenades found their target directly, their explosive presence forced the gunboats to slow down, creating some much-needed distance between us.

Just as a glimmer of relief washed over me, Diego turned to face us with a grave expression. "Bad news, fellows. We've got a MiG-29 heading our way."

Both Arturo and I looked back and upward, following Diego's gaze. Trailing behind the aircraft, a faint trail of smoke emerged from the southern horizon. It could only be the MiG. Our eyes met, and Arturo's shrugged response silently conveyed our shared realization that we were in a dire predicament.

Sitting on the floor, I planted my hands firmly at my sides, steadying myself amidst the boat's relentless movements. Though my gaze remained fixed forward, my mind ventured into a whirlwind of memories—a montage of my life's significant moments. It started with the early days of dating Marcy, the carefree moments of playfulness and laughter. Then, I revisited the dinner at Garcia's when Marcy declared that she would only continue our relationship if I committed to monogamy. In that instant, I knew I couldn't bear to lose her. Marcy was my soulmate, and no one else held such profound significance in my life.

I fast-forwarded to the cherished memory of our wedding at Saint Helens, with Father Dominic O'Brian officiating the ceremony. The radiant joy emanating from Marcy's face, her eyes illuminated with sparkling emerald-green hues, flooded my thoughts as Father Dom pronounced us husband and wife.

But amidst the turbulence of the present, these memories stood as a reminder of the love and life I cherished and fought to protect. Taking a deep breath, I steeled my resolve, ready to confront whatever challenges lay ahead, with the unwavering determination to ensure our survival and the eventual reunion with my beloved Marcy.

I couldn't fathom that this could be the end. The realization struck hard—I would never lay eyes on my precious daughter, Michelle Marie, with her inherited spunk and sassy attitude, again. How old was she now? Just five or six weeks? My thoughts became a jumble. Never before had I been in a situation where I had absolutely no control. In the past, there was always some action I could take to alter the outcome. But now, faced with a missile-equipped MiG-29 closing in on our tiny boat in the vast Atlantic Ocean, I was powerless. Helpless. We were nothing more than sitting ducks, easy prey for this pilot. I could almost envision him relishing the prospect, his lips curling into a sinister smile as he imagined his missile hurtling toward our vessel. Then, the explosive impact, followed by his triumphant radio call, tauntingly declaring a victory for the Cuban Air Force over the "Yankee imperialist pigs." The tears welled up in my eyes, and a single tear escaped, tracing a path down my cheek.

As I brushed away the tear with the back of my hand, an unexpected roar of thunderous engines shattered the air above us. Four F/A-18F Super Hornets soared with breathtaking speed and precision directly overhead. It was as though they had choreographed this spectacular display just for us. In unison, all four of us onboard began shouting, our voices united in fervent patriotism, "USA, USA!"

Diego slowed down our boat as if eager to witness the impending air show. The Super Hornets, mere fifty yards above the water's surface, initiated a sharp ascent. Two of them broke away, streaking toward the MiG, while the other two set their sights on the gunboats.

Amidst the thunderous roar, Diego's voice boomed, "Compliments of Jake T at Boca Chica Naval Station, who spotted the MiG closing in on us!"

I didn't know who Jake T was, but he had single-handedly saved our lives.

The MiG, initially on a collision course with us, suddenly veered to the right, embarking on a wide arc toward the south, relentlessly pursued by the two Super Hornets. Meanwhile, the gunboats, now aware of the imminent danger, reduced their speed to a crawl as one of the Super Hornets unleashed a barrage of machine-gun fire ahead of them. Startled, the gunboats altered their course, making a swift southerly turn, effectively escaping harm's reach.

Overwhelmed by relief, the four of us instinctively came together in a spontaneous group hug, celebrating our survival with ecstatic high-fives and wide, grateful smiles. We were alive, and we were heading home.

I yearned to call Marcy, to convey my undying love, but my phone seemed to have vanished in the chaos.

Diego pushed the throttles forward, propelling our boat to a steady forty miles per hour while a protective formation of Super Hornets enveloped us, their presence serving as a reassuring canopy.

Twenty minutes later, with only eight miles remaining to reach the Boca Chica Naval Base in Key West, a Coast Guard cutter awaited our arrival. We pulled alongside the vessel to refuel, and I was provided with orange coveralls to wear, conveniently concealing my hairy legs. The Super Hornets, having fulfilled their mission of protecting us, bid us farewell as they veered off toward the base to resume their training exercises, preparing for potential air battles over Ukraine. Accompanied by the cutter, we continued our journey toward the base.

Upon reaching the base, our three acquaintances—John, Richard, and Tuck—were there, awaiting our arrival. However, there was now an additional individual who I presumed to be Mr. Hood, their boss.

Handshakes and congratulations were exchanged all around. A suited individual summoned Diego and Arturo, leading them away for what appeared to be their debriefing. Before they departed, I made sure to express my gratitude and embrace both of them.

Mr. Hood then turned his attention to Reinhard and me, with the three amigos following close behind him. Without any formal introductions, he addressed me directly, saying, "Mr. Mancuso, I extend my gratitude for your invaluable assistance in this operation. Rest assured, you will be duly rewarded for your exceptional work. We have a helicopter prepared to transport you to Islamorada."

I nodded appreciatively, replying, "Thank you. I truly appreciate that. But what about Mr. Reinhard?"

Hood glanced at Reinhard and then back at me. "Mr. Reinhard will need to undergo debriefing regarding his time in Cuba. Additionally, there are other individuals who need to speak with him. He will be accompanying us on a flight to Washington, DC."

Reinhard's expression turned to one of concern as he looked at me.

"Excuse us for a moment," I requested, gesturing to Hood.

"Certainly," Hood replied.

I walked a short distance away, with Reinhard following closely. "Listen, don't do anything you don't want to do. If they try to force you into anything, tell them to go to hell. Demand a new identity and relocation. Carve out a new life on your terms," I advised, glancing over at Hood and the amigos, who were observing our conversation.

"And you think they'll grant that?" Reinhard asked, uncertainty evident in his voice.

"They will, and they'll ensure your protection. You don't need their money. Let me ask you, what the hell is it about your program that everyone is so interested in?" I questioned, curiosity piqued.

"Hah, explaining it fully would take more than just a few minutes. But here's a summarized version. You're aware that every place you go is being mapped and tracked by various geo-mapping features on your devices, right? Your locations, purchase habits, even food orders from services like Uber Eats, are all being shared and monitored," Reinhard explained.

"Yeah, I've noticed targeted ads and sometimes even conversations about products showing up," I replied, still facing away from the amigos.

Reinhard continued, "Exactly. Devices like Alexa and Siri are constantly listening, collecting keywords from your conversations at home. Even alarm systems and smart TVs are feeding information. All of this data is processed through algorithms. You've heard of algorithms, right?"

"I have, but I don't really understand what they are," I admitted, turning back to face Reinhard.

"My algorithmic-aggregation program takes all that information and much more. It can analyze what you order and when and aggregate all your social media activity. Let me simplify it—based on this aggregated data, I can predict your thoughts, your movements, and your future actions with a high degree of accuracy. The algorithms even have access to some of your medical records and DNA. If you've done any home testing, those labs are likely owned or operated by third parties, possibly even Chinese labs. It's an oversimplification, but you get the idea," Reinhard explained.

I looked at Reinhard in astonishment. "They have all that information, and your program can make predictions based on it?"

"Not a hundred percent accuracy, but once I finish it, it will be around ninety-five percent accurate. It creates a complete profile for each individual, including facial recognition. However, I won't complete it. I can see the potential commercial benefits, but I also see the dark and malicious applications governments might have in mind," Reinhard said with a hint of regret.

"Wow. Establish yourself as a fishing charter service. Screw them. And let me know where you end up. I want to go fishing with you in US waters," I suggested, offering my support.

"I will, Mancuso. Thank you," Reinhard replied appreciatively.

"Wait, wait. What's the real story behind your first encounter with Galiano and the others?" I asked, eager to hear the full account.

He glanced at Mr. Hood, who was observing our conversation. "Now I understand that the plan was for me to be handed over to the two Cuban men who brought the fentanyl as a down payment for my abduction. They were supposed to take me to Havana and, ultimately, to the Chinese cargo ship."

Curiosity piqued, I asked, "So what happened?"

"The two guys had no intention of taking me to Cuba. They wanted to keep the drugs, the money, eliminate all of us, and illegally enter Florida," Reinhard revealed.

Something seemed off. Was he making this up? I probed further, "But why did Galiano have all that money if the drugs were only a down payment?"

"Because the Cubans had promised to double the amount of drugs if they paid," Reinhard explained.

"So what transpired next?" I inquired.

"Galiano and Castellanos sensed something was amiss from the beginning. And before the Cubans could act, Galiano's henchmen shot them," he disclosed.

"And that's when you fled in your boat with the money and drugs?" I clarified.

"Exactly."

"Oh, and by the way, don't mention anything about Galiano and Castellanos," I advised.

He nodded, understanding the need for caution. We shook hands, embraced, and bid each other farewell.

It was eleven o'clock in the morning. I was on my way to Islamorada, hoping for a possible lunch with Marcy at Habanos in Caloosa Cove Marina. Since I couldn't find my own phone, I asked a guy nearby if I could use his.

I dialed Jote's number and left a voicemail, saying, "Hey, Jote. I'm heading back to Islamorada. I know where Galiano and Castellanos are headed, and I'm aware of drugs being smuggled into the US. But I want to be part of the task force that takes them down. Otherwise, I might just forget what I know. Understand?"

As the helicopter began to lift off, I caught sight of Sergeant Leone and Susan Joyce from the Monroe County Sheriff's Department arriving at the naval station.

Part 3
34
Monday, 2 p.m.

The helicopter ride from Naval Air Key West Station to Islamorada was truly remarkable. Though it was a bit noisy, the breathtaking views of the vibrant blue sky and the emerald-green waters of the Atlantic were simply incredible. Words failed me as I tried to describe the myriad shades of blue and green that emerged from both the bay and the ocean simultaneously. The seven-mile bridge seemed endless from above, resembling a captivating painting, where the dark-blue waters revealed the channels encircled by the light-blue shallows. Undoubtedly, these colors were unlike anything I had seen in the East River or Hudson River.

The Coasties skillfully landed the helicopter on an empty lot across from the Caloosa Cove Resort and Habanos Restaurant. A handful of curious onlookers slowed their cars to witness the grandeur of the helicopter landing. Expressing my gratitude, I gave my hosts a thumbs-up, patted them on the back, and cautiously disembarked from the helicopter.

As I crossed US 1, I caught sight of Marcy walking toward me. Within seconds, I held her in a tight embrace as if I had returned from the brink of death itself.

"I love you," I whispered.

"I love you too," she replied, gently pulling back. "How bad was it?"

Holding her hand tightly, I reassured her, "It wasn't as bad as you might think."

Hand in hand, we began our walk toward the resort. Suddenly, Marcy halted and said, "Joey, you look like you've been to hell and back. So, how bad was it, and where are your pants?"

"My pants decided to stay in Cuba. It's a long story. But how about we grab some lunch? I'm famished, and I'll fill you in on all the details."

Over lunch, I recounted the entire tale to Marcy. She listened intently, offering only a few "Oh my Gods" and shaking her head in disbelief. Although the ending was a happy one, the story didn't seem to bring her the same joy.

As we strolled back to our room, she inquired, "So, can we go back to New York? Perhaps in a day or two? I miss our daughter."

"Well, actually, there's more to the story," I responded.

"Oh, and what might that be?" she asked curiously.

"Galiano and Castellanos are headed to Sarasota, Florida. I've already informed Jote about it," I shared with Marcy.

"Good. Let them deal with it there. The task force can handle the rest," she replied, expressing her satisfaction.

I remained silent as we entered our room, eager to remove the thick and bothersome orange coveralls I had been wearing. Marcy chuckled when she saw me and remarked, "Did you lose your underwear too?"

"It got wet," I explained. She pointed out a strand of seaweed entangled near my privates, causing the persistent itching I had been experiencing. "I'll take a shower," I said, realizing the need for immediate relief.

"And then we can make plans to fly back to New York," Marcy suggested.

The shower provided a refreshing respite, and it also gave me the opportunity to gather my thoughts on why I shouldn't immediately return to New York.

Dressed in a swimsuit and a T-shirt, I joined Marcy in the living room of our room. "Marcy, I've requested to join the task force going after Galiano and his gang," I informed her, awaiting her reaction.

She closed the laptop she had been using and turned her full attention toward me. "Why? You've already done more than enough on this case. You even risked your life by joining the extraction team, which is not your usual line of work. Let someone else handle these drug dealers. You have no obligation to be involved," she argued.

"It's not about the drugs. I feel indebted to Dianne and her unborn baby. I want to ensure that these guys are brought to justice," I explained, emphasizing my personal sense of responsibility.

She remained silent, but I knew she shared the same sentiments about Dianne. I hoped she would understand why I needed to be a part of capturing these murderers. After all, it was my involvement that had initially implicated Dianne, and I felt a duty to see it through.

Following a brief moment of silence, Marcy voiced her concern, "Why do you always have to be involved in every aspect of a case? Can't someone else finish the job?"

I responded with a touch of humor, "Maybe I'm just a control freak?"

She smiled and playfully acknowledged, "I've known that forever. Your compulsion to rearrange the salt and pepper shakers, water glasses, silverware, and anything else on the restaurant table. Yes, you're a control freak. But you don't need to be physically present when they apprehend the criminals."

Her observation was accurate, but it masked her underlying fear for my safety and the risks I took. We had both narrowly escaped danger on multiple occasions, having been shot ourselves. Father Dom and Mr. Pat had also been injured, and just recently, Jack had been shot. It was only natural for her to be afraid.

"I understand your concerns," I responded, empathizing with her. "All I want is to be there when we bring these guys to justice. The task force will handle all the groundwork. I just need the satisfaction of seeing them in handcuffs."

At that moment, Marcy's phone rang, drawing our attention. When she answered, a familiar voice spoke, "Marcy, how are you? This is Jote. Is your husband there?"

Marcy's expression turned serious as she handed me the phone.

"Jote, Reinhard is safe, and I know where these guys are heading," I informed him, walking toward the kitchen on the other side of the unit.

"Hey, Mancuso, glad to hear about Reinhard," Jote responded, his voice filled with relief. "Hang on, almost everyone is back in Miami. SA Michael Donnelly might get reassigned after this mess."

"What do you mean, mess?" I inquired, feeling a sense of foreboding.

"Mancuso, he spent millions of dollars chasing illusions—the fishing boat, Queen of the Seas, the high-speed boat—up and down the Florida west coast. Helicopters, Coasties, countless hours wasted. He doesn't want to hear your name ever again."

I closed my eyes, disappointment washing over me like opening a Happy Meal box and finding an apple and a carton of milk. "Didn't they find the fast boat, the bright-red MTI?" I asked, hoping for a breakthrough.

"They did, near Naples. They boarded it, and there was nothing. Turns out it was just a joyride by a couple of guys. No trace of drugs anywhere."

"So they orchestrated the entire charade as a diversion. These guys are good," I muttered, realizing the extent of their cunning.

"Perhaps too good," Jote conceded. "The truth is, every time we get close to Galiano, he manages to pull a rabbit out of his hat. I wish I could assist more because I want these bastards caught."

"What if you share what I know with Donnelly? They're heading to Sarasota," I suggested, stepping outside the unit for some fresh air.

"If I let him know that you have firsthand knowledge, then Tico and I might have to consider retiring," Jote responded, considering the weight of the situation.

Removing the phone from my ear, I gazed at the sun, closed my eyes, and took a deep breath. Bringing the phone back to my ear, I continued, "It wasn't just a tip. Reinhard overheard the information. The fentanyl is intended as payment for delivering Reinhard to the Chinese in Cuba."

Jote's voice sounded cautious as he replied, "I want these guys caught just as much as you do, but how do we even know if they received the drugs? After all, Reinhard is no longer in the hands of the Chinese. For all we know, they could have disposed of these guys like fish food."

"So, we should just forget about it?" I asked, grappling with the possibility.

"The best I can do is notify the vice group in Sarasota to be on the lookout. If not now, we'll catch them another time. They're not going anywhere," Jote concluded.

Ending the call, I made my way back to the room, where Marcy was packing her belongings.

"What's going on?" I inquired.

"I've booked a flight back to New York from Miami tonight," she replied.

I wanted to ask if she had purchased two tickets or just one, but before I could, she added, "I got two tickets, but if needed, you can change your destination to Sarasota."

"Are you upset?" I asked, sensing her frustration.

Marcy looked at me, her expression filled with concern. "Of course, I'm upset, Joey. You were almost killed by a rocket from a MiG, no less. We came here to relax and unwind, and instead, you've been chasing drug dealers, involving yourself in a foreign country, and being pursued by gunboats and fighter planes. And now you refuse to give up. How would you feel if the roles were reversed?"

I sat on the armrest of the sofa, opened my arms, and replied, "Marcy, I have to—"

"I know, I know, you have to do this," she interrupted, her voice tinged with understanding. "Bring the killers of Dianne and her unborn baby to justice. I know you too well. Just do what you need to do, but please, don't get hurt in the process."

"I don't want you to be upset or worried. I'll be back in New York in a few days," I reassured her.

Marcy walked over to me, and we embraced. She asked, "Will you be meeting Jote and Tico in Miami?"

"I'll drive to Sarasota on my own. I'll need a car," I replied, confirming my plans. "Leave tomorrow; stay with me tonight."

35
Wednesday, 6 a.m.

After bidding farewell to Marcy at Miami International, my original plan was to embark on a drive to Sarasota, heading west and then north on I-75 for approximately three hours.

Refreshed from a restful night, armed with a new inexpensive phone, and having replenished my energy with a satisfying breakfast, I merged onto I-75. I felt revitalized, though my immediate course of action remained uncertain. Well, that is not entirely true. I intended to contact Agnes to enlist her assistance in tracking down a flight involving Galiano and his cohorts. Beyond that, I needed to formulate a concrete plan.

My first call was to Marcy, who shared the joyful news that her parents were en route to bring back Michelle Marie. Everything seemed to be going well on her end, except for the nagging guilt I felt for allowing her to believe I was rendezvousing with Jote and the task force.

Next, I dialed Agnes. "Hey, young woman, how are you?"

"I'm good, thanks. I spoke with Marcy this morning. Where are you?"

"Make a note of this number. It's a cheap phone I purchased because I misplaced mine. I'm on my way to Sarasota, and I require your research expertise."

"Oh, and remember, Mr. Pat is in Naples, which is approximately two hours south of Sarasota. But go ahead, I'm all ears."

I hadn't made the connection between Mr. Pat's whereabouts in Naples and my destination. I mentally noted the proximity.

"Alright, I need you to find flights from Mexico City to Sarasota," I instructed Agnes, providing her with the full names of Galiano and Castellanos. I explained that their arrival could be expected within the next few days, but the timeframe was uncertain—possibly one, two, three, or more days.

"Joey, while you were speaking, I accessed the Sarasota Bradenton International Airport database. Unfortunately, there are no direct flights from Mexico City to Sarasota."

"What about flights from Texas, maybe Dallas?" I inquired.

I could hear the pecking on the keyboard.

"Yes, I do have a few options for that," Agnes replied.

"Likely they're connecting in Dallas to Sarasota. Monitor those flights," I instructed Agnes.

"Are you sure they haven't already flown in?"

"Check the manifests for the past two days just in case."

"Good thinking," Agnes acknowledged. "Marcy informed me that Reinhard is back in the USA and that you'll be joining an FBI task force to pursue Galiano."

"That was the plan we discussed, yes," I confirmed.

"In that case, the task force will have an easier time checking the flight manifests for your targets. They have quicker and more direct access. It might take me longer to do it."

"You know me—I'd prefer we double-check on our end, too, right?" I couldn't reveal that I was embarking on this adventure alone. "How's El Padre doing?"

"He's fine. I'll have JJ also assist in checking the manifests for these flights. Anything else?"

I had momentarily forgotten about our new coder/hacker. "No, I'm good for now. But see if JJ can locate Paul Reinhard. He's supposed to be under DOD protection. The DOD was flying him from Key West to Washington, DC." I proceeded to provide Agnes with the names of the relevant individuals and FBI SA Donnelly.

Next, I dialed Jote's number. "*Oye, Jote—¿Qué pasa?*" I greeted him.

"*¿Qué pasa* with you, Mancuso? Are you in Sarasota yet?" Jote responded, turning the question back to me.

"Hah, that's why you're a detective. You knew I'd show up in Sarasota."

"That, and because you're an effing pit bull with a bone," Jote remarked.

"Well, I'm on my way there. Did you talk to the vice group?"

"*Sí*, Mancuso. Sergeant Roger Gunther is in charge of the Narcotics Unit. I'll text you the number. The sergeant is expecting your call."

"Dude, you're good. Is Gunther a reliable guy?" I asked, noticing a road sign indicating that Naples was just twenty miles away.

"Seems fine and interested, so I think you'll receive a warm reception."

"If it pans out, will you come?"

"No, buddy, Tico and I were assigned to a case here in Miami. If everything works out there, I'll be glad that you and Gunther took down those bad *hombres*."

"Okay, thanks. I'll keep you posted," I replied to Jote before ending the call.

Thirty minutes later, I exited I-75 and made my way into Naples. I wanted to surprise Mr. Pat by showing up at his bar and grill, but I didn't know the exact location or even the name of the place. After contacting Agnes once again, she texted me the address. I stopped my car and entered "Goodlette-Frank Road" into the navigation system. I was just fifteen minutes away. Mr. Pat had mentioned that the bar was located a block away from the beach, but the direction I was heading seemed to be away from it.

Eventually, I found it. Wayne's Bar and Grill sat between another upscale bar and grill and a respectable-looking restaurant. Wayne's had a more rustic appearance, almost like a shack, but it had a waterfront view. The sign displayed, "We open at 4 p.m.," while another sign read, "In case of emergency, call—"

I walked toward the back and discovered a charming, covered deck overlooking the waterway. Wooden tables with drum barrels as legs adorned the deck, with lanterns hanging from the ceiling. Thick ropes served as a railing. The ambiance had a nautical and beachy theme, and it exuded a cozy atmosphere that invited relaxation and enjoyment. A U-shaped bar spanned both the deck and the interior of the restaurant, which I found to be quite unique. I was happy for Mr. Pat; he truly deserved to have this place.

I sat at a table facing the water and dialed the emergency number listed on the sign. I hoped Mr. Pat would answer, but it could also be a direct line to the fire or police department.

After the third ring, a voice answered, "This is Patrick Sullivan."

I smiled, disguising my voice, and responded, "Mr. Sullivan, there's an emergency at your bar."

"Is it a fire?" he asked in his distinct Irish brogue.

"No, sir, there's a man here demanding a Brooklyn lager, a pastrami melt on a bagel, a *cafecito*, and a Rocky Patel Vintage 1999."

There was a moment of silence on the other end. "Joey, is this you?"

"I gave you too many clues. Get your ass here. I can't wait to see you."

Patrick, or Mr. Pat, as we affectionately called him, had served alongside Dom's father, Brandon, in Vietnam. They later ran the bar together. After Brandon's passing, when Dom and I took over, Pat continued managing the bar and eventually joined us at Mancuso and O'Brian Investigative Services. He was like an uncle to all of us. Using the proceeds from his ownership share in our ventures, which we bought back for him, he purchased Wayne's to retire in Naples.

After Patrick arrived, he opened the sliding glass door to the bar, and we embraced tightly. "I love your place," I remarked, looking around at the cozy interior.

Patrick followed my gaze, nodding. "Yes, it's nice, but it could use a little tender loving care. Please, have a seat. Would you like a beer or an espresso?"

Glancing at my watch, I noticed it was only eleven in the morning. "Let's start with an espresso. I'll make it for you."

We entered the interior of the bar, which maintained the same ambiance with plank walls, ropes, and matching decor. Reaching the end of the bar, I positioned myself behind the espresso machine and began preparing the coffee. "Are you planning to change the name?" I asked curiously.

"I was considering naming it Sullivan's Bar and Grill, but the regulars and locals insisted that Wayne's has been here for over fifteen years. People know the name and the place, so I have to think about it," Patrick explained.

"If business is good, there's no need to mess with it," I responded, serving the freshly brewed espresso.

"I'm thrilled with how things are going, Joey," Patrick said, taking a sip. "So, what brings you to Naples?"

"I'm on my way to Sarasota, but I wanted to stop by and say hello, and maybe even recruit you for one more case," I replied with a smile.

Patrick beamed in response. "I'm glad you stopped by, but as for working a case, I'm not sure. It's hard to find good help these days. I'm working twelve-hour days and then some, you know."

"I figured you'd be busy. Don't worry about it. I'll be collaborating with the Sarasota Narcotics Unit," I assured him.

"Tell me more about it while I prepare lunch for us," Patrick suggested.

I followed Patrick into the kitchen and settled on a stool while he assembled some sandwiches. I proceeded to fill him in on the events that had unfolded so far. Returning to the outdoor seating area, we enjoyed our lunch, accompanied by local IPAs on draft and chips.

"This is not your typical case. It sounds like something out of a movie," Patrick commented. "How many pieces are there to this puzzle?"

"I'm hoping it concludes with the apprehension of these guys. I just hope they attempt to smuggle drugs so we can build a stronger case," I replied, taking a bite of my sandwich.

"Based on what you've told me," Patrick began, pausing to sip his beer, "you already have the murders they committed as significant evidence."

"We can't prove that they killed Dianne, and they didn't kill their own two guys themselves. Reinhard is a witness to the two Cubans they killed, maybe just one. But I don't even know if there's a warrant for their arrest on that," I explained, taking a bite of my sandwich.

Pat shook his head in concern. "If they fly in and you can't connect them to the drugs, they'll walk free without a warrant. You better make sure there's a warrant in place."

I realized that this was one aspect I missed about our brainstorming sessions—the collaboration and open thinking. Without hesitation, I picked up my phone and dialed the

Monroe County Sheriff's Department. "Is Sergeant Leone available?" I inquired.

"Hold on," the voice on the other end responded.

"Sergeant Leone here."

"This is Mancuso. Have you issued a warrant for the arrests of Galiano and Castellanos?"

"Good morning to you too, Mancuso. No, we haven't. We only have circumstantial evidence linking them to the murders. I heard Reinhard ended up in Cuba."

"He's back now and under the protection of the DOD," I informed him.

"Great. I have a warrant for his arrest. Bring him in, and maybe he can provide an affidavit stating that he witnessed your boys killing the Cuban on the boat. I'll gladly issue a warrant for them as well. Otherwise, I can't do much," Leone explained.

"What about suspicion of murder?" I asked, feeling a sense of desperation.

"I should have arrested you for obstructing an investigation and harboring a fugitive, Mancuso. You had us running around like headless chickens, and all I have are five bodies," Leone responded sternly.

"Six," I whispered, considering the unborn baby.

"What?" Leone asked, not catching my words.

"Never mind. Thank you, and have a good day," I said, ending the call. I felt frozen, unsure of what to do next. Should I contact the DOD? But how? I only had agents with fake names—Hood, Tuck, Richard, and John, named after characters in Robin Hood novels. And deep down, I knew they weren't really part of the DOD.

36
Wednesday, 1 p.m.

I said my goodbyes to Mr. Pat and hit the road again, heading back to I-75 on my way to Sarasota. Mr. Pat's words echoed in my mind. Arresting Galiano and the others at the airport would be meaningless. We needed to catch them in the act with the drugs.

Jote picked up on the second ring when I called him again. "Yes, Mother," he teased, bursting into laughter.

Ignoring his humor, I got straight to the point. "I need you to find out from SA Donnelly who he contacted at the DOD to get involved."

"I can ask, but you know how he feels about you," Jote replied, his tone skeptical.

"Jote," I interjected, "I need Reinhard to provide a sworn affidavit stating that he witnessed the murder of the Cubans on the boat. These guys are flying in, not arriving by boat with the drugs."

"I'll do my best, buddy, but I can't make any promises," Jote cautioned.

I knew that relying on Donnelly for help was unlikely. He was done with me and the whole mess. It seemed like Galiano and Castellanos might walk away unscathed, and that didn't sit well with me.

Continuing my journey north on I-75, I dialed Sergeant Roger Gunther's number.

A female voice answered after the fourth ring. "Sergeant Gunther."

Taking a brief pause, I introduced myself. "Sergeant, this is Joey Mancuso."

"Hey, Mancuso, I've been expecting your call. I hear you might have a case for us," Gunther replied.

"Text me your address. I'll be there in thirty minutes."

Forty-five minutes later, I found myself sitting with Gunther at the Sarasota Police Department on Adam Lane. As I entered her small office, I noticed Gunther—an attractive woman in her forties—with short brown hair, amber eyes, and cute dimples on her cheeks. She stood up, removed her rimless reading glasses from the tip of her nose, and warmly greeted me.

"Have a seat, please," Gunther invited, gesturing toward a chair.

As I looked around Gunther's office, I couldn't help but notice the set of pictures arranged chronologically, showcasing her career in law enforcement—from her early days in uniform to the present. Fresh flowers adorned her credenza, and there were family pictures displaying her husband, a girl, and a boy.

Sensing my curiosity, Gunther offered to answer the question on my mind. I smiled and leaned back in my chair.

"My legal name is Rogelia," she pronounced it slowly and deliberately, "Rogelia Cabrera Gunther. My great-grandparents from Barcelona settled in Tampa many years ago when the cigar trade moved from Key West to Tampa. As simple as Rogelia is," she emphasized again, "it's hard for Americans to pronounce it correctly."

I crossed my legs, acknowledging her decision to simplify it to Roger. "I understand."

"Now, let's dive into the case. Can you start from the beginning?" Gunther asked, retrieving a legal pad.

For the next twenty minutes, I provided her with the condensed version of events, starting with Dianne and Reinhard's appearance, their request for me to solve Reinhard's murder, and concluding with the extraction from Cuba. It felt like I had repeated this story a hundred times.

"So, you're saying that if I contact Sergeant Leone in Monroe County, he won't cooperate and issue a warrant for these individuals?" Gunther inquired.

"He's dealing with five dead bodies, three of which remain unsolved, not to mention the unborn baby," I replied. "Maybe he'll be willing to cooperate with you, but without any witnesses unless I find Reinhard, it will be challenging."

Gunther nodded, understanding the predicament. "Well, without a warrant for Galiano and Castellanos, I can't detain them unless they are caught in possession of the fentanyl."

I leaned forward, growing more focused. "My office is currently checking for flights from Mexico to Dallas and then to Sarasota to see if they appear on any manifest."

"But you're overlooking one possibility," Gunther interjected. "If these individuals are as skilled as they seem to be, they might opt for private flights rather than commercial ones. Am I right?"

My eyes widened, and I raised an eyebrow. "You're absolutely right. And if that's the case, they might attempt to smuggle the drugs with them."

It was becoming clear that catching them in the act of transporting the drugs would be crucial for building a solid case.

Gunther smiled and acknowledged the challenge. "That's the tricky part. We have over fourteen private airports in the area, not to mention other potential landing locations they could choose."

I closed my eyes briefly, contemplating the situation. "But don't these private planes have to file a flight plan? We could at least check the ones coming from Mexico."

Gunther shook her head. "Assuming they follow legal procedures, they would file a flight plan. But criminals often disregard such regulations," she replied, getting up from her desk. "Would you like a bottle of water?"

As Gunther stepped out to fetch the water, I couldn't help but feel disheartened. With numerous private airports to search, no warrants, and uncertainty about whether they would even have drugs on them, the situation seemed bleak. And my mind kept circling back to Reinhard—was he being held against his will by our own government?

Gunther returned with the water and sat back at her desk. "There's a silver lining, though," she said, pausing my attempt to open the bottle. "Or rather, a potential strategy."

I paused, eager to hear any glimmer of hope. "Please, enlighten me. It's getting increasingly difficult to find one."

"Even better," Gunther replied with a hint of excitement. "Follow me to the squad room. I have my team assembled there."

I followed Gunther into a conference room equipped with a large table and whiteboards covering the walls. She introduced me to her commander, Lieutenant Brett Spencer, six detectives, and one private citizen who served as an investigator for the team.

Gunther updated them on our discussion, providing a condensed version of the fentanyl entry by two well-known dealers. Without delving into all the reference material, she conveyed the essence of the situation.

"My theory is," she continued, addressing her team while standing in front of them, "since these individuals operate out of New Orleans, the fact that they might come here suggests they have a distribution arrangement in Sarasota. Otherwise, they wouldn't bother. So, I want you to lean on every known dealer, confidential informant, the usual suspects, and anyone else who might have information about a large shipment of fentanyl. If it's coming here, they'll be salivating out there."

It was evident that Gunther was highly competent. She knew her field and commanded her team with skill and respect. I felt a glimmer of hope in her strategic approach.

Gunther assigned specific tasks to her team, ensuring that every avenue was covered. She designated two detectives to work on monitoring the airports for any incoming planes, regardless of their point of departure. She instructed the civilian investigator to collaborate with the marine patrol group, focusing on inspecting suspicious vessels and involving the Coast Guard if necessary.

As Gunther mentioned the Coast Guard, I couldn't help but feel a pang of unease, hoping they wouldn't associate me with the previous costly chase for a nonexistent culprit. I certainly didn't want my face on their dartboard.

Another detective was assigned to monitor incoming commercial flights from Texas, including cities like Dallas and Houston. Gunther concluded by emphasizing the urgency of the situation and the need to get ahead of it.

The team members received their clear and concise assignments, and I had confidence in their professionalism and dedication. I expressed my optimism to Gunther, stating, "That was good. If the drugs are coming here, I feel comfortable that you'll find them."

She smiled in response. "You got that right. Now, where are you staying?"

I replied, "I was hoping you could recommend a place."

Gunther seemed one step ahead. "My husband is the general manager at the Lido Beach Hotel. There's a beachfront room there with your name on it. I'll give you directions. Then, at seven, take their shuttle to Columbia Restaurant. My husband and I will host you there."

We walked into her office, and I expressed my gratitude. "Wow, that's very kind of you. I wish my wife was here. She went back to New York after Islamorada."

Gunther surprised me with her knowledge. "Former FBI Special Agent Marcy Martinez. Have her fly down and spend a few days."

Surprised, I asked, "You checked us out?"

She nodded, smiling. "I like to do my homework before working with someone. I know all about you and her. I have a feeling I would like her."

"She's wonderful, and I just might call her to come down. See you at seven, and thank you," I said appreciatively.

With a final exchange of pleasantries, we parted ways, each of us prepared to tackle our respective roles in the operation.

Surprised by Agnes's call, I listened intently to her update on JJ's investigation into Paul's whereabouts after his extraction from Cuba. It seemed they hadn't found any evidence to suggest he was flown to Washington, DC. Instead, there was a possibility that he had been taken out of the country, though they couldn't confirm it.

"Thanks for letting me know, Agnes," I replied, a hint of concern in my voice. "Keep digging and see if you can uncover any more information. I'll do my best to find him from my end."

As we concluded the call, I couldn't shake off the feeling of unease. I needed Marcy by my side, both for her support and expertise. I dialed her number, hoping she would be able to join me at the hotel.

"Hey, Joey," Marcy answered, her voice warm and familiar. "What's going on?"

"Hey, Marcy," I said, relieved to hear her voice. "I'm at the Lido Beach Hotel in Sarasota. It's a bit of a long shot, but I thought maybe you could join me here. Things are getting complicated, and I could really use your help."

There was a brief pause on the other end of the line, and then Marcy replied, "I would love to, but I can't. Mom fell on the steps to her home, and she's in pain. Nothing was broken, but she can't deal with Michelle Marie at the moment."

I was disappointed. "I understand. Take care of her and give her my love."

So it was up to me to unravel the mystery surrounding Paul's disappearance and to Gunther's team to bring justice to those responsible for the drug trafficking operation.

37
Thursday, 6 a.m.

Thursday morning arrived, and with it came a sense of urgency and determination. I had a plan in mind, and I needed Marcy's and the team's assistance.

As I greeted her, I could sense the busyness in the background. Marcy informed me that she was on her way to the office, and JJ was driving them. It was good to know that they were actively engaged in their investigative work.

I wasted no time and delved into the main purpose of my call. "Listen, Marcy, Reinhard seems to have vanished within the labyrinth of government bureaucracy. He's refusing to complete his program because he fears it will be militarized by 'the' or 'a' government."

Concern filled Marcy's voice as she asked, "What can we do to locate him?"

"Let's have JJ and Agnes dig deeper into this. I want to know if there's any evidence of Reinhard being held against his will," I explained. "And Marcy, I need you to leverage your contacts within the FBI to see if they have any information on his whereabouts."

With a hint of skepticism, Marcy inquired, "Do we have any concrete proof that Reinhard is being forcibly detained?"

I paused, acknowledging the possibility that my concerns might be fueled by speculation. "No, we don't have definitive evidence. It's a hunch, but I want to ensure his safety and well-being. Let's leave no stone unturned."

Marcy assured me, "I'll make the necessary calls and see what I can find. FBI Special Agent Michael Donnelly was the one who supposedly called in the DOD. He headed the task force. However, considering the fallout from our previous encounter, he may not be inclined to cooperate."

A tinge of irony colored my response. "It's quite a peculiar situation for you to find yourself on the FBI's shit list. But we'll navigate through it. I appreciate your efforts, Marcy. Let's see if we can uncover anything significant."

We concluded the call, each of us aware of the challenges that lay ahead. While I waited for Sergeant Gunther to pick me up, I couldn't help but ponder the mysterious web of connections surrounding Reinhard's disappearance. There were still pieces missing from the puzzle, and it was up to us to find them and bring clarity to the situation.

As we embarked on our day's mission, the weight of unresolved mysteries lingered in the air. I shared with Gunther the ongoing efforts made by Marcy to uncover information about Paul Reinhard's whereabouts. Gunther expressed her hope that Reinhard was pursuing his own desires rather than being coerced into any unwanted actions.

"Yes, let's hope for the best," I replied, gazing out the window, lost in my thoughts.

Returning to the task at hand, Gunther shifted the conversation toward our agenda for the day. She informed me that the team had apprehended two of their usual suspects, who were now awaiting our interrogation. Additionally, we were headed to meet one of Gunther's former confidential informants.

Curious about the CI, I asked Gunther, "Male or female?"

She turned halfway toward me, offering a slight smile. "Ana Bella, a twenty-five-year-old female. I helped her secure a job as a server at a local restaurant once she got her life back on track. Back when she was fifteen, I had arrested her for involvement in prostitution. She went through juvenile detention and multiple rounds of rehabilitation. When I arrested her the third time, she was still involved in prostitution but had also started using and distributing drugs for her pimp. I convinced her to cooperate and testify against him, which ultimately led to his downfall. In return, we offered her a chance to start anew, and she's been a reliable CI for the past three years."

Curiosity sparked within me, and I inquired, "Is she clean now?"

Gunther nodded, her gaze fixed on the road. "To the best of my knowledge, she has stayed clean. She shows up for work diligently and hasn't had any brushes with the law since then."

"But she still has connections within the community?" I asked, turning my attention back to Gunther.

Gunther's response carried a hint of the realities of a small-town environment. "Sarasota may not be as sprawling as Chicago or New York, but there are still interconnections. We're about to meet her now," she said, pointing to a bus bench where Ana Bella patiently awaited our arrival.

We pulled up to the curb, and Ana Bella entered the back seat of the car, ready to join us on our investigative journey. The pieces of the puzzle were gradually coming together, and with Ana Bella's insights, we hoped to unveil crucial information that would lead us closer to the truth.

"Good morning, Ana. This is Mr. Mancuso. He's assisting us with the case," Gunther introduced me as we greeted Ana, who sat in the back seat. Ana appeared as a cute, petite blonde with blue eyes accentuated by makeup, attempting to conceal the dark circles that surrounded them. Her youthful appearance belied the hardships she had endured in her past.

I turned to face Ana, observing her body language and demeanor.

"Hi, good morning," she greeted sheepishly, crossing her arms tightly around her chest and avoiding direct eye contact.

Gunther attempted to engage Ana in conversation. "Is everything going well for you?" she asked.

Ana responded with a simple "Yep," still looking down and evading eye contact.

It was evident that Ana Bella wasn't much of a talker. I continued our conversation, seeking any information she might possess. "Ana, we need to know if you've heard anything about a shipment of fentanyl coming into Sarasota."

Her response was quick and straightforward. "No, no, nothing," she replied.

I acknowledged her commitment to staying clean but pursued a line of inquiry. "I understand you're clean, but—"

Ana interjected, asserting her sobriety. "I am clean," she blurted out before I could finish my sentence.

Aware of the sensitive nature of our questioning, I approached her cautiously. "I know. But do you happen to know anyone who isn't?"

"Some," she replied, still avoiding eye contact and fixing her gaze on the floor.

Continuing our line of inquiry, I asked, "Have you heard any discussions about prices going down?"

She shook her head and responded, "Haven't heard," maintaining her guarded stance and hesitancy to make eye contact.

Gunther made a U-turn, heading back toward the station. Before Ana stepped out of the car, Gunther reminded her, "Just keep your eyes and ears open. We need to know the moment you hear anything, okay?"

Ana replied with a simple, "Yes, sure," before exiting the vehicle.

As Gunther continued driving, she turned to me and asked for my thoughts on the interaction with Ana.

Reflecting on her behavior, I expressed my concerns. "You know her better than anyone, but I didn't get the right vibes."

Curious, Gunther inquired, "How so?"

I explained, drawing on my observations. "You mentioned she used to be a prostitute. A profession like that often fosters an outgoing, assertive, and sassy demeanor. However, this girl seems subdued, reserved, and unwilling to make eye contact. She's actively concealing the dark circles under her eyes, which could indicate something troubling, like a lack of sleep."

Gunther pondered the possibilities. "Perhaps I've been fooling myself, thinking she's clean."

"Alternatively," I suggested, "she might be trapped in an abusive relationship. Do you happen to know if she has a husband or boyfriend?"

Gunther tilted her head, deep in thought. "I don't know," she admitted, recognizing the gaps in her knowledge about Ana Bella's personal life.

Gunther and I entered the station on Adam Lane, ready to question two individuals who were considered regular suspects in the area. As Gunther parked the car, she briefed me on our upcoming interactions.

"Lance Williams, twenty-two years old, has quite the extensive rap sheet. Mostly minor offenses and misdemeanors, but he's well-connected," Gunther explained. "And then there's Pepe Pascual, a Salvadoran who moved here after crossing the border. We suspect him of being involved with MS-13, a notorious gang, but he doesn't have any visible tattoos that would confirm it. We've brought him in multiple times on suspicion of drug distribution, but we haven't been able to make any charges stick. Are you ready for this?"

"Always," I replied confidently, prepared for the task at hand.

Gunther continued, outlining our approach. "Alright, here's how we might need to handle each of them.

38
Thursday, 11 a.m.

"Sergeant Roger, please have a seat," Lance greeted us with a smug smile as we entered the interrogation room. Gunther and I took our places across the table from him, noticing that he was slouched in his chair but not restrained by handcuffs.

Gunther introduced me, saying, "This is Joey Mancuso, who's assisting us on a case."

Lance couldn't resist making a snide comment. "Joey? Isn't that a kid's name? Come on, brother, you've never heard of Joey DiMaggio or Joey Namath, right?" he mockingly remarked.

Ignoring his attempt at banter, Gunther proceeded with the purpose of our visit. "We need to ask you some questions," she stated firmly, brushing off his comment.

Lance, with an air of defiance, replied, "Yeah, milady. Well, I have a question of my own. Why is it my ass gets pulled in here every time someone takes a shit?"

Deciding to confront him directly, I spoke up. "From what I've heard, Lance, you are a piece of shit. So, every time there's shit on the street, everyone knows you've been around it."

Lance's posture suddenly straightened as he retorted, "It's Sir Lance to you, brother, and I ain't no piece of shit. I'm a respected entrepreneur in this here community." He then looked at Gunther and asked, "Where did you find this New York guy?"

Sensing the tension rising, Gunther placed her hand on my arm to signal for restraint and replied calmly, "Lance, we want to know what you've heard about a new shipment of fentanyl hitting our town."

Lance's face lit up with interest. "Now, this is the business I like. An honest and profitable transaction for both parties," he said with a smirk.

Cutting to the chase, Gunther inquired, "What have you heard?"

Lance played coy, teasing, "My woman, my woman. Let's talk business. How much can that kind of information be worth to your unit? Every week, your guys seem to bust some small-time dealers. This here could be big."

Gunther maintained her professional stance. "We don't pay for information, and you know that," she stated firmly.

Lance attempted to negotiate, asserting, "If I was an informant, you would pay. So what's the difference?"

Firmly shutting down his proposition, Gunther replied, "Then become a CI. I'll sign you up, and we can make a deal."

Lance hesitated, contemplating the offer. "Then I become an official snitch. No way I want that on my resume," he finally responded, revealing his reluctance to become a confidential informant.

We were getting nowhere with Lance, and my patience was wearing thin. "Can I have the room for a few minutes?" I requested, turning to Gunther.

She shrugged and nodded, understanding my need for a private conversation. As she was about to step out, I made a request. "Can you turn off the recordings while I talk to Sir Lance?"

Lance grew concerned, asking, "What are you going to do?"

Gunther walked out, leaving us alone in the room.

I stood up, and Lance instinctively shielded himself, crossing his arms over his face and stomach. "Listen, you little turd," I began, taking a stern tone. "I'm with the NYPD, but I also have other employers who want to ensure the safe arrival and distribution of these drugs. Understand?"

Lance cautiously lowered his arms, his curiosity piqued. "You're a dirty cop?" he asked, testing the waters. "Are you admitting to being dirty?"

"To you, I am," I confessed, trying to maintain an air of authority. "First, because no one will believe you if you talk. And second, because I don't want to kill you. Now, I'll pay you a Grover for any information you can provide. Two more once the drugs are safely in town."

Lance's expression shifted, realizing the gravity of the situation. "No need to kill anyone. So, I come to you with information?" he confirmed.

"Yes, only to me," I emphasized.

Lance's street-savvy humor emerged as he quipped, "Is there, like, a retainer fee? You know, an advance for Lance?"

In response, I pulled out two hundred dollars and threw it on the table, along with a piece of paper containing my cell number. The temptation of the cash was too hard for Lance to resist. He looked at the one-way mirror, shrugged, and quickly pocketed the bills.

I opened the door and called out to Gunther. When she walked back in, I informed her, "Sir Lance here has agreed to keep us informed if he hears anything. Right?"

Lance, now playing along, nodded vigorously. "Yes, yes, that's the agreement."

Gunther smiled and told Lance he was free to go. As he walked away, I couldn't help but ask Gunther, "Is that how you wanted me to play it?"

She chuckled and replied, "Your ad-lib about being a dirty cop was quite original. One of the detectives with me in the room even questioned if you were serious. You had them guessing."

"Well, I hope my acting skills were convincing," I remarked, relieved that my improvisation had worked. "Now, let's see what kind of character awaits us with Pascual."

We waited in the room while an officer brought in Pepe Pascual, and Gunther invited him to have a seat. Pascual, displaying a rough appearance, wore a sleeveless T-shirt that revealed his muscular biceps. His head was shaved, he sported a thick mustache, and he had small earrings in both ears. I couldn't help but wish Jote and Tico were here with me at this moment.

Pascual wasted no time in making a request. "Can we have a working lunch? I've been here two hours waiting for this, and all I got was watered-down *café*." His comment hinted at his dissatisfaction with the situation.

Gunther responded, "Sure, I can get you a tuna sandwich or two. Maybe some tacos instead of our ham-and-cheese delicacies."

Pascual suggested, "I wouldn't mind some tacos."

Turning to me, Gunther asked, "Would you care for a fresh lobster salad or maybe some caviar?"

"I'll have a tuna salad, thanks," I replied, acknowledging Pascual's disapproval of my choice.

Pascual made a face at the mention of tuna, clearly not a fan of it. He then addressed Gunther, questioning their repeated encounters. "Sergeant Gunther, aren't you tired of pulling me in here and having to let me go? How many times now? Four, five? What are you charging me with now?"

"No charges. We just want your cooperation," Gunther calmly explained.

Pascual found humor in the situation. "Cooperation? Now that's funny. You know what I need? I need an agent to help record a new rap song I wrote. Maybe this *hombre* is one?" he said, pointing at me teasingly.

"I am an agent, but not the kind you need. I'd love to hear your rap," I responded, playing along.

Pascual looked at Gunther, seeking her approval. She nodded, giving him the go-ahead.

"I need to stand," Pascual stated, and Gunther waved him up. He positioned himself by the wall and began his rap:

"I'm a legal illegal, and I'm here to stay— I don't really give a fuck what you gringos say. 'Cause I'm a legal illegal, and I'm here to stay."

"That's pretty good. There's some hidden talent there," I complimented him.

Gunther then steered the conversation back to the purpose of their meeting. "Have a seat, Pascual. Here's why you're here. We need to get ahead of a large shipment of fentanyl coming into Sarasota. And since you know the game, you're going to tell us when and where."

Pascual leaned back in his seat and flashed a smile, intrigued by the proposition.

A knock echoed at the door, prompting me to rise. I received three bottles of water and three wrapped sandwiches, instantly recognizing their contents as I opened the bag. Taking one out, I tossed it to Pascual. "There's your tuna 'taco' on white bread."

Pascual swiftly caught it midair and placed it on the table. "Sergeant, I'm flattered that you would assume I possess such information. However, even if I did, I would never willingly share it with the authorities."

"We anticipated your response, and that's precisely why I'm here," I replied. "I mentioned earlier that I'm an agent—a border agent. Let me show you what I have."

Gunther handed me a large manila envelope, and I opened it, revealing several photographs of a badly beaten fifteen-year-old girl. The pictures depicted her in three different poses. "Are you familiar with this girl?"

Pascual glanced at the photos but simply shook his head.

"Her name is Margarita. She is a Mexican national, and she has been sexually assaulted. Moreover, she is now pregnant, carrying your child," I stated.

"What the hell, man? I had nothing to do with that," Pascual objected loudly. "You have no proof."

"At some point during the journey to the USA, you raped Margarita and potentially others," I added.

"Show me the evidence. I didn't do it," Pascual challenged.

"Are you seriously claiming that throughout all your trips, smuggling illegal immigrants and recruiting for MS-13, you never targeted young girls? Come on, man, really?" I pressed.

"You have no proof," he reiterated.

"But we do, my friend. Your DNA is an exact match," Gunther claimed deceivingly.

"I never consented to anyone obtaining my DNA. The judge will dismiss this case," Pascual retorted.

"Do you recall the nasal swab we administered to you when you crossed the border?" I asked.

"Yeah, it was for the COVID test, and the result was negative," he replied.

"Well, Pepe, that swab contained and still contains your DNA. Additionally, the diluted coffee we provided you, which you drank outside while waiting and smoking—that holds your DNA as well," I revealed.

"That's bullshit. You can't use that. You all gave it to me," Pascual argued.

"Yes, but you discarded it on the sidewalk, and we collected the trash," I said.

He picked up the tuna sandwich and slammed it onto the table. "So, what's next?" he asked.

"Here's the deal, Pascual," Gunther said. "As long as you cooperate with us, this border agent won't take you into custody. We have control over you."

"Let me make this short-term. We only need your help with this drug shipment. After that, maybe we can forget the whole thing," I suggested.

"So, all I have to do is inform you if I hear something?" Pascual asked.

"No, it's not that simple. You need to actively inquire about the drugs, not just sit back. And I expect a daily report. It's happening soon," Gunther explained.

"Can I leave now?"

I stood up, approached Pascual, and said, "If you don't cooperate, you might find yourself singing, 'I'm an illegal illegal going to jail.' Got it?"

I leaned back and unwrapped my tuna salad. Gunther was already taking a bite of hers. "Was the rape story true?" I asked.

She smiled discreetly, swallowed, took a sip of water, and replied, "That was a risk, but you know how many girls and boys get assaulted on their way here? Especially by gang members?"

"Sergeant Rogelia, I admire your approach."

In a similar fashion, albeit less dramatically, we applied pressure all over town to the criminals who might have information about our drug shipment. We hoped that at least one of our targets would come through. Private airports and commercial flights were under surveillance. The marine patrol was conducting searches. Everyone was on high alert.

I felt confident about our chances. Roger Gunther's methods aligned with my own. They were unconventional yet within the boundaries of justice. After all, there was no law preventing law enforcement from deceiving a suspect.

The only thing that still concerned me was Paul Reinhard's whereabouts.

At four in the afternoon, I got a ride back to the motel. I had the evening free to enjoy the beach, pool, and tiki bar. Two hours later, after taking a shower, I sat at the outdoor tiki bar. I ordered a beer, and the baby back ribs from the menu, savoring the starry evening.

Breaking the peaceful ambiance, my phone rang. The caller ID displayed "Joey Mancuso."

I double-checked, confirming that the caller ID indeed displayed "Joey Mancuso." "Hello," I greeted as I answered the phone.

"Mancuso, it's Reinhard," a hushed voice whispered.

"Paul? Is that you?" I inquired.

"I can't stay on the line for long. I need your assistance," he urgently pleaded.

"Where are you?"

Before I could gather more information, the connection abruptly cut off, leaving me with a dead line.

39
Friday, 6 a.m.

The unsettling call from Reinhard last night continued to trouble me. "I need your help," he had pleaded before the connection abruptly ended. It seemed that Reinhard had found himself in more trouble than a stray cat in a lion's den. From his initial plea to solve his own murder to his abduction and now his uncertain fate in the hands of unknown captors, his situation grew increasingly dire.

Agnes' efforts the previous night to trace the call had proven fruitless. The phone appeared to be dead, or the SIM card had been removed. Unless Reinhard reached out again, I had no idea how to locate him.

As I sat down for breakfast, waiting for Sergeant Gunther to pick me up, my mind raced through the events surrounding Reinhard's abduction to Cuba by Galiano and his group. Suddenly, a realization struck me. I quickly grabbed my phone and dialed Gunther's number.

"I'll be there in twenty minutes," she answered when she picked up the call.

Gunther picked me up, and we drove to the station where detectives were interrogating the usual suspects. I observed the proceedings, but so far, nobody had any leads on an incoming shipment of fentanyl. It seemed that we were either mistaken about the drugs, questioning the wrong individuals, or Galiano and his crew had an incredibly efficient distribution system.

After two hours of watching the questioning, Gunther led me to an unoccupied desk, and I dialed Marcy's number.

After exchanging our customary "I love you" greetings, I got straight to the point. "Any progress with the FBI?"

"Victoria Stewart, my former boss at the bureau, and I reached out to Special Agent Donnelly," Marcy replied. "He claims to have contacted the assistant director, who then passed it on to the Department of Justice, and they probably reached out to the Department of Defense."

"It feels like navigating a labyrinth, and I'm afraid we may never find out the truth. Damn it. Reinhard sounded like he was in real trouble," I vented my frustration.

"Donnelly assured me that he will follow up and gather more information," Marcy assured me.

I rearranged a few items on the desk as I sighed. "Yeah, well, I'm not holding my breath."

"How are things going there?" Marcy inquired.

"Anyone remotely connected to the drug trade is being questioned. Private airports, commercial flights, marinas—everything is under surveillance, but so far, we've come up empty-handed."

"How long do you plan to stay there?" Marcy asked.

"I'll give it a couple more days," I replied, drumming my fingers on the desk. "I feel like I've mobilized the entire National Guard. From the Florida Keys to this place, the name Mancuso might become synonymous with failure unless we catch these guys."

Marcy teased, "You could always take my last name, Joey Martinez, and move on."

"Thanks, love. I appreciate it," I replied.

"I love you. Bye, Joey."

It was now eleven o'clock, and I grew restless just sitting around. I stood up and began pacing the squad room. All eyes were on me as some team members exchanged glances, probably wondering if I had lost my mind. I glanced at Gunther, but she was occupied on the phone in her office.

"Mancuso, have a seat," said Chris Heffernan, the private investigator assigned to the team, pointing to a chair next to his desk. "By the way, I'm Chris Heffernan. I heard you were with the NYPD for quite a few years."

"Thank you, Chris. Yes, I served for almost twenty years. Now I'm in private practice and consulting for the NYPD, among others," I replied, appreciating his interest.

Chris, in his forties, had a small stature, standing around five-seven. He had a slender build with a touch of gray on the sides of his head. His attire was sharp—a blue suit, white shirt, and a tasteful green tie. His desk was organized, and I noticed the meticulous shine on his shoes.

"Where did you serve?" I inquired.

He smiled, his eyes widening. "Ah, Afghanistan, the last four years. Navy Intelligence. I retired last year after twenty years, holding the rank of major. What gave it away?"

I pointed to his well-polished black shoes. "The spit shine on your shoes. Thank you for your service."

Chris glanced down at his shoes and grinned. "It's become a habit now. After two decades, I can't seem to stop. It feels like I'm not fully dressed unless my shoes are shining."

"What brought you to this place?" I asked.

"At one point, I was stationed at the Naval Air Base Pensacola, and my wife and I honeymooned here. We fell in love with the area and always wanted to come back."

"It seems like an ideal place," I commented.

"It has changed quite a bit, more commercialized, but my wife and I enjoy raising our family here."

I glanced around the room, realizing that as nice as the small talk was, I had other pressing matters on my mind.

"You seem stressed, Mancuso. If the drugs are coming here, we'll find them. We've covered the entire area. One of our confidential informants is bound to uncover something," Chris reassured me.

"It's not the informants I'm worried about, but rather the usual suspects we've been questioning. One of them could be connected to our targets, and word might leak that we're waiting for them. These guys managed to evade capture in Miami and are operating freely in New Orleans. They have a tight-knit network," I explained, expressing my concerns.

"We'll just have to wait and see," Chris replied with a hint of optimism.

As Gunther exited her office, I stood up and glanced in her direction. Chris seized the opportunity to invite me for a drink later that day.

"Sure, let's do that," I agreed as Gunther signaled to everyone.

"Listen up," she announced, addressing the squad room. "We've received a tip that a cargo plane from Jamaica is scheduled to arrive tomorrow morning. Allegedly, the cargo consists of lobsters and shrimp."

"Do we know the importer of the cargo?" I inquired, capturing everyone's attention.

Gunther checked her notes and replied, "RAJO Seafoods."

A smile spread across my face as I took a satisfying deep breath, expanding my chest. "That's them. Rafael Galiano and Jorge Castellanos."

"We'll be at the airport, along with customs, to inspect all the cargo. If the drugs are there, we've got them," Gunther declared energetically.

By seven o'clock, I was back at the hotel after enjoying a few drinks with Chris and two other detectives from the squad. My plan was to order room service and have dinner on the balcony overlooking the ocean. I needed some time alone to think and reflect. Perhaps things were finally turning in our favor.

On the one hand, I felt a surge of enthusiasm at the prospect of apprehending these guys with the drugs. Maybe we could even tie them to Dianne's murder. However, my thoughts kept returning to Reinhard. "One thing at a time," Marcy's voice echoed in my head. I wished I had the advantage of my team's brainstorming sessions, even if it were just through video conferences. As a team, we could piece the puzzle together. But now it was just me, facing this challenge alone.

My dinner arrived, and I instructed the server to set it up on the balcony table. A club sandwich, fries, coleslaw, tonic water with lemon, a thermos of coffee, and a decadent triple-decker chocolate cake.

As I settled down to eat, my phone rang, displaying Marcy's caller ID along with a picture of her, Michelle Marie, and me. A warm smile formed on my face as I answered, "Hi there. How are you guys doing?"

"We're good. Michelle Marie is wondering when you're coming home," Marcy replied.

"Hah, if we're lucky, maybe in two days," I responded, informing her about the cargo plane lead.

"That would be great, but it sounds too easy," Marcy commented.

I took a sip of my tonic water. "You're right; it does sound too easy. These guys are too smart to fly in like that. If only we had the cooperation of the Monroe County Sheriff, we could at least arrest them on suspicion of murder. But that stubborn Leone won't budge unless Reinhard signs some ridiculous affidavit. Speaking of Reinhard, any word from Donnelly, the FBI special agent?"

"Yes, he told Victoria, my former boss, that he spoke to a woman named Megan Wright at the DOD. However, we can't locate her. She's been unavailable for the past two days."

"Does her boss know anything?" I asked, hoping for some lead in this convoluted situation.

"No, the person I spoke to at the DOD said they've never heard of Paul Reinhard," Marcy responded.

"Fantastic. So we've lost all traces of him. Someone has him, and he's in trouble," I exclaimed, frustration seeping into my voice.

"We'll keep working on it here. Agnes and JJ are digging into Megan's background. You focus on your end. There's not much you can do unless Reinhard reaches out to you again," Marcy advised.

"I know. Give Michelle Marie a kiss for me. I love you both," I said, feeling a mix of worry and longing.

My appetite vanished after the call. The cake on the table looked enticing, but I had no desire to indulge. Marcy's words lingered in my mind: "This looks too easy." She was right. No seasoned drug dealers would risk flying in a shipment of fentanyl to a commercial airport, disguised as lobsters and shrimp, using their own names. Or perhaps they had a cunning method to conceal the drugs. The uncertainty gnawed at me.

40
Saturday, 6 a.m.

Chris and I joined the swarm of law enforcement personnel making their way toward the plane. The tension in the air was palpable. As we approached the hangar, I could see agents from the DEA, FDA, and Customs all geared up for the operation. The whole area was bustling with activity, signaling that this was going to be a major operation.

Sergeant Gunther was already on the scene, coordinating with the various agencies involved. She spotted me and gave me a reassuring thumbs-up, which I returned with a hopeful smile. We were all hoping that this operation would yield the breakthrough we needed.

At 10:15, the plane came to a halt, a remanufactured Basler BT-67, a modified Douglas DC-3. The moment of truth was upon us. Police cars strategically blocked the plane, preventing it from going anywhere. Refrigerated trucks were positioned nearby, ready to receive the cargo.

As the doors of the plane opened, a team of officers, agents, and personnel moved in swiftly, ensuring that the situation was secure. I followed closely behind Chris, my SPD card holder hanging around my neck, a constant reminder of the role I was playing in this operation.

The tension was thick as we waited for the cargo to be unloaded. The hopes and expectations of cracking this case were riding on this moment. If our suspicions were correct, and the drugs were indeed concealed within the shipment, this would be a significant blow to Galiano and his crew.

As the first crates were being brought out of the plane, a sense of anticipation filled the air. This was it—the moment that would determine the success of our mission.

Five individuals disembarked from the plane, met by a group of agents. Straining to hear, I inched closer, displaying my newly issued ID hanging around my neck.

"One by one, state your names," one agent requested. The passengers complied, while another agent demanded their passports, and yet another asked for the bill of lading. None of them mentioned Galiano or Castellanos. I yearned to join their huddle and inquire about the two individuals, but it was impossible to break in. Finally, Gunther, positioned within the inner circle, inquired, "Where are Galiano and Castellanos?"

The apparent leader shrugged in response. "They're not onboard."

Gunther pressed further, "Are they coming to Sarasota?" The man simply shrugged again, claiming ignorance.

Someone handed the man what I presumed to be the warrant to inspect the cargo. His face transformed, rage seething from his furious red eyes. He erupted in a Spanish tirade filled with curses.

"We must transfer the cargo to the refrigerated trucks. Otherwise, the dry ice will evaporate, ruining twenty-two thousand pounds of lobsters and shrimp. This is madness!" he exclaimed vehemently.

"Sir, we'll expedite the process, allowing you to proceed with your journey," someone assured him, signaling the agents to board the plane.

Finally, I managed to approach Gunther. "Can I board the plane?" I inquired.

"Not happening. Even we can't go aboard. They have dogs and trained personnel. If there's anything there, they'll find it," she responded.

An hour later, the anticipated search and seizure turned out to be a mere search. No fentanyl or drugs were discovered, only lobsters and shrimp. There was no sign of Galiano and Castellanos either. All the personnel swiftly dispersed.

Gunther stormed toward me, fuming with anger. I could practically see smoke billowing from her ears. "Well, Mancuso, I've been thoroughly humiliated. With all these people here, we now reek of spoiled shrimp."

"Did you confirm this possibility with the Miami PD guys?" I questioned. "They expected drugs, just as we did. Either these guys outsmarted everyone, or there were never any drugs. It's also plausible that we may have shared our plan with too many individuals, and someone leaked it."

Gunther's face flushed red. "Are you suggesting that rounding up all the usual suspects was a mistake?"

Before I could respond to Gunther, my phone rang, interrupting our conversation.

"Yes, yes, where?" I answered the call. "Got it. We're on our way," I said before ending the call.

Gunther inquired, "Who was that?"

"Sir Lance. He says our two boys are landing at Hidden River Airport on a G4," I replied.

"That airport is closed," Chris interjected.

"Shit. Get the team, and don't tell anyone else," Gunther instructed Chris.

Curious, I asked, "How far is that?"

"About twenty-five miles west of us. Did Lance mention if they've landed?" Gunther inquired.

"He said they're about to land. They might have the drugs with them," I shared.

"Now, that would be a happy ending," Gunther remarked, a glimmer of hope in her voice.

"But you're not informing the other agencies?" I questioned, fully aware that I wouldn't have done so myself.

"Would you, after this fiasco?" Gunther responded with a nod.

"What about a warrant?" I inquired, even though I was concerned about jeopardizing the case.

"Don't worry," Gunther reassured me.

Thirty-five minutes later, we arrived at Hidden River Airport. A G4 aircraft was taxiing on the closed runway, and a black van was waiting nearby.

"Wait for the plane to be next to the van. Then close in," Gunther relayed the instructions through her phone.

We waited for five more minutes. "Move in, move in," Gunther commanded.

The three cars advanced toward the plane and van. As the aircraft doors opened, we stepped out of our vehicles.

Gunther ascended the four steps onto the plane, and I followed closely behind as the fourth person in line.

Gunther addressed the first man about to walk out, asking, "Are you Mr. Galiano?"

"I am," he replied with a smile. "And you are?"

"Sergeant Roger Gunther, with the Sarasota Police Department," Gunther introduced herself.

Rafael "Rafa" Galiano was in his mid-sixties, short and plump, with a white mustache and unkempt white hair. He wore a loose-fitting white shirt with his long sleeves rolled up and slacks and sported large dark glasses supported by a prominent wide nose.

"Are you Mr. Castellanos?" Gunther inquired, addressing the man behind Galiano.

"Yes," replied the man, who was hunched down to avoid hitting the ceiling.

Jorge Castellanos was lanky, wearing similar dark glasses to Galiano, a golf cap, a red pullover, and blue jeans. He appeared to be in his mid-fifties.

"Please step outside the plane. We need to ask you some questions," Gunther instructed.

Galiano smiled and gestured with his right hand, saying, "Lead the way."

Once outside the plane, Galiano commented, "Are you the one responsible for detaining my cargo of seafood? You know, it almost spoiled."

Gunther ignored the question and stated, "We have a warrant to search your plane."

"I'm aware of the warrant. I doubt it includes this plane and cargo," Galiano responded.

"Anyone else on the plane?" one detective inquired.

Galiano disregarded the detective and focused his attention on Gunther. "Just the crew, two pilots, and a flight attendant. The shape and beauty of your eyes tell me you're Latina. Are you?"

Gunther firmly asserted, "I'm the one asking the questions."

Galiano nonchalantly said, "Help yourself to a search. We have nothing to hide."

"Why did you land at a closed airport," Chris questioned, "if you have nothing to hide."

"The captain will tell you we had engine problems and wanted to land far from the major city, just in case," Galiano explained.

I glanced at the plane. "That's convenient."

"No, that's responsible," Galiano countered.

Four detectives proceeded to board the plane and conduct a search, while two others opened the cargo area to do the same. Galiano and Castellanos observed as the cargo contents were unloaded.

"Were you in the Keys a week ago?" I asked.

"And you are?" Galiano inquired.

"My name is Joey Mancuso."

"Oh, you're Mancuso. I'm familiar with your name," Galiano said with a grin. Then, addressing Castellanos, he added, "Jorge, this is Mancuso."

Jorge and I exchanged glances, but neither of us uttered a word.

"What do either of you know about Paul Reinhard?" I asked.

They exchanged glances. "I don't know any Paul Reinhard," Galiano replied.

"Right. Maybe you know him as Captain Tony whom you hired to go fishing or, better yet, to do a drug deal?" I suggested.

"Captain Bob, of course. A thief and a pirate. Or I guess those two things are the same," Castellanos spoke up. "We were carrying a large amount of cash because we planned on buying a boat in the Keys. He saw it on the boat and called two buddies to steal it from us."

"Were you buying the boat on a fishing trip? Why carry all that cash?" I inquired.

Castellanos explained, "We didn't feel comfortable leaving it at the hotel. It was safer with us, or so we thought."

"And what happened? You and your two other guys shot his buddies in self-defense?" I pressed.

"Actually, it was Captain Bob who shot his buddies and made us board their boat. He then took off in his boat with our money," Castellanos revealed.

"And the fentanyl?" I questioned.

They exchanged glances once again. Galiano, remaining calm and collected, replied, "We know nothing about drugs."

Realizing I had no concrete evidence to push further, I decided to halt the interrogation. While I intended to eventually bring them to justice for Dianne's murder, at this point, I would have to settle for a drug charge.

After approximately twenty more minutes, Chris returned and shook his head at Gunther.

"Sorry for holding you up. You're free to go," Gunther informed both Galiano and Castellanos.

Galiano shook his head. "I don't blame you, Sergeant. You have a job to do. Perhaps you can join us for dinner while we're in town."

"I don't think so. But thank you," Gunther replied, smiling.

I interjected, "How long are you staying in town?"

"We don't know yet," Galiano responded.

"Maybe I'll join you for dinner soon," I added, then walked away toward Gunther's car.

As I left, I overheard Galiano saying to Gunther, "Keep an eye on this fellow—he's a little hotheaded."

Back at my hotel, I took a seat at the tiki bar and ordered a reposado tequila, intending to savor it slowly. The events of the day had been a complete failure. No drugs were found, no arrests were made, and there were no confessions. On top of that, I now owed Sir Lance eight hundred dollars for the tip he provided. It had been a disappointing outcome all around. The only things we had come across were lobsters, shrimp, and dry ice.

"Dry ice," I muttered to myself, a spark of realization igniting within me.

41
Saturday, 10 p.m.

"Apologies for the late call, Sergeant," I said as Gunther answered her phone.

"No problem. I was just getting ready for bed. What's going on?" Gunther replied.

"Do you happen to know the exact location of the storage facility where the lobsters were taken?" I asked, strolling away from the bustling tiki bar.

"I have the address in my notes. It's somewhere off US 321 in North Sarasota. Why do you ask?" Gunther responded, her curiosity piqued.

"Dry ice," I blurted out with excitement. "That's where the drugs are hidden. They've concealed them within the dry ice."

Gunther's voice held a tinge of skepticism. "How do you figure that out?"

"It's more of a hunch," I confessed while gazing at the moonlit shoreline.

"Mancuso, if you were billed for all the personnel hours, fuel, and expenses you've racked up on hunches, you'd be working for a century to pay it off," Gunther remarked wryly.

"But I'm convinced, Gunther. The fentanyl must be hidden inside the dry ice. When the dry ice sublimates, the carbon dioxide gas is released, masking any other scent. The drug-sniffing dogs wouldn't have detected it," I explained fervently.

"Hmm, it's a plausible theory. I'll give you that," Gunther conceded.

"Does the warrant cover the storage facility? We need to go there immediately," I pressed, my back turned to the vast ocean, gazing at the distant lights of the nearby hotel. A gentle wave brushed over my feet.

"The warrant only extends to the planes," Gunther replied.

"Is it possible to obtain a separate warrant for the storage facility?" I inquired, hopeful yet aware of the obstacles.

"I won't wake up a judge in the middle of the night based on a hunch, especially after the fiasco we experienced today. I'm already in deep trouble with the DEA, and I have to work with them regularly," Gunther stated firmly.

I took a few steps toward the land, away from the soothing ocean sounds. "Can you at least give me the address of the facility?"

Gunther let out a sigh on the other end of the line. "Fine, I'll provide you with the address. But remember, if this leads to another dead end, I won't be bailing you out."

I quickly found a pen and paper, ready to jot down the crucial information Gunther was about to share. The address was noted down meticulously. As I stood there, anticipation coursed through my veins, mingled with a hint of anxiety. The storage facility held the answers I sought, but would my hunch prove to be right?

"Mancuso, I don't like where you're headed with this. If you break into that facility, any evidence you gather won't hold up in court," Gunther cautioned, her concern evident in her voice.

"I understand the risks, Gunther. But if we don't act, there won't be any evidence left. They could easily dispose of the drugs by removing them from the dry ice and transporting them elsewhere. They might have already done it. But I have to see for myself," I explained resolutely.

"I can't officially provide you with the address, or I might end up with a job as a maid at your hotel," Gunther replied, a hint of amusement lacing her words.

"Given that your husband is the GM, I'm sure he'd promote you to a supervisor of hospitality," I quipped, trying to lighten the mood.

Gunther let out a chuckle. "That's hilarious. Okay, off the record, the place is called Refrigerated Facilities of Sarasota. But please, Mancuso, be careful."

With the name in hand, I swiftly accessed Google Maps on my phone. Frustration washed over me as the app revealed that the location was an hour away from my current position. Time was of the essence, and I couldn't afford any delays. Hurrying toward the rental car I had secured, I embarked on the drive. The thought of the suspects staying one step ahead fueled my determination. I imagined them swiftly separating the seafood from the dry ice, distributing the drugs into waiting trucks, and leaving the premises. If my timing was off, all I would find were crates of innocent seafood. Just as I hit the road, my phone rang, displaying Marcy's name on the screen. I hesitated for a moment, contemplating whether to answer or not. Eventually, I picked up, attempting to sound casual.

"Hey there, ready for bed?" I greeted her.

"Finally! Your daughter gave me a hard time tonight. How about you?" Marcy replied, her voice filled with a mix of exhaustion and relief.

I never kept secrets from Marcy, but I knew how much she worried about my impulsive adventures. The recent trip to Cuba had been eventful enough to last for a week. As much as I despised not being completely transparent with her, I couldn't reveal that I was alone and en route to a high-stakes encounter at a potential drug storage facility.

Meanwhile, the Google Maps voice interrupted our conversation, instructing me to continue straight on US 321 for the next fifteen miles.

"Where are you headed?" Marcy inquired, sensing the presence of the navigational assistant.

"Just heading back to the hotel. Had dinner with three of the detectives on the team," I replied, inwardly berating myself for the half-truth.

"Do you want to call me when you get there? I want to make sure you're safe," Marcy insisted, her concern evident.

"No need, we're all good. I want to get some sleep once I return. I'll brief you on today's events tomorrow morning. My love to both of you," I reassured her, desperately longing to protect her from the dangerous path I was about to tread. As we bid each other goodnight, I couldn't help but feel a pang of guilt for not sharing the whole truth with Marcy. Nevertheless, I pushed those thoughts aside, focusing on the road ahead as I embarked on a race against time to uncover the elusive fentanyl and bring those responsible to justice.

My phone rang once again, and without checking the caller ID, I answered with an affectionate tone, "Yes, my love."

A playful voice responded, "Wow, one date, and you're already in love. Impressive, Mancuso. You're quite the romantic."

Confused, I asked, "Who is this?"

"It's Chris, my darling. I heard you're on your way to North Sarasota?" came the reply.

Realizing that Gunther must have contacted Chris, I silently thanked Sergeant Gunther for her resourcefulness. "Yes, I am," I confirmed.

"Wait for me at the corner of Tallevast Road and Twenty-Sixth Court East. It's right off US 321. Got it?" Chris instructed.

"Thanks, Chris. See you there in fifteen," I acknowledged before hanging up. It was a pleasant surprise to know that Gunther had taken the initiative to send Chris to assist me. While Chris was a civilian attached to the SPD drug squad, there was a sense of camaraderie and support between us. At least I wouldn't be facing this operation alone. When I arrived at the designated meeting spot, Chris was already waiting, casually leaning against the driver's side of his car. I parked my car behind his and stepped out.

Chris gestured for me to get in his car. "Get in; we'll go in my car," he said.

I complied, buckling up as he started the engine. "Gunther called you?" I asked, curious about the coordination.

With a smile, Chris replied, "I'm not sure who called. They just said you were in need of assistance and were nearby."

"That's good enough for me. How do we proceed?" I inquired, eager to get started.

"We'll approach the facility and park nearby. As we get closer, we'll assess the situation on foot. Do you have a firearm?" Chris inquired.

"I don't carry," I admitted.

"Is that a personal choice or just for tonight?" Chris probed, referring to my decision not to carry a firearm.

"I'm not carrying at the moment," I clarified, glancing around at the dimly lit surroundings in the industrial area.

"Open the glove compartment. There's a firearm in there. It's unregistered and clean," Chris instructed.

Following his guidance, I opened the glove compartment and unwrapped a cloth to reveal a Smith & Wesson 686. "This is a beauty," I commented, appreciating the craftsmanship.

Chris cautioned, "Let's not get too carried away. That's for a last resort."

We continued driving for about three hundred yards until the facility came into view on our left, with another hundred yards to go. "Let's park here and continue on foot. Stay in the shadows," Chris advised, preparing for our approach.

As we approached, the sight of a single-story warehouse surrounded by a fence topped with barbed wire came into view. The area was well-lit, with lights illuminating the warehouse and the nearby parking lot. A few cars were parked outside, and two individuals were standing by them, engrossed in their smoking break. However, there were no trucks in sight, raising suspicions about the situation.

Scanning the surroundings, I remarked, "I don't see any alarms or lights that we can trigger from here. But with those two guys guarding the entrance, we can't easily get inside."

Chris nodded in agreement, saying, "Looks like we'll have to wait.

We might be late to the party."

Just as we were discussing our next move, the warehouse doors swung open, and two trucks emerged. The sides of the trucks were adorned with vibrant marine scenes, accompanied by the bold letters that read, "Fresh, Fresh, Seafood. From the ocean to your table."

"There must be drugs hidden in those trucks. They might be the last ones remaining here," I speculated.

Chris, already dialing on his phone, responded, "I know. I'm calling the rest of the team. You know what to do."

Curiosity piqued, I asked, "Who are you talking to? Is Gunther there too?"

"Everyone is here," Chris confirmed with a smile.

"Shit, I wasn't expecting this. What's the plan?"

"We wait and see," I replied, my focus now fixed on the unfolding events.

The driver of the first truck stepped out and exchanged handshakes and high-fives with the individuals who had been smoking. Afterward, the driver hopped back into the truck, maneuvering it closer to the gate. Meanwhile, a passenger from the truck got out and opened the gates, allowing the truck to exit. Once outside, the truck patiently waited for the passenger to close the gates behind them.

As the trucks proceeded down Twenty-Sixth Court East in the opposite direction of our approach, all I could see were their fading taillights. Fixated on the truck about to make a right turn onto Tallevast Road, I suddenly noticed flashes of blue and red lights at the intersection. Though I couldn't see the vehicles themselves, the vivid lights pierced through the darkness, illuminating the industrial park.

Curiosity and a sense of urgency surged within me. "What's happening down there?" I questioned Chris, eager for information.

Without hesitation, Chris handed me his car keys. "Drive down there and observe. Do you still have your SPD tag or something similar?"

"Yeah, it's right here," I confirmed, patting my pants pocket. "I'll put it on and head down. I'll go and provide updates."

With that, I swiftly made my way to Chris's car and drove toward the illuminated scene, eager to unravel the unfolding events.

42
Saturday, midnight

As I approached the scene, the flashing lights from the police cars illuminated the tense atmosphere. The officers stood their ground, maintaining their professionalism despite the escalating situation. It was clear that they were handling a delicate encounter, and I wanted to ensure our investigation continued smoothly.

Drawing closer, I positioned myself within earshot of the conversation unfolding between the officers and the truck occupants. The driver, clearly agitated, questioned the legality of the stop, while the officers calmly explained their reason for the intervention—a robbery reported nearby.

Sensing the urgency, the passenger seized the opportunity and requested permission to make a call. My instincts screamed at me, knowing that a single phone call could alert their accomplices and jeopardize our chances of securing further evidence.

From the unmarked car, a man emerged and approached the truck's cabin. Intriguingly, he extended his arm and head through the open window, examining the interior. After a brief exchange with the officers standing by the second police car, he returned to his vehicle and drove away.

Recognizing the crucial moment, the officers engaged in a brief discussion before confidently requesting permission to search the truck's cabin. The driver and passenger exchanged uncertain glances, ultimately acquiescing to the request.

As the officer inspected the truck with his flashlight, he discovered a bag and confronted the driver about its ownership. The driver and passenger stood outside, unable to clearly see from his vantage point, and were instructed to step back and approach the officer for a closer look.

Meanwhile, my attention was drawn to the passenger who had retrieved his phone amidst the officers' distraction. Fearful that he intended to make a call, I raised my voice urgently, alerting the officers to the imminent threat.

Startled, the officers swiftly reacted, and one of them managed to confiscate the passenger's phone before any call could be made. With the situation under control, their focus returned to the evidence at hand.

The officer holding the bag spoke with authority, informing the driver that it contained approximately half a pound of marijuana. He announced his intention to secure the necessary protocols and procedures to process the discovery appropriately and search the contents of the cargo.

The driver, growing increasingly agitated, vehemently denied any association with the discovered bag. "That's not ours. We've never seen that before!" he protested, his voice filled with frustration and desperation.

The officer in charge remained resolute. "Cuff 'em both," he commanded, unmoved by the driver's claims. "We need to inspect your cargo."

Outraged, the driver shouted, "You need a warrant for that!" His pleas fell on deaf ears as the officers swiftly restrained both him and the passenger, securing them in separate police vehicles.

As the scene unfolded, I approached the truck, and the officers' attention momentarily diverted from me. One of the officers promptly questioned my presence, voicing concerns about my unauthorized presence.

Identifying myself, I displayed my SPD drug squad tag, reassuring them of my affiliation. The officer acknowledged my credentials, instructing me to remain in place as they prepared to open the truck.

While the officers initiated their inspection, I noticed another truck making its way toward us. It was clear that time was of the essence, as the approaching driver would likely turn back upon seeing the flashing lights. I immediately contacted Chris, suspecting that he had called in the situation from the facility.

"I think they're headed back to you," I informed Chris urgently. "You alerted the team?"

Panting, Chris responded, "I'm running toward it. I'll stop him if he turns."

Driven by the gravity of the situation, I swiftly returned to my car, executing a U-turn to intercept the oncoming truck. The driver of the second truck had already made a U-turn, intending to retreat to the facility as there were no other viable escape routes.

As I closed in on the truck, I witnessed Chris positioned in the middle of the street, arms raised and waving frantically, his gun in hand. His voice was drowned by the distance, rendering his words unintelligible. The truck seemed to accelerate as it neared Chris, who stood his ground, preparing to act.

In a frantic attempt to avert disaster, I screamed from within the car, "Get out of the way, Chris! Get out—"

But my words were futile. Before Chris could fire a shot, the truck collided with him, launching his body into the air before crashing onto the pavement with a sickening thud. A surge of anger and anguish coursed through me as I muttered, "Son of a bitch," to no one in particular.

Without a moment's hesitation, I exited the car and rushed to Chris's side. He lay face down, moaning in pain, blood flowing from a wound on his head.

Kneeling beside him, I pleaded, "Stay with me, buddy. I'm calling for help." My hands trembled as I retrieved my phone, urgently dialing emergency services, seeking the aid that Chris so desperately needed.

As the 911 operator answered, the urgency was evident in my voice. "Officer down! We need an ambulance at Twenty-Sixth Court East, just north of...Tal...Tallevast Road."

Chris's groans of pain filled the air, his voice strained. "My chest...my chest is killing me," he managed to articulate, the distress evident in his repeated moans.

"Stay still, Chris. Help is on its way," I reassured him, attempting to provide comfort amid the chaos.

The impulse to make a lighthearted remark about his choice to undertake such a perilous endeavor as part of Naval Intelligence crossed my mind, but the gravity of the situation silenced any hint of humor. Perhaps, I thought, I could share a joke later when he had recovered.

Sergeant Gunther, accompanied by another detective and a second police car, swiftly arrived at the scene. She rushed toward us, concern etched on her face. "How bad is he?" she inquired urgently.

"I've called for help. He's complaining of chest pain. You go after those individuals. I'll stay here with him," I responded, my determination evident.

Gunther wasted no time, returning to her car and speeding away. Meanwhile, a SWAT truck sped past me, followed closely by three other police cars. The street descended into chaos, with the sounds of gunfire piercing the night air, each moment feeling like an eternity.

Finally, in the distance, an ambulance emerged, its flashing lights cutting through the darkness. I stood and waved my arms frantically, signaling their attention. "He's experiencing chest pain. He was struck head-on by a truck," I informed the approaching paramedics.

"Thank you, sir. We'll take it from here. Please stand back," one of the paramedics requested, their professionalism shining through the chaos.

Complying with their instructions, I moved away as the EMT crew swiftly attended to Chris. They secured his head, ensuring stability, and checked for any signs of spinal injury. With precision and care, they gently transferred him onto a stretcher, established an intravenous line to administer fluids, and carefully loaded him into the waiting ambulance.

"Are you coming with us?" the paramedic inquired, pausing momentarily as they prepared to depart.

"Which is the most upscale hotel in Sarasota?" I asked abruptly, my question catching the paramedic off guard.

She blinked in surprise, then replied, "I suppose the Ritz-Carlton. But sir, are you coming with us?"

Regretfully, I shook my head. "No, I can't. Please, take off and do whatever it takes to save him."

With a nod of understanding, the paramedic closed the doors, and the ambulance sped away into the night, its siren wailing as it navigated the city streets, carrying Chris, my injured partner, to the medical care he so desperately needed.

43
Sunday, 2 a.m.

The Ritz-Carlton felt like it was an eternity away, an hour-long drive from my current location. Everything in this small town seemed to be situated at least an hour apart. As I contemplated the time constraints, my instincts told me that the individuals at the storage facility had likely managed to contact Galiano. There was a sense of unease that lingered within me. Determined to gain an advantage, I jumped in Chris's car and swiftly entered Hidden River Airport into the GPS. A glimmer of satisfaction crossed my face as I realized it was only a forty-minute drive from where I was.

Time was running out, and urgency gripped me. The quickest escape route for the two criminals would be by plane. Knowing the fentanyl had been discovered, their desperation might have escalated to violence. I couldn't dismiss the possibility that Gunther and her team were currently occupied with the storage facility. My plan was to confront Galiano alone, coaxing him into confessing to Dianne's murder.

Arriving at the darkened Hidden River Airport, the atmosphere resembled a bear's cave during hibernation. The plane sat idle, devoid of any signs of life or vehicles nearby. I parked the car—now realizing it belonged to Chris—behind a hangar, took a moment to confirm the presence of the gun holstered at my waist, and stealthily advanced toward the aircraft. Concealing myself behind the large wheels, I waited patiently.

Fifteen agonizing minutes crawled by until a dark SUV entered the airport grounds. My eyes never wavered from its movement. The SUV parked approximately twenty yards away from the plane, and Castellanos and Galiano emerged, making their way toward the aircraft. The pilot, obediently following their instructions, opened the door, lowered the steps, and a foursome boarded the plane.

It was time for one more passenger.

As the flight attendant prepared to retract the steps, I sternly commanded, "Stand back and do not utter a word."

Assertively, I boarded the plane, my Smith & Wesson leading the way. Only a single pilot remained in the cockpit. With my firearm trained on him, I issued my instructions. "Do not start the engines. Move to the back of the plane, but ensure you raise the steps before doing so." Complying with my orders, he slowly made his way toward the others.

Maintaining my aim, I addressed all four individuals. "Please stand, all of you, and remove your clothing, leaving only your underwear. Young woman, if you are wearing a bra, you may keep it on. Any surprises awaiting us in the galley?"

Galiano couldn't contain his disdain. "You're out of your mind, Mancuso," he spat.

"Undress and be cautious. I'd rather not have this firearm discharge inside the plane. The noise would be quite deafening."

Complying, the pilot began removing his clothing, followed by the flight attendant, who glanced at the others before doing the same. Observing Castellanos eyeing the overhead bin, I quickly intervened.

"Don't even consider it, Jorge. Just take off your clothes. You too, Rafa, quickly."

"Throw them up here," I directed, gesturing with the gun toward an empty space on the floor in front of the seats. The Gulfstream G4 had four single seats facing forward and two more facing backward near my position.

"When I call your name, rise slowly, walk toward me, and sit on the floor here," I instructed, pointing. "Imagine you're all in a cozy hot tub. Young woman, you're up first."

Following my command, the young woman sat on the floor beside me. "Next, the captain. Sit next to her."

"Mancuso, what the hell do you think you're doing?" Galiano demanded.

"Just stand up slowly and make your way here," I retorted firmly.

Galiano stood in his boxer shorts, reluctantly taking a seat opposite the others. "Jorge, your turn. Don't do anything stupid."

Jorge, sporting snug underwear, moved deliberately and settled beside his companion, Rafa.

Confident that no one had any concealed weapons and that sudden movements were unlikely, I maintained control of the situation.

"Rafa, stand up and head to the cockpit. We need to have a chat."

Galiano couldn't contain his outrage. "You damn coward, what are you up to?"

I pressed the firearm against his forehead. "Just get up, *gordo*, and move forward. Do you understand?"

"Lower the gun; there's no need for violence," Rafa pleaded, struggling to stand within the confined space.

As all eyes fixated on his arduous endeavor, he eventually managed to rise and advance.

"Take a seat in the captain's chair and fasten your seatbelt," I directed, standing near the cockpit door but keeping my gaze on the others.

"Now listen, Rafa. I'm not here because of your drugs. Frankly, I couldn't care less about the drugs," I stated, pausing for emphasis. "Well, actually, I do care. Your drugs are responsible for killing thousands of people in the US, especially young individuals. But I'm here to find out why you killed Dianne."

"Who the hell is Dianne?" Rafa queried, beads of sweat forming on his forehead.

"Dianne is the young woman you used to entice Reinhard. Did you know she was pregnant?" I demanded.

"Oh, her. I didn't kill her."

The tension in the cabin was palpable as Galiano pleaded for his life. I kept the gun pressed against his knee, my finger hovering over the trigger.

"Relax, Mancuso," he urged. "Maybe one of my guys did it."

"On your orders, right?" I replied coldly, placing the firearm on his right knee.

"Wait, wait. Don't do this."

"You're all going down for the fentanyl. A murder or two won't make much difference. But I want to know," I asserted.

"I had nothing to do with that, believe me," he gasped, his breath becoming shallow.

I shifted the barrel two inches to the right and fired a shot. The deafening sound reverberated through the cabin, causing everyone to instinctively cover their ears, though it was too late. The scent of gunpowder filled the air.

"You're fucking crazy, Mancuso! What are you doing to him?" Jorge shouted from the floor.

Galiano, with his hands still covering his ears, hunched down. Sweat now drenched his hairy back.

"Alright...I'll confess," he stuttered between labored breaths. I pulled out my phone and activated the recording app. "Go," I commanded.

"Dianne was of no use to us once we had Reinhard. So I ordered her elimination."

"What about the Cubans on the original boat?" I inquired.

"Them too. Jorge gave the order," he whispered.

"Was your deal with the Chinese to abduct Reinhard and take him to Cuba in exchange for the fentanyl?"

"Yes. But the two Cubans were supposed to take him to Cuba. However, they backed out and decided to keep the small amount of fentanyl they were supposed to provide as a down payment."

"So that's why you killed them?"

Galiano began to weep and said, "Yes, that's correct. We couldn't afford to double-cross the Chinese."

"Do you know where Reinhard is now?"

He looked up at me, his nose running. Wiping it with his arm, he replied, "No, I don't know. They rescued him from Cuba. I assume he's here in the US."

"But you still received payment in fentanyl?"

"They honored the deal, which involved us handing Reinhard over."

"What about Captain Tony of The Queen of the Oceans? Is he dead?"

Galiano remained silent as I pressed him for answers. The weight of his nod confirmed my suspicions.

"Did you throw him overboard?" I pressed further. Again, he didn't respond verbally, but his nod indicated the grim truth. Captain Tony had met a tragic end at their hands.

"I need your verbal confirmation," I insisted, knowing the recording would be crucial. "Is that a yes?"

Galiano sighed heavily before reluctantly admitting, "Yes."

With his confession, he had implicated himself in multiple homicides—those of the two Cubans, Captain Tony, Dianne, and her unborn child. Regardless of whether they had found the fentanyl, I now had them on serious charges.

Through the cockpit windows, I could see the flashing lights of police vehicles approaching the plane. The situation was escalating rapidly.

"Go back and sit on the floor," I instructed Galiano, keeping a close eye on him. Meanwhile, I quickly wiped clean the Smith & Wesson and discreetly stowed it away in a hidden compartment within the cockpit.

SWAT teams and police officers surrounded the plane, their long rifles trained on the aircraft. The cabin was bathed in the alternating blue and red lights of emergency vehicles.

Taking a deep breath, I descended the steps with my hands raised. Stepping onto the tarmac, I called out, "We're good here. Come on in."

The authorities cautiously approached, ready to apprehend the criminals and secure the scene. It was finally over, and justice would be served.

44
Sunday, 5 a.m.

The two crew members, Galiano and Castellanos, were apprehended in the cabin by Gunther and her team. As police cars drove the group away, I turned to Gunther with concern. "How's Chris?" I asked, wanting an update on his condition.

Gunther's expression turned solemn as she responded, "He suffered a massive heart attack in addition to the injuries from the truck. He's in critical condition."

Relieved, I inquired eagerly, "Did you find the fentanyl?"

A wide grin spread across Gunther's face as she replied, her eyes opening wide with excitement. "One thousand pounds of it, in clear capsules. No wonder they couldn't be spotted. That was an ingenious call on your part."

Curiosity piqued, I asked, "How much is that worth in dollars?"

We began walking toward her car, and Gunther paused for a moment to calculate. "About one hundred million dollars in street value," she estimated.

I couldn't help but smile at the magnitude of the discovery. "That's a significant amount. Were the DEA agents present during the operation?" I inquired, wondering if they had missed out on the bust.

A hint of disappointment flashed across Gunther's face as she responded, interrupted by the arrival of two officers calling for her attention. "Unfortunately for them, they missed out," she replied before being called away.

Eager to share the latest development, I mentioned, "By the way, I recorded Galiano on my phone confessing to five murders."

Gunther's interest was immediately piqued, and she motioned for a moment to address the officers. They showed her three plastic bags containing the Smith & Wesson and two other firearms before she returned to me.

Curiosity brimming in her eyes, Gunther asked, "Mancuso, how did you manage to pull this off?" Her pointed finger gestured toward the plane. "You stopped the plane, had them undress, and even got Galiano to confess. They didn't overpower you? Three men against one?"

Offering a nonchalant shrug, I replied, "I suppose I'm quite persuasive when I need to be."

Cocking her head, Gunther pressed further, "Did you have a weapon? Surely, you must have been armed."

I shook my head, emphasizing my statement. "I don't carry a weapon."

Gunther's surprise was evident as she continued her line of questioning, her tone incredulous. "Both Galiano and Castellanos had weapons in the overhead compartment. Are you telling me you managed to subdue them unarmed? And is the Smith & Wesson found in the cockpit yours?"

Confidently, I responded, "No, it's not mine. And you won't find my fingerprints on it either." I smiled, shaking my head. "Nope."

Gunther's eyebrows furrowed in disbelief. "So without a weapon, you managed to hold three men, made them strip, and even got Galiano to confess. That's your story?"

I chuckled lightly and replied, "It's all in the way you ask."

Understanding my point, Gunther nodded. "Okay. What are you going to do now?"

Thinking for a moment, I responded, "I have Chris's car. What hospital is he in? I want to visit."

"Sarasota Memorial, about a half hour from here," Gunther informed me.

Nodding gratefully, I said, "That's where I'll be."

Gunther warned, "There will be more questions."

I shrugged and replied confidently, "I'm sure. I plan on flying back to New York tomorrow, so whatever you need, let's get it done today."

Leaving Gunther behind, I made my way to the back of the hangar where I had parked Chris's car. The daylight greeted me, showcasing a beautiful sky painted in various hues of orange, yellow, and blue. Time seemed like a blur, and I couldn't remember when I last slept. The entire Sarasota experience had been a whirlwind. But with the capture of the criminals, the recovery of the drugs, and Galiano's confession, it felt like a triple victory.

Seated in the car, ready to message Gunther about the recorded confession, I noticed two missed calls from Joey Mancuso. My heart sank as I realized Reinhard had tried to reach me. I hurriedly checked my voicemail, but there were no messages. Reinhard had called twice, and I had missed both calls. Damn it.

As I drove toward the hospital, the urge to call Marcy tugged at me, but I held off for the moment.

A few minutes later, I found myself in the cardiac intensive care wing of the hospital, desperately seeking information about Chris. However, no one was willing to provide me with any details.

Feeling a wave of guilt wash over me, I knew I had to stay strong for Chris. He had come to my aid and befriended me. I believe he had an exceptional record and had served our country with honor. I could only hope for the best.

Twenty minutes later, a woman in her forties emerged from a room, accompanied by an older man and woman. The younger woman, overcome with emotion, collapsed to the floor. Without hesitation, I rushed to their side and assisted the man in helping the young woman sit up.

"Hi, I'm Joey Mancuso," I introduced myself, concern etched on my face. "Are you—"

The young woman, her tear-stained face looking up at me, extended her hand and managed to say through sobs, "I'm Jennifer, Chris's wife. He talked about you."

Gently clasping her hand, I spoke softly, "How is he—"

The man interrupted me and introduced himself. "I'm Barry," he said, shaking his head and closing his eyes momentarily. Opening them again, he added, "I'm Jennifer's father, and this is my wife, Nora."

Jennifer, still sobbing, asked without looking up, "You were there?"

I nodded and replied, "Yes, I was."

Through her tears, Jennifer asked, "Did the truck trample him?"

I shook my head, offering a comforting lie. "No, not at all. It was merely a brush, but he fell from it. I'm so sorry."

Barry expressed his gratitude, saying, "Thank you for coming."

"Of course. Again, I'm sorry for your loss," I said, patting Barry's shoulder gently. I nodded to Nora in acknowledgment.

Jennifer looked up at me, her eyes filled with tears, and whispered, "Thank you."

I simply nodded, my gaze locked with hers. Her round blue eyes reflected fear and uncertainty, an image that would stay with me for a long time.

I called Barry aside and spoke to him privately. "Sir, I have Chris's car parked in the lot. Section A. Here are the keys."

Barry accepted the keys, expressing his thanks once again. Feeling a heavy weight on my heart, I walked out of the hospital. Despite the success in apprehending the criminals and seizing a significant amount of fentanyl, the loss of Chris, a man with a loving wife and two children, made the victory feel hollow.

Before arranging for a car service to take me back to the hotel, I noticed a Wendy's across US 41. I needed sustenance, any food, and a cup of coffee to soothe my tired mind.

Sitting at a table, sipping on my coffee, I dialed Marcy's number.

"How's it going?" she asked.

I shared the details of our successes and then broke the news of Chris's passing.

"Oh, I'm so sorry, Joey," Marcy said sympathetically. "Did you get to know him well?"

"Well enough for it to hurt, yes," I replied, a touch of sadness in my voice. "I think he would have survived the accident, but the poor guy had a heart attack. It's unbelievable."

"You're done with everything now, right?" Marcy inquired.

"Almost. I still have a few more questions to answer for the SPD. But other than that, I'm planning on flying back tomorrow afternoon. Please have Agnes book me a flight."

"I'll take care of it personally and text you the information," Marcy assured me.

"Thank you. Oh, and I forgot to mention, Reinhard called me twice from my phone again, but I didn't speak to him. I'm worried about him. It seems he's going through a tough time."

The weight of the day's events settled on my shoulders, and I couldn't shake off the concern for Reinhard.

"Oh, God. Come on back, and we'll think of something. But I'm gratified Dianne's killer will pay for it," Marcy responded, her voice filled with concern.

"I am, too. Kisses. I'll see you tomorrow," I replied, feeling a mix of exhaustion and relief.

After ending the call with Marcy, I dialed Gunther's number to discuss any remaining questions she had for me. I needed to decide whether I could handle them immediately or if I should prioritize getting some much-needed rest at the hotel. My body felt drained, and the adrenaline that had fueled me throughout the day had long dissipated.

Gunther advised me to get some sleep. She assured me that if any further questions arose, I could provide answers over the phone in a day or two. She instructed me to leave the identification tag with her husband at the hotel and informed me that the Sarasota Police Department would take care of the hotel bill.

A small smile crept onto my face as I imagined indulging in a well-deserved surf and turf dinner at the hotel restaurant. I couldn't help but feel a twinge of guilt for finding joy in such a moment, considering the tragic events of the day. However, I saw it as a small personal reward amidst the chaos and exhaustion I had endured.

Part 4
45
Monday, 4 p.m.

I settled into my seat in first class on Delta flight 2711, ready to make the nonstop journey back to LaGuardia. My mind was filled with thoughts of returning home to rejoin the team, but most importantly, to be with Marcy and our daughter, Michelle Marie.

As the flight prepared for takeoff, I heard a familiar notification sound, indicating a new message on my phone. Curiosity piqued, I opened it to find a message from Sergeant Roger Gunther. The words on the screen revealed that Gunther had forwarded the report of my involvement and the discovery of the fentanyl to the US Department of State's Narcotics Reward Program director. I was astounded to learn that there could potentially be a significant reward for apprehending Galiano and Castellanos, with the Department offering payouts of up to $25 million. Gunther wished me a safe flight and signed off.

Father Dom would be ecstatic about this development, grinning from ear to ear. He had always been concerned about taking cases without clients and the strain it could put on our resources. However, reflecting on our past cases, it seemed that we had experienced a stroke of luck with the rewards we had received from the IRS, banks, and insurance companies, and now the possibility of a reward from the narcotics program. I had no idea what the exact state of our bank account was; that was Dom's area of expertise. But I was confident that our balance would be in the seven figures.

Smiling to myself, I glanced out the window and whispered, "Oh shit, talk about happy endings." I quickly forwarded Gunther's message to Marcy, Dom, and Agnes, ensuring they were aware of this unexpected turn of events. With that done, I switched my phone to Airplane Mode and powered it off.

Leaning back in my seat, I closed my eyes and allowed a sense of satisfaction to wash over me. The intense pursuit of Galiano and Castellanos had finally come to an end. These men would face justice for their drug crimes and, in some way, be held accountable for the tragic deaths of Dianne and her unborn child. It was regrettable that they couldn't be charged for the additional lives lost due to their fentanyl trafficking.

With a mix of relief and contentment, I embraced the certainty that justice had been served and a measure of closure could be found. As the plane soared through the sky, I let myself relax, knowing that the chapter of the Galiano-Castellanos chase had reached its conclusion.

My sense of satisfaction quickly dissipated as the thought of Reinhard weighed heavily on my mind. Reinhard, a young man who had achieved great wealth and success through his intellect, perseverance, and groundbreaking program, had noble intentions, believing that his creation would bring positive change to commerce and law enforcement. However, he had failed to anticipate how this technology could be exploited by evil individuals and governments to oppress and control the population. Idealistic geniuses often overlook the potential harm their discoveries can unleash if placed in the wrong hands. Fortunately, Reinhard had realized the potential for misuse and abruptly halted his work, retreating to a simple life as a fishing captain in the Keys.

The unanswered questions lingered in my mind. Who had abducted Reinhard, and for what purpose? Was he being protected from another abduction by an unfriendly government, or was he being coerced to complete his program in a secret location? Who were these enigmatic Robin Hood-like characters, and who were they working for?

The flight finally landed, albeit a few minutes delayed. As I disembarked, leaving the Sunshine State behind me, I was greeted by Marcy's radiant smile and her beautiful emerald-green eyes, bringing a sense of warmth and joy back into my life.

"You have to tell me everything that happened. But I love the outcome of what you accomplished," she said as we exchanged kisses and broke our embrace.

"I'll fill you in during the car ride. How's our little Michelle Marie?" I inquired, eager to see our daughter.

"She's with a sitter at home, and she's been asking for her Daddy," Marcy replied with a smile, since Michelle Marie was far away from speaking her first word.

All seemed well, but the pain of recounting the events and, particularly, the loss of Chris still weighed heavily on me. Senseless deaths always troubled me, and Chris's passing added to the sorrow of this unfortunate series of events.

As Marcy took the wheel and we drove for about twenty minutes, my mind raced with thoughts on how we could locate Paul Reinhard.

"What are we going to do about poor Paul?" Marcy asked, breaking the silence.

I turned to look at her, contemplating the question. "I've been pondering that myself. Tomorrow, I want to gather the team and brainstorm ideas. There has to be a way to find out where he is and ensure his safety."

"The mysterious team of Hood, Tuck, John, and Richard, who do they really work for?" I questioned aloud. "I was told they work for the DOD, but their origins and true identities remain unknown. We have a missing link in the chain, starting from when Special Agent Michael Donnelly contacted the bureau's assistant director, who then passed it on to the DOJ, only to have it disappear when it reached the DOD," I explained.

"Let's not forget about Megan Wright, the woman Donnelly spoke to before she went missing," Marcy interjected.

"I instructed Agnes to dig deeper into Megan's background. She could be the key to unraveling this whole situation if she was involved," I recalled.

"Let's hope she's still alive," Marcy expressed, and I couldn't agree more. I didn't want to see another life senselessly taken.

I glanced at Marcy and closed my eyes, silently hoping for a different outcome. The last thing we needed was another murder. I then suggested, "What if we have your former boss, Victoria, call the assistant director? Do you think she would be willing to help?"

"You mean my old boss who's retiring at the end of the year? I'll give her a call tonight. I don't think she'll mind making waves at this point," Marcy replied, maneuvering through traffic.

"Why would she be making waves? We're simply trying to locate a missing computer genius," I queried, gripping the dashboard as Marcy deftly navigated through the congested streets.

Marcy turned to look at me, her expression filled with concern. "Because maybe someone in the government has their own plans for Paul Reinhard."

I met her gaze and remained silent. It was precisely what I feared. Someone had their sights set on Paul, and it wasn't for his own intentions but rather for the agenda of others.

46
Tuesday, 8 a.m.

I longed for the familiar embrace of the pub, like sinking into a worn leather chair that felt like home—a place to sit, exhale, and find solace. The walls adorned with pictures of celebrities and sports figures seemed to welcome me back, silently saying, "Welcome home, Mancuso."

As I prepared my espresso, I raised the cup in a toast to the faces on the wall. It was time to gather the team around the conference table and delve into brainstorming. Our mission was clear: find Paul Reinhard. Without him, all the recent victories would be rendered meaningless. However, amidst the wins, we couldn't forget the losses, particularly the tragic fate of Dianne and her unborn child. At least Galiano and Castellanos would face justice for their crimes.

Father Dom strolled in at eight-thirty, his voice brimming with warmth. "Well, well, look at suntanned Mancuso. How are you doing?" Dom greeted me.

"Hey, brother. Good to see you. I've got more of a farmer's tan going on," I replied with a grin.

Dom walked behind the counter, joining me, and we shared an embrace. It was a comforting moment as if our connection reaffirmed the strength of our partnership.

"The espresso is ready," I announced.

Dom poured himself a cup, his tone reflecting the worry he had carried. "You have no idea how many rosaries I've said on your behalf, Joey. Especially after that brief trip to Cuba. What were you thinking?"

"I didn't have much of a choice, Dom. Paul Reinhard asked for my help, and I felt compelled to stand by him. But it's all in the past now. Your prayers worked, and here I am," I reassured him. Then, a playful smile tugged at my lips as I added, "You'll be glad to hear that I even said a few prayers myself and four F-18s miraculously appeared."

Dom looked up at the ceiling, gratitude evident in his gaze, before flashing a thumbs-up.

"I can't help but eagerly anticipate the Drug Recovery Fund kicking in. Any idea how much we might receive?" Dom inquired.

"I'm not even sure if we qualify, but it would certainly be a welcome bonus after everything we've been through, right?" I replied, optimism creeping into my voice.

"Let's head to the office and wait for the team," Dom suggested. "By the way, what are your thoughts on the possibility of a subway series this year?"

"I haven't been keeping up with baseball lately, but I do know that both the Yankees and the Mets are having an exceptional year," I confessed. "Attending a game together sounds like a fantastic idea."

Dom chuckled, his laughter laced with a sense of joy. "You're in luck, little brother. A parishioner gifted me two tickets to the Yankees versus the Mets game next week."

A surge of excitement coursed through me, and I eagerly anticipated the respite from our work, immersing ourselves in the beloved American pastime. But for now, it was time to gather the team, fuel our minds with ideas, and devise a plan to locate Paul Reinhard. Our success hinged on uncovering the truth behind the mysterious figures known as Hood, Tuck, John, and Richard and their enigmatic allegiance. Together, we would find the missing link and unravel the web of secrets surrounding Reinhard's disappearance.

I glanced at Dom, a spark of excitement in my eyes, and replied, "You're on."

A few minutes later, the gang walked in one by one. Agnes and Lucy, followed by our newest team member, JJ, and

Marcy, whom JJ had picked up and brought here. The complete team had assembled, but I couldn't help but feel a pang of longing for Mr. Pat's presence at the table.

I warmly welcomed JJ to the team and proceeded to bring everyone up to speed on the recent events in Sarasota, specifically the successful apprehension of the Galiano group. However, our primary focus now shifted to finding Paul Reinhard.

JJ, our talented eighteen-year-old computer whiz, spoke up first. "I have the phone that Paul used. It's your old phone, Mr. Joey. If he calls again and stays on for a few minutes, I can pinpoint his location using a tracking method."

"He called me twice, but I missed it," I admitted.

"I'm aware," JJ replied. "Unfortunately, he hung up almost immediately. However, if he calls again, we'll be ready."

I turned to Agnes and inquired, "Any updates on Megan Wright?"

Agnes responded, "She resides in Laurel, Maryland, approximately an hour away from Washington, D.C. Her phone has been switched off since her conversation with FBI agent Donnelly, and she hasn't returned to work."

JJ chimed in, "Once she turns on her phone, we should be able to locate her as well."

Curiosity piqued, I asked Lucy for the official word on Megan Wright's situation. "Did you manage to reach anyone regarding Megan?"

Lucy nodded, her expression serious. "I made the call, and I was informed that she's currently on leave from the Department of Defense."

Deep in thought, I voiced my doubts. "I highly doubt that Paul is where he is voluntarily. If that were the case, he would have contacted me freely and informed me about his circumstances. He's definitely under some form of duress wherever he may be."

Lucy probed further, raising a critical question. "Do you suspect that our own government has him and wants him to complete his program?"

I turned to face Lucy, my gaze filled with a mix of concern and apprehension, before nodding slowly. "As much as I hate to entertain such thoughts, it's a possibility we can't ignore."

Marcy leaned closer to the table, her voice filled with apprehension. "Allow me to propose another scenario. What if the people holding Paul are merely acting as brokers, intending to auction him off?"

A wave of unease washed over the faces around the table. Lucy's eyes widened, Agnes's jaw dropped, and Father Dom shook his head in disbelief. However, I noticed a mischievous glimmer in JJ's eyes.

"JJ, what's going through your mind?" I asked, curious about his reaction.

A sly smile formed on JJ's face as he replied, "If they're planning an auction, they would have to conduct it either through direct channels or on the dark web."

His words hung in the air, sparking a mix of concern and intrigue among us. We realized that if we wanted to locate Paul Reinhard and thwart the sinister plans of those holding him captive, we would need to navigate the hidden corners of the internet where illegal transactions took place. The dark web held answers, but it also presented a dangerous path we had to tread carefully.

"And if they're using the dark web, you can track them?" I asked, my anxiety evident in my voice.

JJ's eyes gleamed with excitement. "Maybe. You provided me with the list of names. I can search for any chats or mentions of individuals named Hood, Tuck, Richard, and John. If I find anything, I can follow the trail."

Agnes chimed in, acknowledging the slim chances but seeing it as a viable option. "It's a long shot, but it's better than having no leads at all."

I shook my head, expressing my reservations. "I don't know. Are we solely relying on technology and the dark web? Can't we go back to old-fashioned detective work? Knocking on doors, questioning people?"

Father Dom offered an alternative. "We could send Larry and Harry to Laurel and conduct on-the-ground investigations. They can go door-to-door, talk to neighbors, and even try to locate Megan."

I tapped the table twice and turned to Agnes. "What are Larry and Harry currently working on?"

Agnes responded promptly, "They don't have any pressing assignments at the moment. They can either drive to Laurel or fly to DC and start their search."

Father Dom pulled out his phone and opened Google Maps. "It's approximately a four-hour drive on I-95. If they leave now, they could be there by this afternoon. This way, we save on flights and rental cars."

"Perfect. Agnes, get them on it. Instruct them to gather information from neighbors, reach out to family members—let them use their investigative skills. And they should be prepared to stay there for a few days. We need answers," I instructed.

Marcy interjected with a suggestion, her voice filled with concern. "I think it would be wise to check local hospitals and morgues as well. I have a bad feeling about this woman, Megan."

Agnes nodded in agreement. "I can assist from here with that while JJ delves into the dark web."

"Excellent. Well done, Dom. I love it when we can engage in real detective work instead of relying solely on technology," I remarked.

"Technology has certainly been advantageous for us," Agnes acknowledged. "I'll also find out if Megan took any flights recently."

"Good. Yes, technology is valuable, but there's nothing quite like the thrill of uncovering clues and piecing together the puzzle," I added.

Father Dom chimed in playfully, "Just like your fictional heroes, Sherlock Holmes and Hercule Poirot."

"Exactly, Dr. Watson," I concurred with a smile.

Lucy's voice grew more serious as she brought up a case from the past. "Joey, there was a case we worked on about eight years ago. We encountered an individual named Rupert. Does the name ring a bell?"

I furrowed my brow, struggling to recall the specific case. "I can't quite remember the details of the case, but the name does sound familiar."

Lucy jogged my memory further. "We were investigating the murder of Uri Aberman, a staff member at the Israeli consulate here in New York. He was suspected of spying for the Iranians."

Recognition flickered in my eyes. "Uri Aberman, yes, I remember him. So, what's the connection?"

Lucy continued, "There was a man who came to us, using the name Rupert. He claimed to be from the Department of Defense (DOD), but we knew he was CIA. He was involved in all the cloak-and-dagger stuff, secretive meetings, and such. And he provided us with accurate information, confirming that Aberman was indeed a spy."

I nodded as the memories fell into place. "Ah, now I recall. Rupert, the enigmatic figure. He played his part well, and everything seemed to point toward an Israeli execution of Aberman."

Lucy added, "But the case was abruptly taken away from us, and it was never officially solved, given the sensitive nature of the situation. So, what about Rupert? I still have his number. I can give him a call."

A glimmer of anticipation sparked within me. "Yes, let's reach out to him. It might shed some light on our current predicament. Go ahead and make the call, Lucy."

47
Wednesday, 8:30 a.m.

We were all gathered back at the office, except for Lucy, who had informed us that she had contacted Rupert, and he agreed to meet with her alone. Father Dom was at his church attending to his responsibilities. JJ was diligently exploring the dark web, but so far, he hadn't come across any meaningful leads. Larry and Harry had arrived in Laurel, settled in, and started knocking on doors. We were expecting an update from them later in the morning.

Neither Paul nor Megan had turned on their phones, making it impossible for us to track their whereabouts. Marcy inquired with Agnes, "Any news from the hospitals or morgues regarding Megan Wright?"

Agnes responded, "There have been no admissions under the name Megan Wright in any of the hospitals in Laurel, and there have been no reported deaths with that name either."

Marcy expressed her hope, saying, "Let's hope she's still alive. If she is, there's a chance that Larry and Harry can locate her as well."

Agnes continued, "However, I did find something interesting while conducting a social media search. Megan's mother owns a home in Bakersville, North Carolina. There are family pictures indicating they spend time there."

I paused my pen fiddling, and looked up. "If she's in hiding, Bakersville could be a likely place for her to seek refuge. Where exactly is Bakersville?"

Agnes replied, "There's a flight from here to Bristol, Tennessee. From there, it's a one-and-a-half-hour drive to Bakersville. You head south. Alternatively, you could fly to

Asheville, North Carolina, which takes about the same amount of time, but then you drive a bit northeast."

"We need to find out if she's there," Marcy suggested. "But how can we do that?"

Agnes pondered for a moment. "We could send her an Amazon delivery. That way, we would be notified when it's delivered."

I raised a concern, saying, "That might spook her, and she could flee. Besides, if there are others with her, they might receive the delivery instead. Is the house listed on vacation rental platforms like VRBO or Airbnb?"

"Let me check," Agnes responded, diving into her research.

While Agnes looked into it, I turned to Marcy and proposed, "Would you like to accompany me if she's indeed in Bakersville?"

Marcy smiled warmly. "I would love to, but I think it's better if you go. I've been away from my parents for too long, and I don't want to burden them further. Plus, you're more than capable of handling the situation."

"Oh, thank you," I expressed my gratitude to Marcy with a smile.

Agnes then informed us, "The home is listed on both services, and there's a local Realtor managing it."

"Excellent," I responded. "Give me a minute to come up with a plan."

I walked over to the pub area and grabbed a bottle of water, thinking about the best course of action. An idea started to form in my mind.

Returning to the conference table, I addressed Agnes, "Call the Realtor and pretend to be a neighbor from Laurel. Mention that Megan received an Amazon delivery of hiking boots in Laurel by mistake, and you want to mail it to the house. Ask if she's still there. Use a burner phone to make the call so she can't trace our caller ID."

Agnes got on the phone with the Realtor, speaking with her head down. She flashed us a thumbs-up before ending the call. "She confirmed that Megan is still at the house and has extended the booking for three more weeks."

"Book me a flight to Bristol," I instructed Agnes. "We need to speak to Megan."

Father Dom chimed in with raised eyebrows, "Business class?"

"We have some extra funds coming in, Father Frugal, so it's okay," I replied.

At ten-thirty, Lucy returned to the office, wearing a concerned expression on her face. I immediately asked, "What's wrong? Is there a problem?"

Lucy took a seat and said, "This guy Rupert has been promoted within his agency. He wants to help us, but we need to be cautious because we're being watched and monitored."

My eyes widened, and I whispered, "Watched and monitored? How?"

JJ stood up, went to a storage closet in our office, and retrieved some equipment.

Curious, I whispered to Agnes, "What's he doing?"

Agnes whispered back, "He's got detection gear. He's going to sweep the office for any listening devices."

I realized the severity of the situation. If someone had been eavesdropping on our conversations, they might already be one step ahead of us, and Megan's safety could be at risk.

We all sat frozen in thought, contemplating the potential implications, as JJ meticulously searched the office for any signs of surveillance.

Finally, JJ shook his head and reported, "I haven't found any listening devices, but it's likely that someone has been monitoring our calls and computer searches."

The gravity of the situation weighed heavily on us. We needed to proceed with caution and ensure Megan's safety as we delved deeper into the investigation.

JJ nodded in understanding. "I'll continue my dark web searches from my laptop and ensure I have the necessary security measures in place. It's always better to be safe than sorry."

Agnes added, "I'll arrange for burner phones for everyone in the office. We'll switch to those for any sensitive communication."

Marcy chimed in, "Joey, please be cautious when you go to meet Megan. We don't know who we're up against, and it could be a dangerous situation."

I acknowledged their concerns and replied, "I understand the risks involved, but we can't afford to sit back. We have to move forward and gather as much information as possible. We'll be cautious and vigilant."

Lucy interjected, "Rupert is looking into these rogue groups within the DHS. Hopefully, he'll be able to provide us with more information soon."

I pondered for a moment and then said, "Keep me updated on what Rupert finds. I'll trust him for now, but let's remain cautious. We can't blindly rely on anyone."

Agnes nodded in agreement, "We'll take it step by step and adapt as necessary. Safety and thoroughness are our top priorities."

I turned my attention back to JJ, asking, "Keep me posted on any significant findings from your dark web searches. And remember, be extra careful with your online activities."

JJ assured me, "I'll continue my work with the utmost caution, and I'll keep you informed of any relevant discoveries."

Agnes then stated, "As for your travel to North Carolina, Joey, we'll make sure you have all the necessary arrangements in place, including a rental car and accommodations. We'll also monitor any updates on Megan's whereabouts."

With a determined look, I replied, "Thank you, Agnes. Let's stay focused and gather as much information as we can. We need to find Paul and Megan and uncover the truth behind all of this."

As the team continued to strategize and take precautions, we remained aware of the potential risks and challenges ahead. It was crucial to proceed with both caution and determination in our pursuit of the truth.

I observed Marcy's expression, a visible grimace etched on her face, reflecting the weight of our circumstances.

"Mr. Joey, I had Agnes purchase these AirTags," JJ interjected, revealing four compact round tags. "Take them with you. If you encounter someone or something that we need to track, place an AirTag on them or it. We'll be able to monitor their location at all times."

I looked at JJ, blinking in acknowledgment. "Good thinking," I commended him for his resourcefulness.

In a matter of moments, Larry contacted us with an update. Sensing the urgency, Agnes informed him that our cell phone connection was compromised and instructed him to call me on my new cell phone from a landline.

Considering Larry's lack of a personal landline, he would need to find someone's home or locate a public phone in Laurel to make the call.

Twenty minutes later, Larry's voice came through the line. "What's going on?" he asked, eager for an update.

I proceeded to explain the possibility of our phones being monitored and instructed Larry to acquire local burner phones for both him and Harry.

"Larry, here's what I need you to do. In twenty minutes, text Agnes that you've discovered Megan Wright is driving to Hilton Head, South Carolina, to spend her leave time there."

"I've got it," Larry acknowledged.

"Now, tell me, what have you found out?" I inquired, eager for any new information.

"Not much, aside from the fact that she's on vacation with her husband and six-year-old son, according to the neighbors. However, they don't know the specific destination. Megan's husband works as an engineer for the local utility company, and they're generally a quiet family. That's about all we've gathered so far."

"Okay, that's helpful. If there's nothing more to uncover, consider heading back. Remember to maintain communication with us and be cautious," I advised Larry, emphasizing the importance of his safety.

"That plan will keep them busy chasing Megan in Hilton Head," Marcy remarked, seeking solace in the prospect of diversion.

"Indeed, or at least create some confusion," I replied, sharing her sentiment.

Agnes interjected, distributing copies of paper and phones to Lucy, Marcy, Dom, and JJ. "I've made copies for everyone. These are the burner phone numbers for each of us. They're fully charged and ready to use."

An hour later, we dropped off JJ at his place, and Marcy and I returned home, allowing me time to pack an overnight bag for my impending trip to North Carolina.

Following a late lunch, Marcy, Michelle Marie, and I settled in our living room, the gravity of our situation enveloping the space.

"I don't want you to worry about this trip," I began, attempting to assuage Marcy's concerns.

Marcy quickly extended her hand to halt my words, determination evident in her eyes. "I will not worry anymore. I can't. When you left the police force, I was relieved that you were no longer carrying a firearm. However, even in your private investigative work, there have been close calls and brushes with life and death. I was once abducted during a case, and another time, while I was pregnant, intruders entered our own apartment and restrained me. Mr. Pat and Father Dom have been shot in previous cases," she recounted, her voice wavering as tears welled up.

I moved closer, wrapping my arm around her, offering solace in my embrace.

Gently wiping away her tears, Marcy continued, "Allow me to finish. During our vacation last week, you were on the verge of being struck down by a Cuban MiG in the ocean. I've been consumed by worry, but I've reached a point where I can't let it consume me anymore. I understand that these are the risks you must take, and while I still harbor concerns, I've spoken with Father Dom, who shares in my worries. We have both placed our faith in God and entrusted Him to protect you."

I lowered my head, planting a tender kiss on her forehead, gratitude and love filling my heart. "Thank you for your understanding, and I apologize for causing you and Dom so much worry. I also worried when you carried a firearm. We take on these cases, often unaware of where they will lead us, like the current one. But please know that I'm not seeking danger for the thrill of it. I—"

Marcy gently interrupted, placing her index finger on my lips. "I know, and there's no need to explain. Just be careful and approach each situation with caution, as I know you can. Right now, we're facing numerous unknowns. Foreign governments are seeking to abduct Paul, and our own government may have its own agenda in this matter. We're up against powerful forces that couldn't care less about someone like you. So please, exercise utmost care."

Her words resonated deeply within me, reaffirming the need to navigate this treacherous path with vigilance and strategy. With Marcy's unwavering support and Father Dom's prayers, I embarked on this mission, fully aware of the dangers that lay ahead.

48
Thursday, 9 a.m.

After a nearly two-hour drive from Bristol, I arrived at the Bakersville residence of Megan Wright's mother. The picturesque summer day showcased a vibrant blue sky, and the lush green mountains provided a serene backdrop. Wildlife freely roamed, with deer and rabbits enjoying the peaceful surroundings.

A woman in her seventies greeted me at the door with a warm smile. "Good morning," she said cheerfully.

"Good morning," I replied. "Are you Megan's mother?"

"Yes, I am. I'm Donna Ashton. We weren't expecting anyone. Are you a friend of Megan's?"

"Mrs. Ashton, my name is Joey Mancuso. May I speak with Megan and her husband?"

"Please come in," she invited, gesturing for me to enter.

Stepping inside, I found myself in a spacious area that seamlessly blended the living room, dining area, and kitchen. An impressive fireplace adorned one side, flanked by two large windows that offered breathtaking views of the mountains.

"I'll fetch them for you. Please have a seat," Mrs. Ashton offered kindly before making her way through a covered patio and into the expansive yard beyond.

Within moments, a man and a woman, presumably Megan and her husband, entered the room. I rose to greet them, but their expressions lacked the same warmth I had seen on Mrs. Ashton's face.

Approaching me with a hint of suspicion, the man spoke first. "Who are you?"

"My name is Joey Mancuso. I'm a private investigator and a consultant to the NYPD," I introduced myself, emphasizing my affiliation with the police department to establish credibility.

"The NYPD? Why are you here?" the man inquired, with Megan standing by his side.

Noticing the dining table, I gestured toward it. "May we sit and discuss this?"

"Of course," the man replied.

All three of us moved to the table and took our seats.

"And you are?" I inquired, facing Tom while Megan sat beside him.

"I'm Tom Wright, and this is my wife, Megan. Now, why exactly are you here?"

Tom, a tall and handsome man in his forties, possessed black hair with hints of gray creeping in at the sides. Megan, also in her forties, exhibited an attractive appearance, with brown hair and striking green eyes.

"The NYPD has nothing to do with this. However, I was working with an FBI task force in Florida. I'm currently searching for a man named Paul Reinhard," I explained. As soon as I mentioned Paul's name, Tom's gaze shifted toward Megan, who grew visibly worried, blinking rapidly and crossing her arms.

"I believe Mr. Reinhard is in some kind of danger, potentially being held against his will," I continued, scanning the room. Leaning forward and speaking softly, I added, "I also suspect that those who are holding Reinhard might be looking for Mrs. Wright to ensure she doesn't reveal what she knows."

"She knows nothing," Tom swiftly interjected.

"Maybe she does, maybe she doesn't. She might possess enough information to make certain individuals uneasy. That's why you took leave, isn't it? That's why you're here?" I countered.

"As I said, Mancuso, Megan doesn't—"

"But I do," Megan interrupted her husband.

"We don't know who this guy is. You don't have to say anything," Tom cautioned Megan.

"You're right. You don't know who I am. However, if I had any ill intentions toward you, I wouldn't have come alone. My sole interest is locating Reinhard. He hired me in Florida because he feared for his life. All I want to know, Mrs. Wright, is who you spoke to after Special Agent Donnelly contacted the assistant director, who then passed the information on to the DOJ," I explained, stressing the urgency.

Megan hesitated, grappling with her decision.

Recognizing the need to push the case and present Paul as the victim, I continued, "Look, Mr. Reinhard's girlfriend was murdered in Florida. She was pregnant with their child. Someone abducted Reinhard and took him to Cuba. He was on the verge of being shipped against his will to China. Two others and I managed to extract him from Cuba. I simply want to ensure his safety and ascertain that he's not under any form of coercion. I need your help."

Megan's eyes widened at my account. She swallowed hard and whispered, "The assistant director never called the DOJ. There was a man in his office, supposedly from the DHS, who assured him he would handle Reinhard."

Finally, progress. "What is the name of that man?" I inquired eagerly.

As Megan hesitated to respond, we heard the sound of gravel being compressed on Little Mountain Road, indicating a vehicle approaching.

"Are you expecting anyone?" I asked.

"No, but it could be the neighbor up the road," Tom replied.

"Is there another way out of the house that doesn't lead to the road?" I inquired.

"We can walk down the tree-filled hill on our property to a creek by the road. But beyond that, there's nothing—just the road with very little traffic," Tom explained.

The sound of the approaching vehicle grew louder. Thinking quickly, I instructed them, "Tell your mother to say you went somewhere for the day if anyone knocks on the door. I'll follow you down in a minute. Now, go."

Concerned about their son Charlie, Megan pleaded, "What about Charlie?"

"Bring him with you," I replied, reassuring her.

Megan shouted for her son, who was upstairs in his room. "Come with us. We're going down the hill to the creek."

Charlie, excited for the adventure, swiftly made his way downstairs.

The three of them exited through the covered patio door, informing Mrs. Ashton of what to say. Meanwhile, I remained behind to observe if the vehicle would stop at their house.

As expected, an SUV pulled up the driveway, and two casually dressed men stepped out, knocking on the front door. I discreetly moved out of the living room and took cover on the covered patio. If Mrs. Ashton was in any danger, I would intervene. If not, I could easily evade the men by escaping into the small forest behind the house and reaching the creek.

"Hi, good morning," I heard Mrs. Ashton greet them.

"Hi, good morning," one of the men responded. "We work with Megan at the DOD and heard she was here. We just stopped by to say hello."

"Oh my goodness, she's going to be disappointed to hear that. She, Tom, and Charlie went to spend a night or two at Linville Falls. Can I tell her who was here to visit?"

"We'll be back to surprise them. Maybe we'll come back for a barbecue. Do you mind if we walk around and enjoy your beautiful property?" the man suggested.

"No, please help yourselves. Feel free to check out the hot tub on the open patio," Mrs. Ashton replied.

As they began exploring the property, I remained hidden, keeping a watchful eye on the situation, ready to act if necessary.

After the men left, I walked back inside the house to avoid being seen during their inspection. As they conducted a thorough inspection of the property, I found myself in the bathroom, aware that the entire house was visible through its generous-sized windows.

Once they completed their inspection, the two men returned to the front door and knocked again. Mrs. Ashton opened the door, and one of the men asked if he could use the restroom. Mrs. Ashton directed him to the upstairs bathroom, citing an issue with the septic tank downstairs. I listened as he flushed the toilet above me and descended the stairs. Would they leave or intend to stay longer?

Finally, the men thanked Mrs. Ashton and made their way back to their car, driving down the gravel road. I was confident that Tom, Megan, and Charlie would have heard their departure and taken cover.

Leaving the bathroom, Mrs. Ashton approached me and asked, "Mr. Mancuso, is Megan in danger?"

Uncertain of the situation, I replied, "Oh, you know how it is with all these government agencies. I'm sure it was just a friendly visit, maybe seeking information. I wouldn't worry too much." I hoped my words were reassuring, although I couldn't be certain myself.

Fifteen minutes later, Tom, Megan, and a breathless Charlie emerged from the woods.

"That was fun, Charlie," I said, addressing the young boy.

"Yeah, someone built a little bridge from the property over the creek," Charlie replied with excitement.

Megan inquired about how it went, to which I responded, "Your mother handled it like a pro. But yes, they were indeed looking for you."

Megan expressed her gratitude, saying, "You stayed behind to protect Mother. Thank you."

Turning to Tom, I added, "I think it would be wise for you both to go somewhere else."

Tom nodded in agreement, understanding the necessity of temporarily relocating. "It'll only be a few days. Once I find Reinhard, this will be over. Now, Megan, I need that name, please."

Megan hesitated before responding, "Xavier Thompson, with DHS."

49
Thursday, 11 a.m.

After Mrs. Ashton, or Donna as she preferred to be called, offered to make sandwiches for the road, I decided it might be best to wait a while before leaving. I wanted to give the men who had visited the house enough time to clear out and avoid any potential risks. My main concern was that they might linger in the area, waiting to see if anyone emerged from the property. The road to downtown Bakersville had numerous twists and turns where they could easily hide.

Donna's suggestion was met with approval from everyone, and Megan went to pack a few essentials. Meanwhile, I motioned for Tom to join me on the covered patio, away from earshot.

"Do you have any firearms?" I asked him, trying to assess our level of preparedness.

Tom nodded and replied, "Yes, I have two pistols and a rifle. Why do you ask?"

"I don't mean to alarm you, but it's better to be prepared in case those guys have any malicious intentions," I explained, my gaze shifting to the sliding glass door through which Megan was packing.

He considered my words and said, "I'm not sure if I want to take Charlie with us now."

"Perhaps leaving Charlie here with Donna while you two go on a short trip could be a good idea," I suggested.

Tom hesitated but eventually agreed, his eyes fixed on Megan in the master bedroom. "Megan might freak out, but it's a sensible plan."

"I'll drive with you until I have to head north to Bristol. Let me borrow one of your pistols, and I'll return it to you later down the road. Where were you thinking of going?" I inquired.

"I was considering heading south to Asheville," Tom replied.

"Good. Donna told them that you went northeast toward the Linville Falls area. I'm not sure if they bought it," I informed him.

An hour later, we were on the road, with Tom and Megan driving ahead of me. I kept a watchful eye for any suspicious vehicles that might be tailing us. We stayed together on US 226 until we reached Red Hill, where we would part ways. Tom would continue heading south to Asheville, while I would head north toward Bristol.

Pulling over to the side of the road, Tom approached my car, and I returned his pistol, which he discreetly concealed in his pocket.

"I believe you and Megan are in the clear now. This is my cell number. Call me if anything happens," I said, extending a piece of paper. "And may I have your number as well?"

"Thanks for everything, Mr. Mancuso. I hope you find this Reinhard person soon," Tom expressed his gratitude.

"I'll contact you immediately," I assured him.

Once I reached US 19, I dialed Agnes's number.

"Young woman, how's it going?" I inquired, expecting an update from her end.

"Hi, Joey. JJ is still monitoring the dark web. No hits so far. Lucy hasn't heard from Rupert, and Larry and Harry came back with no more information on Megan. How about you?" Agnes reported, keeping me informed.

"I need you to perform a 'cybernoscopy' on Xavier Thompson, most likely associated with DHS in DC. He's the individual Megan confided in regarding Reinhard's situation, and he informed the bureau's assistant director that he would handle it," I explained, referring to Agnes's comprehensive research on individuals.

"Ah, I see. So, you've found Megan," Agnes deduced, recognizing the situation.

"And it seems they found her too. Two men came looking for her. Perhaps we've bought ourselves some time, but now we need to locate Reinhard."

Agnes inquired, "Should I book a flight back to New York for you?"

"It depends on what you uncover about Xavier Thompson. I might consider paying him a visit in DC. He could be the quickest route to finding Reinhard, assuming he's willing to see me," I replied, considering the possibilities.

"Understood, boss. I'll collaborate with JJ to gather all the information we can find on Thompson. If there's any dirt to dig up, we'll find it. He's connected, and you need to know," Agnes assured me, ready to delve into her investigative work.

"Excellent. Keep me updated on your progress," I instructed, confident in her abilities.

"I'll continue the research and get back to you with any substantial findings. You'll be staying at the hotel in Bristol until tomorrow, correct? We can discuss our next steps then," Agnes confirmed our plan.

"Yes, that's right. Let's reconvene tomorrow and decide our course of action," I confirmed, visualizing the path ahead.

With ample time left to reach Bristol, I unpacked the sandwich Mrs. Ashton had prepared for me. I discovered an oversized brisket with melted Swiss cheese nestled between slices of homemade white bread. The sight was appetizing, and I savored each bite, ensuring not a single crumb found its way onto my clothes.

After two hours, I arrived back at the Fairfield Inn & Suites Hotel in Bristol when a knock resonated through my room, capturing my attention.

I opened the door to find the familiar faces of the two men who had previously visited the Bakersville home. Their attire remained casual, sporting jeans and pullover shirts, but now one of them had a windbreaker on, revealing a noticeable bulge under his left arm.

Curiosity piqued, I inquired, "Can I help you?"

"Mr. Mancuso, we have some questions for you. Can we come in?" the same man who had done all the talking at the house requested. He appeared to be around my age, with aviator sunglasses and an athletic build that hinted at his possible military background. He whispered with a slight smile.

The man in the windbreaker, who seemed more physically imposing with his oversized biceps, also wore sunglasses of the same style. His square jaw gave him a rugged look, suggesting he was the muscle behind the friendly façade.

Preferring to keep the conversation outside, I replied, "I'd prefer we talk out here."

"Mr. Mancuso, my name is Josh, and this is George, my associate," he introduced, presenting his credentials. "We're with the DOD, and we have some questions we'd rather ask in private."

As he spoke, George slid his hand under the windbreaker, prompting me to assess the situation. Deciding it was best to defuse any potential tension, I stepped back and gestured for them to come inside. However, I remained vigilant, keeping an eye on George for any sudden movements.

Then, an opportunity presented itself. I approached George, who towered about four inches above me, and seized his windbreaker, starting to pat him down.

George forcefully pushed me away, his voice filled with irritation. "Get the hell away from me."

"Yes, he's armed. We're authorized, Mr. Mancuso. No need to worry about that," Josh assured me.

Respecting their request, I stepped back and motioned toward the seating area. "Please, have a seat," I offered.

Josh and George surveyed the surroundings before settling on a two-seater sofa while I took a position across from them.

Curious about their intentions, I inquired, "What is it that you need to ask?"

Josh wasted no time in getting to the point. "What were you doing at the Ashton home in Bakersville?"

It became apparent that these agents had observed my car at the scene and now confirmed their suspicion by spotting it in the hotel parking lot. Additionally, they likely had prior knowledge of my destination by monitoring our calls before we switched to burner phones.

"Same thing you were there for. I wanted to speak to Megan Wright. Unfortunately, she was not there," I replied.

Josh sought further clarification, asking, "About what, sir?"

Not in the mood for an interrogation, I decided to lay it all out. "You know I'm looking for Paul Reinhard, and I believe you know where he is. I thought Mrs. Wright might have a clue where I could find him. But now that you're here, maybe you can enlighten me."

Josh and George exchanged glances, their expressions revealing a silent communication.

"We know what you've already done for Mr. Reinhard, and the department appreciates your help. We know the extraction from Cuba was hairy. But now your role is over, and there's nothing else for you to do," Josh responded.

Leaning in, I made my intentions clear. "If you tell me where he is, and I get the chance to speak with him, I'll consider ending my search. It's that simple."

George couldn't resist a smug remark, asking, "You'll consider?"

Josh's stern gaze silenced George as if commanding him to stay quiet. It seemed the larger man wasn't supposed to have a speaking part in this conversation.

"Mr. Mancuso," Josh pleaded, his tone softer, "you, of all people, should know that there are others who want to kidnap Mr. Reinhard. We have him under protection at the DOD. There's no need for you to continue your quest. He's safe and secure."

I responded with a smile, injecting a touch of familiarity, "By the way, no need to call me Mr. Mancuso; you can call me Mancuso. Mr. was my dad. Anyway, if he's truly safe and content where he is, he can tell me himself."

Josh's argument continued, "You don't seem to understand—the same way we found you, these other non-friendlies could be on your tail, and you'll lead them to Reinhard. Can't you see that?"

Their reasoning made sense, assuming these men were genuine and, indeed, protecting poor Paul. But what if they had ulterior motives for him?

"Tell you what, let's call your boss, Xavier Thompson, and have me get in touch with Reinhard," I proposed.

The exchange of glances between the two men and Josh's disapproving frown confirmed that I had struck a nerve by mentioning Thompson.

Josh stood up, signaling George to follow suit, indicating that our conversation was coming to an end.

Josh issued a stern warning, "We have warned you, Mancuso—cease and desist your search for Reinhard. Do not interfere in a national security situation. Nothing good can come of it. Understood?"

I stood my ground, matching his intensity. "The only security I'm concerned about is that of Reinhard. I don't deal with national big-picture stuff."

Josh moved closer, attempting to intimidate me. "Go back to New York and continue doing your little private detective work with your team. Take care of your family and your brother. You don't want the US government on your case. We can create many problems for you."

His threats didn't faze me. Instead, I took a step toward him and deliberately burped. It was a deliberate act of defiance.

Josh closed his eyes, visibly disgusted by my behavior.

"I hope you like brisket," I taunted. "Now, I don't take kindly to threats. I trust that was simply a suggestion."

"Take it any way you want. Stay the hell away from this," Josh retorted. He turned on his heel and walked out of my room, with George following closely behind.

At least I confirmed that these guys were indeed working for Xavier Thompson, the same person who intercepted Paul's call. However, the question still remained: were they the good guys protecting Paul, or were they forcing Paul to complete his program against his will?

50
Thursday, 2 p.m.

I returned to my room with a double-cheese Whopper and fries, a meal I hadn't indulged in for about fifteen years, ever since I found a Band-Aid in my last one, nestled between the tomato and lettuce. After carefully inspecting the food this time, I leaned back, smiled, and let the memories of my years on the force wash over me.

Although it wasn't a Whopper, it reminded me of a time when Lucy and I were parked on West Thirty-Fourth Street in Midtown, devouring burgers and fries from Five Guys. It was 2015, and just as we were enjoying our meal, a 10-10 call blared over the radio: "Ten-ten, shots fired at a bar at 237 West Thirty-Fifth Street."

Lucy swiftly started the car, exclaiming, "Tell them we're responding. We're only a block away." As I relayed the information, Lucy shifted gears, activated the lights, and maneuvered us into traffic, causing our entire meal, which sat on the dashboard, to catapult toward us. Mustard, ketchup, mayo, and the rest of the menu splattered all over our clothes. My khaki pants were drenched, resembling a urinary mishap. We were the first to arrive at the scene of an attempted armed robbery, which turned out to be unsuccessful as the bar owner managed to fend off the robber with a knife after two shots missed. One point for the good guys, although the uniforms who arrived later reported to the precinct that Detective Mancuso had wet himself at the scene.

Returning to the present, after my unexpected visitors had departed, I sent a text to Agnes and JJ, informing them that I had placed an Airtag on one of the guests. I asked them to trace its location and keep me updated. Perhaps it would lead me to Paul or reveal their destination, potentially back to DC.

My phone rang, displaying Agnes' name on the caller ID.

"Hey, Joey, got your text. Your guys are heading to the airport."

"Keep me posted if you can track where they're flying. Any updates from the dark web?" I inquired.

"JJ is still on it, but nothing significant yet. Lucy is here with me, and we're on speaker," Agnes replied.

"Hey, Lucy, any word from our elusive contact, Rupert?"

"Nothing, my dear. Hopefully, he's trustworthy and can provide assistance. I'm just waiting for his call," Lucy responded.

"Agnes, any progress on your research about Xavier Thompson?" I asked, eager for any new information.

"Xavier Thompson, a retired Air Force colonel, served in Air Force Intelligence during the Afghanistan war. He retired without any blemishes on his record, but there was a close call with a court-martial. He had provided false information regarding a drone strike that resulted in the deaths of twelve innocent civilians. However, the blame was shifted to the drone pilot, who is currently serving a five-year sentence. Thompson now works for an undisclosed department within the DOD and resides in DC," Agnes relayed the information.

"How the hell did he manage to avoid the court-martial?" I exclaimed in disbelief.

"Mr. Joey, this is JJ. They pinned it all on the drone pilot," JJ chimed in.

"Of course they did," I scoffed. "You know what? Find out where that pilot is and get me the full story about Thompson from him. It might come in handy."

"On it, Mr. Joey," JJ acknowledged.

"Do you have any names for the two guys who visited you? I can run a search," Agnes offered.

"No, just Josh and George. I doubt those are their real names. Let me know as soon as you have their destination, and book me a flight to wherever they're heading. I have a hunch about those two," I instructed.

"That might take a while before we can track their landing," Lucy interjected.

"I could use the downtime. Is Marcy available?" I inquired.

"No, she's currently meeting with Bevans and Associates. They might have a case that aligns with her expertise," Agnes informed me.

"Great. I'll catch up with her later then."

"Father Dom wanted you to know that he's on a retreat with some parishioners until Saturday," Agnes added.

I smiled, disposed of the Whopper remains, and walked outside to find a suitable spot to get rid of the lingering smell. "Saving souls, one retreat at a time. Good for him. Let me know when you have any updates."

Next, I called Tom and Megan to check in on them. Tom informed me that they were staying at a friend's house in Hendersonville, North Carolina and that everything was calm. It was a relief to hear that they hadn't checked into any places that could be traced. I couldn't help but feel a twinge of guilt for potentially putting Megan in danger with our phone conversations.

After a three-hour nap, Agnes woke me up with an update. Josh and George were heading west, possibly to Colorado, but the exact location was uncertain.

"There are several military bases in Colorado. They could be headed to one of those," I speculated.

"I'll see what I can find. Maybe we can narrow it down," Agnes said before ending the call.

Feeling groggy and anxious without a solid plan, I decided to take a cold shower to clear my head and shake off the fatigue. As the cold water poured over me, I tried to gather my thoughts.

Just as I was drying myself off, my phone rang with an unknown caller ID. It was Marcy.

"Joey, how are you?" Marcy asked.

"Glad you called. I'm doing alright. And how about you?" I replied.

"You sound like you're in a submarine. Where are you?" Marcy chuckled.

I couldn't help but smile at her comment. "In the bathroom, just took a shower. How did the meeting with Bevans and Associates go?"

"It went well. They have a client who suspects industrial espionage and wants our help to investigate. What do you think?" Marcy explained.

"That's your area of expertise. If you think we can assist, go ahead, and take the case. It's been a while since they've given us something," I replied.

"I'll discuss it with the team and get back to Bevans. And what about you? Still in a holding pattern in Tennessee?" Marcy asked.

"Something like that. It looks like I'll be heading west," I replied.

"Agnes is researching military bases in Colorado. Do you think they might be holding Paul in one of them?" Marcy inquired.

"It would make sense if that's where they're headed, but at this point, it's just speculation. We'll have to wait another hour or so to find out if they actually land in Colorado," I explained.

"Alright, we'll talk later then," Marcy said before ending the call.

Marcy's call brought some encouragement with the potential new case for our white-collar crime division. However, the current situation with Paul Reinhard felt like chasing a beach ball in a football stadium, bouncing in every direction without a clear destination.

After contemplating whether to reach out to Paul or not, I decided to take a chance and send him a text message. I typed, "How are you, buddy? How are things your way? Can we meet for a beer soon?"

As I hit the send button, a sense of anticipation mixed with worry washed over me. I wondered if Paul still had the phone or if it had been discovered by someone else. The thought of calling him directly crossed my mind, but I hesitated, afraid that it might raise suspicion if the phone was no longer in his possession.

I hoped that if Paul did have the phone, he would have it silenced to avoid drawing attention. Waiting for his response felt like an eternity, filled with questions and uncertainties about his situation.

Twenty minutes later a text came in. "Can't meet. I'm in a hole and need your help."

51
Thursday, 10 p.m.

As Agnes provided me with information about the Cheyenne Mountain Air Force Station, my mind raced with thoughts about the situation. The fact that the base's mission was to collect data and intelligence through various means raised concerns about Paul's program being exploited for their purposes. The thought of our own government forcing someone to complete such a task was unsettling.

Agnes suggested that perhaps they were offering Paul a significant amount of money to compel him to finish the program. While I doubted money was a motivating factor for Paul at this point, it was difficult to predict what might drive him.

The crucial question remained: How could I rescue Paul from the clutches of the base? Agnes reminded me that finding a solution to this problem was my responsibility.

As I pondered my next move, Agnes mentioned that part of the station was open to civilians, and there were additional attractions like a zoo and an archaeological site. This information sparked a glimmer of hope in me. If there was civilian access to the base, there might be a way to infiltrate and retrieve Paul without raising too much suspicion.

"I'll need more details about the civilian access and the surrounding areas," I told Agnes. "We need to find a way in that doesn't jeopardize Paul's safety or our mission. Keep digging for any additional information you can find."

Agnes assured me that she would continue her research, and we ended the call with a renewed determination to devise a plan to rescue Paul from the Cheyenne Mountain Air Force Station.

I felt a surge of concern as Agnes informed me about Father Dom's unexpected absence from his scheduled Masses. It contradicted the information we had that he was on a retreat with parishioners until Saturday. Something didn't add up, and it worried me.

"Agnes, this doesn't make sense. Father Dom should be on retreat. Did Father Andrews mention anything else? Did he try to contact Father Dom?"

Agnes replied, "Father Andrews said he tried calling Father Dom multiple times, but his calls went unanswered. He's concerned that something might have happened to him or that there's an emergency requiring his presence."

I furrowed my brow, pondering the situation. It seemed like the threads of various mysteries were converging all at once—the disappearance of Paul, the involvement of the government and military, and now the unexpected absence of Father Dom. I couldn't shake the feeling that these events were interconnected.

"I need you to reach out to Father Andrews again," I instructed Agnes. "Ask him if he has any additional information or if there's anything unusual happening at the parish. We can't afford to overlook any possibilities."

Agnes assured me that she would contact Father Andrews immediately and gather more details. I settled back in my seat as the flight took off, my mind consumed with thoughts of Paul, Father Dom, and the impending mission at the Cheyenne Mountain Air Force Station. Little did I know that the challenges awaiting me in Colorado would be greater than I had imagined.

I closed my eyes and tried to calm my racing thoughts. Marcy and Lucy were on the case, and I had to trust in their capabilities. JJ's update about tracing the last signal on my phone to Colorado Springs provided a glimmer of hope.

Perhaps it meant that Paul was also in the same vicinity, and I might be getting closer to finding him.

But my focus shifted back to Father Dom. His sudden disappearance was alarming, and I couldn't help but consider the worst-case scenarios. Did he meet with foul play? Was there an accident? The possibilities were distressing, and I wished there was something I could do at that moment.

During the two-hour-plus flight to Dallas, I felt a sense of helplessness, unable to take any immediate action. I mentally went over the possibilities and tried to devise a plan for when I landed in Colorado Springs. Finding Paul was my primary objective, but now I also had to uncover the truth about Father Dom's disappearance.

I knew that the next leg of my journey would bring me closer to the heart of the mysteries surrounding Paul and Father Dom, and I was determined to uncover the truth and ensure their safety.

52
Friday, 9 a.m.

I found myself in the restroom as soon as the seatbelt sign turned off, urgently dialing Marcy's number. Without waiting for her to respond, I blurted out, "What the hell is going on?"

Marcy's voice sounded concerned on the other end. "I'm here at the rectory with Father Andrews. Last night, Father Andrews went out to have dinner with some parishioners, while Dom stayed back at the rectory with no plans to leave. That was the last time Father Andrews saw him."

Lowering my voice, I expressed my worry, "Marcy, you know Dom. This isn't like him. And why would he text Agnes about being on a retreat? What's happening? Have we started tracking his phone?" The questions poured out of me, my anxiety reaching its peak.

"Take a breath, Joey. We're doing everything we can to gather more information. Dom's phone is still here, in his bedroom. Nothing has been touched," Marcy reassured me. "But you're right; it's not a good sign that he left his phone behind. We're also checking on the church's van. It's still parked there."

As Marcy spoke, the words of Josh, the spook from my time in Bristol, resurfaced in my mind. "Go back to New York and continue with your other private detective work; take care of your family and your brother. You don't want the US government on your case. We can cause you many problems." The key words "take care of your family and your brother" echoed ominously, casting doubt on the situation.

"Marcy, I think we're facing a serious problem," I confided, sharing my thoughts.

She responded with disbelief, "I can't believe anyone would do something like that. No, it can't be true."

"It all depends on who they are, Marcy. At this point, I don't trust anyone anymore. Maybe they know I'm getting closer to the truth, and now they have Dom to hinder or slow me down in finding Paul."

Marcy tried to inject some reassurance into her voice. "Joey, if that's the case, I'm sure someone will reach out to us. They wouldn't harm Dom."

"We can't be certain of that," I replied, urgency lacing my words. "The moment I touch down in Dallas, I'm flying back to New York. We need to figure this out."

Our conversation ended, and I exited the restroom to find a woman glaring at me impatiently. Apologizing quickly, I returned to my seat, checked my watch, and let out a sigh. Two more hours left on this flight, and all I could think about was Dom's disappearance.

After a tense conversation with Marcy, I felt a growing sense of urgency and concern. Father Dom's disappearance had taken a sinister turn, and I couldn't shake the feeling that it was somehow connected to Paul and the mysterious individuals who had been targeting us.

As the plane taxied to the gate in Dallas, I quickly gathered my belongings and made my way to the terminal. Turning on my phone, I saw a flurry of missed calls and messages from Marcy, Lucy, and Agnes. I dialed Agnes first, needing to get an update on the situation.

"Agnes, what's the latest?" I asked, my voice filled with urgency.

Agnes sounded worried as she replied, "Joey, we've been trying to trace Father Dom, but there's no sign of him. Marcy and Lucy are speaking with the local authorities, and we're doing everything we can to find him. But there's still no word from Paul either."

I sighed, feeling the weight of the situation. "Agnes, I don't think this is a coincidence. It feels like someone is intentionally trying to disrupt our search for Paul. Dom's disappearance, it all adds up. We need to stay vigilant and consider every possibility."

"I know you're all doing your best. Just focus on getting me back to New York."

"Joey, if you're right, that's exactly what they want you to do. We are—" Agnes began to say, but I interrupted her, my voice filled with concern.

"Has anyone checked the hospitals?" I asked urgently.

"That and more. No sign of Dominic O'Brian," Agnes replied, avoiding using the word 'morgue' to spare me unnecessary distress. "We're also looking into camera footage near the church, hoping to find any leads."

"Keep searching, Agnes. Leave no stone unturned. I'll call you from Colorado," I instructed her before ending the call.

The situation perplexed me. If they had Father Dom, what did they want from me? I had no leverage or bargaining power. Was it our own government behind this? Or perhaps a foreign entity, like the Chinese, who believed I had Paul and wanted to negotiate? The lack of clear answers only added to my frustration.

As we approached the gate in Colorado, I was on my feet, ready to deplane, much to the flight attendant's disapproval. I sat for a brief moment, gathering my thoughts, before hastily exiting the aircraft.

Once in the airport, my singular focus was finding Xavier Thompson, the retired Air Force colonel who now worked for an undisclosed department within the DHS. He was the one who intercepted the FBI call about Paul. I pulled out the sheet of paper Agnes had prepared with our burner phones and immediately dialed Lucy.

Without exchanging pleasantries, I cut to the chase. "I need Thompson's number. Can you get it from Rupert?"

Lucy understood the urgency in my voice and replied, "We already have it for you. JJ noticed Paul's text to you, but he couldn't trace the location of the phone."

"I'm certain Paul is in the Cheyenne Mountain station. His message about being in a hole must refer to the cave," I shared my deduction.

"Alright. No updates on Father Dom yet, but we're doing everything we can. I'm sure he's safe," Lucy reassured me, trying to instill hope.

I closed my eyes, silently acknowledging that hope was all we had for now. "Thanks, Lucy. Keep me informed and send me Thompson's number."

Sitting alone at an empty gate, I anxiously awaited the text message. As soon as it arrived, I dialed Thompson's number. However, my call went unanswered, and there was no voicemail to leave a message. Frustration welled up within me. It seemed Thompson was deliberately avoiding my call.

The journey ahead was uncertain, and the stakes were higher than ever. But I was determined to uncover the truth, even if it meant facing the unknown and risking everything I held dear.

My phone rang, and without glancing at the caller ID, I swiftly answered. "Mr. Thompson—"

"Joey, this is Marcy. We have a lead on Dom. A parishioner witnessed him leaving the rectory with two men. Dom willingly got into their car, and they drove away. JJ and Agnes are currently reviewing the surveillance footage from nearby cameras."

"Did the parishioner notice whether the men sat in the front and Dom in the back or if one of them joined Dom in the backseat?" I inquired, hoping for more details.

"They were wearing suits, and indeed, one of the men sat in the back with Dom. I understand what you're thinking," Marcy responded.

"Exactly. It doesn't seem like Dom went willingly. I'm trying to get in touch with Xavier Thompson to unravel this situation, but he's not answering my calls."

"Even if you manage to reach him, who knows how forthcoming he'll be with information?" Marcy cautioned.

"I might need some leverage against him. Did we dig up anything on the drone pilot who took the blame for Thompson's intelligence mishap?" I inquired, hoping for a potential angle to work with.

"Give me a moment," Marcy requested. After a brief pause, she resumed, "Yes, we did find something, but we temporarily put it on hold. The pilot's name is Bruce Frazer. He's currently serving time at Leavenworth military prison in Kansas. He has about one more year left on his sentence."

Suddenly, my phone rang again, but the caller ID appeared as "blocked." Without hesitation, I tapped the green button and greeted, "This is Mancuso."

A mechanical voice emitted from the other end, sending a shiver down my spine. "Mr. Mancuso, if you wish to see your brother alive again, cease your pursuit of Paul Reinhard. Return to New York, and within the next forty-eight hours, we will release your brother."

53
Thursday, 5:30 p.m.

Finally, the call I wanted the most came in.

"Mr. Mancuso," he greeted me in a somewhat amiable tone, "welcome to Colorado Springs. I hope you're here as a tourist because otherwise, you have no business being here."

"Listen, Thompson," I began assertively, "what do you know about my brother?"

"Your brother?" he responded with surprise. "He's a pastor at a Catholic church in Brooklyn. Why?"

"You had no involvement in his abduction?" I demanded, seeking answers.

"I'm sorry, Mancuso, but I have no idea what you're talking about," he claimed.

"I'm tired of playing games. I've had enough of the secrecy and lies. If anything happens to my brother, I'll hold you personally accountable. And I will uncover how you managed to escape unscathed while Bruce Frazer took the blame for innocent lives lost."

Silence enveloped the conversation for a few moments. "Mancuso, perhaps we should meet in person to resolve this. I can arrange for a car to pick you up. I'm confident we can clear up any misunderstandings," Thompson proposed.

"Where should we meet?" I inquired, my skepticism still lingering.

"You were attempting to find your way to the Cheyenne Mountain Space Force Station. I can have you driven there," he offered.

And end up in some damn hole like Reinhard? I wanted to retort. "How about we meet in a public place instead? What about the zoo outside the base?" I suggested.

"Sounds reasonable. I'll send a car for you," he agreed.

"Thank you, but I'll arrange my own transportation," I replied.

Twenty-five minutes later, I arrived at the entrance of the Cheyenne Mountain Zoo. Three individuals who didn't resemble typical tourists stood near the prominent zoo sign. Approaching me was a tall, handsome man in his fifties. He wore light-gray slacks and a blue button-down shirt and carried a folded gray jacket over his left arm.

Extending his hand, he introduced himself, "I'm Xavier Thompson."

My initial inclination was to refrain from shaking hands, but I ultimately extended my hand and shook Thompson's. He glanced around and gestured toward a bench near the entrance. "Let's talk," he suggested.

We took a seat on the bench while his two companions maintained a distance of about twenty yards.

Without wasting time, I began, "I don't want to beat around the bush. You're aware that I'm searching for Paul Reinhard. I'm genuinely concerned for his well-being and, frankly, his freedom."

Thompson nodded, signaling for me to continue.

"I believe he's here, likely being coerced to complete some program against his will. Furthermore, I've received warnings both from your agents and a computerized voice on the phone, urging me to cease my efforts, or else my brother's abduction could take a darker turn."

"And you suspect the involvement of the US government in all this?" Thompson inquired.

I spread my arms and opened my palms. "You tell me."

"Mancuso, I understand that national security matters might not be what you want to hear about. Josh and George, my two agents, have made that clear to me. Much of this information is classified, but I'll try to give you a general overview. The computerized message you mentioned? Not our doing. Josh and George instructed you to stop at my request. Furthermore, we have no connection to your brother's disappearance, and I've already directed the New York FBI office to investigate it thoroughly."

"My wife—"

"Yes, I'm aware," he interjected, "she's a former FBI agent. We're currently in the process of contacting her."

I surveyed the bustling crowd entering the zoo, resting my elbows on my knees. Opening my palms, I posed the question, "Is Paul Reinhard here?"

Thompson leaned back. "I'm afraid you've made a wasted trip. No, Reinhard isn't here, and we have no intentions of compelling him to complete any program."

A smile crept onto my face. "Now you're feeding me a load of nonsense. We traced the phone I lost during the extraction from Cuba, the one Reinhard found on the boat, to this location. He's been texting me from it."

Thompson reached into his jacket pocket and produced a black phone. "Is this your phone?"

I examined it closely. "No, it isn't."

"Use your burner phone and call your original number that you have."

I followed his instructions, dialing my own number. The phone Thompson held began to ring, and he answered, establishing a connection between us. "I'll leave it on for your people to trace it. Your phone was cloned, and today we found this phone here at the base."

"Today, after eleven days of Reinhard being missing. Quite the coincidence, don't you think?" I remarked skeptically.

"As soon as we learned you were coming here, we assumed your team had traced the location of your phone. That's why we initiated a search," Thompson explained.

I stood up to stretch my legs. "So, who had the cloned phone?"

Just as I asked, my burner phone received a second call. Thompson instructed me to answer it. It was JJ on the line.

"Mr. Joey, are you talking to Reinhard on the phone at the Cheyenne Mountain Zoo?" JJ asked.

I glanced at Thompson, who had a smile on his face.

"Yes and no. It's a long story. I'll call you back," I replied to JJ before disconnecting the call.

Thompson also ended his call with my burner phone. "You have a talented team working with you. But they have managed to deceive all of you."

"Who had the clone?" I pressed.

"You met agents Hood, Richard, John, and Tuck in Islamorada," Thompson revealed.

"Yes, all bogus names, of course. But what about them?" I inquired.

"We have our reasons for using aliases. It's part of the job. In any case, the clone was hidden in one of Hood's carry-on bags."

"And conveniently, you discovered it today."

"Yes, we did."

"Are the Robin Hood characters here?" I asked, suspecting the answer.

"I suppose that was obvious. This is where things become classified. Let's just say that Hood and John are here. Unfortunately, we've lost contact with Tuck and Richard."

"When did this happen?" I questioned, feeling perplexed.

Thompson hesitated. "We're working on the case, and we can't allow you to interfere any further. You're making it difficult for us to carry out our duties."

I sat on the bench, gazing up at the bright blue sky. Closing my eyes, I tried to recall the events. "Sergeant Leone and Deputy Joyce from the Monroe County Sheriff's Office showed up at the Boca Chica Naval Station in Islamorada as I was leaving. They were supposed to take Reinhard to DC for debriefing. That's when you lost Reinhard and your two agents, right?"

"I want to locate Mr. Reinhard just as much as you do, but—" Thompson started.

"Don't give me any more excuses," I interrupted. "Leone had a warrant for Reinhard's arrest in connection with the deaths of the two Cubans in Islamorada. And you handed him over?"

"Leone insisted on questioning Reinhard. Tuck and Richard volunteered to accompany Reinhard to Leone's station. It was all happening right there in Key West," Thompson explained.

I shook my head in disbelief. "It's unbelievable that a county sheriff could take someone in federal custody without you guys intervening. Especially after the trouble we went through to extract Reinhard from Cuba."

"That's why Tuck and Richard went along," Thompson replied.

"It's completely out of character for your agency to allow that. So now they're all missing? The sergeant, the deputy, and your agents with Reinhard?" I asked, seeking confirmation.

"Yes. The bureau has sent a team down there to work on the case alongside two of our agents. And I repeat, you need to stay out of it," Thompson insisted.

"After everything that's happened, do you honestly think I'm going to listen to that?" I retorted.

"You have your brother to think about, right?" Thompson's response angered me. It felt like a veiled threat.

"Listen, Thompson, if anything happens to my brother, I'll dig deeper into your Afghanistan misinformation and the scapegoating of Bruce Frazer, the drone pilot."

Thompson frowned, straightened his posture, and sternly said, "Save yourself the trouble, Mancuso. Although it's classified, Frazer was court-martialed and imprisoned for being under the influence of narcotics. I proved that my information was correct. Frazer had been given the right coordinates. So let's leave it at that, and don't ever repeat what I just told you. I have nothing to do with Father Dom's disappearance."

I stood up, walked away from the bench, and started searching for a taxi. I needed to decide—should I head back to New York and assist in the search for Dom or go to Key West? The uncertainty gnawed at me as I made my way to the airport.

54
Friday, 8 p.m.

As I settled into my seat on the plane, I booked a flight to New York and another one to Miami International Airport. It pained me to have to return to the Keys without helping in the search for Dom. At the airport, I purchased a new burner phone and immediately called Marcy to check for updates.

"Any news?" I inquired anxiously.

"You need to come back here," Marcy replied. "The bureau is now involved in the case, and JJ just found the car used in Dom's abduction in Queens. We haven't informed the bureau yet. What do you think?"

"That's great news," I said, feeling a glimmer of hope. "But I'm uncertain about who I can trust anymore. Do you know the agents who are assisting?"

"I do. They both work in the criminal division. I would trust them," Marcy assured me.

"Don't contact my old burner phone. It's been compromised. This is my new burner number. There's a flight leaving at 12:40 on United that will get me to LaGuardia by 1:30 in the morning."

"I'll arrange for a sitter and pick you up. What did you find out about Paul?" Marcy asked.

"How's Michelle Marie?" I inquired, wanting to hear about my daughter.

"She's teething and asking about you," Marcy chuckled.

"Of course she is. Good news about Paul. He's not here. I'll fill you in on the details when I arrive. Contact the agents and inform them about the car's location. Maybe Lucy and I can join the investigation. I love you."

"Love you back, Mancuso. Take care," Marcy replied.

As the plane reached cruising altitude, I ordered a double shot of tequila. The news of the car's discovery had filled me with enthusiasm, but fatigue began to set in. I sipped my drink, and before I knew it, we were landing at O'Hare for a layover. Rather than disembarking, I decided to stay on the plane, bribing the flight attendant for a couple more tequilas before drifting back to sleep. The next destination was New York City.

At LaGuardia Airport, I stepped out into the terminal, scanning the crowd for Marcy. It didn't take long for me to spot her smiling face and her waving arm beckoning me over to the car. I tossed my bag in the backseat, hugged Marcy tightly, and kissed her.

"Any news?" I asked eagerly as I settled into the car and buckled up.

"We're heading there," Marcy said, merging into traffic and making her way toward the destination. "The bureau and NYPD have a stakeout at a single-story home on 172nd Street in Queens. They located the car, and then a man drove out of the house. We followed him, and he picked up an Asian-looking man at the Democratic People's Republic of Korea Embassy and brought him back to the house. As far as I know, they're still there."

"So now we have North Koreans involved in this. Do they have any photos of the two men?" I asked, hoping for any leads that could help us locate Dom.

"I'm sure they do, but I haven't seen them yet. But there's more," Marcy said, her tone becoming more serious as she changed lanes.

I leaned in, my eyes wide with anticipation. "What is it?"

"JJ intercepted messages on the dark web about an auction for a computer expert. We believe it's for Paul Reinhard."

"That explains why they're in New York City. Many countries with an interest in Reinhard have embassies or consulates here," I replied, connecting the dots.

Marcy glanced to her right and made another unexpected lane change. "So, what exactly happened at the Boca Chica Naval Station? I thought the DOD agents were supposed to fly Paul to DC."

I recounted the events, explaining how Sheriff Leone and Deputy Joyce arrived with a warrant for Reinhard and left with Tuck and Richard. None of them have been seen since.

"Oh, my God. You think the sheriff and the deputy are involved in this?" Marcy exclaimed, shock evident in her voice.

"I think we have two more homicides in the Keys. It's possible that either Tuck or Richard contacted the sheriff, arranged for Reinhard's arrest, and then got rid of both the sheriff and the deputy," I speculated.

Twenty minutes later, we reached Seventy-Third Avenue and 172nd Street, greeted by a chaotic scene of flashing red and blue lights from police vehicles, unmarked cars, fire trucks, and EMT vans. Yellow crime scene tape marked the area, hindering our progress on Seventy-Third Street.

My heart sank. What had happened? Why were the EMTs present? Had someone been killed or injured?

Marcy parked the car in front of a nearby home, and we stepped out. We were about a hundred yards away from the house where all the commotion emanated. The air was filled with tension and uncertainty.

"I have my NYPD consultant credentials," I said to Marcy, urging her to do the same. The uniformed officer guarding the crime scene tape was an old acquaintance from my time on the force.

"Charlie," I called out, recognizing him. "What the hell is going on here?"

"Mancuso, how you doing?" Charlie greeted me. "We have a DOA and another person seriously injured. That's all I know. Oh, and the house caught on fire."

"We need to go in there," I insisted, showing him our credentials.

"You're on this case?" Charlie asked, surprised.

I nodded. "Very much so."

Charlie lifted the crime scene tape, allowing Marcy and me to enter. We hurried toward the house, about twenty yards away. As we approached, I noticed two stretchers being wheeled out of the house. The first one carried a body bag, while the second was still too far back to identify.

Out of breath, I stopped and bent over, placing my hands on my knees and taking deep breaths to recover. Marcy asked if I was alright, and I motioned for her to give me a moment.

"Come on, before they take the stretchers away," Marcy urged me, aware of the urgency. We resumed our pace, heading toward the EMT van.

The two bureau agents, whom Marcy knew, noticed her and approached. As we reached the EMT van, she introduced me as her husband and emphasized our need to see the victims.

Both agents instructed the EMT to unzip the body bag, revealing the deceased individual inside. One of the agents asked if I recognized him.

Closing my eyes briefly, I said a silent prayer before responding, "His name is supposedly Agent Richard with the DOD. I need to see the other victim."

I turned toward the other van, where I could see Father Dom's head wrapped in gauze and slightly elevated on the stretcher. Marcy confirmed his identity.

"How is he?" I inquired as I stood by his side. One of the FBI agents signaled the EMT to proceed.

"He's unconscious, with various injuries to the body and head. Likely broken ribs and a cut to the back of his head from a blunt object," the EMT informed us.

"What are his vitals?" I asked, concerned.

The EMT responded, "Oxygen levels are very low, blood pressure is high, but we'll stabilize him immediately."

"I'm going with him," I stated firmly, turning to Marcy.

"Go. I'll stay behind and find out more," Marcy assured me. "Where are you taking him?"

"New York-Presbyterian in Flushing," the EMT person replied hurriedly as they closed the doors and the ambulance began to pull away.

I nodded to Marcy, acknowledging her plan to gather more information at the scene. With a sense of urgency, I quickly made my way back to the car and prepared to follow the ambulance to the hospital.

55
Saturday, 7 a.m.

Marcy had arrived at six with coffee, bagels, and some fresh clothes. I had been by Dom's side all night as the EMT crew performed necessary procedures. Dom lay there, connected to various hoses through his nose and mouth. The incessant sound of the ventilator was starting to wear on my nerves.

I updated Marcy on what had taken place. Upon our arrival at the hospital, Dom underwent an MRI, revealing an acute subdural hematoma—an accumulation of blood outside the brain causing pressure. He underwent a procedure called "burr hole trephination," during which a hole was drilled in the subdural hematoma to suction out the blood. Currently, Dom is relying on life-support equipment to help him breathe and receive nourishment.

"How is he doing now?" Marcy asked, her concern evident.

"It's too early to say," I replied. "The doctors managed to alleviate the pressure on his brain by removing the accumulated blood. However, he's still classified as being in serious condition, even though his vitals are stable."

"He would want us to pray," Marcy said, her voice filled with faith.

"That's exactly what I've been doing all night—here and at the chapel while he was undergoing the procedure."

"Lucy and Agnes are on their way," Marcy informed me. "I've told the rest of the team to wait until they move Dom to his room. We can't all be in the ICU at once."

Though I heard Marcy's words, my mind was elsewhere, and I simply responded, "Good, good."

"Do the doctors have any prognosis?" Marcy inquired gently.

Without meeting her gaze, I answered, "The prognosis remains uncertain for now. Based on the limited information I've gathered from the doctors, younger individuals tend to have a better chance of survival. And since Dom received immediate treatment, his chances are further improved. The doctors seem cautiously optimistic about his recovery."

Marcy moved closer and clasped my hand. "He's going to pull through. Remember, he has a connection to the higher power. By the way, Father Andrews will be coming in later."

I took comfort in Marcy's words and the knowledge that our dear friend Father Andrews would be joining us soon. Together, with unwavering faith and support, we would navigate this challenging time and remain by Dom's side, believing in his strength to overcome.

I didn't reply. Father Andrews could give Dom his last rites, just in case. I couldn't help but reflect on all the times I had put myself and those close to me in life-and-death situations. Dom, now twice, Marcy, Mr. Pat, Jack Ryder, and myself. Was it all worth it? We were private investigators, not frontline crime fighters. But it seemed that our line of work, dealing with murders, came with its fair share of danger. Perhaps it was time to retire to central Florida, spend my days fishing, and maybe even open a small sports bar near a football stadium in Tampa or Jacksonville.

"A penny for your thoughts," Marcy said, interrupting my musings.

I turned away from Dom to look at her. "Have you ever been excited about moving to a small town, buying a house with a picket fence, getting two dogs, and having a bunch of little Mancusos?"

Marcy's brows furrowed. "Is that what's been on your mind?"

"That's what I've been thinking," I confessed. "If Dom doesn't make it through this, I'm done with this dangerous game. I can't keep putting all of us in jeopardy of losing our lives because of our work. It's not fair to anyone, especially not you and Michelle Marie. Or anyone else."

Before Marcy could respond, Lucy and Agnes walked into the room. We embraced each other, and Marcy brought them up to speed on Dom's condition.

Agnes spoke up, "Mr. Pat wanted to fly up as soon as I told him, but I advised him to wait and we'll keep him informed."

"Thank you, Agnes. I'll give him a call later," I said gratefully.

After a moment of silence, Lucy asked, "So, what happened?"

Lost in my thoughts, I hadn't answered Lucy's question. Marcy took the lead and explained, "It appears there was a confrontation at the house. A loud explosion occurred at the back of the house, drawing all the neighbors out of their homes and causing chaos. Three men took advantage of the commotion and disappeared into the crowd."

"You mentioned that someone brought a person from the North Korean Embassy," I interjected.

"Presumably, one of the men who ran out is the person they brought from the embassy. The identities of the other two are still unknown," Marcy clarified.

"So, those would be Reinhard and the so-called Agent Tuck," I speculated.

Lucy was intrigued. "How do you know?"

I recounted the events that took place at Boca Chica Naval Station involving Sheriff Leone and the others.

"We believe the North Koreans were there to either bid on or pay for Reinhard, and they most likely intended to take him back to their embassy," Marcy explained.

"Good Lord, that would have been the end of Reinhard," Agnes remarked.

Marcy continued, "Tuck or the North Korean shot Richard, the deceased individual at the scene. We're not sure of the motive, but they set a fire as a diversion to make their escape."

"And those bastards beat up Dom and left him behind to burn," I muttered quietly.

Everyone turned their gaze toward Dom. Agnes inquired, "Was he badly burned?"

"No, luckily, there was a retired firefighter living next door who rushed into the house and rescued Dom and Richard from the fire," Marcy responded.

"And they managed to escape?" Agnes asked.

Agnes's question triggered a thought. I grabbed my burner phone and dialed my original number. If Reinhard answered, great. If not, I could try Agent Xavier Thompson, who had the clone phone.

There was no answer. Then I remembered that Thompson had called my burner earlier. I scrolled through my contacts and found his number.

"Mancuso, what's going on?" Thompson asked.

"Before I tell you, I need to know Tuck's real name. It's of utmost importance," I asserted.

"Mancuso, you have to understand that—"

I was not in the mood for bureaucratic nonsense. "Listen, Thompson, Richard was shot and killed, most likely by Tuck, just as they were about to sell Reinhard to the North Koreans. They escaped after nearly killing my brother. So, you're either with us or against us. What is Tuck's real name?"

There was a brief silence. "Thompson?" I prompted.

"His real name is Zacharias Brown, but he goes by other aliases as well. We all do," Thompson finally revealed.

"We need to issue a BOLO for Zacharias Brown," I told Marcy, keeping Thompson on the line. "I need all his known aliases too. This guy isn't getting away."

Reluctantly, Thompson provided me with two additional names, which I quickly relayed to Marcy so she could include them in the BOLO with the bureau.

"Thank you, Thompson," I expressed my gratitude before ending the call.

"I'm going to call JJ and have him research these names for any known associates here in New York," Agnes stated, taking charge of the task.

Suddenly, an alarm blared above Dom's bed. The blood pressure readings on the monitor started rapidly increasing.

Panicking, I rushed to seek help, but before I could, a team of doctors and nurses rushed into the room.

"Everybody out!" a nurse shouted, her voice filled with urgency.

Desperate for answers, I asked, "What's happening?"

One of the medical professionals responded, "He's having a seizure."

56

Saturday, 10:15 a.m.

After twenty minutes of anxiety, as we waited outside Dom's door, the doctor came out.

Dom's condition had stabilized once again, but the doctor warned us that these seizures could recur as the pressure subsided, and there was also a risk of potential hemorrhages. He was still in a precarious state, requiring close monitoring by a nurse. We were asked to give him space and remain outside the room.

We gathered in the hallway, contemplating our next steps.

"What are you going to do?" Marcy inquired, concern evident in her voice.

"I'm staying right here until he regains consciousness," I firmly declared.

Lucy chimed in, "I've requested police protection for Dom. We'll have a uniform stationed outside his door twenty-four seven."

"Excellent, Lucy. Thank you. I doubt anyone will attempt anything, considering Tuck, or Zacharias, is on the run with Reinhard, and the North Korean operative is back at their embassy," I responded, acknowledging her proactive approach.

Marcy added optimistically, "Let's hope Zacharias is greedy and tries to sell Reinhard again. If he does, it might lead us to him. Otherwise, if he decides to flee, Reinhard becomes unnecessary baggage."

A nurse approached us, politely requesting that we relocate to the waiting room. We complied, finding a secluded corner where we could continue our discussion in hushed tones.

"Let's brainstorm this. Suppose Zacharias succeeded in selling Reinhard. What would be his next move?" I pondered aloud.

Lucy promptly replied, "He'd most likely leave town, assuming one of his aliases."

"I'm not so sure," Marcy interjected. "He knows that the Department of Defense is actively searching for him. Would he risk using his known aliases?"

"He might have other identities that we're unaware of," Lucy speculated. "But with his face plastered everywhere now, I doubt he would risk trying to flee via an airport."

"I agree," I concurred. "We have to consider that he wasn't planning to take Reinhard to a country that would pay for him. Going to China or North Korea seems unlikely."

Agnes chimed in, posing an important question, "So, are we assuming he's on the run, or is he planning to negotiate for Reinhard's release?"

We exchanged thoughtful glances, realizing that the answers to these questions could determine our next course of action.

I said, "This guy didn't strike me as a computer whiz. If he tries to sell Reinhard, he needs to know how to connect to the dark web and navigate that world. But he ran without a computer, so he would have to set up somewhere else and find a way to get access."

Lucy posed the question, "So, are you thinking he's on the run without Reinhard?"

I replied, "I suppose it depends on how much money he has. Reinhard is worth millions to him, and he was close to striking a deal with the North Koreans."

Marcy chimed in, sharing her insight, "My guess is he's going to try the North Koreans again. He won't find a new buyer at this point."

Curious about my perspective, Lucy asked, "What would you do, Joey?"

"I would contact the North Korean mission, arrange the deal again, and have them pick me and Reinhard up at a predetermined location. Part of the agreement would involve a wire transfer and safe transportation out of the USA. That's what I would do," I explained.

Agnes added, "That seems like the most logical course of action. It's unlikely that he would attempt to set up a completely new deal. But how do we prevent that?"

Lucy suggested, "We could set up a perimeter in front of the Korean Mission and search every car entering."

"That would keep Zacharias out if he sees the increased security," I acknowledged. "But if he realizes that, he might just decide to eliminate Reinhard and make a run for it."

Marcy pointed out the challenge, saying, "We can't monitor every vehicle leaving the embassy. The bureau or NYPD won't be able to do that."

Inspiration struck me, and I smiled as I said, "What if we had a way to know when, where, and how the Koreans are planning to execute that plan?"

"That would change the game entirely," Marcy remarked.

I stepped outside the hospital, pulling out my phone to dial Xavier Thompson's number.

Thompson answered, "Mancuso, we're doing everything we can on our end to locate Agent Brown."

"Probably not everything," I replied confidently. "Here's what we think is going to happen..." I proceeded to explain our supposition, finding shelter under an awning to escape the scorching heat.

"And you assume we can do that?" Thompson questioned.

"Come on, Xavier. You probably already know what I had for breakfast this morning. I'm sure you're aware of what's happening in there. Just give me a call, and we can take it from there," I suggested.

"That would be completely out of order. We need to follow protocol," Thompson insisted.

"Isn't this a matter of national security? How would you explain losing Reinhard to the North Korean government?" I questioned.

Thompson responded, "The State Department would have to give us the green light, Mancuso. I can't act on my own in dealing with a foreign government."

"Exactly. And that process could take weeks as it moves up the chain of command. Meanwhile, Reinhard could be in Pyongyang, and your guy Brown would be lost forever. The higher-ups in DC would not be happy about that," I pointed out.

"It's a tough call," Thompson admitted.

I pressed on, stating, "Listen, Thompson, they won't be using an official car for this operation. No flags or typical markings. If you give me a call when you have the information, no one will ever know what happened. I have a plan."

"That's what I'm afraid of. You've had a plan since you encountered and lost Reinhard in Islamorada a few weeks ago. And from what I've heard, your actions have added millions to the national debt," Thompson quipped.

His response puzzled me. It seemed like he was leaning toward agreeing, yet he chose to make light of our efforts. I expected a more serious tone if he had no intention of helping me.

"Well, I expect that call," I stated confidently, adopting an assumptive posture.

"We'll see," Thompson replied before disconnecting the call.

57
Saturday, noon

Returning to the waiting room, I gathered the women together. "Okay, I have a plan in motion. Agnes, get in touch with Larry and Harry. Have them call me immediately, or better yet, ask them to come here. Marcy, reach out to your agent friends and let them know to be prepared to apprehend Zacharias and recover Reinhard at a moment's notice."

Lucy asked, "What's the plan?"

I shared the details of my plan with the women, omitting the identity of the person who would be giving me the necessary information. If things went awry, it was best that they were not aware of my source.

"Let's go check on Dom," I suggested.

Upon entering Dom's room, we found him alone, which was a positive sign. He was being closely monitored from the nurses' station, and a uniformed officer stood guard outside the room with whom Lucy had been speaking.

I requested to speak with a doctor while Marcy and I stayed by Dom's side. Lucy and Agnes would return later. Before Lucy left, I pulled her aside to discuss another matter.

About twenty minutes later, Doctor Alberto Gonzalez entered the room, his name tag clearly visible.

"How is he, Doctor?" I inquired as he examined Dom's medical chart.

"You're Mr. Mancuso, his brother?" he confirmed.

"Yes, sir, and this is my wife, Marcy," I said.

Doctor Gonzalez nodded in acknowledgment. "We were considering the possibility of performing another trephination procedure to drain more blood, but it doesn't appear necessary at this point. His vital signs are stable, and we conducted an EEG, which indicated normal brain function.

These are positive signs. He is showing signs of improvement, but recovery will take time," the doctor explained.

"When you say time, are we talking days, weeks, or even longer?" I inquired.

"I can't provide a definitive timeline. It varies from patient to patient. However, your brother is progressing well," Doctor Gonzalez replied.

Expressing our gratitude to the doctor, Marcy and I took seats next to Dom's bed, feeling a sense of relief and optimism.

Things were starting to look better. We had a plan in place, or at least I believed so, to apprehend Zacharias Brown and rescue poor Paul Reinhard. However, the success of the plan hinged on Thompson's cooperation. I had to believe that he would find a way to help us. Allowing North Korea to kidnap Paul would be a career-ending mistake for him, and I was determined to ensure that everyone would know about it.

Marcy brought up the question we had discussed earlier. "Should we talk about the question you asked?" she inquired.

Before I could respond, Larry and Harry entered the room, displaying their credentials to the uniformed officer stationed outside the door.

"I'll get some sandwiches while you talk to the guys. Anything for you both?" Marcy offered.

Larry and Harry politely declined the offer as we began discussing the intricacies of the plan. It was a complex strategy that relied on some element of luck, but if executed properly, it would yield the desired results. I made assurances that I would cover all expenses, and they needed to be ready at a moment's notice.

Once the guys left, Marcy returned to the room with sandwiches. Dom remained connected to tubes and a ventilator, its monotonous sound filling the room. However, I took solace in Dr. Gonzalez's encouraging words.

"So now we wait?" Marcy asked.

"I didn't want to mention it in front of Lucy or Agnes, but I'm counting on Thompson to call me with the information I need to set things in motion," I replied.

I shared the details of the plan with Marcy, but I sensed a momentary hesitation from her.

"What's wrong? You don't like the plan?" I questioned.

Marcy unwrapped the sandwiches and replied, "There are just so many variables that could go wrong."

"I have contingencies in place. If I receive the right information, it should work. Just make sure the bureau agents are prepared," I reassured her.

We ate our sandwiches, and I made sure to keep my phone charging. Running out of battery at this critical juncture was not an option.

The hours ticked by, and it was already six o'clock. No calls had come in yet. Nurses came in and out to tend to Dom, who remained in critical but stable condition. As much as I wanted to stay by his side, I knew that I had to leave the moment the call came, and Marcy would stay behind.

At eight o'clock, my phone rang, displaying an unknown caller ID. "This is Mancuso," I answered.

A voice on the other end instructed, "Ten tonight. From the home base. Black Mercedes pickup at 210 East Forty-Six Street. Sparks Steak House. Back to home base. Say yes if understood."

"Yes," I responded, and the call abruptly ended with a click.

58
Saturday, 9:15 p.m.

"Larry, Harry, are you both in position?" I asked on the phone. "Yes, yes," came their affirmative responses.

"You know what to do," I reminded them.

"Marcy, are your people ready?" I inquired.

"So they said," Marcy replied.

"I'll inform you the moment the target car leaves the home base," I assured them.

Parked in our SUV across from the Permanent Mission of the Democratic People's Republic of Korea on Second Avenue, my plan was to follow the car and keep everyone informed of its movements. Larry would be the first in line, Harry the second, and I would be the last resort if everything else failed.

At exactly ten o'clock, a black Mercedes rolled out of the mission.

"Target on its way on Second Avenue," I reported into the phone.

"Ready, ready," came the replies from Larry and Harry.

"Turning right on East Forty-Fourth Street, as expected," I updated.

I trailed behind the Mercedes, maintaining one car's distance.

A few moments later, I informed, "Turning right on Third Avenue."

I followed closely behind the Mercedes but allowed some space between our vehicles. I didn't want to raise suspicion.

"Turning right on Forty-Sixth Street for the pickup. Be ready," I alerted Larry and Harry.

As anticipated, there was a bustling crowd of people getting in and out of cars in front of Sparks Steak House. The North Koreans had chosen this location as a convenient cover for their pickup.

I remained one car behind the Mercedes, observing Zacharias Brown and Paul Reinhard getting into the vehicle.

"Packages in the target car. It's your turn, Larry," I communicated.

"On it," Larry replied.

I watched as Larry began to pull out behind the Mercedes, but suddenly, a flashy red Lamborghini swooped in and cut him off.

"Boss, I've got a problem," Larry reported.

"I see it. Harry, be ready," I instructed.

"No *problemo*," Harry replied confidently.

As the Mercedes turned right on Second Avenue, Larry remained one car behind, with me trailing behind Larry.

"Now, Harry, now," I urged.

Harry had parked his car illegally in the bus lane on Second Avenue. The moment he spotted the Mercedes turning, he swiftly pulled out, maneuvering out of the bus lane, and forcefully rammed into the right side of the Mercedes.

Harry's impact pushed the Mercedes one lane to the left. Larry promptly stopped his car in front of the Mercedes, effectively blocking its path, while I positioned my vehicle on the left side to prevent a quick escape. The target car was now successfully blocked.

"You're on, Marcy," I informed her on the phone.

I was just about to step out of the SUV when I noticed Zacharias exiting the Mercedes alone. He briskly started walking toward Forty-Sixth Street, and I swiftly made my way toward him. At least I knew Paul was still inside the car.

Zacharias glanced back twice toward the accident but failed to spot me approaching from his right. I pressed my phone against his back, causing him to tense up. "You move, asshole, and you're dead."

He turned his face to see who was behind him, then smirked and said, "You will not shoot me in cold blood, Mancuso."

I yelled into his right ear, "You're a fucking spy, Brown, and the penalty is death. I'm going to carry out that penalty right here if you force me. My brother is dying in a hospital bed, thanks to you," I said firmly. "Now kneel and drop facedown."

The sound of approaching sirens grew louder, the police cars illuminating the surroundings.

Two uniformed officers rushed toward us. I addressed them, "I'm Mancuso, working with the NYPD. Federal authorities want this man for espionage and murder. Cuff him."

"Show me your hands, sir," one officer demanded.

I spread my arms wide, holding my phone between my thumb and index finger while maintaining pressure on Brown with my right foot.

"Step away from the man and show me an ID," the officer ordered.

"I'm putting the phone down and pulling out my creds," I complied. Brown attempted to stand up as I placed my phone on the pavement.

"Sir, stay down and cross your legs with your hands behind your head," the other officer commanded, standing near Brown.

I quickly retrieved my credentials and showed them to the

officer standing beside me as the flashing lights of the police cars illuminated our surroundings.

"You're Joey Mancuso, Midtown South Precinct. I know you, Mancuso. I'm Jason Carter from the precinct," the officer identified himself.

Although I didn't recall knowing Jason, I played along. "Hey, buddy, good to see you. This guy is a bad *hombre*. Make sure you cuff him. I need to get back to the accident. You mind?"

"Hey, John, this here is Mancuso, the legend," Jason informed his partner.

"Brother, I need to get back there," I insisted, pointing toward the accident. "Go, go, we got this, Mancuso," Jason assured me.

I hurried back to the cars, which were now surrounded by police cars and unmarked vehicles. The diplomat from the mission was causing a scene, arguing that Paul Reinhard, being a diplomat, should be returned to the mission with him.

Paul, flanked by two intimidating North Korean men, stood behind the diplomat.

"Excuse me!" I shouted. "Who are the FBI agents in charge?"

One of the agents approached me. "Are you Mancuso?"

"Yes, I am," I confirmed.

"Is that Paul Reinhard?" the agent asked.

"Yes, he is, and he's not a diplomat," I replied.

The agent turned to the diplomat and stated, "Mr. Chang, you're free to go, sir. But Mr. Reinhard," he pointed at Paul, "stays with us."

Chang huffed and muttered what were likely curses in Korean.

I noticed Larry standing behind Paul. I blinked at Larry, and he placed his hand on Paul's shoulders.

Paul looked at Larry, then at me. I nodded to Paul, signaling that everything was okay.

He nodded back and smiled.

Larry and Paul took advantage of the chaos and darkness to discreetly leave the immediate scene.

As soon as I saw Larry and Paul depart, I made myself inconspicuous and vanished from sight.

I called Lucy to update her on the situation. "All good on our end. You take over from Larry."

"Got it," Lucy confirmed.

I left Harry behind to deal with the likely ticket he was about to get and the tow of his car, which had lost the front bumper. A minor price to pay for the results achieved by my plan. Father Andrews, with two parishioners, had planned to stay with Dom overnight. The ventilator and other life-support equipment had been removed. Dom was breathing on his own, albeit not conscious yet. But everything pointed to a speedy recovery. I was home unwinding from the adrenaline high at midnight when I got a call from Xavier Thompson. "Mancuso, well executed, but we have a problem. Where is Paul Reinhard?

I could sense Thompson's frustration on the other end of the line, but I maintained my playful tone. "I think he left the country."

"Left the country? Are you serious, Mancuso? You better have a damn good explanation for this."

I chuckled lightly. "Relax, Thompson. I'm just messing with you. Paul is safe, and he's not going anywhere. But he's been through a lot, and I think it's best if we give him some time to recover before bombarding him with questions. We can arrange a meeting once he's in a better state."

Thompson let out a sigh. "Mancuso, you're pushing the limits here. I need answers, and I need them soon. This is a matter of national security."

I understood Thompson's perspective, but I was determined to protect Paul from unnecessary stress. "Look, Thompson, I've been working tirelessly to ensure Paul's safety, and I won't jeopardize that now. We'll have our debriefing, but it needs to be on Paul's terms. Give him a week or two, and I'll arrange a meeting at a neutral location under controlled conditions. That's the best I can offer."

Thompson grumbled on the other end, clearly unhappy with my proposal. "Fine, but don't think I'm letting you off the hook, Mancuso. We'll be in touch."

With that, Thompson ended the call, leaving me with a mix of relief and anticipation. I knew the road ahead wouldn't be easy, but I was determined to protect Paul and ensure justice was served. It was time to regroup, gather more evidence, and prepare for the next steps in our pursuit of the truth.

59
Sunday, 10 a.m.

I was at home, busy preparing a delectable breakfast spread for Marcy, Lucy, Agnes, JJ, and myself. I took pride in my culinary skills, and today's menu consisted of my signature ham and cheddar cheese omelet, cooked to perfection, accompanied by golden hash browns, toasted Cuban bread slathered with butter, and steaming cups of *café con leche*.

Before we dug into the delicious feast, JJ took it upon himself to sweep the apartment for any potential listening devices. We wanted to ensure our conversation remained confidential and secure. The thrill of engaging in spycraft always added an extra layer of excitement to our endeavors.

With the table set and the food served, we gathered around, ready to indulge in both sustenance and discussion.

Marcy broke the silence, expressing her satisfaction with our operation the previous night. "That went well," she remarked, prompting nods of agreement from the rest of us.

I chimed in, sharing the minor setback we encountered when the Lamborghini disrupted Larry's plan to rear-end the Mercedes. "Yes, the Lamborghini threw a wrench in Larry's approach, but luckily, Harry came through as our backup, and it all worked out in the end," I explained.

Agnes, ever curious, inquired about Paul's whereabouts. "Where is Paul? It feels like we've been hearing about him for so long, and I was hoping to finally meet him."

I glanced at Lucy, giving her the cue to address Agnes's query. Lucy responded with a hint of mystery, "Let's just say that Paul is currently enjoying some well-deserved rest in an undisclosed location. He might even be leaving the country soon for a minor surgical procedure. It's all for his own safety, you understand."

The room filled with laughter, a shared understanding of the need for secrecy in our line of work.

Mentioning the impending debriefing with the Department of Defense, I couldn't help but inject a touch of humor. "The DOD is fuming, but they'll have to settle for a debriefing via a Zumba meeting."

Marcy joined in the laughter, playfully correcting me. "Zoom, Zoom, Mancuso," she quipped, adding to the lighthearted atmosphere.

I shifted the conversation, looking forward to celebrating our successes in the near future. "Once Dom is back on his feet, we'll continue our tradition of a celebratory dinner. This time, we'll do it in style at Sparks Steak House."

Excitement filled the room as JJ expressed his delight. "Oh my God, Sparks! I've never been there."

I shared a knowing glance with Agnes, suggesting she enlighten JJ about our company's protocol when it comes to new employees and celebratory dinners.

Agnes gracefully placed her hand on JJ's arm, ready to explain. "That's right, JJ. It's our tradition that the newest employee treats everyone to dinner. So, this time, the honor falls upon you."

A mix of anticipation and camaraderie filled the air as we savored our breakfast and made plans for both the future and a well-deserved feast. Together, we were a team bonded by trust, humor, and a shared sense of adventure.

Epilogue
Monday, 8 a.m.

Sitting in the comfortable confines of the O'Brian Cigar Club, adjacent to the pub and just steps away from our office, it's a quiet morning with only you and me. I'm settled into a plush leather recliner, savoring a cortadito, and I trust you're enjoying your surroundings as well. Our cigar club has thrived, attracting a diverse membership who relish in the pleasure of fine liquor and high-quality cigars. The revenue flows smoothly, bolstered by the distinct clientele we attract compared to the pub.

Typically, Dom would join me at half past eight in the morning, but today he is back at the rectory, recuperating comfortably after his harrowing experience. Marcy made sure to reach out to our mother, Briana, who promptly flew up from The Villages in Florida to stay with Dom. The two of us spent all of Sunday at the rectory, catching up with Dom and enjoying the company of our mother. It had been a while since I had seen her, and her presence was a welcomed one. However, once Dom made a full recovery, she would return to her friends, social gatherings, and golf at The Villages. I was glad she could be among her peers and enjoy the activities she loves.

We have much to discuss. This case, as you've witnessed, kept us on our toes from the very beginning. Marcy and I only had a brief respite in Islamorada for two days before our friend Paul arrived, donning his iconic Elton John sunglasses and sharing a gripping tale of potential murder.

So, let's delve into the events surrounding the lobster poachers at the Topsider on the day Paul reached out to us. While I was engrossed in conversation with Paul, I missed the entire incident, but Marcy filled me in. It appears that these individuals were vacationers from out of town, a middle-aged man accompanied by a teenager. They were observed heading toward the water with nets and lobster tickle sticks. A concerned resident warned them that it was not lobster season and they should refrain from engaging in their suspicious activities. However, they disregarded the warning and continued their venture. Before long, the Florida Marine Patrol arrived, waiting for the opportune moment to catch them in the act of poaching lobsters. The authorities successfully apprehended the adult culprit, who now faced a hefty fine and the possibility of spending ten days in the local jail. As for the teenager, he received a warning. The teenager's mother, on the other hand, became quite agitated with the patrol personnel and nearly found herself in legal trouble as well. It seems even in lobster season, one cannot catch them unless they venture three hundred yards out into the bay.

The incident served as a reminder of the various elements at play in our surroundings, the interconnectedness of our endeavors, and the need for vigilance in our community. As we reflect on these events, we can appreciate the delicate balance between our covert operations and the everyday challenges faced by others.

Patrick Sullivan, affectionately known as Mr. Pat, our beloved adopted uncle, is thriving in Naples, Florida, with his bustling bar and grill. Despite his desire to visit Dom up here, we were fortunate that Dom's recovery was swift, allowing Mr. Pat to remain in Naples. However, he did manage to connect with Father Dom through a successful Zoom call (finally getting the hang of it!).

Ana Bella, one of Sergeant Gunther's valuable confidential informants from Sarasota, has made significant progress in her life. When I first encountered her, she exuded a sense of vulnerability, avoiding eye contact and wearing heavy makeup beneath her eyes. Concerned for her well-being, I asked the sergeant to check on her, suspecting that something was amiss. It turns out that Ana Bella had successfully overcome her drug addiction but was trapped in a dangerously abusive relationship with her boyfriend. Thanks to the sergeant's intervention, Ana Bella was provided with a new home, and her boyfriend was sternly warned never to harm her again.

Sir Lance, the informant who alerted me to Galiano and his plane's arrival, received his well-deserved reward of two thousand dollars and continues to pursue his entrepreneurial endeavors in Sarasota.

Now, I know you're eager to hear about the fate of the "bad *hombres*." Just bear with me; we're getting there.

Captain Tony, the owner of The Queen of the Seas vessel that transported Galiano, the boys, and Paul to Cuba, unfortunately, met a tragic end. His body was never recovered and is presumed to have been lost at sea in the treacherous Florida Straits. He became one of the many innocent victims entangled in this complex web.

You may recall the four F/A-18F Super Hornets that swooped in to rescue us from the impending threat of the MiG. I discovered that Jake T, the kind benefactor who orchestrated their timely arrival, is an air traffic controller stationed at Boca Chica Naval Station. It was Jake T who first spotted the MiG closing in on us and promptly dispatched the Super Hornets to our aid. To express my gratitude, I've ensured that Jake T receives a year's worth of craft beer subscription, with a monthly delivery of specialty brews. I owe him a debt of gratitude that extends far beyond a simple gesture.

Tragically, Sheriff Leone and Deputy Joyce from the Monroe County Sheriff's Office met an untimely demise. Their lifeless bodies were discovered washed up at Fort Jefferson in Dry Tortugas National Park near Key West, leaving behind two more innocent victims in this tangled web of events.

Give me a moment, if you will. I need to take a brief stroll. As you know, I have a troublesome knee that needs replacement.

But let's continue. Megan, Tom, and their son Charlie were able to return to Laurel, Maryland, and enjoy their lives without fear. I made a mental note of Megan's mother's home, the serene Little Mountain Retreat in Bakersville, North Carolina. It seemed like the perfect getaway for Marcy, Michelle Marie, the in-laws, and me. I could already imagine the mouthwatering aroma of sizzling steaks on the grill, enjoyed on the covered patio while watching an exciting football game on the TV.

Bruce Frazer was the drone pilot who was incarcerated for his actions while under the influence and mistakenly firing a missile at the wrong target in Afghanistan. This information is strictly confidential between you and me. Unfortunately, it was a devastating incident that claimed the lives of twelve innocent people. The government chose to keep the incident under wraps, and we understand the reasons behind their decision.

Thanks to Xavier Thompson, the retired Air Force colonel working with a DHS agency in DC, I was able to set my final plan in motion, ensuring that Paul was saved from an unexpected and undesired trip to North Korea. Xavier facilitated a secure video call and personally debriefed Paul.

Agent Zacharias Brown, also known as Agent Tuck, has been apprehended and awaits trial for the charges of murder and espionage. I hope he faces the full extent of the law. Even if justice falls short, he will spend the majority of his days confined to solitary confinement, with only one hour of daylight.

Jack Ryder and Max have returned to their home at the docks of Miami Beach Marina, fully recovered from Jack's gunshot wound. Jack completed his latest novella, "Murder at the Beach Cove Hotel," and submitted it to the editors. He claims that I owe him all the details of my adventure as payment for what he endured. I suppose I'll have to negotiate royalties with my dear friend.

Harry, the unfortunate soul who crashed into the Mercedes, received a ticket for his actions. I covered the fine and also provided him with an additional $1,200 for the repairs to his car. Now, Larry and Harry are requesting company life insurance following our daring plan to prevent the North Koreans from kidnapping Paul. Perhaps it's worth considering life insurance for everyone on the team.

You know, this reminds me that I never fully discussed with Marcy what would have happened if Father Dom hadn't made it. I was ready to call it quits on our detective agency, as we had experienced far too many close calls with death. I'm not sure if I'll revisit that conversation or not. Let's see what the future holds. I love what we do, and we're damn good at it.

I sat and leaned back in my chair, taking in all the developments. Galiano and Castellanos, as you're aware, were apprehended by Sergeant Gunther in Sarasota. The list of charges against them is extensive, including murder, drug trafficking, RICO violations, and more. They won't see the light of day for a very long time. Three life sentences mean they'll be locked up until their dying breath. You know what I mean, right?

The pilot and flight attendant who were involved in the operation received five-year sentences. Hopefully, that will serve as a lesson to them.

Now, here's the exciting part, my friend. The Department of State's Narcotics Rewards Program contacted us and informed us that we're entitled to a five-million-dollar reward. We just have to navigate through a million pages of paperwork to claim it. Hallelujah, baby, it's payday!

But here's something that concerns me. Who was listening in on our communications and monitoring our activities? It feels like we were an open book to everyone. Xavier Thompson's contacts were aware of all our moves, but who else had eyes and ears on us?

Alright, I know you're eager to hear about Paul Reinhard. As you recall, in the midst of the chaos after the Mercedes incident, Larry rescued Paul and handed him over to Lucy as part of my plan. Well, I'm pleased to inform you that Paul underwent some discreet cosmetic work at a clinic in upstate New York. Nothing too extravagant, just a few touch-ups here and there. Afterward, Paul, now going by the name Victor, obtained a new passport and a whole new identity. He boarded a plane bound for a destination that I can't disclose to you. Sorry, my friend, you know how this works. But hey, if you ever go big-game fishing in the Atlantic, you might just hire Captain Victor without even realizing it. Just don't get too nosy and ask him if he's ever been to Islamorada, or he might have to toss you overboard.

It seems Marcy has taken on the industrial espionage case from Bevans and Associates. This is fantastic news. It means we're expanding our capabilities at Mancuso & O'Brian Investigative Services. Maybe this case won't involve firearms and people losing their lives. That's my hope, at least. But you know how unpredictable things can be in our line of work.

It was a night of celebration at Sparks Steak House, where we gathered for our well-deserved celebratory dinner. Father Dom, along with my mom, joined the entire team, along with their loved ones. We even extended the invitation to Marcy's parents, Rosa and Alberto. JJ, our newest team member, was relieved to know that he wouldn't have to foot the bill for this special occasion. It was clear that JJ would be a valuable asset to our team.

As the evening ended, I playfully handed the check to Father Dom. Everyone at the table anticipated his reaction, knowing what was coming. When he saw the eight-thousand-dollar tab, his eyes bulged, and for a moment, it seemed like he might have a stroke. But I leaned in and reminded him, "We made five million, remember?" He let out a sigh, took a deep breath, and then burst into a smile. Without missing a beat, he pulled out his credit card and playfully threw it onto the table.

The unexpected reaction from Father Dom caught everyone off guard, and the whole table erupted in laughter. At that moment, we knew that life was good.

I'll be back soon. *Ciao!*

The end.

Now, here's a synopsis of A Seed For Murder. A Joey Mancuso, Father O'Brian Crime Mystery, Book 11.

This chilling story broke on NBC News 4/17/23: Two Chinese nationals were charged with operating a secret police station in NYC, The station, which was in an office building in Chinatown, was set up to "monitor and intimidate" critics of the Chinese government, the Justice Department said.

Author Parr amazingly captured the story way ahead of the news channel in this thrilling, page-turner novel.

Introducing the latest addition to the thrilling Mancuso and O'Brian Crime Mysteries series - "A Seed for Murder"!

In this gripping tale of industrial espionage and murder, author Owen Parr takes you on a journey into the world of genetically modified crops, exposing a web of deceit and greed that will keep you on the edge of your seat. Did Myrna Tucker really commit suicide, or was there something more sinister at play? With NuvoSeed fearing that their intellectual property has been stolen and the company on the brink of a lucrative sale, could they be hiding the truth about Myrna's death and the server breaches from the acquiring company?

Enter the dynamic duo of Mancuso and O'Brian Investigative Services. Led by former NYPD homicide detective Joey Mancuso and Father Dominic O'Brian, this team of experienced investigators will stop at nothing to uncover the truth. With the addition of Joey's wife, Marcy Martinez, and the skilled computer researcher, Agnes Smith Persopoulus, they have the perfect combination of skills to tackle this complex case. But they're not alone - they also have Jimmy Johnson, a brilliant computer hacker, and Lucy Roberts, Joey's former partner and mentor at the NYPD, on their side.

Based out of an Irish Pub and Cigar Bar in the Financial District of New York City, this eclectic team will take you on a thrilling ride through the underbelly of the city as they unravel the truth behind Myrna's death and the theft of intellectual property. Fans of James Patterson, Nelson DeMille, Michael Connelly, and Lee Child will be captivated by the twists and turns in this thrilling crime mystery.

Don't miss out on the latest addition to the Mancuso and O'Brian Crime Mysteries series - get your copy of "A Seed for Murder" now and join the hunt for justice!

A note from Owen

Thank you for taking the time to read or listen to this story. My aim is always to entertain fans of crime mysteries, and I hope I have succeeded with this latest release.

While I strive for realism and conduct thorough research, I must admit that for the sake of storytelling, I may have taken a few creative liberties here and there.

Your feedback is always welcome, and I encourage you to reach out to me at Owen@owenparr.com. I would also greatly appreciate it if you could spare a couple of minutes to leave a review of the novel on Amazon.com. For independent authors like me, reviews are incredibly valuable.

Please take care of yourself, continue reading, and enjoy yourself. If you haven't read the entire series, I invite you to go back and start with the first book. I'm confident that you will enjoy them all.

A special thank you goes to Randy McCarten, whose voice brings the audiobook to life. His talent and skill in audio production and narration truly work their magic throughout the story. Thank you, Randy.

Other titles by Owen Parr

Operation Due Diligence. An Alpha Team Spy Thriller-Vol 1
Operation Black Swan. An Alpha Team Spy Thriller-Vol 2
Operation Raven—The Dead Have Secrets-An Alpha Team Spy Thriller-Vol 3

A Murder on Wall Street—A Joey Mancuso, Father O'Brian Crime Mystery-Vol 1
A Murder on Long Island—A Joey Mancuso, Father O'Brian Crime Mystery-Vol 2
The Manhattan Red Ribbon Killer—A Joey Mancuso, Father O'Brian Crime Mystery-Vol 3
The Case of the Antiquities Collector—A Joey Mancuso, Father O'Brian Crime Mystery-Vol 4
The Murder of Paolo Mancuso—A Joey Mancuso, Father O'Brian Crime Mystery-Vol 5
The Abduction of Patient Zero—A Joey Mancuso, Father O'Brian Crime Mystery-Vol 6
The UNSUB—A Joey Mancuso, Father O'Brian Crime Mystery-Vol 7
The Labyrinth—A Joey Mancuso, Father O'Brian Crime Mystery-Vol 8.
A Deadly Scam—A Joey Mancuso, Father O'Brian Crime Mystery-Vol 9.
The Islamorada Murders—A Joey Mancuso, Father O'Brian Crime Mystery-Vol 10

Jack Ryder Crime Mystery-Novellas 1, 2, & 3 The Case of the Dead Russian Spy; Murder Aboard a Cruise to Nowhere; Murder at the Beach Cove Hotel.

How to Sell, Manage Your Time, Overcome Fear of Rejection—
A Non-fiction, Self-Improvement Book

All titles are available at Amazon.com, BarnesandNoble.com, and other online retailers and as audiobooks at Audible.com.

Owen Parr

Printed in Great Britain
by Amazon